P

Elli

A Second Chance Novel

"Elli—A Second Chance Novel, is an amazing book; it's a delightful and uplifting read while it touches upon one of the most serious diseases facing us all today—cancer. The book never preaches — it entertains with wonderful humor. I recommend this book — it's simply excellent in so many ways! A keeper — not to mention that every last penny of the author's share goes on to battle cancer. Bravo!"

Heather Graham, New York Times Bestselling Author

"DeSalvo writes with warmth and wit. Her characters leap off the page and into your heart. It is a fun read where deals, dogs and disaster blend seamlessly in a fast paced story of second chances."

Cherry Adair, New York Times Bestselling Author

"Ms DeSalvo has created a family unit out of frightened and broken folks, introducing a southern crew of characters that are a true delight! This southern charmer is sure to please most readers."

InD'Tale Magazine

"This debut novel features an adorably plucky heroine, a hot Cajun hero and a cast of hysterically eccentric family members who trip over each other to chew up the scenery. DeSalvo has created some truly memorable characters, and the blog posts she uses at the beginning of each chapter to show Elli's battle with cancer are moving."

RT Bookreviews

Jewell

A Second Chance Novel

Tina DeSalvo

To my mom, Ann, who was always ready to go for a ride anywhere, attend a party or social event at any time or visit with friends or strangers in any location. She enjoyed life and creating the memories her mind stopped holding onto in her last years. Thank you for showing me how to be present in each moment...and to always, always, always have fun.

This book is also dedicated to all of you who have lost a loved one to dementia and Alzheimer's while they physically remained in your life.

For more information on Dementia and Alzheimer's please visit: www.alz.org

Chapter

1

Cane, Louisiana
Fall

Hello God, it's me, Mignon Duet. I hope You don't mind me speaking to You in my head again, while the world is going about its business around me not knowing we're having this conversation. I guess that's what you do when you get old. Have conversations in your head. Come to think of it, I've heard some old people talk to You aloud, too. That makes them sound crazy though. And then their families try to excuse it by saying they got religion in their old age. I know the truth, just like You. They don't even realize they're talking aloud. They think they're talking in their heads like I'm doing.

Hmm, I am talking in my head, right?

Yes. I am. Otherwise the people in here would be looking at me sideways instead of shopping in this old house looking for bargains. My only granddaughter is selling things for the family who owns this old stuff. Junk, mostly. Not that all old stuff is junk. Look at me. I'm quality, even though my brain isn't so sharp anymore. I'm not junk to be tossed away, even though I'm old. My brain is rusty; the gears in my body don't work so well. I have a cane and pretty beige orthopedic shoes to help me move along. And I have my granddaughter, Jewell, ma sucrée, *my sweet. She helps me move along, too. Mainly, she shares her brain with me.*

Jewell is never very far away from me. Thank God...er...Thank You. She reminds me of things I need to do and she finishes my sentences when I can't. You know, she even takes me with her to work, like she did today. Not that this place is much of a job, if you ask me. She used to take me to mansions. Big New Orleans mansions. I liked going to big mansions. I felt special sitting on their fancy chairs, drinking sweet tea from heavy crystal glasses. Now we're in a dusty bungalow in the country. Not that that bothers me much. I like the country. I'm from the country. At least, I think I am. No...I'm sure I am. Anyway, Jewell isn't so sure I'm from the country— even though I told her I used to live on a plantation with Twinnie. Ah, I sure miss Twinnie, God.

When I talk about Twinnie, though, it seems to make Jewell sad. Ma sucrée looks sad a lot lately. Why is that? I don't think it has to do with Twinnie or me getting childlike sometimes and needing her to hold me. I think it has to do with the legal problems she's having. The ones she says I shouldn't worry about. But I do. And it makes me scared, God. Really scared.

I don't want anything to happen to her. It breaks my heart to think she has problems. When I see her eyes look so full and sad and troubled, my insides tremble. I'm so frightened for her that I cry myself to sleep at night. God, can You help ma sucrée not be sad? Can You make her problems disappear so we can be together...so that she doesn't have to leave me...alone?

Oh, mon Dieu, my heart is pounding so hard now. My hands are shaking. I know that this is what "totally alone" feels like even though there are a few people nearby shopping in this strange place. I don't know any of them. I don't know where I am. It's getting hard to breathe and Jewell's big brown eyes lock onto mine. She smiles at me...and I feel relief, comfort.

"I know you," I tell her.

"And, I know you, Mimi."

I feel peaceful knowing I'll always recognize Jewell's chocolate colored eyes, her straight nose, her rosy lips and her café au lait complexion. I will always recognize her, won't I?

Jewell looks scared, too, as she stares hard inside her open cash register as if she can make the money there multiply by sheer will. I can't tell her how frightened I am now. She has her own problems. She shouldn't worry about me. She's young. She has her life ahead of her. Mine is over. She needs to be free to find success again and to find happiness. Maybe even a good man. I should free her from the burden of having to take care of me. That's the right thing to do...but, if I free her, dear God, I will be totally alone...

...and so will she.

***

Jewell pressed on the gas pedal of her old pickup truck a little too hard, throwing both Mimi and herself against their seats in an unexpected jolt.

"I know you want to get out of here in a hurry, but you don't have to give us whiplash in the process," Mimi told her, speaking the formal French that was her first language and the one she and Jewell preferred to speak to one another.

Jewell eased off the pedal. She drove with her Airstream camper in tow down the bumpy dirt road of the Simoneauxs' property onto the smooth two-way state highway adjacent to it. She glanced at her plump grand-mère who was now staring out of the closed side window. White hair styled with a tight perm and dressed in her Sunday best, she sat on the clean but faded tan cloth front seat as poised as if she was seated on a satin Chippendale chair at a formal dining table in Commander's Palace restaurant in New Orleans. She didn't know how Mimi managed such perfect posture after two long days of sitting around the estate sale, especially when arthritis had set painfully in her worn bones years ago. Mimi might complain about a long list of things, but her personal aches and pains were not among them.

She was a remarkable woman. She had been when she was a young, energetic grandmother raising her unwed, rebellious teenage daughter's child and now, as an elderly, frisky lady fighting to stay relevant in a confusing world. It broke Jewell's heart to know that her time with the most important person in her life was limited both because of her age and because of advancing dementia. Once Mimi was gone, Jewell would be left alone with only her wonderful memories of this woman. She intended to have no regrets to mar their challenging but loving life together.

Mimi turned, looked directly into Jewell's eyes. "You're glad this job is over, huh, *ma sucrée*? I can see it in your troubled eyes."

Jewell blinked, refocused on the road in front of her. "Yes, I am, Mimi." She was glad to be leaving the Simoneauxs' property where she'd worked for the last week. The minute she'd walked into the poorly maintained 1920s bungalow, she'd felt like a Civil War cannonball had hit her in the chest. This was not the type of estate furniture and household property she would've been called to appraise and sell before her career plummeted to the depths of the muddy Mississippi River.

"Me, too," Mimi agreed. "You know, this was more like a garage sale than a pretty Magazine Street store. Or *was* this just a garage sale?"

"It was an estate sale," she sighed. The worst estate sale she'd ever facilitated in her professional career.

"Hmm. I think it was a garage sale." Mimi crossed her arms over her ample breasts and thick belly. "If you want to have a garage sale," she insisted, "you can have one closer to home in New Orleans and save us the hour trip into the bayou country."

"I didn't want to have a garage sale, Mimi."

"Then why did you have a garage sale? You don't make any sense. I don't understand."

Jewell looked at Mimi. Her brows were furrowed. She looked confused. She really didn't remember why they were at the Simoneauxs'. "I took the job here because no one will hire me in New Orleans," she said, keeping her voice even as she started the GPS on her phone to direct them to their next destination.

"You have dirt smeared on your face, *ma sucrée*," Mimi said, pointing to Jewell's chin. "You always have dirt on your face. You did as a child, too."

Jewell glanced at her reflection in the rearview mirror. Nothing wrong with Mimi's vision. There was a smudge of bayou dirt on the underside of her chin several shades darker than her complexion. She wiped it with the heel of her hand, quickly inspecting the rest of her face. No dirt. Just her dark hair, already coming out of the ponytail. "Did I get it all?" She lifted her chin for Mimi to inspect.

She nodded. "It's déjà vu with the dirt." She smiled. "And, with the way you look." Mimi shook her head. "You wear your hair the same as you did in college. Maybe if you took it out of that straight ponytail and added that pretty royal purple streak that people are decorating their hair with today, it would be nice. You're a pretty girl. A little color would look good on you. Change is good. If your memory is good, that is. Otherwise, change can be a confusing." She smiled, but it didn't reach her eyes. "Now, you could get one of those trendy tattoos. That's a change that isn't confusing. It would follow you around. Especially if it's on your derrière." She laughed. "You're too conservative for that. I'm not though. I should get one." She pursed her lips. "Come to think of it, a tattoo wouldn't be right for either of us. We're not sailors. Sailors are the only ones who should have tattoos. Sailors and pirates."

Jewell smiled. *And, maybe an antiquities expert celebrating getting an advanced degree,* she thought, placing her hand low to the side of her hipbone just below her bikini line. "You know, tattooing has been around a long, long time. It's been in the Polynesian and Native American cultures and it was even found on the mummified remains of ancient Egyptian priests and priestesses."

"I didn't know there were Egyptian pirates." She frowned. "You know a lot of things. You just don't know fashion. Now, that's something I know." There was a twinkle in her eyes. "I can still sew well enough to make you a sophisticated white brocade sheath pretty enough to turn every grand Madame's head for Friday lunch at Galatoire's. You'd have to discard those jeans, that baby blue company golf shirt and the rubber boots you always wear, though. Wouldn't hurt to wear pretty stilettos."

"As a matter of fact, it might hurt. My boots are fun, practical. They make me smile. Stilettos make me wince." Jewell tucked a long strand of hair that had fallen from her ponytail behind her ear. "I'm actually comfortable in my own skin just like this, Mimi."

She adjusted the rearview mirror to get a better view of her vintage Airstream camper behind them. It truly was their home away from home. A wave of fatigue and a little bit of despair and loneliness swept over her. She suddenly just wanted to stop for a little while, crawl under her favorite patchwork quilt, take a nap and shut out the worries of Mimi slipping away, of rebuilding her career and any one of a thousand things weighing on her mind like a ship's anchor set in a stormy sea.

Instead, Jewell continued driving along the winding bayou road and negotiated a sharp curve a little too fast. Mimi slid on her seat, causing her safety belt to lock across her heavy breast.

"Oh, *mon Dieu*." She tugged on the seatbelt but it didn't budge. "I'm taking the streetcar next time."

Jewell checked for traffic behind them. Not another vehicle was around, so she stopped in the middle of the road. She quickly refastened Mimi's safety belt, then, resumed driving again. "No street cars around here," she smiled. "Doesn't look like there's any public transportation or even any cars."

"If you don't have to wear a safety belt on a streetcar, I don't see why you have to wear one in an old truck." She pulled on the belt to keep the extra slack over her folded arms. "If you weren't already in trouble with the law, I wouldn't wear this uncomfortable thing."

"Thank you for being so considerate."

"So, we're going to our next job, now, right?"

"Our final interview for it." Jewell prayed it went well. They needed this job, and it was especially great that the new client was so receptive to Mimi's coming along. If Jewell wasn't totally convinced that her grand-mère enjoyed going on jobs with her, she'd find different work that suited both of them. Something that would keep Mimi with her as long as possible.

One look at Mimi reassured her that she was doing the right thing. Her skin wasn't as supple as it once was, her plump body not as firm and her blue-green eyes weren't as clear, but Mimi looked like the same prideful woman who had raised her. Just more faded. Jewell made sure Mimi maintained her weekly appointment to style her white hair at the neighborhood salon she'd gone to for the last forty years. Jewell ironed all of the dresses Mimi wore in just the way her grand-mère liked. She shined Mimi's tan orthopedic shoes just as she preferred, too. It was why she looked as fresh and styled today as she did yesterday and all the days before. If only Jewell could do something to Mimi's brain so it would function as it had before.

You have arrived. Destination on your right.

"Now how does that lady know where we're going or where we've been?" Mimi asked, as she always did when the GPS announced their arrival. Jewell didn't mind hearing the same questions and stories from Mimi over and over again. Sure, she sometimes let her mind drift as Mimi recounted the same story she'd told eight dozen times, but in the end, Jewell appreciated that Mimi wanted to share her thoughts instead of remaining quiet for fear or embarrassment that she was doing something wrong. She had seen in her eyes and in her expressions how difficult not remembering was for Mimi.

"The lady in the GPS is just smarter than us, I guess," Jewell answered as she turned into the Sugar Mill Plantation drive. "We're here." Her old tan pickup truck looked incongruous in front of the locked, glossy white gate of the plantation. Jewel shook off fatigue, looked at the closed gate in front of them—not feeling locked out, but filled with anticipation for what would be waiting for them when it swung open. She looked through her truck window and let the modern world fall away.

"Can you imagine this place if the white vinyl fencing around the property was gone and the asphalt road behind us was just a narrow dirt horse-and-buggy path?" Jewell whispered. The land wouldn't look very different than it had over two hundred years ago when the first sugarcane crop was standing tall on a similar, warm October day. The plantation that she couldn't see, but knew was down the road, would be welcoming with its windows and doors spread open to the fall breeze and arriving guests.

It would really be good if she got this job at this nice historical property, so like many of the places she'd worked when her career was arrowing upward. The phone conversation with Elli Bienvenu a few days earlier had sounded promising, Jewell thought as she turned off the truck's well-worn engine. It gave a few extra knocks before it silenced. "You know, Mimi, the owner, Elli, seems friendly, smart—and best of all, in need of our services to appraise and sell her barn full of stored furniture and things."

All Jewell had to do was have a successful meeting with her today, get her to sign a contract and begin work tomorrow. The only stumbling block could be if Elli or her husband had heard of how badly the Simoneauxs' job had gone. The way news traveled in small towns like Cane, that was a real possibility. Even though she'd climbed through the muck under the house and nearly went to battle with a raccoon to recover some cool antiques, she hadn't been able to sell them for what they were worth. She'd invited the top antique dealers from New Orleans and Baton Rouge to attend, but they hadn't shown up. Inviting them was a risk since there weren't many good antiques in the home. Inviting them when they wanted nothing to do with her was an even bigger risk. In the end, what little that did sell, sold under value. To make matters worse, she ended up having to donate more of the Simoneauxs' property to Goodwill than she'd sold.

Jewell just had to hold out hope that even if they had heard of her underperformance, she could reason with Elli about realistic expectations for the Sugar Mill Plantation project. If not, Jewell would simply lower her fees and appeal to the fact that Elli was on a tight deadline. She knew Elli needed to have everything cleared out of the barn before the set crew arrived in a week to prepare for the movie being filmed there in two weeks. Even if she wasn't able to sell what Elli didn't want to keep, at least she could get the stuff out of the way for the movie crew.

"She's going to hire us, Mimi." Jewell blew out the breath she hadn't realized she was holding. "I know it."

"It doesn't sound like you know it." Mimi said, her tone a little rough. Jewell glanced at her. She was having a bit of a mood swing. She often did that when she got tired, hungry or bored. Sometimes it happened for no reason other than that she had mood swings. Mimi's doctors had told Jewell that was all part of life with dementia. Mimi unsnapped her safety belt and sighed. "Just your optimism talking about knowing this and that. Always been your problem."

Jewell laughed. "I don't see why optimism is a problem. I'm an optimist, but I'm a pragmatic, logical, methodical researcher, too. Nothing wrong with me wanting to go through Elli's old stuff, either."

Jewell's heart raced, and an excitement danced in her soul as it always did when she thought of being able to explore places where people had tucked away things from long ago. Things too precious to throw away yet, too old or odd to fit into their modern lives. She looked at her grand-mère. The same had been true for Mimi before she came to live with Jewell. She grabbed Mimi's arthritic hand, and squeezed it gently. Her skin felt as dry and fragile as parchment. Sensing her grand-mère's mortality scared Jewell. Mimi was everything to her. Everything. She was the only real family she had.

"We'll have fun, Mimi. We're on a grand adventure together. It'll be a treasure hunt."

"Or a trip to the dump," she said, still sounding irritated. She shook her head, making the tight curls in her white hair bob. Jewell didn't let her grand-mère's attitude bother her. She knew her mood would improve. It always did.

Jewell glanced at her cell phone. They were thirty minutes early. The ten-mile drive from the Simoneauxs' home had been a lot faster than the GPS directions indicated. It would be okay for her to arrive fifteen minutes early to meet a client, but thirty would make her seem too desperate...which, of course, she was.

"Do you hear it?" Mimi asked, her voice laughing lightly. This was the fastest Jewell had seen her grand-mère's mood improve, ever. "It's me and Twinnie giggling as we run through those cane fields." She leaned her head back and inhaled deeply. She closed her eyes and a tear slipped onto her cheek. "I miss Twinnie. Do you think she remembers me?"

A lump formed in Jewell's throat. Her body ached with wanting to say yes to her grand-mère but her heart broke with not being able to do it. She just couldn't say something she wasn't sure she believed was true.

Twinnie might not exist. If she did, she might be dead or in a nursing home in New York City or right here in Cane. How had Mimi lost touch with this person that was so important to her? Was she her sister? A cousin? A twin?

Or had she never existed?

"I'm old. My brain is mushy, but..." Mimi paused and her cloudy blue-green eyes locked onto Jewell's with such sadness and hope, and some other emotion that Jewell couldn't identify—for she'd never seen it before. "I do remember things. I also know things, *ma sucrée*. I know you took that garage sale job because you wanted to come to this area to see if the stories I told you were true. I heard you asking questions about Twinnie." She sighed. "I might not remember yesterday or today well, but I remember this," she waved her hand out her window toward the tall cane fields shimmying like a living, breathing thing. Jewell didn't know if it was the way the sun shone on the dark green blades of cane, the fertile sable soil or the white puffy clouds in the cornflower sky, but it looked like a picture that was colored with new crayons.

The sunlight also shone on the four rings of imitation semiprecious stones on Mimi's hand like Mardi Gras beads tossed from a Fat Tuesday float—a reminder that Mimi may appear normal, but dementia had changed her. It had even turned her churchgoing, God-fearing grand-mère into a bit of a kleptomaniac. Jewell had learned through research and discussions with Mimi's medical team that dementia could distort her grand-mère's ability to reason. It could cause her to make up stories to fill in the gaps of her memory. As sad as it made Jewell to identify the changes, she had to remind herself that Mimi did not act as she had just a few years before.

A perfect example of that was how she had cased the costume jewelry table at the Simoneauxs' estate sale for forty-five minutes. She acted like a seasoned thief before executing the heist for the four rings that were jammed on her arthritic right hand and the three rings resting above the thick, bent knuckles of her left hand. Even if Jewel had wanted to deny she had done it, her two workers and about six customers all witnessed and pointed out her poorly executed pilfering.

"If I'm to find Twinnie," Jewell began, carefully picking her words, "I need more to go on than 'I lived on a plantation near a bayou with Twinnie.' I need a surname or something less ambiguous. I need one solid detail. The name of the bayou would help."

So, what was the truth with Twinnie and Mimi being raised on a plantation? Those things may or may not have been true, Jewell realized with the logical aptitude that made her a good researcher. The emotional capacity that made her a loving granddaughter had her wanting to gift Mimi with her dear Twinnie while she could still know who she was. It was logic and emotion that Jewell had struggled with over the last two weeks as Mimi spoke with increasing frequency of Twinnie and the plantation they played on. So her logical side said it was time to expand her business outside of New Orleans where she might get a fresh start, and her emotional side said she should expand it in an area where she could research if grand-mère's stories were fantasy or truth.

Jewell glanced at her grand-mère who was rubbing her forehead. In an abrupt movement, Mimi rolled down her window and took in a deep breath. "Smells like home."

Jewell's mouth went dry. The plantation her grand-mère had claimed was hers when she saw it in the movie they had watched wasn't visible a mile down the road on the other side of the locked gate. Mimi had never called the plantation she said was hers by name. The sign for the Sugar Mill Dog Training Facility and Kennel would mean nothing to her. So, why would Mimi say *this* land smelled like home, when they had been near, or on, other homesteads with sugarcane nearby?

It was strange. As an American and Louisiana historian and an antiques explorer, it was her job to chase the possible trail to uncover old stories. The research she'd done on the Sugar Mill Plantation to prepare for the meeting today had not turned up any connection to

Mimi's paternal Duet family or her maternal Tassé family. Jewell had paid particular attention to that.

"Mimi," she whispered, trying to level her emotions. She wanted logic to calm the buzz she felt from the possibilities Mimi's long-term memory had triggered in her romantic treasure hunter's head. She continued speaking French both as a comfort to Mimi and herself. "Is it possible you're remembering the scents of a childhood visit to the country or here in Vacherie Parish? Or, maybe, it smells the same as you remember when the harvested cane was carried into the New Orleans French Market."

Mimi shook her head and rolled her eyes but didn't defend her statement any further. "This cane looks ready for harvest," she said. "Ripe. Sweet."

"When did my urban grand-mère turn into Farmer Brown?"

What does she smell? Maybe it would be familiar to her, too. She rolled her window down. All was quiet except for the shushing sound of the cane waving in the light breeze. She inhaled deeply. The humid, warm fall air eased into her lungs, filling it with the organic scents of earth, cane and open sky.

Wouldn't these scents be the same on any sugarcane farm? Or did each farm have its own particular nuance? Would a person's brain store all of the impacts on their senses from a casual visit? Did the mind of a person with dementia tap into places in the brain that others without it did not? Jewell had more questions than she'd had when she started this day and she really wasn't sure how to get the answers she sought since her dear Mimi was not a reliable source.

Jewell started to consider her options for investigating this mystery but decided it was best to stay focused on the meeting with her client first. She could get lost in the hunt. "We're twenty-three minutes early," she said, glancing at the time. "I don't care."

"You'll look desperate if you go too early," Mimi grumbled. "Well, a spool of thread is a spool of thread and not a bolt of silk cloth."

Jewell got out of the car and walked to the speaker and keypad. She pressed the call button. A smooth male voice immediately responded.

"About time. I thought you'd never get here. Come straight in. We've been waiting since half time and the game is almost over." The buzzer sounded and the gate swung open.

Jewell looked at the speaker for a moment, pretty certain that the man, probably Elli's husband Ben, thought he was talking to someone other than her. But, then, maybe he did know who was speaking to. "He said to come straight in, Mimi," she said, climbing into the truck. "I'm not sure he really knows who he let onto his property."

"Oh, that's not good." Mimi looked at her granddaughter. "I bet he's a mass murderer." She whispered as if the man she was talking about was listening. "He had a real appealing voice on that radio. I heard him. I bet he's handsome, too. Mass murderers are always handsome. It's how they trick their victims into their snares." She shifted in her seat to look at Jewell. "You have your gun, right?"

"Yes. Under my seat." Well out of Mimi's reach, she thought with relief.

Mimi lifted her red nylon handbag. "Mine is in my purse."

Chapter

2

"Mimi, no! No gun," Jewell said, still speaking French and using a firmer tone. She drove through the open gate onto the Sugar Mill Plantation property. Once the gate closed behind the camper, she slammed on the brakes. Her truck and camper slid on the well-maintained shell driveway.

"We've got to protect ourselves against mass murderers. You know that." Mimi folded her arms over her chest and hugged her purse with the gun.

Jewell turned to face her grand-mère, trying to keep her voice steady even though her heart was hammering in her chest. God, she hoped she didn't really have a gun with her. "We retired your gun when you turned eighty-five, Mimi." Jewell knew she was speaking louder and faster then she should. She couldn't help it. "I want the gun."

Mimi rolled her eyes and pulled the gun from her purse.

Jewell gasped. She did have one. It was a long barrel .22 revolver. "Where did you get this gun?"

She was grateful Mimi at least handled it safely, pointing it away from both of them. How she'd managed to carry the thing around without Jewell knowing was unbelievable. The barrel had to be six inches long!

"Oh, *mon Dieu*," Jewell cried. "Mimi, that's dangerous." God, she hoped she had the safety on.

"Don't get your thong panty in a twist." Mimi rolled her eyes and looked at the dull gray gun that seemed old and poorly maintained. "It's not like I have bullets."

"Thank God." At least she wasn't fully armed.

"I took them out of my purse to get to my lipstick when I went to the Simoneauxs' bathroom." She frowned. "I think I forgot them there. Maybe on the counter next to the sink. Maybe."

How would she ever explain the bullets to the Simoneauxs? "Mimi, I'm officially retiring this gun and all of your ammunition—again. Give me the gun." She looked at her grand-mère to make sure she'd heard her. She extended her hand. Mimi handed the gun to her properly with a harrumph. "I mean it. If you can't drive a car, you can't operate a firearm. No more guns." Jewell checked to make sure it wasn't loaded. It wasn't.

"No law in the state of Louisiana says that."

"Better than that, the law of your twisted-thong-panty granddaughter says it." She stuck out her hand again. "May I have your purse, please, Mimi?" She wanted to see if there were any other dangerous items inside of it, or any items she may have stolen from the Simoneauxs' house. She usually checked Mimi's purse for items she'd picked up because she liked them, without regard to the fact that they didn't belong to her.

"I gave you my gun. I'll keep my purse."

"Mimi," Jewell said firmly.

"I'll need my lipstick when we get to the big house." She opened her purse, took her lipstick out of it, then handed her the purse. Jewell looked through it and didn't see anything else that shouldn't be in it. She gave it back to her grand-mère.

Jewell placed the gun under her seat and resumed driving down the road. They passed the Sugar Mill Plantation Kennel first, which didn't sit well with Mimi.

"*Mon Dieu.* I thought we were going to the pretty plantation house I saw in the movie. My plantation. This is a dog pound." Mimi shook her head. "I'm confused."

They drove past a group of old slave houses. It appeared they'd been converted into offices. Jewell figured that they must've been used for the kennel. Across the street were a large wooden building and a huge fenced yard with agility apparatuses.

"I'm really confused now. It doesn't seem like a mass murderer would have time to make such a fine-looking dog pound," Mimi conceded, staring out the window.

"Not a mass murderer. Elli and Ben Bienvenu. They own the plantation and the kennel."

The road continued past the kennel, slicing through a thick, healthy crop of sugarcane fields with a narrow bayou bordering it on one side and acres of sugarcane on the other. She drove around a sharp bend and turned to face the magnificent Sugar Mill Plantation home. Jewell's heart fluttered in her chest just like it did when she found a special heirloom in a dusty old attic. Yes, this building was a treasure. A prized antique.

"Yep, that's it!" Mimi laughed and clapped her hands. "But it isn't pink anymore. I liked it pink best."

"It was probably only painted pink for the movie you saw it in," Jewell replied absently. Her attention was on the beautiful plantation that had her heart racing.

Jewell immediately spotted the back door that Elli had instructed her to use in their earlier conversation. She wanted to walk around to the front, to see the main entrance, but that hadn't been her instructions. She'd have time to explore later if she got the job.

Dear God, I want to get this job. I need it.

After Jewell made sure Mimi's gun remained tucked under the seat next to hers, they exited the truck. She didn't know who stumbled more in the race to get to the door, her or Mimi. "Holy cow, Mimi," she said, speaking French. "I think I need your cane more than you. I can hardly stand with the way my knees are shaking." She knew her voice sounded like a high school girl talking to her crush, but, my goodness, how could it not when she got to touch and smell and walk through such an amazing piece of history. On top of that, she was getting to take Mimi to this amazing place that might or might not be relevant to her childhood. Even if it wasn't, Mimi thought it was and that made her grand-mère happy.

Jewell hesitated pressing the doorbell. She was still studying the one-hundred-forty-five-year-old hand-forged nailheads in the doorframe. She thought of the slaves or free men of color who would have forged these nails right here on the plantation. They probably would've worked near the bayou, needing a water source.

Jewell squatted and pressed her hand to the gray wooden planks beneath her feet. It felt thick with years of paint buildup but she could tell by the length of the planks and the way they were laid that the wood was cypress. "Mimi, can you imagine how tall the cypress tree must've been that formed these boards? It must've been from one of the ancient cypresses that were as tall and wide as the sequoias in Yellowstone National Park."

"Huh," Mimi grunted as she expertly applied her lipstick. When she finished, she pressed the doorbell, which didn't *ding* but sounded more like heavy wind chimes.

Jewell stood, touched her nervous stomach, then dropped her hands at her sides. "Remember, we don't have the job, yet."

"Then you better be on your best behavior and stop that excited breathing. You sound like you're having sex with an athletic man."

"Mimi!" Jewell felt her face blush. Her grand-mère had never spoken of sex with her until the dementia advanced.

"Oh, don't be so virtuous." The door opened, but Mimi continued. "Sex is good and fun. Don't you know that? Haven't you had it before?"

Jewell placed a finger to her own lips and made a *shhh* sound to her grand-mère. Mimi placed her index finger on her freshly painted red lips looking innocent and childlike. She wanted to hug her precious, precocious grand-mère, but turned toward the opened door instead.

"Shame. Now, everybody's stopped talking just when the conversation was getting interesting," the man who answered the door said. Jewell dropped her hands to her side, blushing again.

This man with the deep, easy voice was tall, lean and impossibly handsome with eyes as light green as a barn cat's. He was wearing an untucked New Orleans Saints jersey and faded jeans. He looked down at Jewell and smiled. Her stomach did an odd little flip.

"You're not holding two extra-large meat-lovers' thin crust pizzas and cheesy breadsticks." He looked at Mimi and grinned a good-humored grin. "Neither are you." He leaned against the doorframe and looked at Jewell's bright green rubber boots with the red ladybugs imprinted on them. "Cute boots."

She blushed, and forced herself to stand still and not shuffle. She never had been embarrassed for wearing these boots or any of the two dozen others with fun designs she owned, so why now? His tone wasn't mocking or demeaning. It was just...well, playful. Flirty. Was Elli's husband flirting with her? Now she was annoyed. "It's good for dealing with whatever dirt and trash I have to step on," she said, eyes steady on his.

"Which apparently is an issue when delivering pizza." He nodded toward Mimi. "Which you clearly are not doing. You two are not the pizza delivery boys, huh?"

Mimi shook her head. "We're not boys. Are you blind?"

Jewell's eyes widened but the corner of his lips twitched telling her he was amused by Mimi's response.

"No ma'am. I can see just fine." He smiled at Jewell. It was both friendly and spoke of his virility at the same time. How did he do that? Did he do it on purpose? Jewell suspected he did. But, then again, she wasn't one-hundred percent sure. Better not think too much on it or she might ask him about it. She needed this job too much to risk not getting it by saying something foolish. Mimi on the other hand, had no agenda. She said and asked whatever popped into her mind whether it made sense or not.

"What did you do with my cistern?" She asked, talking behind her finger still on her lips.

He grinned and shrugged his shoulders. "Can't say."

Jewell reached over and gently urged Mimi to lower her hand. She frowned like it was Jewell's fault that she'd forgotten it was there. Then, Mimi looked at Elli's husband and gasped. "Is it game day?" She tugged on the hem of his Saints black and gold football team jersey.

"Yes indeed, ma'am. They're down by six against the Atlanta Falcons. Fourth quarter."

Mon Dieu," she wobbled passed him, into the house. The four rubber tips on the bottom of her swan-neck, quad-cane left marks on the waxed wooden floor. Pride had her once refusing to use the cane like she now refused to use the walker which would better suit her mobility level. "They're playing the dirty birds. I can't miss the Saints playing the dirty birds." She disappeared from view, almost giving Jewell heart failure.

"Mimi. Wait." She moved past Elli's husband who was now smiling a big white shiny smile. "I'm sorry. I'll get her. Excuse me." God, she'd never be able to convince Elli and Ben that Mimi wouldn't cause any disruptions with her work, now.

"Who dat...who dat..." Jewell heard Mimi cheering but already couldn't see her. "Who dat say dey goin to beat dem Saints."

"Down the hall past the stairs to the left," Jewell heard from behind her, his voice even with a hint of humor. "Game's on the TV in the parlor."

Jewell looked at him over her shoulder. He stood a head taller than her five-feet-eight inches. Despite being frazzled by Mimi's nervy behavior, she smiled back. "She really loves the Saints," she managed, knowing her statement was a poor defense of Mimi barging into his home. "She's been a fan since the first day they were organized. She was actually at the press conference announcing that a franchise team was awarded to New Orleans." She paused and shook her head, realizing nerves had her about to tell him personal information about why Mimi had actually been there on that day. *Relax, Jewell,* she reminded herself. *Don't be so upset by what Mimi's actions might mean to getting this job.* "My fault. I should've planned better so she could've watched the game."

"I see. Picking a random house, trespassing so your..." He looked at her a moment, "...grandmother I presume, can watch the Saints play the Falcons—that's how you remedy your lack of planning?"

"Trespassing?" Jewell stopped at the foot of the rich walnut stairs with its simple newel-posts. She paused a moment to listen for her grand-mère's voice. She heard Mimi speaking in a nearby room, telling someone that the Saints were going to beat the dirty birds. Probably Jewell's future client, Elli.

Not a good start.

She turned to face Elli's misinformed husband with the bad attitude. "We're not trespassing. We may have entered the home uninvited, but we were invited onto the property." Turning on her heels, she headed off to do damage control.

"You were invited to deliver the pizza we ordered. Or so I had thought." His words had her turning to face him again. He was now leaning against the wall opposite the stairs.

Why was he always leaning on something? He sure seemed fit enough to hold up his own body weight. It was easy to see that he worked out with the way his broad shoulders tapered to his narrow hips and straight long legs. So why was he assuming this "not a care in the world" pose? It didn't make sense. Jewell's instincts told her that this award-winning dog trainer actually would be like a cat. He might look calm and easy going, but he'd pounce and devour without a moment's notice.

"I'm sorry for the confusion," she began, feeling her already electrified nerves for the meeting with her potential client amp-up because of this misunderstanding with her husband. "I was invited here by Elli. I'm here to talk to her about a project." His eyebrows arched. So, he didn't know about their meeting. Awkward. Everything about their meeting had been awkward. "I'm early," she said, like that would explain why he didn't know about the meeting.

His eyebrows shot up again and she all but heard him say, *Really, so that's why I didn't know about it? Because you're early?*

Jewell shrugged, extended her hand. "I'm Jewell Duet, All Things Antique." She looked over her shoulder toward where Mimi was yelling at the television. "You must be Ben Bienvenu. Elli's husband?" Mimi's voice grew louder. Jewell turned, not waiting for him to respond. "Please excuse me. I have to go to my grandmother."

She walked into the parlor where the roar of the crowd at the Saints game was blaring over the TV and sportscasters were announcing that the Saints were on the eight-yard line, ready to score.

Her grand-mère sat on a high back Duncan Phyfe sofa, reupholstered in a powder blue silk. Next to her was a good-looking man sprawled on an early 1980s ugly brown recliner. He wore a Saints football jersey and had a bottle of beer in his hand. A Beagle and a Labrador mix were sitting upright on the floor next to him. They were looking at the TV as intently as Mimi was. Jewell was struck by the complexity of life there with the mix of restored antiques, comfy man's furniture, hominess and a bit of hospitality.

The man in the chair saluted her with his beer. "I assume you don't have the pizzas."

"She's here to see Elli," the leaner said.

"Her, too?" he asked, nodding to Mimi.

"Yes. She's with me." Jewell rushed toward him, extending her hand. "I'm Jewell Duet, All Things Antique. I was just telling Ben that I have an appointment with his wife."

The man in the recliner grunted. "Knucklehead, there, will never have a wife. Especially, not mine."

Jewell swallowed back the frustrated shriek in her throat, looked at him with all the calm and dignity she could muster, then at the man she'd thought was Ben. He was smiling and leaning again. "She's early."

Dear God. This initial meeting with her potential client was not going well. She should've waited the extra 23 minutes.

If Elli would've been there, the identity confusion over her and Mimi being the pizza deliverers and the leaner guy being the homeowner would never have happened.

"Who Dat! Go Saints. Go. Two-yard line. They will get this. Woo-hoo," Mimi cheered.

The noisy distraction with Mimi probably couldn't have been prevented regardless.

Ben, the smiling-leaner who wasn't Ben and Mimi narrowed their focus on the television as the New Orleans Saints completed an easy screen pass and scored a touchdown to tie the game. The smiling-leaner, who had left his wall to sit next to Mimi on the nineteenth century sofa, was now giving her a gentle but full-on hug followed by a couple of high-fives. Ben was cheering from his recliner and his dogs were barking to join in the excitement.

Despite her nerves, worry and frustration, Jewell started to laugh. The scene did not fit the historic parlor with its old wood and marble, but it felt right and good. Then she remembered that she was an outsider, there by default. Her smile faded. The man that wasn't Ben extended his hand to Mimi. "I should introduce myself." Mimi looked at his hand a long moment and Jewell knew she was confused about what to do with it. Her eyes narrowed and she slapped his knuckles. Really hard. The sound echoed in the room, silencing the cheering, laughing and even the barking.

"Mimi!" Jewell shouted. "I'm so sorry. She gets a little confused sometimes. Please forgive her."

Ben started laughing, a full-on belly laugh. "Hell, she did exactly the right thing with this rascal knucklehead," he said, his Cajun accent heavy. "That was exactly right, Mimi."

"I'm not your Mimi." She told him with all sincerity. "I have one grandchild from one daughter. And you're not her. She is." She pointed to Jewell. "Oh, shhh. I can't hear the announcers." No one pointed out to her that she was the only one speaking.

Jewell looked at the men who were both actually smiling. They seemed to be enjoying Mimi's strange behavior. The smiling-leaning charming man who wasn't Ben walked over to Jewell with his hand up in the air.

Really, he was going to high-five her too?

She awkwardly lifted her hand and slapped it. "Who Dat," she said with confused and diffused enthusiasm. She felt awkward, uncertain. Not usual things for her. She started to speak in a rambling, un-Jewell-like way. "The extra point is good...yay...They're up by one...only twenty-seconds left on the clock. If the Falcons can't run it back on kickoff, they might have time for one Hail Mary pass...could get lucky...odds are against them."

"You know football, huh?"

She motioned toward her grand-mère. "It's a religion in our home." She extended her hand to him. "You know who I am. I didn't get your name?"

He captured her hand in a firm handshake, then covered it with his other hand in a gentle hold. It was totally inappropriate, flirtatious and challenging. Then he smiled an outrageously charming smile, more disarming than his earlier ones. Jewell knew in an instant that there must be a slew of brokenhearted women all over south Louisiana pining for this man. He seemed to enjoy the sport of flirting. She didn't like this man. She didn't want to play his game, nor tug-of-war with her hand to reclaim it, so she just stood there, looking at him with her best professorial look, telling him without words, *you're acting like a naughty schoolboy, and I'm not impressed.* He immediately released her hand. So he was charming and astute. That was interesting, and a little unsettling.

"Beau. Beau Bienvenu," He said, glancing at Mimi who was telling Ben all of the reasons a Hail Mary pass wouldn't work with the special team defense the Saints had. "And who is the young lady with the old school Catholic nuns' disciplinary hand?"

"My grandmother. Mignon Duet." Jewell had already explained to Elli that she brought Mimi with her to all of her job sites and guaranteed that she wouldn't interfere with her performance, so she saw no need to explain it to Beau.

"That knucklehead is my cousin," Ben said to Mimi in response to her question about who was the man talking to Jewell.

"I'm actually the more brilliant knucklehead in this family." Beau laughed. "He does have the best girl in the state of Louisiana, though. I will concede that. I'd say that's not too bad for a man who chases dogs all day."

"Speaking of his wife," Jewell began, "I'm early for our appointment...as you already know." She glanced at Beau as she pulled out her cell phone from her jeans pocket and

looked at the time. "It's about appointment time now."
"Elli's late," Beau smiled. "She's always late."

"I'll call her," Ben said, looking at the TV and not moving.

"Shhh," Mimi fussed looking at Jewell. *"Tu parles trop, ma sucrée."*

"Yes, indeed. Sounds like you were scolded," Beau laughed.

"Shhh, Mr. Knucklehead. You talk too much, too." Mimi told him, repeating in English what she'd said to Jewell.

Jewell put her finger to her lips and shook her head when he was about to say something to Mimi. He probably wanted to correct her and tell her his name wasn't actually Mr. Knucklehead. Not a good idea since the Saints had lined up for the kickoff. A run back and field goal would put the game into overtime.

They all leaned in toward the TV.

The Saints kicker dropped his arm and rushed toward the football and connected in the most perfectly beautiful kick with the longest hang-time Jewell had ever seen. It dropped in the end zone into the arms of a Falcon receiver. It was not returnable and a fair catch was called. The Falcons had the ball on their own twenty-yard line. You could hear the disappointment in the deflated roar of the Falcon home crowd but not Mimi's.

"Who Dat, Who Dat, Who Dat sayin' dey goin' to beat dem Saints," Mimi cheered in English, then turned to speak to Jewell in French. "Not the Dirty Birds. Fifteen seconds left on the clock. You saw that, my girl. I love a victory on the road." Jewell looked at Beau and Ben, who were staring at them like they were aliens who'd just landed in their living room. They both might be Cajuns with Cajun accents, but they clearly didn't speak Parisian French.

"Here we go. Watch for the Hail Mary," Mimi shouted as the Falcon quarterback dropped back, and three defensive lineman rushed in with the remainder of the Saints defensive players pulling back to cover the Falcon receivers rushing down the field. The quarterback cocked his arm back and released the ball in a long, high arching spiral that dropped into a group of Saints and Falcons players forming a tangle of arms, legs and helmets on the fifteen-yard line. The officials jumped into the shoving, groping heap to figure out who had the ball with just ten seconds left on the game clock.

"Oh, *mon Dieu.* I think I need a little white heart pill," Mimi said to no one in particular.

"You don't have little white heart pills, Mimi." Jewell told her, making sure she was well. "Your heart is healthy and so are you. You're just excited." Jewell looked at the TV. "Saints intercepted," she shouted. "Look, Sam 'Spiderman' Brown has the ball."

"Saints win, Mrs. Duet," Beau said, giving her a high-five.

Mimi picked up a dog magazine on the table and started to fan herself with it. "Mr. Knucklehead, I never doubted it."

"Of course you didn't."

The telephone rang and Ben answered it. "Pizza delivery's here." Ben told Beau and hiked his thumb at him like a hitchhiker. Beau looked at Jewell and smiled that disarming smile that made her insides swishy. She had no doubt he'd spent many hours mastering that particular smile.

"Are you sure it's pizza delivery? It could be another home invasion," Jewell said.

Ben rolled his eyes. "Yes, I'm sure. It's Cousin Brad's boy, T-Brad. I buzzed him through the gates. You get the door, Beau. You're paying. You lost the bet on the half time score. I'll call Elli."

Jewell sat next to Mimi. She looked tired. The excitement of the game had exhausted her and she had the glassy look in her eyes that she got when her mind drifted off. The dementia had been progressing more this last year. The evenings were the worst. Her doctor had said the confusion in the evening was a common condition referred to as *sundowning*. When the sun went down, her confusion got worst. This dark room, the strange surroundings and the strange men all added to her current dazed state.

"Are you feeling well, Mimi?" Jewell asked, finding easy, simple conversation could keep her calm and present.

"Yes, but I'd like to put my feet up to watch the post-game show. I like when they go inside the locker room and the players take off their shirts. Can you get me the footstool?"

Jewell looked around the room. "I don't see one here." Then she realized it would be the perfect opportunity to leave. She spoke to her in French. "Let's go back to the camper where you can relax in your favorite chair and put your feet up."

"It's in the nook next to the fireplace," she said continuing to speak French to Jewell. She pointed to the right side of the old marble and wood fireplace centered on the main wall in the parlor. There along the wall, about thirty-six inches high from the floor, was white raised panel wainscoting.

"Mimi. There's no nook next to the fireplace." Jewel glanced at Ben who was sitting on his recliner, leaning forward and petting his dogs. He'd just disconnected his cell phone.

"Elli said she'll be here in about fifteen minutes. She ran into cousin Ruby at the grocery store and was delayed. She apologized."

"There's no need to apologize. If anyone should apologize it's me for rudely arriving early and disturbing your game." As she spoke to Ben, Mimi stood and slowly walked to the fireplace, barely keeping her balance with her cane. "Mimi?"

Mimi ran her hand along the side of the wood panel adjacent to the fireplace. A click sounded, loud and heavy. The panel swung open to the left on hidden hinges. Mimi reached inside the open door and pulled out a footstool. The walnut wooden legs were a bit dull with dust, but the detailed embroidered padded top was clean, colorful and unmarred. She closed the door with a snap and carried the footstool to the sofa.

"Twinnie and I helped Momma embroider this. Isn't it pretty? Magnolias were Momma's favorite." She sat on the sofa, placed the footstool on the floor and put her feet up on it.

"Mimi?" She murmured, as she glanced at Ben who was staring at them with a bewildered expression on his face. It was nothing compared to the expression on Beau's face as he stood under the arched opening of the parlor with paper napkins in one hand and two pizza boxes in the other.

Chapter 3

Beau and Ben exchanged a speaking glance. They were cousins and best buds long enough to read each other's looks without saying a word, a convenient skill learned while playing hide and seek as kids. Sound traveled in the cypress bayous, and a nonverbal exchange kept them in the game longer than the rest of their cousins. It was an instinctive skill they had developed even before Beau had been adopted into the family by Ben's Uncle Ronald and Aunt Bernice when he was eight years old. They had always seemed more like family than friends even when they first started playing together in kindergarten.

Beau knew Ben was as shocked by the old lady opening the secret nook near the fireplace as he was. His cousin's eyes were steady and his expression contained, but Beau knew he'd had no idea that the hiding spot existed, and he'd lived in the house longer than anyone else in the family. That included Tante Izzy, who had been born in the house. If Ben didn't know every nook and cranny, then neither did anyone else.

Still, Beau decided he'd ask Tante Izzy when she returned from her casino trip if she knew of it. Not only had his years as an attorney taught him never to leave anything to chance or supposition, his personal experiences had, too.

Ben started to get up out of his chair, and Beau put his hand on his shoulder and pushed him back down. "No," he said quietly. "Let the ladies play out whatever their game is." Ben nodded.

"I'll take a few slices while it's still hot," Ben said, and slid four slices of pizza from the pizza box Beau held with one hand onto the top paper plate that Beau held in his other hand.

"Here are some napkins." Beau gave him a handful. "I know you'll need them." Beau walked to where Jewell spoke softly in French to her grand-mère. It wasn't Cajun French, he noted, or he might be able to pick up a few words and figure out what they were saying. Instead they communicated with the sophisticated French spoken in France. Who were they? What did they want? Were they planning to use Elli as part of some surreptitious scheme? If so, for what ends? Or, were they what they first had appeared to be—a sweet, but awkward granddaughter chasing after her grandmother?

Hell, he'd even thought the granddaughter was sexy and pretty in an exotic sort of way. Creamy café au lait skin, wide milk chocolate eyes, full shapely lips and interesting arching brows. She was...alluring. In fact, everything about her labeled her as a hottie, a fox, a knockout...from her full round, high breasts, well-shaped curved derrière, trim narrow waist to her fluid, almost rhythmic movements. She looked like sex on a lazy Sunday afternoon. That is, everything except for the way she dressed.

Her neat but old jeans, blue golf shirt and brightly painted ladybug Wellies knock-offs were average, unremarkable and bordering on plain. It was a strange mix. He would've thought someone with her shape and sensual nature would be in a micro mini skirt, plunging neckline and man-killer heels, and wearing more makeup than the little bit around her eyes that she had on now.

Yeah, it was as weird as her alluring scent—warm, sweet and a little bit spicy. Did she wear that fragrance to distract, misdirect? There was definitely more than what appeared on the surface. He'd bet his law practice on that.

Beau placed the pizza boxes and paper plates on the coffee table in front of them. "Hungry?"

Mignon Duet and Ben's dogs immediately moved toward the table.

Ben snapped his fingers and his dogs heeled. No surprise there. Jewell grabbed her grandmother's arm to stop her from opening the top pizza box. Her grandmother didn't look very happy about it.

Jewell Duet, why was that name so familiar? *All Things Antique* didn't ring a bell, but her name sure did.

"What? I'm hungry," Mignon complained. Beau noticed that her granddaughter's cheeks blushed a pretty pink as she subtly shook her head in silent communication with her grandmother. So she could telegraph her thoughts to the old lady as he and Ben did.

Beau opened the box and smiled at the grandmother. "Do you like meat-lovers' pizza?" he asked, pulling a slice onto a plate with a napkin.

"I prefer olives and artichokes, but this will do," she said taking the plate. He handed her a fresh napkin.

"Would you like a slice, Jewell?"

She shook her head, causing her long silky ponytail to swish across her back. "No, thank you." Her eyes darted to the footstool as if she wanted to examine it, but she didn't want to be obvious about it.

"You said your business is *All Things Antique*?" Beau asked Jewell, pulling the chair that was near the fireplace closer to the sofa. Closer to her enticing scent. Ben reached around him and grabbed a couple more slices of pizza and gave a crooked forced smile to the ladies, before going into the kitchen, the dogs at his heels. Jewell's fragrance certainly didn't seem to affect his cousin one bit. He actually may not have even smelled it. Interesting.

Beau kept his eyes locked on her. Her eyes were bright, anxious. "Um, yes. You've heard of my business?" she finally answered, her voice steady, even.

"No." He took a bite of pizza and chewed. "Where are you from?"

"New Orleans."

"How did you and Elli meet?"

"She mentioned getting my phone number from my direct-mail flyer and from speaking with one of my clients here in Cane." She picked up the crumbs from her grandmother's lap and placed them onto a napkin. "I just finished their estate sale today."

"More a garage sale if you ask me," Mignon said around a mouthful of pizza. "Only good thing they had there was this nice collection of rings." She put the pizza on her lap and the paper plate on top of it before extending her hands for Beau to see the rings. He stood, leaned over the coffee table to look at the old battered rings.

"Very nice." He smiled and Mignon smiled back at him. He glanced at Jewell who was looking down at the footstool again. "Your name sounds familiar."

"She's very famous," Mignon interjected. Jewell placed her hand on her grandmother's knee. Beau knew it was to silence her. So, she didn't really want him to know who she was. "Not as famous as her momma." Mignon nodded and wagged her eyebrows.

Jewell stood. Her scent wafted over him. "I think we should reschedule our appointment with Elli." She took a clean napkin and wiped the table near her grandmother. "It's going to be late by the time we get back to New Orleans. Besides it has been a long day. We should be heading home."

"I am home, *ma sucrée*," Mignon's tone left no room for discussion.

"I know I said we might sleep in the camper here at Sugar Mill, Mimi, depending on when Elli wanted us to begin work, but we really should head back to New Orleans now."

"Oh, *mon Dieu*. Do you have rocks for brains? I said I'm home." She looked at Beau. "Get me a blanket. I can sleep right here in front of the fire." She looked at the fireplace. "Where's the fire? Why isn't there a fire? There's always a fire in the evening. Even in the summer. The gentlemen's pipes don't smell so bad when they're in here and the fire's going and the flue is open."

What in the hell was going on here? Beau stood. He'd told Ben not to show his hand, but he had about enough of this cryptic story telling from the old lady. "Jewell, what is she talking about?"

"I...uh..." she stammered.

"Hello," Elli shouted from the back entrance of the house. A dog howled and another barked to echo her master's call. Beau heard her hurried steps as she and two of her dogs raced into the parlor and straight to Jewell who easily patted them on the head. Elli's short wavy blonde hair was in its usual perfect sassy mess. Not that he knew anything about cosmetics, but he could see that it had been applied with a light expert hand, making her pretty light blue eyes pop and her full mouth shine. She looked like she was in hurry, but not one bit anxious. In fact, she looked coolly sophisticated in her dark jeans, tan California bohemian blouse and fancy running shoes, "Oh, I'm so very sorry I'm late." Her dogs, Doe and Jenny, circled around Jewell and sniffed her ladybug boots.

"Oh, no you don't," Elli said, pulling the dogs away from Jewell. "They have a thing for rubber boots," she smiled. "They practically maimed Tante Izzy when they first met her. They tried to rob her of her shrimp boots and knocked the poor woman down in the garden in the process. Excuse me. I'll be right back."

Elli dragged Doe and Jenny out the front door and quickly returned. She gave Jewell the kind of warm hug that was usually only shared by old friends, not women who had never met before. It wasn't lost on Beau how different the women were standing there, one blonde and fair in running shoes and the other with creamy caramel-colored-skin and long, very dark, silky hair wearing ladybug rubber boots. Yet, there were similarities, too. Both were tall, lean, with intelligent eyes.

"I'm sorry, the dogs are so much better behaved than when I first got them, but..." she shrugged and didn't finish her sentence. She didn't have to; their earlier rambunctious behavior did it for her. "I hope Ben and Beau made you feel welcome," she smiled, "and this guy didn't turn all his charm on you," she laughed looking at Beau. "The last female visitor I had here needed oxygen after meeting Beau," she laughed.

"Not because of me," Beau smiled. "She had asthma. Allergic to dog hair."

"Funny it didn't bother her in the hour before you arrived and started flirting with her."

Beau threw up his hands in surrender. "I'm sticking with my defense. Dog hair."

Jewell was smiling. A pretty, wide-mouthed, unguarded smile. For a few moments he thought about how nice it would be to see her smiling at him over a nice dinner with good wine at Antoine's. Then he caught sight of the grandmother from the corner of his eyes staring at the fireplace. She looked confused and maybe even a bit annoyed. He better keep his wits about him with this woman, he thought, looking at Jewell again. She had skills. If you could call smiling like she did *skills*. Hell, yeah. He called that a skill.

"Well, I'm just glad they didn't ignore you both because the Saints game was on," Elli continued.

"They beat the dirty birds," Mignon interrupted. She threw up her hand to give Beau a high-five, which he immediately obliged. "I don't remember the score, though," she frowned. "Tell her, Mr. Knucklehead. Tell her the final score."

Elli laughed. "Yes, Mr. Knucklehead, tell me the score."

Beau couldn't help but laugh, too. "17 to 14."

"That's football, right?" Elli grasped Jewell's hands and tugged. "Let's go into the kitchen for some tea, organic lavender cookies and MoonPies. We can discuss business there," Elli said, then turned to Beau. "Where's Ben?"

Elli was suddenly swept around and into the arms of her husband in a huge, embrace. "Here I am, *chère*. Missed me?" He kissed her full on the lips. She looked up into his Bienvenu spring green eyes, and Beau had a moment of real envy seeing how much she loved him...and he loved her. It wasn't the first time he felt it and it certainly never lasted more than thirty seconds, but he got it nonetheless. He glanced at Jewell, who was smiling a timid, sweet, tender smile looking at them.

"I had a man who loved me like that," Mignon announced. "Kissed me a lot, too." She nodded and her tight curls bobbed. "Too bad he was married."

"Mimi," Jewell groaned. "Dear God. I'm sorry."

"Don't you apologize, *ma sucrée*." Mignon shook her head. "It was a grand love affair. And I got your momma from it. Without her, I wouldn't have you."

"Elli, I'd love that tea now." Jewell stood abruptly.

"I'm staying here," Mignon announced. "I want to take a nap." She immediately leaned her head against the back of the sofa and closed her eyes.

Jewell looked at Elli. "I'm so sorry. I did explain the situation to you. She's vocal but she won't interfere with my work."

"She's darling." Elli left Ben's side and grabbed Jewell's hand, then led her out of the room, saying over her shoulder, "You two men don't mind making sure Miss Mignon is comfy, do you?"

"She already looks comfortable to me," Ben said, waving his wife on. "What in the hell is going on with these women?" He whispered, looking at the old lady who was fast asleep and making little snuffling sounds. Ben walked to where Mignon had opened the secret nook. Beau joined him.

"It can't be good." Beau said, his voice hushed even though he didn't think there was much of a chance that

Mignon would wake. He stepped closer to where Ben squatted and ran his hand along the side of the wainscoting. The latch released with soft snap. "I'll be damned." The door swung open and Beau bent over and looked inside the dark, wooden nook. "Empty."

"It wasn't about thirty minutes ago."

Beau pulled out his cell phone and started a Google search of Jewell Duet. Who was she, really? Why was her name so familiar to him? He typed in her name. "Well, I'll be a son of a..."

"What?" Ben interrupted.

"She's Dr. Jewell Duet." He looked at Ben. "She's the leading antiquities expert in the state of Louisiana. And she was a professor at Tulane University up until the spring semester when she was asked to step down." He looked at Ben. "You don't remember her? She used to be interviewed on the news whenever they needed an antiquities expert. Then, she was on the news a lot this past spring and summer because she was charged with felony theft."

"Were there any dogs on agility courses or in any rescue trials in any of those news stories she was in? Or were there any football games or scores?" Ben said, one brow cocked. "If not, I'm sure I never saw her on the tube. I don't have time for idle TV watching, cuz."

With a shake of his head, Beau grinned as he leaned against the fireplace mantel. "Well, it's a good thing I'm watching out for you and the family. You might just get sucker punched otherwise. I read. I watch. I observe. It's why I get paid the big bucks."

"Not by me," Ben grunted, "which reminds me. You still didn't bill me for those contracts you drafted."

Beau rapped his knuckles on the wall near the secret latch, not happy that a thief was in his family's home. "We're talking about the sexy brunette that smells like smooth sex in a fast car. Stay focused." Beau looked at his phone again, his stomach knotting the more he read.

"According to this news report, the New Orleans DA has a solid case against her. They have everything but the proverbial smoking gun. The stolen items have never been recovered." He sucked in a breath and looked at Ben. "Crap, man. This is really bad. She's accused of gaining the family's trust and confidence, gaining access to very valuable pearls, diamonds and gold, and stealing it. She did this at one of the estates she was working. I remember the news accounts now. Apparently, she picked the wrong people to rob. I don't see a name, but from what I remember, they went after her like soldiers battling an invading army. The family is Old New Orleans money. Connections. They threw their influence at her like heavy artillery."

He searched a few more items, feeling his muscles tense in his shoulders and neck with each article he clicked on. "Yeah, here it is," Beau said. "The reason we never heard who the family is." His eyes met Ben's. "A gag order was issued, so the exact details of the case weren't released to the media. Interesting. The article says the gag order was issued by Judge Marcus Brunello to protect the privacy and security of the victims." Beau rubbed a hand over the tight muscles at the back of his neck. "That's unusual in a theft case. In a sexual assault case or one involving minors, yes. For theft, that is highly unusual procedure."

He remained silent as he read further, and then continued. "It doesn't reveal anything more." He looked at Ben. "This is the New Orleans judicial system, so who knows what's really going on here. The rational thinking is that the judge is privy to all the facts of the case, so for him to place a gag order, he must have seen just cause for it." Beau thought about that a moment. "He must've thought the victims needed to be protected or there was sensitive information that he wanted sealed either because of the investigation or because of who may have been damaged by the information." Beau looked down at his phone again. "It's very unusual." He swiped his finger across his phone as he read silently, before speaking again. "Well, there hasn't actually been a conviction...yet. Dr. Duet's case still has to go to trial."

"Great." Ben blew a heavy breath. "My wife hired a known thief and invited her into our home to look through our personal things."

Beau looked at his phone in silence reading another newspaper article that he had pulled up. "I'll have to research this further, make a few calls. I have more questions than answers, Ben. We do know a few things though from these articles, and from what I remember from cocktail discussions with some of my peers." He started lifting a finger for each point he made. "First, the DA and the legal community think she's a thief. I don't know why we shouldn't believe that, too." He cursed under his breath. "She hasn't been convicted yet, and there are a lot of pieces to this crime we don't know, but we do know that she had opportunity being there to work at the family estate." He lifted a second finger. "We also know that she's a hell of a researcher and she's really good at what she does."

"Talk about overqualified for the job of cleaning our dirty attic and shed."

"Or not qualified at all to clean anything," Beau interjected. "Probably nobody wants to touch her in New Orleans with a ten-foot pole. She's definitely unemployable."

Ben grunted. "Except by my wife. We get her by default." Ben shook his head. "Her troubles will make her more desirable to Elli—she wants to save the world. When Dr. Duet comes back in here, let's ask her what the deal is with the charges against her and the secret nook." Ben ran his hand over the hidden latch to release the door again. The door swung open. Mignon sat up in her seat and looked right at them but she didn't say a word. She grabbed the footstool and carried it to the nook and placed it back inside and closed the door.

"Momma said we should keep everything tidy for the morning." She turned, but instead of walking back to the sofa, she climbed into Ben's recliner. After a minute of struggling with the handle to lift the leg-rest, she gave up and closed her eyes. Beau walked over to her and lifted the leg-rest for her. He got an old quilt from where it was folded in a basket behind the sofa and laid it over Mignon. She might be trouble. She might be up to no good. But she was an old lady who looked lost and tired right now.

"You're a pathetic softy."

"No," he said, denying what he knew was the truth. "It's better to keep your friends close and your enemies closer. At least until you figure out if they *are* your enemies. I don't think we should confront Jewell yet. We need more information. We need to be prepared for whatever excuses or stories she tells us when we do confront her. Besides," he moved away from Mignon and motioned for Ben to follow him. "You know that addendum with the generational trust and special clauses we had to high step around when we executed the will for you and Elli to inherit Sugar Mill Plantation?" Ben nodded. "Remember how no matter how hard we tried, we couldn't connect all of the dots in that trust from two generations ago?" Ben nodded again. Beau looked at Mignon and blew out a breath. "Well, it's possible we're looking at a dot."

"Or the expert researcher has figured out a way to contrive a dot."

Beau nodded. "Yes, indeed, cuz. Yes, indeed. The granddaughter might be running a confidence game for her biggest theft yet."

***

"I'm glad you're taking the job to clear the barn properly," Elli said, placing her teacup on the matching saucer. "I'll be nearby or just a phone call away if you need anything." She smiled a soft smile. "I'll be busy completing preparations before this big budget movie can be filmed here. I won't be here for the set carpenters when they arrive to start early construction, but I've had several meetings with them. Everything is organized for their arrival. They are a relatively small group. I'll be here for the larger crews to get situated on the property, so they'll be the least disruptive as possible to the kennel. They'll be bringing in the heavier equipment, trailers. Ben has to continue working with the search and rescue dogs that are in a critical stage of training. He has contractual obligations to deliver the dogs ready for service in just weeks." She took a sip of tea before continuing. "I can't believe he agreed to let them film such a huge production here when he has to get the dogs ready for graduation at the same time." She smiled. "I know he'd prefer not to have the distraction but he's doing it for me and Joey. He knows how much we enjoy having movies filmed here."

Elli placed her hands flat on the rough-hewn cypress plank table. Jewell figured that four or five generations ago, this table had been crafted by slaves or free men of color on the plantation. She wondered for a moment if Elli knew that. Had she looked on the underside for the initials or markings of the craftsman who created the centerpiece for the kitchen? Had the current Bienvenu family ever considered how their ancestors or their long-ago workers had prepared meals on this table or what topics of conversations were shared around it?

Would future generations wonder what the current Bienvenus did around this very table? God, Jewell loved history, the connections that existed between today and yesterday.

"Our seven-year-old son, Joey, is at Boy Scout camp," Elli continued, and Jewell refocused her attention on the conversation with this happy, content and confident woman. "When he gets back, we're going to take him to the beach for fall break. He's very disappointed he'll be in school most of the time the production crew is setting up. He loves the behind-the-scenes stuff. Me, I love the orchestrating, the gathering of all the best components to bring it together to create something spectacular."

"Are you producing movies again?"

"No. I'm just dabbling in one little piece of the big puzzle." Elli laughed. "It's all I really want to do now. I get to bring amazing directors and producers here to Sugar Mill where they can let their imaginations create movie magic. This is a magical place, you know?"

"Yes, I do." Jewell looked up at the wavy lead glass kitchen window, knowing exactly how difficult and remarkable it was for that to be created in the 1800s. Yes, she understood how magical this place was down to its foundation. "You and Ben are blessed to live here. It's nice that you share your home with the movie industry and therefore the world."

Elli smiled and took a sip of her tea. "You know, my husband gets that. He's a perceptive and sensitive guy even though he has a snarling bark from time to time. It's just like the flash and blasts in a movie." She laughed. "It looks intimidating, but it isn't real. He's so fair-minded...such a softy. He's darling."

Jewell actually heard Elli sigh. Wow. She'd heard her mom sigh over a guy once, but she'd done it in front of the man who drove a brand new red Ferrari. And, she'd faked it. This was the real deal. She didn't know women actually sighed like that for real.

"Well, I'm setting up the bunkhouse down the road by the kennel nice and cozy for us," Elli continued. "Joey is thrilled we'll be staying there. He says it'll be better than Boy Scout camp. The reality is this movie will make it almost impossible to live in the house." Elli shrugged her shoulders. "I hope staying in the bunkhouse will keep my husband sane. He'll be happier closer to his dogs with so many people around. I'm having his recliner moved to the bunkhouse, too. He'll get a kick out of that." She smiled a sweet, gentle smile that made her blue eyes shine.

"I've worked on a few movie sets in New Orleans and around the area," Jewell said, "as an antiquities consultant, to make sure the scenes were set correctly or that certain props were handled in the right manner." She laughed thinking about how little the last set designer knew about cooking on the plantation in the 1860s. She wanted the scene to be set with slaves cooking inside the big house, when all cooking had actually been done in yard kitchens in that era. "I totally understand the disruptions. There are so many people rushing around, so much equipment, too."

"Exactly." She placed her hands flat on the table. Jewell felt it was a signal that she was bracing for a more businesslike discussion. "The movie carpenters and crew preparing for the shoot at the end of next week will start arriving before the weekend. Maybe even midweek. That's when we're scheduled to leave. I'm sorry I won't be here."

"Don't be. I have a lot of experience leading projects. Just tell me what you need."

She smiled. "This must seem like a little thing compared to the important investigations and expeditions you've led."

"Not at all. Each site holds its own intrigue no matter how much or what is there."

"What an interesting life you have." Jewell liked hearing the esteem in Elli's tone. She hadn't felt that in some time. "The plan is for the carpenters to start building sets in tents on-site but they'll have to get into the barn to stage everything sooner rather than later. Are you certain you can clean the barn in just one week?"

Jewell nodded. She would do it if it required her to stay up 24-7. "I do what I say I'm going to do, Elli."

"And, you don't mind staying in your camper?"

"No. I told you. It's home away from home for Mimi and me. It's familiar and comfortable for her and for me, too.

"I want to make sure you understand some things too, Elli." Jewell's heart was racing. She felt full disclosure was necessary with her new employer although she wouldn't let her legal problems and Mimi's dementia affect her performance. "I've already mentioned Mimi's behavior and my need to keep her close to me." Elli nodded, reached across the table and squeezed Jewell's hand in a show of understanding. It made what she wanted to tell her about being charged with felony theft so much harder.

She didn't want this kind, generous, open person to think poorly of her. She liked Elli. It felt good to see that she liked her back. That was a rare thing since she had been accused of being a criminal. What difference did having friends matter if she ended up in prison anyway? Oh, God. She couldn't let her mind drift to negative thoughts of being imprisoned. She had to shut that down before it drowned her in a wave of despair.

She pulled her hand from Elli's. The absence of human contact made her feel every bit as alone as she actually was. "Elli, I respect you and feel you should know..."

Beau and Ben walked into the room. Jewell stopped speaking. Both men were frowning. It set off alarm bells for her.

"Is Mimi okay?" She stood and started to walk out. Elli grabbed her hand. It oddly eased her racing heart but she still wanted to rush to check on her grand-mère.

"How's Mignon?" Elli asked the men, looking at Jewell.

"Sleeping like a baby," Beau said with a smile, then thumbed his finger at Ben. "In his chair." Jewell let out the breath she was holding and sat in the kitchen chair. Her head felt light, her knees weak. She really had to learn to control her anxiety, her worry that something terrible could happen to Mimi. If she didn't, how would she deal with it if they were forced apart by the judicial system or when her grand-mère reached the inevitable end of her life?

Elli and Beau laughed. Jewell looked at them confused and remembered the comment made about Ben's recliner. She really should just leave now. But the unsigned contract on the table anchored her to her seat.

"Did you take a picture of Mrs. Mignon in Ben's chair?" Elli asked. "I want to send it to the family." She looked at Jewell. "No one sits in Ben's chair, except Tante Izzy."

"Oh," Jewell turned to Ben, who was smiling instead of frowning as she'd thought he would. "I'll get her out of your chair."

He shrugged. "I guess if I let one old lady take a nap in it, there isn't a problem with another one."

"You're so lucky that first old lady isn't around to hear you call her that," Elli laughed. "Tante Izzy is his aunt. She's the Bienvenu matriarch and keeper of all the family secrets. And, if you aren't careful, she's a self-appointed matchmaker, too. Except, somehow Beau has managed to stay away from her hocus pocus tricks."

Beau grabbed a MoonPie off the plate on the table, and smiled a boyish grin.

Ben hugged Elli. "Well, we stayed out of her clutches too, *chère*." He kissed her on the cheek. "We did just fine without her love potions."

Elli laughed. "She tried to give us some kind of spider spit concoction," she told Jewell.

"This is Isaure Claudette Bienvenu you are speaking about, right?"

Beau looked at her, his eyes steady. He was studying her like she would study a new document she'd discovered. Did he not like her asking about Isaure Claudette? Did he wonder why she'd asked about her? Jewell didn't really care what he thought. It didn't affect her, her work or her search for Twinnie one bit. It was his problem to sort. Not hers.

"We are certainly speaking of Tante Izzy," Elli answered. "And if you value your ear drums, don't call her Isaure in her presence." Elli laughed. "I guarantee, if she wasn't out of town right now, she'd be interrogating you to find out who you are, who your people are, and who's your momma?"

Jewell's mouth went dry. Best she stay away from Tante Izzy. Of course, the matriarch might very well be exactly who she needed to speak to for some answers—or at least some leads in finding Twinnie or in eliminating the claim of Twinnie's existence in Cane. If she was as much a busybody as they said, the woman probably knew the history of the people of Cane and nearby towns. She'd know if someone named Twinnie had ever lived around there.

"How do you know of Tante Izzy?" Beau asked, shoving the last of the MoonPie into his mouth.

"I always research the properties where I work."

He grunted, looked at Ben, and then turned his attention back to her. "Even when you haven't been hired yet?"

"It's good business," Elli said, saving her from having to respond. "You always go into an interview with a potential employer prepared."

Jewell smiled at Elli. Yes, she did that and more. She wanted to know everything for professional knowledge and because of her insatiable curiosity. In this instance, however, she also had researched Isaure and the others in the family from the same generation as Mimi for more personal reasons. From what she'd discovered in her investigation on the family lineage there were three Bienvenu siblings—Martine Louise, Isaure Claudette and Benjamin Aguste. Ben's grandfather, Benjamin, was deceased. She couldn't find any current information or a local address on Martine. So, Isaure would be the easiest one for Jewell to interview by default. If speaking with Isaure turned up nothing, then she'd find Martine or other people of that same generation to question.

Besides looking for people to interview about Twinnie, she had to consider if they were actually Twinnie. Jewell had looked into the possibility that Martine or Isaure was Twinnie. The fact that their last names didn't match any of Mimi's familiar names or were called Twinnie made either one an unlikely match.

Isaure's age wasn't a match either. She was about eight years younger and Twinnie had to be about the same age as Mimi according to her stories. But, Martine's age did match. Not that having the age connection revealed anything. Thousands of women were born the same year Mimi was in Louisiana—if Twinnie was even born in Louisiana. Following that thread now meant there were millions of age appropriate possibilities in the world.

If Jewell was to scale it back and limit it to people who lived on sugar plantations that existed or once existed in Louisiana, then she would only be looking at a mere fifteen hundred of them. Geez. That would take years of research. Dementia wouldn't give Mimi years. At best, she had months to find Twinnie if Mimi was going to recognize her...and with her trial so fast approaching, she didn't even have that.

So, with the odds so stacked against them, she had decided to ask Mimi directly if Martine was Twinnie. Another iffy proposition, again because of the dementia. Mimi hadn't hesitated. She flat-out said no.

Dead end. Until Mimi opened the secret nook and pulled out the footstool. Was it possible another plantation had the same kind of hidden nook and a similar footstool inside?

"You know, we all prepare thoroughly for our work, too," Elli said, still discussing Jewell researching the Bienvenus before she even secured the job. "You, Beau, are the worst or best of us all."

They started teasing each other over who was the most OCD with their work. As they laughed, recanting stories of excess, Jewell thought about how her quest had changed in an instant right in front of the handsome Bienvenu dynamic duo.

Then the conversation circled back to Isaure. "The one person who is never prepared, but always manages her way through things, is Tante Izzy," Beau said, his eyes twinkling with pleasure.

"Well, I look forward to meeting Tante Izzy," Jewell said, not really meaning it, thinking of all of the reasons she should stay away from her. She looked at Beau. His dark, pensive earlier expression had told her that he wouldn't like hearing her say that. His brows were furrowed now, and she found a little pleasure in teasing him about it. "Where is she?"

"Oh, she's with the quilting club on a casino bus trip to Shreveport." Elli laughed. "She'll be back tomorrow."

"Enjoy the quiet and calm," Ben said, leaning over to scratch the big bloodhound behind its ear.

Jewell didn't give voice to the fact that life with Mimi was never quiet and calm.

Beau leaned against the kitchen cabinet and crossed his arms over his chest. Jewell suspected that even though this man exhibited quiet and calm right now, he wasn't really any closer to that than Izzy and Mimi were.

"Ben, Jewell will begin work in the morning."

Beau stood up straight but didn't say a word. His body language said enough of how he didn't like hearing that news. Elli picked up the pen Jewell had placed next to the three-page contract on the table when they first sat down to meet. "Can you and Beau help her hook up her camper to a good power source near the barn?

Ben nodded, then lifted the refrigerator door up and open. He pulled out four bottles of water and placed them on the table. Then, as an afterthought, he handed one to Jewell.

"Thank you." She was moved at his gesture of hospitality.

Elli started to read the contract when Beau moved in closer to her. "Do you mind if I look it over?" He pulled a chair next to her.

"I guess it doesn't hurt to have another pair of eyes review it. Besides you are my attorney." Elli looked at Jewell. "Beau practices law here in Cane. He has a lot of us Bienvenus as clients." She laughed. "He has a lot of others from the area, too. He's got a nice-sized practice, a diverse one, too. Right, Beau? Contracts, family law, real estate and whatever legal dealings come into your office."

"Oh, I'm just your run-of-the-mill good ol' country attorney," he answered, not looking up from the contract he was reading. "That's me. I get paid with chickens, fish and pats on the back."

Elli laughed. "Hardly." She rolled her eyes. "He's very good."

Jewell forced herself to relax her tense shoulders and pasted a smile on her face. She didn't care what Beau did for a living. Well, that wasn't entirely true. She wouldn't have cared if he was a carpenter or beekeeper. The fact that he was an attorney, a very good attorney, gave her pause. Her contract was simple, honest. Yet, having an attorney studying it with intense focus made her more nervous and anxious than she already was. She needed this job. She didn't need an overzealous country lawyer messing things up for her.

Elli flipped the pages as she read through the document and lifted the pen to sign the contract but Beau stopped her. Jewell's heart skipped a beat. Oh, no, she prayed, please don't let him ruin this.

"I don't think your out-clause is strong enough," he told Elli.

"I'm fine with this, Beau." Elli frowned. "We're only talking about having her clear out the old equipment barn, and catalog, value and sell the items in there. Everything is clearly stated in this contract. Any additional work will be negotiated and if necessary an addendum agreed upon by both parties will be added."

Ben walked up to the table. "Do y'all have to do this, now?" he asked. "Can it wait until the morning? Maybe Elli and I can discuss it."

"Since when do you get involved with my dealings?" She shook her head and rolled her eyes. "I've got this."

Ben looked at Beau and shrugged. "Elli has a lot of experience with this sort of thing. She's comfortable with it. Do you think there are reasons for her not to be?"

Before this got too heavy and her job was derailed by over lawyering, Jewell spoke up. "I'm willing to adjust the contract to expedite things if you want," she said, looking at Elli. "As long as we keep my fee schedule in place." She just wanted this deal to be sealed. She needed the paycheck and she needed access to the area to look for Twinnie.

The three Bienvenus began to discuss whether or not they needed to beef up the out-clause. It quickly became clear that Beau thought Elli and Ben needed to be better protected from Jewell. He didn't say exactly why, but from what she could gather from the undercurrents, it was totally because he mistrusted her. She knew it was his job to mistrust and anticipate possible problems, but after her disappointing weekend, and after months of dealing with her own lawyers' indirect legalese, she felt bruised by his strong position against her. That was silly of her. He was, after all, Elli and Ben's advocate, not hers.

"Okay, just write in what you think needs to be in there," Elli told Beau. She looked at Jewell and gave her a resigned smile. "This is all just academic. We're going to have a great relationship."

Jewell smiled but she felt like crying. It felt awful to have her integrity questioned, even in the name of good advocacy. Even if there was just cause with the theft charges levied against her. But, did they know about them? She hadn't had a chance to discuss it with Elli. Was it fair to her to enter this agreement without her knowing? She would tell her. After the deal was made and not in front of Beau. If Elli wanted out of it, she would walk away.

Beau took the contract and added two additional sentences to it. He turned the page toward Elli to read. She shook her head and rolled her eyes. "I agreed to stronger language, but don't you think this is overkill, Beau?"

"Maybe. As your attorney I recommend you initial it, Elli." She turned to speak to Ben quietly, then, on a sigh, initialed the contract.

Beau handed the document to Jewell. She read it. Her face heated, her temper simmered just below the surface. So this was what the legal allusions were all about? Did he really think he needed this to protect his clients from her?

"A morality clause?" she said, not knowing where she found the strength to keep her voice so calm. A freakin' morality clause. It stated that Elli could sever the contract *for any act by Jewell of misconduct including (but not limited to) an act of dishonesty, theft or misappropriation of property, moral turpitude, insubordination, or any act injuring, abusing or endangering others*. And—for not following the standards of good citizenship.

She looked at Beau. He stared back at her. In his clear, peridot eyes she saw it. This Cajun hard-ass country lawyer knew about the theft charges against her. Did he know about her mother, too? Without showing him the emotion roiling and burning in her gut, she initialed the modification and signed the contract. What choice did she have?

Chapter

Beau realized that Elli had adopted Mignon and Jewell just as easily as she had adopted the three misfit shelter dogs that Ben had tried to pass off as part of her inheritance when she first came to claim her inheritance of half of Sugar Mill Plantation. They were the dogs that lived in the house with them, their son, Joey and Ben's old faithful mutt, Lucky. It was crazy to think that she would have added one more dog to the misfit pack if money and begging had worked with the movie-dog-handler she'd rented a designer dog from in hopes to impress Ben when she had first come to town.

No doubt about it, his cousin's wife had a huge capacity to love. She also wore her heart on her sleeve, Beau thought as he watched her adjust a soft, comfy pillow behind Mignon's head and tuck the blanket under her orthopedic shoes. Elli's dogs seemed to adopt the old lady, too, he realized as they settled protectively on the floor around Ben's recliner where Mignon slept. The dogs were a loyal lot, but they ran all over Elli when Ben wasn't around.

Just like Jewell and her feisty grandmother would if he wasn't there to stop them.

"She'll be just fine," Elli told Jewell who was standing awkwardly in the middle of the room. Elli sat on the sofa with Ben who had just come into the room. She picked up her iPad. "She's nice and comfy and resting soundly." The big bloodhound, Doe, jumped on the sofa next to and on top of Elli. Ben snapped his fingers; Doe groaned and jumped back on the floor. She settled near Mignon again.

"I'm happy to stay here with your sweet grandmother and get a little work done. You won't have to worry about anything while you get the camper set up." Ben stretched his arm over the back of the sofa, resting his hand on Elli's shoulder. She kissed him tenderly on the cheek, and then nodded for him to get up. "Ben and Beau will help you."

Beau saw Jewell nod and swallow hard. She looked like she wanted to cry. But—points to her—not in the open, hugely dramatic, "Look at me, I'm a sad woman" kind of way. She held her emotions below the surface, like she was trying to hide it; only her eyes gave away her pain.

Man, she was good at playing this confidence scam, he thought. She could win an academy award for this performance.

She didn't overact the sad emotional damsel role and she certainly didn't miss an opportunity to play the victim. Even in this subtle way of pretending to hide her feelings. Like she'd be able to hide this kind of emotion if it was real. He remembered how he'd felt the first time someone genuinely offered to help him when he was down in the bowels of bad luck. It had felt like an anvil landed on his chest, crushing his lungs and squeezing his heart.

This act here really pissed him off.

"Thank you," Jewell told Elli, her voice whisper soft. "I won't be long." Ben stood and she smiled at him. "Thanks." Her eyes shifted to Beau. "Thank you, too, Beau."

Beau saluted Elli as he walked out of the parlor with Ben, Jewell and four of the seven dogs.

"Look at that," Ben held up his cell phone as soon as they reached his truck which was parked near Jewell's camper. Jewell kept walking toward the camper and now was out of earshot of the men. "I've got to go to the kennel and check on a sick Lab. He needs his meds before bedtime." He grinned a tight, fake smile, showing a lot of teeth and mischief.

"You have staff for that." Beau folded his arms over his chest. "You'd rather shove a pill down an angry, slobbering dog's throat than deal with this disaster your wife invited to camp in your yard, wouldn't you?"

Ben shrugged. "You know where she needs to plug into the power. Water hose is right outside the barn near the western corner. It shouldn't take y'all long. If you have any problems with it, just step aside pretty boy. Seems like the Professor can take care of herself."

"Yeah, but who will take care of you two bat-shit blind people that let the thieving Professor Capable and her way-too-familiar grandmother homestead on your property?"

Ben laughed, opened the door for his dogs to jump into his old work truck and quickly took off down the road to the kennel.

Beau watched him drive away as Jewell returned, walking up behind him. He hadn't heard her approach but he sure as hell smelled her sweet, distinctive sexy scent. It was stronger than it had been earlier. Why in the hell was that? Did she apply fragrance just to set up her camper, or to allure him and Ben?

"Let's get this over with," she said sounding angry. Not a tone for someone trying to allure another human being. "Before someone misconstrues our unchaperoned meeting in the twilight as moral turpitude, or an act of poor citizenship. Don't want to violate my contract."

He turned to face her. The dark orange and peach glow of the setting sun reached up from the distant horizon, through the thick, heavy branches of the nearby oak and cypress trees into the lavender and violet sky. Jewell stood in silhouette, with her back to the beautiful fall sunset, her arms folded over her full breasts. She was a beautiful woman who looked like she was standing exactly where she was supposed to be standing in the universe at that moment. Beau could appreciate the art of that scene, but it ticked him off that she looked so right in a place where she shouldn't be.

He shook his head. "It really is a damn shame we didn't meet in the Carousel Bar in New Orleans or in the blues tent at Jazz Fest," he said, his voice deep, soft. Yeah, too bad he had concerns that this sultry woman was trying to scam his family. That put her off-limits.

It was crazy he was so attracted to her, he thought. Hell, he normally wouldn't have even considered being with someone who by most accounts was guilty of the crime she was charged with, but his body seemed to be overruling his ethics. Hell, his hands heated at just the thought of how he wanted to slide them over her nice, firm, womanly body. And, damn it, she would've been fun for an intelligent conversation over dinner about history or something interesting, too. There wouldn't be any of the usual fluffy dinner convo he had no interest in, like fashion faux pas of the stars or some reality TV show couple's breakup. Life sure wasn't fair. He was just three feet away from the sexiest woman he'd ever seen and she was a flippin' criminal. Yeah, he saw the humor in it and the damn frustration. He couldn't remember a time he desired a woman, a stranger, like he did this one. She was the forbidden fruit.

Beau let the arousing thought of a hot liaison seep into his body, knowing it could never be, but enjoying how the impossible possibility felt.

"*Cochon*," Jewell's scolding voice cut through his nice little moment. "Snap out of it," she said, staring hard into his eyes.

In French or Cajun French he knew what *cochon* meant. Yep, he probably deserved being called a pig for where his mind had gone. "No offense," he offered with all sincerity. "I should've guarded my thoughts better."

"You shouldn't have those thoughts in the first place."

"First of all, you have no idea what my private thoughts are, really." He looked at her and cocked a brow. "You aren't a mind reader are you?" She narrowed her gaze at him and frowned. "Yeah, that's what I thought. Secondly..."

"Secondly, I'm here to do a job and not to be concerned about what your thoughts are, how you do or don't control them or how you have a God-given American right to have your thoughts." She sighed. "Look, Beau, I suppose you're a nice guy. I guess some women find you charming and want to be your girlfriend, but, me...not so much. Not interested. Frankly, I'm not sure I even like you. I certainly don't appreciate the hostility you've shown me. So, let's get on with finding the power outlet to plug my camper into. Do you know where it is?"

Beau looked at her a moment. He was dazed from the fact that he'd been put in his place, damn quick and rightly so. "Uh," he managed, so unintelligently, that it made him laugh.

She dropped her hands to where she had a leather tool belt strapped around her nicely curved hips. He hadn't noticed it before. It seemed excessive and over prepared to have it, considering they were just plugging in her camper. Beau smiled.

"You weren't a Girl Scout by any chance?"

She cocked her head and looked at him like he was asking her to explain Cantor's theorem, which he wouldn't be surprised if she knew. He pointed to the huge, police-issued flash-riot control mag flashlight that was slipped into one of the belt's loops. It was the kind the military used to knock a violent enemy into submission. "You don't plan to whack me in the head with that, do you?"

"Not if I'm unprovoked." She smiled a half smile, obviously finding humor in her own comment.

"Then I will try not to provoke you." He pointed to the shed. "The power should be over there." He smiled at her back as she walked toward her camper and away from where he'd directed her. She had called him a pig. Ha. He chuckled. That wasn't the way he would've expected her to play out her confidence game. Shouldn't she try to charm him in return?

He walked away, toward the shed, figuring she'd catch up with him eventually. He needed more evidence to figure out what was going on with her and her grandmother. Usually he was dead-on reading someone's intent, a necessity he'd learned very young when dealing with his unpredictable biological parents and their drinking buddies. If he didn't want to end up bruised and broken, he had to be able to look into their eyes and figure out quickly who was a happy drunk, who was a mean drunk, who looked like a happy drunk but wasn't, and who was just a plain ol' son of a bitch. You could read a lot in someone's eyes. Especially pure evil and insincerity.

In the end, the best thing he'd learned for survival was to just stay the hell away from them all, take his younger brother and hide in the cypress woods until the booze left his parents and their party partners passed out and were rendered mostly harmless. That was another lesson he learned, you never walked within striking distance, even if the gator was sleeping.

Beau entered the barn, switched on the fluorescent light and immediately located the outlet Ben had mentioned earlier. Thirty seconds later Jewell walked into the barn carrying a long heavy-duty shore cord and an extra-long black water hose.

Beau extended his hand for her to give him the cord. "I'll plug it in for you."

"I got it, thank you." Jewell walked around him and plugged it in herself. Beau didn't think she sounded like she really was thankful. She seemed like a woman who also believed in staying out of striking distance. But damn, she was adorable in her red plastic ladybug boots and that fierce scowl on her face. Both were better suited to a five-year-old, and yet somehow both made her look sexy as hell.

He really needed to get laid.

"Where's the water spigot?" She dropped the extension cord on the ground in a neat circle with the female end of the cord resting on top.

"Outside the barn somewhere." He said, annoyed at her frustratingly hostile attitude. "Watch for snakes while you look for it." Yeah, she might act like she knew about the human kind of snakes, but let's see what she thought of the slithering, reptilian kind. He hadn't seen any snakes around the house or barn since he was a child, but she didn't need to know that.

He saw the tiniest bit of a hesitation, a flinch. It was hardly noticeable, and he would have missed it had he not been waiting for it. Oh, the woman was quick witted. She caught her involuntary reaction before it manifested into a full girly scream or leap onto a chair. Beau smiled.

He let his Cajun accent thicken, his delivery slow to almost an easy promenade. "*Chère*, want me to come and chase away those nasty venomous water moccasins and those nocturnal snaggle-tooth coons and possums? They start hunting about this time of night."

She turned on her cute ladybug boots and reached with deliberate, slow, very purposeful movements for that damn black 24-inch heavy-duty mag flashlight. Hell, she could have been a gunslinger going for her six-shooter. She slapped it into the palm of her opposite hand, and the light flashed on.

"Maybe I should just tag along to protect the creatures you may happen on with that thing there, *chère*. Yes, indeed."

She looked at him and smiled a contained smile. "What makes you think *you're* so safe around me, *cher*? Yes, indeed."

"Because I have an app, darlin'." He reached into his pocket and pulled out his cell phone. He touched the screen and a light illuminated the darkness, then started to spin in tiny prisms into the darkening night like a disco ball. Music started to play, "Night Fever" by the Bee Gees. "People fled the '70s as fast as they could because of this stuff and because of white polyester leisure suits. I'm guessing an antiques lover and historian will run from it, too, like it was poison sumac."

Jewell started to laugh a full-on genuine laugh. "Okay. Okay. You win. Just turn that off. I'll have nightmares of an army of men and women wearing white patent leather platform shoes, deep-V plunging stretch jumpsuits and gold chains line dancing in the sugarcane fields."

Beau found himself laughing along with her and really enjoying it. It bothered the hell out of him that he was. It had sneaked up on him, too. He usually was more guarded with his feelings and able to joke, tease and navigate a conversation without actually being affected by it when he needed to. He needed to now. Still, her humor and infectious laugh managed to get to him on some visceral level. Not good. He'd be in big trouble if he wasn't careful and didn't step up his "A" game.

He tapped the screen to turn off the app. "Yeah, I see an end to crime, wars and mass destruction. All we need are the right apps to control the world."

"So you're all about world domination, huh?" Jewell turned and started to walk out of the barn to look for the water spigot.

"Isn't everyone?"

"Nah. I just want clean water, cool air and a good night's sleep."

"I bet you are about more than that, Dr. Jewell Duet." Beau followed her to where she'd stopped in front of a water spigot. She didn't look at him, wince, or change her expression one iota as he half-expected she'd do when he used her title for the first time. He had no doubt she heard him and realized why he dropped it in. She'd know he was telling her that he knew more about her than she had shared. "I bet you don't do much without a purpose. I bet you..."

"I think you should call the 1-800-gambling helpline for compulsive betters...I bet, I bet, I bet." She bent to connect the water hose and her jeans strained nice and tight in all of the right places. Beau didn't mind taking a moment to appreciate the fact that Dr. Jewell Duet had a real nice derrière. The kind men wanted to fill their hands

with and women always worried looked too big. She
turned and started to head toward the camper, uncoiling
the hose as she walked. Beau leaned against the wood
siding of the barn and watched her purposeful, yet sexy-
as-hell stride. She had an innate, natural sensuality that
came from her knowing that she was so damn hot. Or did
she?

She might very well be playing him. Yeah, the
Professor was smart. She wasn't chatty about what her
plans were, and she certainly didn't trust him. Beau didn't
blame her for that. He'd made it clear when he added the
clause to the contract which side he was on. And, it did
feel like there were sides. Why was that? Did she see a
reason to be his enemy? Elli and Ben's? The Bienvenus?
Did she just worry that if he were watching her too closely
she wouldn't be able to execute her con?

Why is she really here?

Beau walked into the barn, grabbed the cord and
dragged it to the camper. To get his answers he could
approach her in one of two ways...as a hostile witness and
try to scare, threaten and intimidate the answers from her,
or he could cajole, charm and entice the answers from her.
He laughed softly. No way would the esteemed Dr. Duet
scare or intimidate easily. His instincts, which were
usually dead accurate in such matters, told him the good-
cop approach would have to be it. Decision made. He'd
turn on the charm and have her eating out of his hand.

***

"That's really clever, Jewell," Beau said, annoyingly
complimenting her again, for the fiftieth time in the last
ten minutes, on something mundane she'd done. "Did you
paint those red wood wedges you placed under the tires to
keep the camper from rolling?"

"Are you trying to inveigle me?" Jewell asked, hands
on her hip, looking at the tall, lean, handsome Beau
Bienvenu—still wearing his New Orleans Saints jersey like
another man would wear an Armani suit. "Geez. Enough
with the compliments on how well I set up the camper,

take care of Mimi, handle the flashlight and the other dozen things you have been sucking up to me about. She shook her head. "Look. I get why you used the belt-and-suspenders approach with the restrictive clauses in the contract. I don't like it but I get that you felt you were protecting Elli and Ben's exposure, vulnerability. It was unnecessary, but you wouldn't know that. I'm a stranger." She sighed. "That is done. You did your job. This insincere complimenting on triviality is something else." She looked at him directly in the eyes. "What, Beau? What's this all about? What do you want? And, if you say sex, I want you to know, I have given you much more credit than to be so prosaic." She shook her head, again. "No. I can tell this isn't about that."

She turned to face him. She might as well be direct with him if she had any hopes of getting Mimi into the camper and both of them to sleep that night. She could tell this man was tenacious. She knew what he really wanted, or at least she thought she did. Should she take a stab at it to see if she was right? An intelligent guess? Or wait for him to show his hand?

"I'm hurt, Jewell." He leaned against the camper and crossed his ankles. Geez, the man was tall—he blocked the narrow path that led to the camper door alongside of where she'd parked her truck next to the camper. "I'm just being curious and friendly. Showing you southern hospitality."

"Then offer me a glass of sweet tea and finger sandwiches, or coffee and beignets. Stop with the insincere compliments."

She carefully walked around him, her body rubbing against her dusty truck so she didn't rub against him. Then she sat on the camper steps and looked up at him. "It's getting late. I need to get Mimi to bed. Let's be direct. You've exhausted me with this nonsense. Just say what you mean." She narrowed her eyes and looked at his easy, relaxed expression. He would stand out there with her all night until he got what he wanted. Forget that. "This is about Mimi finding that footstool in the hidden nook by the fireplace, right?

He squatted eye-level with her. "What the hell was that about?"

"I'm not sure."

"I thought you were going to be direct with me," he answered sounding annoyed.

"I am. I don't know how she knew to find the footstool in the hidden nook." She looked up at the sky and exhaled. If things were as simple as the multitudes of complex galaxies in the sky, it would have been easier. "I don't understand a lot of what is happening with her these days. It's the dementia." She sighed. "It's other things. I'm trying to sort it out." She looked at him as she stood. "You can rest assured it will not affect my ability to do the job Elli hired me to do. I'm very good at what I do, Beau."

"Maybe too good for what you're doing. Maybe, not good enough." He stood and looked down at her. "Don't mess with my family. I may seem like an easygoing man, but when it comes to protecting my family, rest assured I am nothing but iron, grit and endless determination."

"You don't seem that easygoing to me." She shook her head. "Dog with a bone."

"Damn right I'm a dog with a bone."

"No." Jewell pointed toward the brown, black and white beagle carrying a large ham bone coming from the house. "There's a dog with an extraordinarily huge bone coming toward us."

Beau grunted. "That's BJ. If BJ has a bone, you can bet...uh, know...that Jenny and Doe will be around fighting for it." Just then, before the words had settled, the bloodhound and the Lab mix that had been nestled around Mimi earlier came running toward the beagle, tongues lolling to the sides of their mouths, ears flapping behind them. BJ put the bone down, sneezed once, picked it up and took off around the barn into the darkness. "Never a dull moment with those animals."

"Should we be worried about the night crawlers harming them?"

"Nah. Just females that smell as good as you carrying riot-control flashlights."

"You never let up, do you?" She walked away. It was time to bring Mimi to bed. The camper air conditioner had been on long enough to cool the inside of the small space and the beds were already made from the night before when they slept in the camper at the Simoneauxs'. She didn't owe Beau a friendly good-night or any other explanation about Mimi. Frankly, she'd had enough of speaking with him. He'd made his position clear. He wouldn't tolerate anyone, especially her, harming his family. And she was going to have access to expensive and private family items.

She also understood that he would continue to flirt with her if she hung around outside with him for no other reason than to get what he could from her. What that meant exactly, she wasn't sure. Maybe it would be for his physical pleasure, like just about every man she'd ever known. Maybe it would be to try to gain information from her. Maybe it would be for both. The way she figured it, either-or-both were all for his benefit, not hers.

Her phone buzzed with a text. It was Elli. *Come to the house ASAP, Mimi's awake and upset.* She started to run toward the house.

"What's wrong?" Beau called from behind her.

She heard him, but didn't answer. All she cared about was getting to Mimi. She knew how she acted when she was confused and upset. She could be argumentative, even a bit physical, or she could curl into a fetal position and cry like a child. She could also just be talkative, anxious, but fairly normal. In the worst of cases, there was usually something more than just the dementia causing the extreme anxiety or symptoms. Medical causes or a sundowning episode. She had to get to her to assess what was going on with her now. She raced into the house, not sure what she would find.

"Ma sucrée," Mimi yelled as soon as Jewell walked into the kitchen. She was holding salt and pepper shakers tightly in her hands but acted as if she didn't know they were there. "Tell this woman to call the doctor," she said in English then slipped into French, "Twinnie is infirmed. She's got a fever. Oh, *mon Dieu.* Not you." She looked at Beau who rushed into the room. She hurried up to him, hugged him with the shakers still in her hands. "Monsignor Jacques," she began speaking English again. "Please. Don't give her the last rites. She just needs a doctor."

Beau looked at Jewell. "What is she talking about?" His eyes were narrowed with concern. "Is she sick? Did she call me a priest or ask for one?"

Jewell shook her head no, but it was meant more to dismiss his questions than to answer them. She approached Mimi and spoke to her softly. "Mimi. Mignon. Come sit a moment in the kitchen chair. Let's talk." She smiled gently, and waited for Mimi to release her arms from around Beau's waist. She looked up at him as she stepped away and smiled a childlike smile.

"Monsignor Jacques, please say a prayer for Twinnie."

"I will and I will say one for you, too." He smiled a kind, genuine smile that seemed to calm Mimi enough for her to let Jewell lead her to one of the ladder-back kitchen chairs. She sat and Jewell knelt in front of her, unable to hold her hands as she wanted because she clutched the salt and pepper shakers in them. Jewell knew she was too upset to ask her why she held them. The reality was, it might or might not have any significance.

"Everything will be fine. Let's think about how lovely the night is for a moment." She waited for Mimi to nod in agreement. "It's a warm night. Not too hot. The stars are bright and beautiful. The moon is out, casting a nice glow in the sky and on the trees, making them look silvery."

Mimi nodded again and Jewell kept talking about familiar things that she knew. It seemed to comfort her as it always did. As she spoke, she looked at the back of

Mimi's hands, lifting the loose skin to check for skin turgor. The skin didn't return back to its normal position for a few seconds. Because of that, plus how dry her lips looked, Jewell was convinced her grand-mère was dehydrated.

"Elli, would you mind if Mimi had a cool glass of water?" Dehydration with dementia, plus being in an unfamiliar place, could cause confusion. Additional confusion resulted in increased anxiety.

"Of course." Elli poured some bottled water she got from the refrigerator into a glass and gave it to Mimi. "Would you like anything else, sweetie?"

"Yes," Mimi answered in a childlike voice. "I'll take *madeleines*."

"I don't think Elli has little butter cakes," Jewell interpreted.

"I have other sweets, though," Elli opened the pantry and filled a pretty blue flowered dessert dish with different store-bought and homemade items. She placed it on the table in front of Mimi. "There's quite a variety there," she laughed softly. "Chocolate chip and sugar cookies. A cinnamon oat granola bar, a MoonPie and a praline."

"Praline?" Mimi said, looking at Jewell. "Here?"

Elli turned the dessert dish so the caramel colored sugary treat faced her. "Yes. Here it is." She handed her a paper napkin. "You like pralines?"

Jewell didn't give Mimi time to answer, "You like sugar cookies." She turned the dish so the cookie faced her.

Mimi placed the salt and pepper shakers in the middle of the table with extra care. "I always take pride in doing my job just right," she said, giving the pepper shaker an affectionate pat on the side of the pebbled glass. With a smile on her face, Mimi picked up a cookie and looked at Jewell as she chewed. "You like how I take care of the salt and pepper, *ma sucrée*?"

Jewell looked at the shakers which stood about three to four inches tall, with polished sterling silver caps on top. These shakers looked to be vintage and consistent with early 1900s designs. They were probably mass produced. Mimi could very well have had similar shakers in her home growing up. "Yes. I like the way you take care of them, Mimi." She looked into her grand-mère's tired eyes and noticed how pale her skin was. "You should drink the water, Mimi. You may be a little dehydrated from the long, warm day and not drinking enough. And, from the side effects of your medicines." She glanced at Elli. "It would explain her anxiety."

"Drink up," Elli encouraged her.

She did. She drank all of the water in one long drink, and then wiped her mouth with the back of her hand. "I was thirsty," she laughed.

"Seems like things are under control now," Beau said, reaching to take the praline from the plate.

"He took the praline," Mimi whispered.

"Is that a problem?" Beau asked. "I love pralines. It's a sweet temptation."

"That's for sure. Men like Praline," Mimi said. "But, don't seem right that a priest does." Jewell just wanted the damn praline to disappear and all discussion to cease about it.

"It's all yours," she said, shoving the plate toward Beau.

"I feel like I've walked in during the middle of an intricately plotted movie and have no idea what is going on." He took a bite of the praline. "Did I miss something?"

"It's just a Mimi conversation," Jewell said, hating to imply it was the dementia that was making the conversation sound so confusing. She just didn't have anything else to say to explain what they were talking around. Nothing she wanted to share, anyway. She exhaled. "When you're finished with your cookie, Mimi," she said, "we're going to turn in."

"Turn into what?" she asked with all sincerity.

Jewell smiled. She was so darling and said the cutest things when she took things literally. The more advanced the dementia developed, the more she missed nuances and intent.

"Don't turn into anything or anyone else, *chère.*" Beau told her, patting her on the shoulder. "I see absolutely no reason for you to do that. You are perfect just as you are."

Jewell rolled her eyes. "You're such a flirt."

Elli laughed. "That he is. But he does it so well."

"Damn straight, I do, darlin'." Beau snatched another cookie from the plate.

Jewell stood. "Well, I think it's time for Mimi and me to turn in...into sleeping women." She helped her grand-mère stand. "Mimi, the camper is set up right outside. Your bed is ready for you."

"Where is Monsignor Jacques going to sleep?" She looked at Beau finishing off the cookie. She cocked her head studying his smooth angular face. "You aren't Monsignor Jacques. You're too handsome." She looked at Jewell. "Who is he?"

Jewell waved good-night to Elli as she led Mimi toward the door. "He's the man you met earlier tonight, Mimi. Mr. Knucklehead."

Chapter 5

"Fire her," Beau told Elli and Ben as he walked into their kitchen.

"It's 6:45 A.M. Can we at least wait until seven?" Ben didn't glance up from whatever organic cereal concoction he was eating. He was dressed in his usual work jeans and black T-shirt with his pack of four dogs sitting at polite attention around the table, waiting for the handout that Ben wouldn't give them. He would, however, signal them at the end of breakfast that it was time for a morning run with Elli. Except for his old dog, Lucky, who just wasn't as capable of keeping up with the others, they all seemed to love the daily outing.

Once Elli left with the dogs, Beau knew Ben would dump the chunky organic cereal Elli lovingly prepared for him every morning into the trash and eat something sweet and unhealthy that he actually liked. It was a morning routine they had settled into that his cousin and his bride seemed totally happy with, though Beau didn't find it appealing in any way.

"Good morning to you, Beau." Elli handed him a cup of coffee. Black. Just as he liked it. The mug was from her favorite I heart MY DOG collection that each had a photo of one of their dogs on it. This one had a photo of Jenny, her sweet Lab mix. "You have court this morning?" She motioned to his navy suit slacks, pale yellow, athletic-cut dress shirt, gold cuff links and baby blue loosely-knotted tie. Elli would know his suit jacket was hanging in the car. She also knew that while he always dressed in a tie, dress slacks and sports coat for the office, he always went into the courtroom in a suit. Her question about his going to court was meant to distract him from what he was really there to talk about.

"Yes. Court's at 9:30." He gave her a pointed look. "This is more urgent." She shook her head. He tossed a folder full of articles he'd printed from the Internet on the table in front of Ben. "It's clear that Elli doesn't want to get rid of the Professor. But I think after you read what's in there, y'all will agree that it has to be done." He pointed to the folder. "There's just cause to dissolve the contract."

Elli leaned against the kitchen cabinet, dipped her tea bag into her cup, and shook her head. "I don't want to dissolve the contract."

Ben opened the folder and started to read through its contents.

"She was charged with felony theft, Elli. She went to work for a prominent family in New Orleans. Although there's a gag order, keeping their name from being released, I was able to find out from my sources that it's the Monroe family." He sipped the hot, dark coffee, keeping his gaze steady on his cousin-in-law. He knew exactly how tenacious and loyal Elli was, but he also knew that in the end she'd be reasonable. It just might take a while. By which time Jewell might very well steal them blind.

Elli stood across the room from Beau, holding her tea mug with the photo of Doe, the noisy bloodhound on it. "Ben told me you mentioned this to him last night. And I told him I knew about it."

"You what?" Beau could have been knocked over with a feather. "And you still hired her? When did you find out?"

"Before I called to hire her." Her eyes softened. "You don't think I'd hire someone without checking them out first, do you, Beau?"

"What good is checking them out if you hire them anyway when you find out they're a thief?"

"Alleged thief," Elli corrected in a stern voice. "Jewell also told me. She didn't know I knew. I hadn't told her. I didn't see any reason to." She shrugged. "After you left last night, and before Ben got back from the kennel, she texted me, said she knew it was late but had something important to discuss with me. I met her at the camper and that was that."

Beau looked at Ben. Was his cousin okay with this? Ben just lifted his brows in response. *What in the hell does that mean?*

"Did she tell you any more about her case?" Beau continued.

"No. She said she couldn't because of the gag order."

Fair enough, Beau thought. "Well, I did more digging." He pointed to the folder. "You should know all of the facts, Elli." She gave him one of those *whatever* expressions. He took it as an invitation to continue. "She was hired to catalog and value property for the Monroe family's St. Charles Avenue estate after the matriarch died. As unusual as it is in our modern world of strategic inheritance planning, Mrs. Monroe had no declared heirs and no will." Beau put his empty mug on the counter and folded his arms over his chest. "Her lone grandson subsequently inherited the property. Jewell was given full access to the property to appraise and recommend what to do with all of the movable goods." He sat across from Ben. "Sound familiar? It's exactly what she's doing here."

"Apples and oranges," Elli stated. "There isn't an entire estate to appraise. Just old neglected stuff in the barn." She sighed.

"That's true, but I wouldn't go as far as saying it's completely different than what you have here," Beau said, his tone friendly. As frustrating as he felt about Elli's kind nature right now, it was what made her such a special person. He stood and walked to the coffee pot for a refill. "We know that she is accused of stealing valuable family jewelry, but we don't know exactly how she did it." He filled his cup. "Did she swipe them when no one was looking? Talk someone into handing it over to her?"

"My bet is on a heist," Ben said, leaning back in his chair. "A sophisticated one with retractable cables and night vision goggles. Maybe she shimmied down a cable from a balcony and did contorted gymnastic moves so as to not set off the alarm system as she made her way through a web of lasers." Elli shook her head and narrowed her gaze to show her disapproval, but her eyes gave away that she wasn't angry with her husband. She was used to the way he and Beau constantly joked with one another. "Oh, and maybe, her grandmother helped her. Do you think she was an accomplice?"

Beau took a deep breath and looked at his cousin. "Of course not," he said, his voice low, serious. "Mignon couldn't have tiptoed past the sensitive alarms in her orthopedic shoes, no matter how many handstands she did."

He smiled, then before their messing around went any further, his eyes settled on the folder on the table. It seemed to draw his attention as if it had special powers. The seriousness of the situation weighed down on him again, as it had just moments before Ben started with his playful scenario.

"While the imagery of all that is humorous," he began, his tone serious, "the situation we have here isn't." He tapped the folder.

Ben sobered. "He's right, Elli," he told his wife. "Tell us what you found out, Beau."

"I know that it was Claude Monroe, the grandson and lone heir, who filed charges against her." Beau returned to his chair, not happy with the way Elli was frowning at him. This time her eyes matched her expression. She was indeed unhappy with this conversation. Beau directed his attention to Ben, who at least seemed open to listening to what he was saying. "He's also the one who asked the judge for the gag order on not releasing the name of his family and the details of how the items were stolen. He requested it because he was concerned for his security. He felt like if people knew how vulnerable the family was and how much they were worth, it would put a big target on his back." He shrugged. "The bottom line for us is that you have to consider that if a person is capable of stealing what doesn't belong to them once, they can do it again."

Elli sighed and sat in the chair next to Ben. "Beau, a person is innocent until proven guilty. I know you believe that. You should know as well as anyone else that often not all is what it seems to be on the surface." She looked at him with big blue insightful eyes. What she said was true some of the time, but not all of the time. He couldn't risk the 'not all of the time' with his family. "Look what happened to Abby and me. I was just recently released of all suspicions, but because she's CFO, and they are still trying to follow the money trail, she's still under investigation in the case involving the crook who scammed and embezzled from us. He stole from us. We were the victims, and we were the ones who were investigated." She waved her hand in dismissal. "It's nonsense. Innocent until proven guilty. End of story."

"She has a point," Ben said, in a monotone voice, as he continued to read from the folder.

"I think it is highly suspect that she arrives here at Sugar Mill with her elderly grandmother and that grandmother finds a hidden nook ten minutes after arriving. A nook that no one knew about in what... at least thirty plus years, maybe longer?"

"Beau has a point," Ben said, his eyes focused on what he was reading from the folder. "Of course, if she's trying to steal from us like she allegedly did on a previous job, why would she have her grandmother reveal a secret hiding spot? That's strange." He glanced over to his wife. "What does she gain by doing that? Why not just gain access to the property and steal what she wants?"

Beau felt an odd twinge in his chest as he observed the couple's silent communication. He'd never had that kind of connection with a woman. Not that he needed or wanted it. He did just fine with the ladies without exchanging meaningful glances filled with subtext.

"She's a smart lady," he told them. "You don't get a doctorate degree by being top of your remedial classes. With her current legal problems, she has to know we will be watching her closely. She'll have to be clever to gain our confidence. To get away with theft." He nodded. "She might have an intricate plan laid out that has more twists and turns than Bayou Dos Gris." He ignored Elli when she sighed in disapproval. "She may have discovered that secret nook in some old book, documents or architectural drawings. Maybe she found some old building plans for Sugar Mill." He turned the mug in his palm. "She must do a lot of research as an antiques expert and as a professor. It's conceivable that she's stumbled on old documents that the average person would never see." He rested his elbows on the table. "Old papers that may have hinted or revealed information on our little family secret with our missing heir."

"Or, maybe, and hear me out, fellas," Elli began, her eyes wide, her brows lifted and sounding a bit too dramatic, "maybe she's just an antiques expert who's down on her luck, has been falsely accused of a crime and is in need of work. Imagine that. Jewell Duet is exactly who she says she is with no ulterior motives." Elli slapped the table, causing Jenny, the Lab mix, to bark once in surprise.

Ben leaned back in his seat and folded his arms over his chest. "Elli, let's say that Beau's right." He hesitated a moment, and Beau saw that Ben didn't like seeing his wife frown. He leaned forward, covered her hand gently with his. "Just for argument's sake, *chère*. Shouldn't we at least know how we'd be affected by a devious scheme to con us into believing she's a missing heir? Shouldn't we be prepared?" He tucked a curl behind her ear. "If we're aware that Jewell may know of the trust fund that was set aside in Great-grand-pépère's will for his missing daughter, Martine, she can't dupe us, right?"

Beau cleared his throat. "It's not that simple." He looked at both of them who now had their light eyes intently focused on him. "Sure, we can be vigilant." He exhaled. "But, we have to be smarter than the Professor. We have to scrutinize, analyze and most importantly realize that everything she is doing could be to bring her to her end goal."

"I don't have time for that," Ben said, looking at Elli. "You don't either with that big-budget movie coming here so soon and with us taking Joey to the beach for fall break when he gets back from Boy Scout camp."

Beau nodded. "Safer to turn her around and send her back to New Orleans then."

"I don't want to do that." Elli looked at Ben. "I like her. I don't think she's trying to do what you two fear."

"There's a good bit of money in Aunt Martine's trust with the original sum and the interest collected over the last seventy-two years," Beau reminded them, not adding the additional funds with the investments he and Ben's father had made through the years with the interest.

"That could be very tempting for someone who needs money. Who's down on their luck," Ben added. "Worse-case scenario, she cons us." He looked at Beau who wasn't happy with the way this train of thought was shaping up. "She gets the trust but she can't take our home away from us or change our lives. That would be unfair and wrong. It wouldn't really change any of our lives, but for you, Elli, it would change something in you. You'd have to live with the knowledge that someone you trusted and defended took advantage of us. That would hurt you. I don't like risking that."

"I appreciate your concerns," Elli said to Ben. "I love that you are concerned about me. But, the bottom line is that I really don't think Jewell is trying to steal from us. I just don't."

Beau blew out a breath and scratched his freshly shaven jaw. "I hate that she might be scamming my family. End of story. And, to be honest, the first moment I laid eyes on her, bells went off..."

"Oh, really," Elli's voice lifted, her eyes brightened.

"Don't get all romantic on me. I don't believe in that crap. Remember, it's me, the guy who lives for the one-week affair." He shook his head. "No, they were warning bells. I know scams. I know the kind of people who run them. I cut my baby teeth watching the biggest reprobate feed his family, and especially his heavy drinking habits, on the scam." He paused to refocus his thoughts on the problem at hand and not old history. "Bringing Dr. Duet here and taking the risk isn't just about us and how we'll all feel getting duped," he said, not wanting to sound insensitive but wanting them to realize all of the ramifications. "If the real Aunt Martine shows up two years from now, or her son or daughter does, we need to be good wards of the trust and make sure their money is here for them. And, if not for them, for the entire Bienvenu family."

"I understand your concerns about this, Beau," Elli said, looking upset. "It's not fair to put this worry on Jewell if she is innocent, though."

Beau leaned back in his chair. "Jewell isn't my concern. Our family is. I'm sorry if that sounds cold to you." He took a sip of his coffee. "When Ben's father died, he named Ben and me trustees of the Martine Trust. I take my responsibility seriously. Just like I know Ben does."

Ben squeezed Elli's hand. "He's right." She nodded.

"And, I know you both know this," Beau continued, "but let me remind you that on Martine's one-hundred-and-twenty-fifth birthday, this special trust will expire and all of the money in the trust will be distributed to every single living heir of her father, Aguste Bienvenu. We need to be good wards to all of them, too." Beau leaned his elbows on the table. "And, consider this. Jewell can certainly try to claim ownership of the entire plantation. She could claim Martine was wronged in some way and that the plantation is rightfully hers and her heirs. Anyone can sue over just about anything in Louisiana."

"You're creating a worry where there is none," Elli pursed her lips like she'd just eaten a sour grape.

"Someone has to worry for the family." He looked at Ben, knowing Elli was already feeling some sort of loyalty and empathy to Jewell and Mignon. "Like I told you when we were hashing out the twisted wills of what you and Elli inherited," he continued. "There are some Napoleonic laws and court decisions that have been rendered that, if applied in this case, would definitely affect your lives. If nothing else, it would drag y'all into the courts for years because of the will's complicated legal nature. This isn't a path you want to go down unless it is absolutely necessary. You certainly don't want to fight this expensive battle because a con artist and her grandmother seem nice."

"I hear what you are saying, Beau," Elli said, shaking her head. "And, considering I was once a victim of a con, completely blindsided by it, I can't say I entirely trust my judgment on this." She sighed. "I want to, though, because my heart and head are telling me Jewell and Mignon are good people. I can tell you that I don't agree with your worries, but I recognize you're an intelligent man with our best interest at heart. I will be cautious. I care about our family, too. I'll keep my eyes open. I just can't be part of an injustice executed on Jewell and Mignon. I can't. And, I think Ben agrees, right?" She looked at her husband, and he nodded.

"Is there anything I can say to change your mind?" Beau asked, knowing that he'd reached an impasse, but having to try one more time.

"I can't fire her. That wouldn't be fair to her without evidence to do so. She hasn't been convicted of any crime with the Monroe's estate. The charges against her may be totally false. And she hasn't done anything to scam or con us or even hint that she plans to." She narrowed her eyes and shrugged her shoulders. "Besides all of that, I need her to perform the work I contracted her to do." She smiled a half smile. "We have good happy lives. Let's enjoy them, now. *Joie de vivre,*" she added, massacring the French pronunciation but doing it with complete enthusiasm.

"Damn, she's cute," Ben grinned, looking at Elli, "and sexy when she tries to talk Cajun." He winked at his wife but when he returned his attention to Beau, the light faded in his eyes. "I stand by Elli's decision," he said.

Beau knew Ben was concerned. He'd seen Mignon open that hidden nook and was shocked by it. He just didn't want to worry his wife about this any further. "I've got some dogs to train. Elli has a movie crew to prepare for." He pretended to shudder, then leaned over to kiss his wife on the cheek. "And we have to do it all before we leave for the beach. You, cuz, I'm sure, have some legal crap to deal with." He stood, placed his bowl of cereal and empty coffee mug in the sink. He gave Elli a tender kiss on the lips. "I'll see you at lunch," he told her. He turned to Beau. "Walk out with me." When they stepped outside, Ben spoke as they made their way toward their parked vehicles. "You're going to keep digging, right?"

"Hell, yeah. I won't let anyone steal from my family."

"For her to stake a claim on that money, Beau, she'd have to produce the heir." Ben opened his truck door and motioned for Lucky to jump in. "A legitimate heir. The long-lost Bienvenu daughter, Martine Bienvenu." He motioned for Beau to look behind him toward the back door of the house where Mignon Duet was shuffling toward the back steps, awkwardly using her cane for balance. She was wearing an off-white robe and tan orthopedic shoes. "Dig away."

"I've got some time before I have to leave for court. No time like the present." Ben got in his truck and drove away. Beau rushed to Mignon and helped her up the steps into the house. "Good morning, Mignon."

"*Bon matin.*" She smiled up at him. Her hair was mostly styled in front, but the back was flattened from where she'd slept on the pillow. Beau noticed that she fumbled to hold her cane in one hand. On closer inspection, he realized that was because she had the glass salt shaker in her hand. The pepper shaker was in her other hand. Why weren't the shakers on the kitchen table where they belonged?

When they got inside the house, she walked slowly over the smooth wooden floor into the kitchen. *"Bon matin,"* she told Elli, placing the salt and pepper shakers in the middle of the table, taking an extra moment to adjust them so they were neatly placed.

"Good morning," Elli said, her eyes bright and friendly. "Would you like some coffee?"

Mignon sat at the table and smiled at Beau who sat next to her before answering Elli. "With boiled milk and sugar."

"That's how Tante Izzy likes it," she said, putting a small blue ceramic pot on the stove. "Cane sugar, I presume is your preference, too." She paused a moment, looked at Beau and frowned. "I know what you're thinking," she whispered. Mignon didn't seem to pay attention to her. She was too busy adjusting the salt and pepper shakers on the table again. "If she is *you know who* then the person with *you know who* would've just knocked at the door and said...*you know what.* The person with *you know who* wouldn't have come here for work with her, not saying anything about *you know who.*"

"Maybe the person with *you know who,* doesn't have enough proof to get *you know who* declared *you know what* in a court of law. Yet. Or she isn't *you know who* at all."

"I once got declared in a court of law," Mignon said, "Not like Tony Gustavo, who kept taking off his clothes in Jackson Square and climbing up with Andrew Jackson on his horse." She clucked her tongue. "The statue, not the real Andrew Jackson. He's been dead a long time."

"You were declared?" Beau asked, moving his chair closer to Jewell's grandmother. Having Mignon walk in without her fierce protector might actually give him the chance to figure out what her granddaughter was up to. "For what?"

She wiped the salt shaker with the hem of her sleeve. "I did not have to go to the mental house in Mandeville with Tony. If that's what you're asking." She shook her head and laughed. "Don't burn the milk, now," she instructed Elli. "You have the flame too high."

She clearly didn't want to answer his question, Beau realized, so he decided to get other answers for now. He could check court records to find out what she was talking about. He smiled at Mignon. "I enjoyed hearing you speak French last night," he continued, making sure his voice was easy, friendly. "I do love the sound of Parisian French. It has a different rhythm than Cajun French. Are you from France?"

"Cajun French sounds muddier," she laughed. "It's country talk. *Tu comprends?*" When she looked at him he saw that her eyes looked clear and focused. The lines from her pillow and the disheveled hair told him she hadn't been awake long, but her mind seemed clearer this morning than it had been the night before.

He nodded. *"Comme ci, comme ça.* So-so," he repeated in English. "I understand a little."

"Qui," she said with a heavy French accent. "I was born there." Her tone was light. Her expression friendly. "But we came to America when I was a baby so I don't remember it. I was too young when we came to America. My momma was from France, though. She insisted we know the language of our heritage. I did the same for my Jewell."

Okay. They were getting somewhere. And, she hadn't called him Mr. Knucklehead or Monsignor Jacques. She knew who he was and she'd given him a clue to who she was. "What was your mother's name?"

Before she could answer, the back door flew open in the mudroom, and Jewell raced in. Her eyes were wide. Her footsteps heavy and clumping. She wore shiny purple, nearly knee-high rubber boots with yellow sunflowers. A rose red, cap-sleeve, form-fitting nightgown fell about five inches above her shapely knees. Her hair was loose, silky wild and uncombed.

And, she wasn't wearing a bra.

Beau leaned back in his chair and folded his arms over his chest. "Hello, Boots." He was unhappy for her intrusion, but didn't mind the view.

"Oh, thank God," she said on an exhale rubbing the back of her neck and lifting her shoulders. "Mimi, you can't just wander off. You have to tell me where you're going."

"Oh, don't get your thong panty in a twist," Mignon said waving a hand in dismissal.

Beau laughed at Mignon's quick response. The flustered Dr. Jewell Duet shot him a heated look.

He raised his hands in surrender.

Jewell plopped into a kitchen chair, placing the flat of her hand over her chest. Beau noticed that she was breathing hard and her large breasts filled out her nightgown quite nicely. He kept his gaze off them, however, remembering her reaction the last time his eyes strayed to where they shouldn't.

He also kept his eyes away from where the red fabric clung to her hips. It was best that he didn't try to confirm if she was indeed wearing a thong as her grandmother insinuated. Instead he focused on her long, straight, mussed hair. He had a sudden urge to run his hand over it to settle all of the strays. She was a mess.

A damn cute mess.

"I'm sorry that we barged in on your morning," she addressed Elli.

"You should put a bell on her, Boots," Beau said, seeing the fire and challenge leap into her milk chocolate brown eyes. She didn't respond, but he heard her disapproval loud and clear.

Beau reached for the loose papers about Jewell that Ben had left on the table and tucked them into the folder.

"We're all awake and getting on with our day, Jewell. Ben already left for the kennel." Elli smiled. "We like company," she said as she handed Mignon her cup of coffee.

"Merci," she responded, cautiously taking a sip. Suddenly, Jewell stood. Then clearly remembering her state of undress, crossed her arms over her chest.

"Elli, do you mind if I leave for just a few minutes before returning to get my grand-mère?" She motioned to indicate her manner of dress, not noticing that Beau was watching her.

"Of course not. Take your time."

"Thanks. Enjoy your coffee," she told her grandmother. "I'll be right back." Jewell rushed out of the house.

"I thought she was dressed just fine," Beau said, grinning. "Now, Mademoiselle Mignon." He shifted to face her, deciding he'd better get some answers before the watchdog granddaughter returned. "You said your mother..."

"I'm glad you liked what she was wearing." Mignon interrupted, smiling. "I sewed that princess cut nightdress for her. She doesn't usually like to wear red, but she always wears what I make for her." She stood, using the table for leverage. "You like what I'm wearing, too?" She swooshed the robe by swaying back and forth. "I'm pretty, huh?"

"Oh, yes indeed." Beau nodded. He liked this lady. She might be a con artist, but she was a charming one. He appreciated charming. It took a bit of self-deprecation, confidence, humor and intelligence to pull it off.

"You should see me in my violet Persian taffeta suit. Now, that is something. I made the same style for the Queen of Rex in 1973 for the Maids' tea. It was gold silk Dupioni. *Magnifique.*" She kissed her fingertips in a very

French gesture. "Then, I changed the design just a bit to flatter my figure and *voilà*. I was as good as any Mardi Gras royalty."

"So you're a seamstress?" Elli asked, sitting with a fresh cup of tea in the seat Jewell had vacated.

"Not a seamstress, sweet girl. *The* seamstress." She nodded.

Beau's phone rang. He looked at it.

"Excuse me, ladies." He stood and answered it right away. "Hi, Dad." He walked into the parlor. As he exited the room, he heard Mignon tell Elli that she would look good in the powder blue organza A-line gown with the jeweled collar she had stored for years since a debutante refused to pay her after she'd commissioned it.

"Son." Just from that one word and the deep solid tone from his dad, he knew there was a problem.

"What's wrong?"

"A client of yours was picked up for DWI an hour ago. Hit and run with a mailbox and a couple of garbage cans."

Beau sighed. His dad knew he hated DWI cases. "Who is it?"

"Stanley Boudreaux." Not again. The man had more money than Midas with the success of his seafood wholesale and distribution business. He had a sweet, beautiful young wife and five smart, terrific children. Yet, he couldn't control the beast in him and refused to get treatment. No matter what kind of lawyering he did, or what connections Stanley had, the man was at the end of this dangerous gamble he'd taken with his life. The law was solid with DWI cases and the District Attorney had given Stanley one too many chances already, if you asked Beau.

"This makes me sick." Beau ran his hands through his hair. "A different street or just a few minutes later, and he could've hit the garbage collectors picking up those trash cans."

"He's asking for you. Refused a Breathalyzer and blood test."

"Shit." He hated this part of his job. He could turn down a new client he didn't want to represent, but a long-time client who had turned to the bottle two years ago, he couldn't abandon. Staying loyal to a man who took a chance on him as a young lawyer fresh out of school meant something. "I'll be there within thirty minutes. I've got court this morning anyway."

Beau walked back into the kitchen. "Duty calls."

"Do you need an assistant?" Mignon asked. "I'm a good assistant. Ask Jewell. And, I can dress as nice as you, too."

"Thanks for the offer. This one I have to fly solo on."

"That's what got Jewell in trouble." She harrumphed. "If I was with her she wouldn't have gotten into trouble."

Oh, hell. Now, she was ready to tell him what he wanted to know when he couldn't stay to hear it. Maybe Elli could get the scoop. He looked at his cousin's wife and she looked at him with narrowed eyes and a shake of her head.

"Innocent until proven guilty," she told him before turning to Mignon. "Now, tell me some stories about the King of Carnival Rex parade in New Orleans. I've only been to parades here in Cane. You must know a lot about New Orleans Mardi Gras history."

"I bet you really want to know what the men wear under their king's dresses." She winked.

"I'm out of here." Beau made a mad dash for the door. He wanted to be out of earshot of that conversation PDQ or he'd never be able to look Mignon in the eyes again.

"You are naughty, Mignon," Elli exclaimed.

"Oh, thank you."

Chapter

Jewell climbed to the top of the dry, splintered wooden steps and reached the upper level of the barn. The steps bowed under her weight and held. She was grateful for that and the fact that there actually were stairs. She had climbed ladders with missing rungs and knotted ropes with frayed fibers to reach stored treasures and junk in countless attics over the years. In all instances, the climb was as thrilling as the ascent to the precipice of a roller coaster.

The anticipation of what she would find made her heart race, her soul excite. She absolutely loved being in the midst of old, neglected spaces. The older and more neglected, the better. That meant the potential for finding a forgotten piece of the past was greater. She carefully stepped into the vast attic space, turning her head so her headlight shone on a mountain range of canvas-covered items.

Holding her breath she paused, getting a feel for the space. Shadows wrapped around her, making her feel like she wasn't alone in a place where she was the only person. Dull, natural light managed to beam through dusty windows. An overhead bulb was black. Useless. Jewell was used to creeping around poorly lit, dirty places.

This upper level storage area in the Sugar Mill Plantation barn was no different. Memories varied from place to place, but the familiar musty scents of warm humidity and mold mingling with mouse and roach droppings and old dust never did. She never got used to coming across a scurrying mouse or leggy spider or working under a curtain of spider webs, either.

Spiders, mice and creepy touching shadows were just part of her hunt, her job, her passion. If she had to forge through those uncomfortable obstacles to get to the treasures, to the history, she did it. The reward, the adrenaline rush, the connection with memories that leaped into the modern world was worth the muck and spooks.

She made a slow circle, itching to get started. "Wow. There's so much stuff in here." She smiled, her heart beating faster and happier in anticipation of the work she had to do. This was going to be so much fun, but the reality of her deadline encroached on her excitement. She only had a week to go through it all, catalog it, see what Elli and Ben wanted to keep, sell or get rid of, and then find a little time to research if and where Mimi's Twinnie ever existed. One week. There was no way to extend the deadline on this job either. Filming started in two weeks. Elli had told her that meant the set construction crew would be there a week before that to build the sets and place the lighting.

One week and countless treasures to discover.

"Oh, geez. I need to clone myself," she whispered, as her headlight caught bright threads of spider webs that hung thicker than the chipped wood-slatted walls in some areas and thinner than lace necklaces in other areas.

She slipped on the weathered black leather satchel that perfectly fit her iPad over her neck like a heavy necklace. It was a Civil War confederate courier's bag that she'd bought at an antique shop on Royal Street. She knew the better bargains were to be found away from the touristy French Quarter, but she fell in love with the courier bag the day she spotted it while walking home from high school one winter's day. It was hanging on one of the wrought iron security bars in the antique shop's window, looking old, faded and magnificent. She was studying the Civil War battles fought around New Orleans in her Louisiana History honors class, and this bag seemed to bring the accounts of the horror of war and triumphs of victory to life for her. It connected her to the history that totally fascinated her. When she slipped the bag onto her body for the first time, she felt part of something important. During the life of this courier bag, it had carried important war documents and lovers' letters; she would be forever part of that history.

She'd integrated herself into the past by being a steward of what was able to survive centuries into the present time. The superficial world of her mother truly wasn't important, as she had always known it was not. This bag was the proof of it.

With a contented breath, Jewell rubbed her hand over the smooth, soft leather that lay over her heart. "Time to get to work."

***

Beau walked into the barn, loosening his silk tie. It was a warm fall day, as most October days in south Louisiana were, but the stale, unmoving air in the barn made this day seem even warmer. Dust motes floated in sunlight streaming in through the door, lifting upward on an air current he didn't feel. As he walked in, dust swirled over his once clean Ermenegildo Zegna shoes. He shrugged and continued farther into the barn. The hollow sound of a distant TV greeted him.

Beau walked toward the stairs that led to the upper floor where he assumed Jewell was working. He spotted a broom hanging on a nail next to a couple of crawfish traps. The broom probably hadn't had a human hand touch it in a decade. Ben was so busy at the kennel—first establishing it and now keeping up with the success he'd made of it—that he didn't have time to clean out a barn he rarely used.

Beau stopped when he spotted Mignon sitting in front of an open window on the other side of the barn. She was seated in a wooden rocker. Her feet were elevated on the same footstool that she'd removed from the hidden nook the night before. A TV tray was next to her, with a tall iced water bottle, a bowl of grapes and a roll of paper towels. As he neared her, he first heard and then saw the small TV set up on a stepladder in front of her. Long rabbit ear antennas allowed her to catch, although very snowy, *The Ellen DeGeneres Show*. The volume was turned up pretty loud, but not as loud as he might have expected for someone her age. The TV was plugged into an extension cord that snaked out of the open window off to God knew where. She looked cozy and happy.

"*Bon matin,* again, Mignon. I hope you're having a good morning," he said, smiling at her. She turned to look at him: A miner's type headlight was strapped to the top of her head with an apparatus that reminded him of one of his cousin's headgear for her braces. The light was turned off.

"You look good. I didn't know it was Sunday."

"Sunday?" He wasn't sure he'd ever follow this woman's train of thought. What did him looking good have to do with Sunday? "I don't understand what you mean?"

"You coming from church dressed in your Sunday best? You even have your Jesus shoes on." She lifted her orthopedic shoes. "These aren't my Jesus shoes. My Jesus shoes are black."

Beau smiled. "No, ma'am. I'm coming from court, but my case was postponed." *And from jail,* he thought with a sour feeling in his stomach. At least, he didn't have to fight to get his client out. Stanley had to stay the mandatory three days in jail for refusing the field sobriety test on his third offense.

"You in trouble, like my Jewell?" She asked with all sincerity. Suddenly, Beau heard something fall overhead, then the sound of stomping.

"What did she do that got her in trouble?" The footsteps pounded louder and then, Jewell shouted.

"Mimi. Mimi. Are you hungry? You want a snack?"

Beau watched as Jewell half raced and half slipped down the stairs near the back of the barn. Like her grandmother, she had a miner's headlight on her head. It was turned on.

"Oh, *mon Dieu,* you want to break a leg, or neck or something?" Her grandmother responded, and her voice echoed from a speaker attached to the waistband of Jewell's jeans. On the windowsill he spotted the broadcasting end of a baby monitor. Jewell had heard his conversation with her grandmother and clearly didn't want her talking about her legal troubles.

Jewell walked over to them, brushing off dust and spider webs from her royal blue long sleeve T-shirt with her company logo emblazed on the front. Beau looked down and saw she was wearing rubber boots again, only this pair had gray, black and white raccoons and cypress trees on a sky blue background.

"It's not Sunday," Mignon told Jewell.

"No, he's probably dressed for work," she answered, not having the same trouble understanding her grandmother's conversation. "Why aren't you at work?" she asked, looking at him.

"Court case was postponed. Didn't you hear?" He nodded toward the monitor on the windowsill.

"I half-heard." She tilted her head and looked at him sideways. "I also half-heard you on my monitor being a busybody."

"Hazards of the job." He reached over to pull a long strand of spider web from her hair. She shied away at first, but let him remove it without protest; her eyes steady on his. Shy one second, bold the next. As bold as her fragrance. What was this all about, he wondered. And why in the hell did her rich, milk chocolate colored eyes heat his flesh? Elli had said she would be cautious. He better damn well make sure he was, too.

"Thank you." She looked away. He still felt her heat.

Something moved on her head. Where the spider web had been he noticed a spider remained. "Hold still, you still have a spider in there."

"Oh, God. I hate spiders." She raised her shoulders up around her neck and shivered, then leaned forward for him to get it.

"I wouldn't have thought you could be arachnophobic in your line of work," he grinned, dusting the spider off his hand.

"Not arachnophobic. Just arachno-disgusted." She pulled the band from her ponytail and shook out her hair. "You got them all, right?"

"All but the brown recluse." Her head jerked up. "Just kidding." He watched her refasten her long dark ponytail, understanding now why she didn't let her hair hang free. He liked it loose, though, remembering how it looked when she raced into the kitchen looking for Mignon wearing her thin red nightgown. He was certain he'd like seeing her silky strands skim the soft curve of her derrière when her head was thrown back in passion too.

"Not funny. I've been bitten by a brown recluse." She rubbed her arms, and then scratched her head.

"Sorry." Her Achilles heel. Not that he'd use it against her. If she tried to execute a con against his family, he'd simply use legal means to strong-arm her to leave Cane. "Well. I unexpectedly have the rest of the day off. I thought I'd see what you two were up to."

"Jewell is up there and I'm down here with Ellen. I like Ellen. She's from New Orleans, you know." Mignon faced the TV. "She sure can dance real good. Like Jewell's momma."

"Mimi," Jewell interrupted. "Are you drinking your water?"

Mignon picked up her water bottle and took a long drink. "Happy?" she looked at Jewell and frowned. "Go back to work and let me watch my Ellen dance. Take him with you." She sighed. "If I could climb all those stairs, I would help y'all." She looked at Beau. "You have work clothes?"

"These are my work clothes." He turned his palms up and shrugged. "I do have my exercise clothes in the car. I usually go to the gym after work." He looked at Jewell. "You need my help?"

"No."

"That's a silly question," Mimi rolled her eyes and told Jewell something in French. "And, I just told her that she gave you an even more ridiculous answer." Her eyes twinkled. "Especially since she just told me she has enough work upstairs for two weeks instead of one."

"You're having trouble with the workload, Boots?"

"Not at all," she looked at her grand-mère then pasted on a fake smile.

"That's better. I told her to be polite to our company. See, she's doing a good job." Mignon turned to smile at Beau. Where her granddaughter's smile was forced and strained, hers was sweet and approachable. Beau had a flash of an image of a formidable younger Mignon flirting with a man just coyly enough to have him do her bidding.

Mimi waved him off. "Go change. You can use my headlight." She took it off her head and handed it to Beau. Her hair stuck straight up where the head straps had once held it down.

Jewell walked over and finger combed her grandmother's silver curls. "She never shares her headlight with anyone," she murmured. Then, she spoke a little louder. "I guess I can use your help until lunch." She gave him an up and down look. "I hope you have a strong back."

"Pushing paper all day builds up back muscles better than you know."

Ten minutes later, Beau entered the dank and dirty top floor of the barn, a place he'd absolutely no interest in spending ten seconds in, much less a couple of hours before lunchtime. He had a healthy appetite, not much ruined it, but he guessed dealing with the crap in storage might do the trick. He flipped on the headlight as he entered the room. Jewell was in front of the only window, a rag in one hand, a bottle of cleaner in the other. She looked wholly domestic. Knowing she was a scholar with a lot of initials after her name doing manual labor here did something to his insides. How far the high and mighty had fallen. He might not trust New Orleans' once most interviewed Louisiana history professor, nor her motives for coming to Sugar Mill. He might totally think of her as a criminal. He even might understand all the reasons people made bad choices and be sympathetic to it up to a point. What he had no patience for was how those bad decisions dominoed negatively into the lives of the innocent. Yet, in this moment as he watched her dodging the spiders she feared to stretch overhead to wipe away layers of dust, he felt sorry for her.

"I can reach the top," he said, taking the dirty rag from her. "Looks like there is just as much gunk on the outside as on the inside."

She sighed. "Yeah. It would be faster for me to bring more lights up here than trying to clean that window. I'd need scaffolding or a lift-bucket truck."

Beau picked up his cell phone and punched in the number of his cousin, Steve. Steve was the general manager of the local cable television company. He had access to bucket trucks. He also was long-winded

"Hey, *coo-zan*." Before he could utter another word, Beau was interrupted.

"Is it true Stanley Boudreaux got himself another DWI?"

Well, if Steve knew about Stanley, then everyone else in Cane knew. There was no stopping the news from spreading fence post to fence post or from beauty shop to pharmacy. Especially when the news started from the one person whose mailbox met the front end of Boudreaux's fire engine red Lexus. That person would be cousin Ruby.

And, cousin Ruby loved to be at the head end of the gossip telling.

"I can't talk about it." He ran his hand through his hair, knocking the headlight he'd forgotten was there. The light shot up at the ceiling, illuminating spider webs hanging like shredded sheets on a clothesline. God, he hated this dirty place almost as much as he hated dealing with Stanley Boudreaux. He yanked off the headlight, holding it in his free hand, and began to pace.

"Come on, man. Just give me a little inside info that Ruby doesn't know yet. It doesn't have to be important. Just something like his wife was on the phone with him when he wrecked or he was wearing women's underwear..." He laughed. "Ruby will hate it if I know something she doesn't. It will be a great practical joke."

"For you." Beau grumbled. "Not me. I've been on the wrong side of Ruby's wrath. I don't intend to be there again."

"Are you talking about the *misère* you and Ben had when you stuffed live crawfish in her mattress? What, you were twelve?"

"It feels like yesterday. My ears still ache where she *peeshnicked* me. She has the most powerful thumping fingers in all of south Louisiana. I guar-an-tee."

Steve laughed. "Oh, man-oh-man," he said when he finally caught his breath between the laughter. "Here I was worried I had to argue around your high ethical morals regarding attorney-client privilege to get info when it is Ruby's finger thumping-*peeshnicking* wrath I have to make a case against." He grunted. "I don't have a chance in hell, do I?"

"Nope." Beau glanced at Jewell who was staring at him, clearly having a hard time following his side of the conversation. No doubt about it, he'd be explaining to her that *peeshnicking* was thumping someone in a sensitive spot with their flicking finger. She turned, and began looking in the dresser drawers closer to her. A Mona Lisa smile gently filled her face. Damn, but that smile made him feel warm inside.

That was dangerous. It could weaken him, if he didn't guard himself better.

He turned his back to her. "So, Steve, I called you because I need a favor. Can you send a bucket truck to Sugar Mill? A window in the barn needs to be cleaned ASAP."

"Let me check the schedule." Beau heard Steve's fingers clicking on a computer keyboard. They could joke and tease with one another, but Beau appreciated how quickly family was ready to help family. There was a security in standing shoulder-to-shoulder with the Bienvenu clan. Even for the small things. "Just the one window, huh?"

"Yep, just the one."

"You will owe me."

"Ben will owe you."

"You're going to tell him that, right?"

"Hell, yeah."

"I'll send the truck over after lunch. Oh, and Beau, would you ask Ben what's up with that pretty brunette staying at his place?" He chuckled. "I hear she looks a lot like Mila Kunis, is that true?"

Beau looked at Jewell. Mila Kunis. He hadn't considered that she looked like her before. She wasn't her twin, but he guessed she did have enough similarities with her big round eyes, full lips, pretty round face and dark silky hair to make the connection. "I don't know," he answered knowing he had to say something. "Where did you see her?"

"I didn't. Ann did."

Beau didn't like the way this conversation was going. Steve's wife was Cane's second most active gossiper after Ruby. And he knew that meant that news about the Mila Kunis stranger in town was spreading across Cane as fast as the news about Stanley Boudreaux busting up Ruby's mailbox with his red Lexus.

"Ann was shopping at the Simoneauxs' estate sale and the pretty brunette started asking her questions about the longtime families of Cane, including the Bienvenus." Beau knew she'd have happily answered those questions, too. "She said the brunette was curious. Real curious. And pretty. Have you met her yet?"

Beau turned the headlight in his hand and shined it at Jewell. "Yeah, I met her. I'll look for your truck, cuz." He hung up the phone as Steve started to talk some more.

"I assume I am the 'her' you're referring to?" Jewell said, surprising Beau that she was so direct. She'd been mostly evasive with everything else they had discussed. He supposed she was curious what his cousin had said about her.

"Yeah, apparently the people who met you yesterday at the Simoneauxs' are talking about you." He exhaled and leaned against the cabinet closest to him. "They say you look like Mila Kunis."

Jewell started to laugh. It was a full, generous and unguarded laugh. "Of all the things I thought you might say, that was not one of them. Mila Kunis?" She wiped a tear from her eye. "Well, that's a first."

He smiled, unable to stop himself as her contagious laughter shot through his blood like heated kerosene in a hurricane lamp. It was so damn unexpected that it completely startled him. He stood and started to walk toward the dirty window to regain his balance.

"Cane has been pretty star struck," he said, not daring to look at her. "Since Elli brought the first movie to Sugar Mill, everyone is always seeing celebrities in the faces of newcomers."

He gazed out the window at two fat gray squirrels racing along a hooked old branch of the live oak. The one in front stopped, turned to face the one behind it with its tail straight up and vibrating. He or she didn't look happy.

Beau found himself sympathizing with the squirrel getting dressed down by the -squirrel with the twitching tail. He shook his head and turned toward Jewell.

"A few weeks ago," he said, picking up the story he had begun, "a man painting the lift-span bridge down the bayou was mobbed by a few dozen women carrying autograph books, cameras, food and personal items of lingerie. Someone had spread the rumor that he was Ashton Kutcher and that he was pretending to be a painter as some sort of research...or method acting thing for a role he would be playing in a movie being filmed in New Orleans."

Jewell's eyes shimmered with her laughter. "That's so funny. I love small towns with personality." She began to open the drawers of the chest closest to her to see if anything was left inside.

"There is no short supply of personality here, that's for sure."

"Well, you tell the chatty people of Cane that I am in no way remotely in the movie or entertainment industry. Definitely not my thing. I have an aversion to it. In fact, I think I'm allergic to it since I was a little girl. I used to break out in hives every single year that I was forced to perform in the annual dance recital. I didn't at first when I was a spunky three-year-old toddler, but from the time I hit grade school until I refused to step on stage in high school, I'd get all red and splotchy and itchy. I..." Her head jerked up, but she quickly dropped it back down to continue looking in the drawers. It was clear that she was sorry she'd revealed so much of herself to him. "Anyway, I'm not remotely the Mila Kunis type."

She bit her lower lip. Beau was good at reading people, and that little nip of her pretty pouty bottom lip told him she was forcing herself to keep her mouth shut. The way her shoulders lifted and tensed, he knew she was unhappy she'd said what she had about herself. So, there would be no more personal revelations for a while. He had no idea why that little story of her fear of performing at dance recitals was a big deal. It wasn't like she had revealed some career or life changing event. Her comments seemed innocuous. Yet, she obviously didn't like telling him anything about herself, even if it was about a childhood experience that had nothing to do with her today. Well, he guessed considering her recent legal troubles, he understood that she still hated being in the limelight.

"Allergy or not," he began, staring directly into her huge, magnetic eyes, hoping to catch any nuance or tell that might give him more understanding or insight into this woman. It might just help him to know how in the hell to deal with her. "You have that sexy, exotic, prettier-than-the-average-bear good looks that translate into something special. Different. To the droves of bargain shoppers you impressed at the estate sale, you look pretty enough to be a celebrity. Those crazy shrimp boots you wear make you eccentric enough to fit the image, too." He shrugged his shoulders. "I can see it."

Jewell looked at him and cocked her head like BJ, Elli's beagle. She looked bewildered and damn cute. Then she blinked a few times and returned to digging in the drawers. Her smart professorial brain was probably processing his compliment, evaluating its purpose and trying to figure out if she could use it to her advantage.

"Grab an end," Jewell said, her voice even and all business. "Let's turn this dresser around toward what little light there is up here so I can look for identifying markings on the back and start cataloging the furniture."

They shuffled their way to the window. Once the dresser was set in place, Jewell took a magnifying glass from the leather tool belt she wore. She crouched in front of the rear of the chest and started studying it.

"What are you looking for?" Beau asked.

"Wood grain to type the wood. Manufacturers' markings or a signature from the craftsman. A child's etching or family stamp. Anything, really."

Beau slipped his headlight on his head and turned it on. He crouched down near her. Big mistake, he thought. When he first saw her in the barn he thought he'd gotten a whiff of her sexy, sweet, earthy scent that had assaulted him the night before, but now, he was certain of it. His entire body reacted to it even before his brain had a chance to know what was pleasing it so damn much. He stood and took a step back.

"It looks old to me," He knew he sounded annoyed.

"Not that old, really." She shrugged, stood, took a step away from him. *Not far enough.* Her scent was still stoking his flesh, burning his blood. "It looks like it's red oak. Mass production. I'd say from the '70s."

"1870s? The plantation was built around then."

"1970s. About the same era as your disco app."

He bit back on a smile. It was one thing to play nice with her, to win her confidence so he could protect his family; it was another thing to actually enjoy a playful convo with her. That would mean he'd let his guard down.

Big mistake.

She slipped her iPad from the black leather case around her neck and typed something onto a spreadsheet. "Is that your diary?"

"Pretty much." She pulled a drawer completely out of the dresser.

Beau tried not to stare at the way her body moved smoothly with purpose and grace. This whole antiquities study was more sensual than he would've ever considered. He titled the head lamp up and shined it up into the dirty rafters.

"You know, I'm kind of surprised how useful dis' here head lamp is for somethin' other than going out at night lookin' for frogs', me. Yep, sure is good for froggin', for sure." He made his Cajun accent intentionally heavy and playful. He tilted his head up and then to the side and then to the other side, causing the light beam to bounce off in different directions. "It's like a movie premiere in the barn."

Jewell looked at him playing with the light. "Are you bored?"

He stopped, faced her and blinded her for a moment. She squinted with annoyance. "Oops, sorry, Boots." He twisted the headlight so it shined behind him. "Not really bored. It's just that all this stuff looks like junk to me."

"Well, from what I can tell, these four items are." She laughed. "The only thing I found of note is the plantation era crystal and brass ink well I put in the crate next to the wall near the window. I found it in the first bureau..." The monitor at her waist began to cackle and Jewell stopped speaking to listen.

Beau recognized the voice immediately. It was clear and strong. Her Cajun accent stronger. His Tante Izzy was back in Cane. Jewell looked at him, clearly not certain what to do about the new arrival. She didn't move to go downstairs right away as the two old women interacted; he and Jewell remained flies on the wall as the women's voices came through the baby monitor on her belt.

"Is that da *Price is Right* you watchin'? Speed-up da TV so I can hear it better." His aunt demanded, sounding querulous. "I guess if you like *Price Is Right*, you ain't half bad."

"Maybe I'm not half good, either," Mimi responded. "In my opinion, being good is overrated. Especially at our age."

Tante Izzy made a rude noise. "What you mean, our age?"

***

"I'm not as old as you are," Jewell heard Izzy Bienvenu tell Mimi on the monitor, and in person as she stepped onto the bottom stair. Beau was already walking up to his aunt, arms spread open to give her a welcoming hug.

"Well, look who's back from her ladies-gone-wild-trip to the casino. Go to any burlesque shows?" He kissed her on her wrinkled cheek and engulfed into his arms the tiny lady in the turquoise velour sweat suit, lemon yellow flowered T-shirt and matching lemon yellow Keds.

She closed her eyes and absorbed the hug for all of ten seconds, then swatted him. "You know we did." She looked at Mignon. "Who dat?"

"Tante Izzy, let me introduce to you Mignon Duet." He smiled. "Mignon, this is Tante Izzy." Jewell watched as her grand-mère stood with polite dignity and extended her hand to Izzy.

"Oh, *mon Dieu,* you is wearin' five rings." Izzy looked at Mimi's hand for what must have been thirty seconds and Jewell would swear she heard the tick of a clock, the drip of water from a leaky spigot, and the swoosh of sand in an hourglass. Fear that this sparky woman would criticize her Mimi for her fashion faux pas had her leaping into action. She rushed forward to diffuse what might be shaping into a difficult moment, but Tante Izzy was a beat ahead of her. She lifted Mignon's hand and inspected the rings. "I wish I had thought of dat, me. It sure is pretty."

Mignon nodded. "They were the only nice things at the Simoneauxs' sale," she told her. "It was more a garage sale than an estate sale, if you ask me."

"Suzette Simoneaux, God rest her soul, was as cheap as dey come." Izzy nodded. "If she din't have bad taste, she'd have no taste at all." She looked at the rings again. "'Cept for dem dere rings. Dey sure are nice. I like da purple flower one best."

"I want you to have it, then." Mimi yanked on the purple ring for a few moments before getting it over her thick arthritic knuckle. She handed it to Izzy who was very pleased to own it and told her so. "You know, da stuff in dat recently departed woman's house was cheap. God rest her soul," Mimi said, repeating Izzy's words. She pointed to Jewell. "That's what I told *ma sucrée.*"

Izzy turned to face Jewell, noticing her in the room for the first time. She threw up her hand to shade her eyes. "*Mon Dieu,* you goin' bull-eyein', girl?"

Beau reached over and flipped off the light on Jewell's headlight. "She's looking for her prince amongst the frogs, Tante Izzy," he said with a grin.

"I am not." She took off the head lamp, then refastened her ponytail that had slipped from the band in the process.

"Best prince around is right in front of your nose." She nodded, then her head jerked to look down. Her eyes widened and her mouth moved a few times before she spoke. "Did you get dose shrimp boots at da Simoneauxs', too?" Jewell smiled and turned her right boot from side to side so Izzy could see it better.

"No. I bought these in New Orleans."

"I gotz me some pink ones with daisies on 'em. But I like da raccoons and cypress trees you got dere."

"Thank you," Jewell said, then extended her hand. "I'm Jewell Duet, Miss Isaure. I'm very pleased to meet you."

Izzy threw back her shoulders, stood as tall as her five-foot delicate frame allowed and narrowed her eyes as she looked up at Jewell who was at least eight inches taller. It was like green ice freezing her soul. "And here I waz startin' to like you." She shook her head. "Fer somebody with good fashion sense, you sure don't know nuttin'." She harrumphed. "Who told you to call me dat?" She snapped. "Someone who don't value dey'z ears."

"Don't you talk to *ma sucrée* that way. I thought you were a nice lady. That's why I gave you my prettiest ring," Mignon snapped, her voice firm. "She might not know nothing about some things, but she knows a lot about other things. She's smart. She's a doctor."

"A doctor?" Izzy seemed to give that some thought a moment. "Well, I guess I can forgive you dis one time. Last time I went to da doctor was when I was *malade* in

1999; he used my given name, too. Dat is, until I set him to straights. He's never made dat mistake again and I'm betting you won't either." She nodded again. Then smiled. "You da new doctor dat took our Dr. Camille's place while she's on her month-long vay-cay-tion?"

"She's not a medical doctor, Tante Izzy. She's a professor. A Ph.D. doctor of Louisiana history," Beau said.

"A good one, too." Mignon added. Then sat in her chair. She eased back and lifted her feet back onto the footstool.

Tante Izzy looked at Jewell a minute. She was studying her, but it didn't make her uncomfortable or uneasy. She was looking at her as she had seen Mimi looking at someone she wanted to get to know better, only Izzy's eyes were sharp and clear. "Nobody tole me you was here. Why didn't you call me on my cell phone, Beau? Oh, dat reminds me. My phone is broken again. But it did work earlier dis morning, so youz could've called me before."

"She just arrived yesterday. Where's your phone?" She reached into her sweat suit pants pocket and handed it to Beau. He leaned against the wall behind him and looked at the phone and smiled. He tapped on the screen twice and handed it back to her. Jewell noticed he still held his head lamp in his hand. "Fixed, darlin'."

"How'd youz do dat?" Tante Izzy looked at the phone.

"You had it in airplane mode." He smiled. There was a kind, amused expression on his face.

"Again?" She harrumphed and Jewell remembered with longing of the many times she had to reset or reboot Mimi's phone because of the countless things Mimi had done to mess it up. Now, she was incapable of using one unless she had a lot of prompting. A lot. "I don't knowz why it keeps doin' dat. Hmm. Don't looks like you called about da Doctor," she said, looking at the screen.

"I thought she'd be gone by now," he said.

Jewell looked at him. "Not until I've finished my job."

"Boots is determined to clean the barn and sell off all that old junk upstairs."

"It's what I was hired to do. It's my job, and you know it."

"You sell old stuff?"

"Nobody does it better," Mimi said.

"Actually, I'm an..."

"I like to hire da best," Izzy said, now speaking directly to Mimi. "How much does she charge?"

"She's not cheap. Not like Suzette Simoneaux."

"God rest her soul," Izzy and Mimi said at the same time.

"Hmm." Izzy mumbled, narrowing her eyes and pursing her lips. "I ain't cheap either."

"Tante Izzy," Jewell said, deciding it was best she took control of this conversation. "You should know that I have a specialized expertise in..."

"I haz an oil well on my land. And I just had a run of good luck at da casino. I won blackout bingo two times."

"Two times?" Mimi clapped her hands. "That is lucky."

"I'll take her." Izzy extended her hand to Mimi and the two elderly women shook. "I need a good fall cleaning in my houz. And if'n I can make a few dollars on sellin' my old stuff, I can go back to da casino and play blackout again."

"You can sign the contract after my nap," Mimi said, enjoying herself.

"Wait, you should know that..." Jewell began, but Izzy spoke right over her as if she didn't know she was speaking. She probably didn't since she was so focused on Mimi.

"I prefer to do business after my nap, too. Does she do windows?" Tante Izzy asked.

"Nope, but apparently I do," Beau said, laughing.

Jewell turned to Beau. "What in the world just happened?"

"I think you got a job with another Bienvenu family member," he said, his voice deep, his expression suddenly strained. "But don't spend your paycheck, yet, Boots."

"Dat is a pretty footstool," Izzy said to Mignon. "Do you do needlepoint?"

"Not lately. I just darn socks, hem pants, repair seams." She pointed to the sewing basket next to her with a few items of clothes and socks. "*Ma sucrée* is always ripping a seam or tearing a hem. She's a little rough on clothes." Jewell noted that there were only three threaded needles left in the pincushion in the side pocket. "My momma did this needlework on the footstool. Isn't it *manifique?*"

Izzy nodded. "My momma was good at needlepoint, too. She loved to embroider flowers on pillows and cushions. I'z good at hand sewing, too. You know, I'm vice-president of da Cane Ladies Quilting Club. I was president, but it was interferin' wit my nap too much."

Beau moved from the wall and walked to stand next to Tante Izzy. "Have you ever seen this footstool before, Tante Izzy?"

"No. But da flowers sure look like my momma's." She nodded and moved closer to the footstool. "I has a framed piece in my dinin' room that my momma did. It looks a lot like dis, but wit bright spring colors."

She looked at Mimi, and Jewell thought by the wide expression in her cloudy green eyes that maybe she would tell her grand-mère something that was revealing about the footstool. Something that might help clarify why Mimi thought her mother had embroidered it, or dispel the belief that her mother had.

"You know," Izzy began, looking at the footstool again. "Dis is sure a pretty footstool but I likes spring and summer colors best."

"Goes with your hair better," Mimi offered easily.

"You like my hair color?" She smiled and patted the tight short permed blue-gray hair with her narrow palm. "Margie put in a new Fanci-Full rinse for the casino trip."

"It's a pretty, cool silver color. I bet you'd look good with one of those new colors the young girls are using. I told Jewell she should put some purple or pink in her hair."

"I'd like pink in my hair, me." Izzy said. "I heard you can use fruit punch to gets a pretty color, too."

"I like fruit punch," Mimi said smiling. "Don't we have fruit punch in the camper, Jewell?"

"Uh...Beau?" Jewell turned to face him and mouthed the word, *Help.*

"If she doesn't, Mignon, I'm sure Elli has some," Beau said with a smile.

Jewell turned to fully face him. "You don't know what fire you are stoking here."

A horn blew from outside the barn. It sounded deep and heavy, as if it belonged to a big truck. "That must be Steve with the bucket truck," Beau said to Jewell as he walked away.

"Oh, good, I need some branches trimmed at my house," Tante Izzy said, walking toward the door.

"I thought he was coming after lunch," Jewell said, following them. "I need to get lunch for Mimi. Do you think he would mind waiting while I fix her a sandwich?"

"I think he's here early to mooch a lunch," Beau said.

"I'm hungry, too," Tante Izzy said, just before she walked outside to talk to Steve.

"And, Mignon, you may be in luck," Beau said, mischief in his voice. "Steve might have one of those big five-gallon containers strapped to the back bumper of the bucket-truck filled with a fruit punch sports drink. Isn't that what is put in most of those five-gallon containers for their heat-exhausted workers?"

"Do you think the sports drink works as good as fruit punch?" Mimi asked.

"No," Jewell nearly shouted. "No." she repeated, controlling her tone. "Mimi, if you want color in your hair, I'll bring you to the salon you've gone to for the last forty years. Please, don't dip your head in a vat of fruit punch."

Chapter

Nothing had happened as she'd expected or planned since coming to Cane and Sugar Mill Plantation, Jewell thought as she spread mayonnaise on slices of wheat bread for the seven sandwiches she was making for five people. It started with the awful estate sale at the Simoneauxs' and continued now to playing chef and hostess to this impromptu lunch. If she was to complete her job to Elli's needs and satisfaction and still carve a little time to search for the possibly nonexistent Twinnie, she had to get to work in the barn.

Jewell looked out the window as she reached for sliced ham. In the shade of a couple of mature crepe myrtles, Mignon and Izzy were seated in lawn chairs pointing up to Beau in the lift bucket cleaning the barn window. She couldn't hear them, but she knew they were directing him to the task, which he'd jumped right into without being asked.

Such a nice gesture.

Or was it? Did he have an ulterior motive? She felt small and petty thinking that, but he'd made it clear that he didn't trust her and didn't want her around. Yet, here he was cleaning the upper barn windows for her. She supposed he probably reasoned if she was going to stay until the job's completion, providing more light to do her job would speed things up.

She hated to admit it, but the handsome man in the bucket cleaning the barn window was proving to be a big help. He not only was getting more light into the barn for her to work effectively, but his strength had come in handy when moving furniture around. He might be a paper-pushing lawyer, but his cut muscles straining against the high-performance exercise shirt and sweat pants indicated that he pushed and lifted heavier weight around. The man was fit, lean and in every way...gorgeous. Ugh, tall, dark, handsome, successful and smart. On top of that he smelled good, too. He was just the kind of man that her momma warned her about...warned her to not let go of.

"If he's all that...has an expensive car and a great job, marry him. Do whatever it takes to get him, Jewell."

Yeah, Beau was exactly the kind of man her momma wanted for her daughter and especially for herself. Jewell shook her head. Not her type. The best man for her rode a bicycle to work, or took public transportation. He spent hours with his nose in books researching an obscure fact that no one had ever heard of nor ever would care about. He'd wear duct tape on his glasses because he didn't want to take the time away from his research to spend in the mall getting his glasses fixed. He would be excruciatingly boring and nothing like the man her mother told her to go after. Like the men her mother had chosen for herself even when her mother was a rebellious sixteen-year-old. Jewell sighed, her hand paused over the unfinished sandwich she was assembling.

God help her, but the man she'd been searching for was the man she created to be the antithesis of her mother's desires. What if the truth was that she actually wanted what her mother wanted? Jewell shook her head.

No. Impossible.

Another car pulled up, a red Cadillac, and a petite, squarely-built woman in her forties with fluffy red hair got out. Jewell was grateful for the distraction. The woman wore burnt orange Capri pants with shamrock green polka dots all over them. Her button-down blouse was the same color as the polka dots and her four-inch high heel mule shoes were tan leather. Her movements were large and energetic as she rushed up to Izzy and Mimi. Mimi was frowning and her eyes were a bit bewildered. She knew her grand-mère well enough to know that a new face could confuse her and cause her anxiety. When it belonged to someone who was hyper, it was a given. When Mimi was anxious, she often became defensive and offensive. Jewell rushed to finish the sandwiches, placed them on a platter she'd already arranged with bags of chips and grapes, grabbed a handful of napkins and hurried outside.

Steve waved to her as she rushed past. He stood at the back of the truck, near the rear controls and a five-gallon container with God only knew what inside of it. "It'll cost you, is all I'm saying," she heard Mimi tell the redhead. "Supply and demand."

"I gots her first," Izzy said with a nod. "She ain't cheap. You cain't afford her. You don't have an oil well on you property."

"Hello, ladies." Jewell pasted a smile on her face. The redhead swung around, a huge smile on her face.

"A garden lunch, how nice," she said, her Cajun accent smooth, her voice friendly. "Let me help you with that." She grabbed the platter from Jewell's hand without her affirmation and placed it on Mimi's TV tray, which was set between the elderly women. "Hi, I'm cousin Ruby. Ruby Bienvenu. I love your shrimp boots."

Jewell laughed. "Nice to meet you." Jewell shook her hand. Never had her rain boots been referred to as shrimp boots before coming to Cane. She shouldn't be surprised, she supposed, considering the number of shrimpers who lived in the community.

Jewell handed Mimi a napkin, then gave one to Izzy. She told them to help themselves to the sandwiches.

"Please, help yourself to a sandwich, Ruby." She handed her a napkin. "There's plenty."

"Why, thank you." She smiled and reached for a sandwich. "You know shrimp boots were the talk of Cane a while back. My husband's second cousin twice removed who lives down the bayou has a shrimp shed. He told me that when *Forrest Gump* was filmed, the props and wardrobe people sent out a call to collect as many used shrimp boots as they could get their hands on. They wanted them for Tom Hanks to wear in the movie. For every pair they received, they replaced it with a brand new pair." She laughed and waved her hand with the sandwich in it. "The dirtier and rattier it was the better. Shrimpers were coming out of the woodwork bringing in their old seafood-smelling, disgusting boots to the shrimp sheds down the bayou. Most had tucked notes inside for the star, too."

"Jewell's boots are not smelly and disgusting," Mimi snapped. Her lower lip jutted out in a frown. "She keeps them clean."

Ruby looked at Jewell, her eyes wide. "I wasn't insinuating she had dirty boots, Miss Mignon." She waved the sandwich again as she spoke. "In fact, I like her boots. A lot."

"Are you going to eat that sandwich or wave it around like a rag swatting flies?" Yep, Mimi was definitely anxious. Her comment wasn't as bad as it could've been but her tone certainly was impolite.

"She doesn't usually play with her food," Izzy offered. "She cleans her plate nice and good."

Ruby rolled her eyes. Looked at her sandwich like she thought about not eating it, then she took a bite. Jewell liked her. She was a cliché. She looked exactly as she would have expected a woman named Ruby to look. She was straightforward. Uncomplicated. Nothing confusing there. Not like Mr. Wonderful in the bucket washing the barn window. She glanced up. He was giving the window a final wipe, his arm stretched high over his head. The muscles in his back bunched with each movement. Muscle and sinew. When he finished, Steve started lowering Beau in the bucket.

"You know, you don't look like Mila Kunis at all. You have the same coloring and sensual aura but, I would never mistake you for her." Ruby said. "Of course, I am a bit of an expert on the subject of celebrities. I subscribe to *People Magazine*." She nodded, like that explained it all.

"I gets dem when she's done," Izzy added. "Da pages are nearly worn t'in, too."

"You do have a familiar face, though," Ruby said staring at her. "I can't put my finger on it. My blood sugar must be low. I had a light breakfast." She took a second sandwich. "Are you going to eat with us, Jewell, or are you an organic like Elli?"

"I eat healthy and I eat organic food whenever possible, but I'm a New Orleans gal. I mostly just enjoy eating good food."

"Did I hear someone say food and eat?" Steve asked as he and Beau walked up. He reached for a sandwich. "If I had known there was going to be a party, I would've brought my wooden paddle and cast iron pot to make a jambalaya."

"Dat would've been good," Tante Izzy nodded. "Better yet, we can tailgate under da oak for da LSU game. Dey's is playin' in dat special out of town game on T'ursday. Bring you radio."

"We like Tulane. Never cared much for LSU," Mimi announced, leaving Steve staring at her with his bottom jaw hanging open. "Sorry. I know it doesn't seem right to be a Louisiana voting citizen and feel that way but there you go."

"Tulane is a Louisiana college at least," Tante Izzy said, jumping to their defense. "Better dan dat fancy Texian Yale law school Beau went to."

"You went to college in Texas? Wait, she said, Yale. That's in New Haven, Connecticut," Jewell said, offering the tray of sandwiches to Beau. He took two.

"*Tex-i-an, sucrée*, not Texan," Izzy corrected, using Mimi's pet name. Hearing someone say it other than Mimi tickled Jewell and she laughed softly.

"A Texian is anyone who isn't from here. A stranger. An outsider," Beau explained. "It was an expression that started when the Texans first came into South Louisiana to begin working the oil fields. Pretty much the only outsiders back then were from Texas or so it seemed to the locals."

"And Oklahoma, too," Jewell added. "I guess anyone who wore cowboy boots and spoke with a western drawl sounded Texan to the locals."

"Elli used to be a Texian before she married Ben," Tante Izzy clarified. "She'z from Hollywood. You two is from New Orleans, and that ain't Texian. Y'all is city girls."

"I'm a plantation girl," Mimi said easily, having all of the Bienvenus turning their heads, giving her their full attention.

"I thought you were from France," Ruby stated as if it was fact. "At least that's what I heard from some people who heard you and Jewell speaking French to one another at the Simoneauxs' garage sale." Ruby sighed. "I guess Ann got her information wrong." She looked at Steve pointedly, then took a bite of her sandwich. He smiled, then took a bite of his sandwich, too.

"I was at a garage sale?" Mimi asked Jewell. "Did I buy anything?"

"You got your rings there, and it wasn't a garage sale," she corrected. "It was an estate sale."

"Was it at my plantation?" Mimi asked.

"Which plantation are you from, Mignon?" Beau asked, his light eyes steady on Mimi. *Of course, this moment would not slip by Beauregard Bienvenu,* Jewell realized. He said he was like a dog with a bone. Her heart began to pound fast and hard in her chest and her ears. Before she could do anything to interrupt or stop her grand-mère from making the biggest mistake of her aging life, Mimi smiled and waved her hand like a queen would wave her scepter. The regal wave was directed at the big beautiful plantation to their right.

"Sugar Mill—*c'est ma maison.*"

"Sugar Mill?" Tante Izzy gasped, standing. "You is saying Sugar Mill is you home? Oh, *alors pas*. You confused. You live in dat camper trailer. You must have dat old-timer's."

Mimi shook her head. "No. I have dementia." She looked at Jewell for confirmation.

Jewell nodded sadly, searching for the right words to interject that wouldn't irrevocably hurt Mimi's spirit and soul. The first time she claimed to be home after the Saints game, no one challenged her. Her words had just passed by. Now, she wasn't so lucky. What could Jewell say now that would change the course of what Mimi had so innocently set in motion from what she honestly believed...What Jewell wasn't sure she believed but would never tell Mimi. Besides protecting her, explaining what her grand-mère was speaking of would have other repercussions. There would be unemployment. Eviction. Financial worries. And there would be unfulfilled dreams for Mimi.

Jewell wouldn't allow that.

She stood next to Mimi, grasped her hand in hers and looked at each of the Bienvenus one at a time. No one said a word. They were waiting for her to explain what Mimi had meant claiming Sugar Mill was her home.

"Mimi believes she once lived here at Sugar Mill plantation," Jewell stated, purposely not offering Mimi's dementia and confusion as an excuse to negate her grand-mère's beliefs. She wouldn't embarrass her grandmother in front of these people she seemed to like. Not in front of anyone.

"*Mon Dieu*. It sure sounds like da old-timer's to me." Tante Izzy walked to stand directly in front of Beau, leaning her head far back to look into his eyes. "Da half of my friends dat aren't dead talk nonsense like dis. Da other half dat ain't got da old-timer's, forget where dey live most times I'm driving dem home. And the other half don't remember dere chil'ren's names." She glanced at Jewell a moment and asked her in Cajun French if she believed what her grand-mère was telling her.

Jewell swallowed hard past the lump in her throat. Mimi was staring at her. The hope and need in her cloudy eyes for her granddaughter to believe her was clear. Jewell felt it like a vise around her heart. "I do." She told her in French. Then, she spoke to Beau in English. "Can I have a word in private with you, Beau?"

"Oh, crap," Steve told Ruby. "I hope this isn't going to be one of those never to be shared attorney-client privilege conversations."

Ruby had her phone in her hand, poised to make a call. "Me, too." She narrowed her eyes at Steve. "Let's make a pact. Let's keep each other informed on whatever we find out about Mignon's claim on Sugar Mill."

Steve shook hands with Ruby. "Absolutely, cuz."

Tante Izzy walked over on thin but strong legs and smacked Steve in the back of the head at the same time she dug her fingers in the fleshy part of Ruby's arm.

"*Oo yi yi!*" they complained at the same time.

"You two sound like school chil'ren. So, I'll treat you dat way." Tante Izzy scolded. "Dis is family business. Don't y'all forget it. It's personal. We stick togedder. Nobody is goin' to say nuttin', you hear me?"

"Yes, Ma'am," Ruby and Steve said at the same time, guilt lowering their voices.

"I'm sorry, Tante Izzy." Ruby sighed. "I would never disrespect or be disloyal to the family."

"Damn right you won't."

***

Jewell walked in silence with Beau to the front steps of the plantation. He suggested that would be the best place for them to talk so no one could hear them or interpret their body language. In the three-minute walk there, she quickly assessed what her goals needed to be.

Right now, she knew she'd have to focus on just a couple of things. First she'd finish the job she was hired to do because she needed the money, she had to repair her damaged work reputation, and she owed it to Elli, who was counting on her. Secondly, she needed to stay around Cane and Sugar Mill Planation to search documents and records to find out if Mimi's claims were true that this plantation or another one had once been her home. Thirdly, and this had been what had driven her to come to Cane in the first place, she had to see if her grand-mère had a sister called Twinnie who was still alive. She hadn't yet figured out how to accomplish those goals, however. She'd have to trust her decision-making skills and her ability to focus.

"Okay. You have my undivided attention," Beau said, as they reached the front of the plantation. Jewell looked out in front of them where the live oaks and cypresses created a wide esplanade from the bayou side to the formal entrance of the plantation. This was how guests would have arrived for balls and social events, by horse drawn carriages.

Jewell exhaled and looked up into thick limbs extending their arms overhead to create a canopy of dark green leaves and wiry gray moss. The fall didn't bring the dramatic colors of a changing season in south Louisiana, but it did bring a darker, richer hue.

"It's so beautiful here," she said, turning to face Beau who was sitting on the third step leading to the grand *galerie* of the Acadian style plantation. He rested his forearms on his knees.

"Yes, indeed. It is," he agreed, looking toward the bayou. Jewel nodded. "It helps to have our conversation in this peaceful, special place." She inhaled deeply, taking in the earthy scents of moist soil, healthy foliage, fallen leaves and nature. "Thank you for speaking with me in private."

She sat on the step just above him, so she was closer to eye level with him. He slid to the same step she was on.

He didn't like being in the inferior position. Fine. That was okay. She could understand that. Jewell stood.

"I ask that you to listen to what I have to say, Beau. Don't cast judgment as judge and jury. Please keep an open mind."

He nodded.

"I'm here to work for Elli and Ben." She looked at him, expecting to see an eye roll or some expression that said he didn't believe her statement. She was pleased that there was none. The fact that he maintained a poker face gave her marginal relief. "I need this job. I want to do a good job for them. A great job, really. That's my primary reason for being here."

Jewell swallowed past the nerves. She wiped her wet palms on her jeans, then moved down a step so Beau wouldn't see that her legs were unsteady.

"It was when we arrived for the job that Mimi announced to me that this was her home." Now, here would come the eye roll for sure, she thought. She waited for it, but it still didn't come. He leaned back onto his elbows.

"Go on."

"There were hints before then. More like statements and claims really. They were disjointed. Odd. Even for her slipping mental abilities. It didn't make sense to me."

"What kind of things did she say?" he asked, keeping his eyes steady on her.

"Well, she first started talking about someone named Twinnie. She didn't mention any plantation at that time." Jewell took in a deep breath, remembering the first time she spoke of Twinnie while they were enjoying an evening meal on their front porch. That evening she had only mentioned how they'd hide their peas in their sleeves at the dinner table and feed them to the pigs afterwards. "She would often just talk about how she missed her."

"How long ago did she start speaking of Twinnie and the plantation?" Beau asked, bringing her back to focus on what needed to be said. What needed to be accomplished.

"A few months back." She shook her head and brushed away a few blades of grass that stuck to her rubber boot. "It was so odd to hear the stories at first. I didn't believe her." She looked at him. "I'm not sure I believe her now. But, the footstool..." She sighed. "This was my grand-mère telling me these strange things. She was the one who had always told me stories of her growing up in a convent in New Orleans with her mother, Adelise, after they had arrived in New Orleans from Lisieux, France."

"How old was Mignon when she said she came to America?"

"Eight months old." She said, not really liking the way he worded his question. Jewell all but heard the word "allegedly" thrown in there.

Beau bit his lower lip as he thought about that. "Where was her father?"

"Her father, Jean Duet, had died in transit from a shipboard illness." Jewell didn't like this tit-for-tat slow Q&A thing they were doing. She didn't have the nerves or patience for it. So she didn't wait for his next question to tell him what she knew. "I looked for a record of his death. I couldn't find any. I did find his birth, baptismal and confirmation records in a small Catholic church just outside of Lisieux."

"So the man, Jean Duet, did exist?"

Jewell nodded. "I didn't find their matrimonial certificate anywhere nor did I find his name on any ship's manifest." She extended her legs in front of her and crossed her boots at her ankles. "Not finding the documents doesn't mean they don't exist, though. I may not have looked in the right place. Yet." She shrugged. "Or it could mean they were destroyed in a fire, or boxed in some obscure place. All I know is that Mimi had said her parents had eloped and moved to a port city where they worked until they raised the fare for their passage."

"Did you ever meet your great-grandmother? Hear this story directly from her?"

"No." Jewell shook her head. "Mimi had my mother late in life...in her early forties. By the time I was born, Adelise was deceased. She had died in a traffic accident. She was in her seventies. I have a few framed photos of her with Mimi in my home. One was taken on the docks in France when she was departing for America. She's holding Mimi in her arms. Two suitcases were near their feet." She smiled. "Adelise was beautiful."

"I imagine she was," he said, smiling for the first time. "Do you look like her?"

She shook her head. "Not at all. She was petite. Light eyes." She smiled. "I may have her dark hair and nose." She touched her nose with the tip of her finger and shrugged.

"I look like my father. Except for this. This is all Momma." He tapped the tip of his straight nose.

She laughed softly. "We wear our history." She looked down the tree-lined esplanade to where a blue heron had just landed along the bayou's edge near a white A-frame swing. "You know, talking about other people's history was how I spent most of my day at the university." She shook her head. "Sharing my personal family history feels odd. This is uncomfortable and difficult."

"*You* asked to speak to me," he said, his tone even.

"Don't misunderstand me. I'll tell you what I know." She had to. She knew that Elli and Ben trusted Beau to advise them. For him to believe her motives and not recommend that Elli and Ben fire her, he'd have to hear Mimi's entire history.

"You were telling me about Jean Duet," he prompted.

"Yes. Well, because I was unable to locate a ship's name, I had no further leads to help locate Jean Duet's grave. I tried other ways to find it."

"What did your great-grandmother say about where her husband was buried?"

"Mimi always told me that her mother had told her that Jean Duet had been buried with the thousands of other poor souls who didn't make the long arduous journey. He'd been buried in a paupers' cemetery along the Mississippi River somewhere. I tried to find it, but..." she shrugged. "There were a few religious men who tried to mark the lives of the dead with graves, but..." she shrugged again and sighed, "nothing."

Beau put his hand on her shoulder and squeezed. He did it easily. Automatically. She could see by the furrow in his brow that the story touched him. She imagined in his work as a small town lawyer, he heard many sad and tragic stories that would tear at a person's heart. He cared. She'd seen it with the way he hugged Tante Izzy, with the way he'd warned her not to harm his family. How did a man who cared about others manage to deal with the realities of the awful parts of the world that ripped into his work?

Jewell touched his arm briefly as a sign of understanding, then dropped her hand to her lap.

"Oh, hell." He frowned, his head dropped forward. "I can't like you, Jewell. I can't be softened by how nice you appear. By the way you care for your grandmother." He turned his head to look at her. "I can't."

"We don't have to be enemies, Beau."

"Friends?" He blew out a breath. *"Merde."* He cursed again in Cajun French. "We can only be adversaries, Boots. I have to protect my family. I can't make any mistakes where they're concerned." He shook his head. "No. We definitely can't be friends. Friends need to trust one another."

He looked at her; his rich green eyes looked so honest, so vulnerable and yet, so determined. It frightened her. He frightened her. How he made her feel when he looked at her frightened her.

"You will not blindside me because I want to believe you," he said, his voice strong, determined. "Hell, I do want to believe you, but I don't. God, that would make life a lot less problematic. You weave a good tale, *chère*. I'll give you that."

His words stung. Bruised her pride. Yet, she wouldn't let her personal feelings detour her mission. She was fighting for Mimi—the dear woman whom Jewell shared nearly every part of her history with, the woman who heartbreakingly would soon not remember her, or that history. That thought was impossible enough to deal with every day. She didn't need to add any useless emotions to the mix.

"I've asked you not to judge me hastily, Beau," she began, her voice firm, confident. "You haven't heard the entire story that got us to this conversation. I *trusted* that *you'd* be fair minded." She paused, waited for him to acknowledge he understood what she was saying.

He nodded. "I'm sorry. You're right. I'm listening."

A rush of gratitude swept over her. *He was going to be decent, civil and maybe even with a little luck, just.* She stood and moved in front of the steps. She needed distance from him. She didn't want her appreciation of his cooperation, her respect for his kindness and her empathy for his defense of his family to keep her from fulfilling her promise to Mimi. The bottom line was—he had openly told her he didn't believe her. That was a tall hurdle to clear.

"So, I had the family story that was told to me my entire life," she began, facing him with her arms folded over her chest. "I had no verification that my grandfather came over by ship from France and was buried in a riverside pauper's grave. My grand-mère had a few dear friends, cloistered nuns at the St. Therese Monastery, who verified she and her mother were seamstresses there and lived at the convent for many years."

She reached up and refastened the elastic that had slipped to the end of her ponytail.

"Fast forward to a few months ago," she continued. "Now I have my grand-mère who has advancing dementia starting to claim that she spent her childhood on a wonderful Louisiana plantation with Twinnie." She put her hands on her hips. "Twins? Sisters who look like twins? What's their relationship? Or, has her dementia confused real life with a movie scene that she may have seen at some point in her life? You know, the long-term memory is usually better than the short term. Does Twinnie represent that long-term memory or a confused memory?" She threw up her hands. "I just don't know. But I owe it to Mimi to find out. She deserves to find her sister, friend, whoever she is, while she has the ability to recognize and enjoy her. While she's present enough in this world to understand. Soon, she might not remember. She's already had a few episodes where she didn't even remember the person she raised as her very own child...*me*." Jewell's voice caught. A heavy lump formed in her throat. "She's already forgetting me."

Beau was on his feet, reaching for her, drawing her up and into his embrace before she took her next breath.

"Don't. Don't be so nice. I can't take it. I can't accept it. Especially when you were just my adversary a few minutes ago saying you don't trust me. Don't be nice to me, Beau."

"I'm still your adversary." He rubbed her back with his strong wide palm. "This is just...damn, I don't know what the hell this is. Shhh. I know it doesn't make any sense. Just give us a few moments here. Okay?"

He pulled her tighter against him. He smelled so good. His body felt warm. Safe. She no longer felt like she was on the blasted ledge alone in a Cat 5 hurricane. He had her. No matter how much he distrusted or disliked her, he wouldn't let her fall into the bottomless, scary, lonely cyclone. A tear slipped down her cheek. At least, for this moment, she was safe. In the next, he'd probably release her and let her plunge to protect his family.

She gripped the tight, thick muscles of his shoulders. She knew her fingers would leave marks where they held, but she couldn't ease away. She couldn't stop the tears either. They embarrassed her, but she didn't have the strength to let go, turn away. Stand on her own. Just a few moments, he'd said. She sucked in a breath. God, it was so hard to breathe.

"Don't cry, Boots." He wiped a tear with his thumb. Then another. "You're trembling." He blew out a heavy breath, and in a fast swift movement, he gripped her ponytail into his hand as he flattened his palm at the back of her head and pulled her face forward to his. "You make me so damn crazy."

Then he kissed her. His mouth wasn't gentle. It was firm and angry; the kiss seemed to be drowning with as much conflicting emotion as was churning inside her body. It was the vortex of the tornado. It had everything to do with the twisting and spinning of dealing with the people they loved and needing a dizzying moment to let their bodies feel something else...Like heat and desire.

"No. This is wrong," Jewell said, not realizing she was speaking French. "We can't."

She gripped her fingers around Beau's short, silky dark hair and pulled in tighter to deepen a kiss that was already impossibly deep. Who was this woman yanking on this man's hair as he tugged on hers in a desperate kiss? Beau's hands slid from her head down her sides over her hips until he cupped her derrière. She heard him groan as he angled his head to gentle the kiss, to slow the slide of his tongue over hers. Never had she felt this kind of sensual wanting before. Never had she been so lost in the feel of a man that she forgot about responsibilities, reputation, whatever damn else she was supposed to remember. Jewell grabbed his derrière and pulled him tighter against her.

"I am two seconds from throwing you over my shoulder and carrying you into the house and onto a bed," he said, squeezing her bottom. "One second."

"*Arrête!* Stop!"

"I got it the first time."

Jewell stepped back. She immediately felt the 80-degree temperature of the day cool her skin as if it was an arctic blast. "Oh, God." She turned her back to him but not before she saw his huge black dilated pupils rimmed by light green. He was so sexy.

Temptation.

All the things that her mother told her sex was supposed to be about but never was. Her mother was wrong. Jewell knew sex with Beau would be wonderful. Perfect. Not the means to a better life that her mother claimed it was.

He ran his hand through his hair again. Then, he reached to gently smooth her hair. "You are a hot mess, Boots. Damn hot."

She felt her face heat, blush.

"I'm sorry. I shouldn't have let that happen."

"No, Boots. *We* shouldn't have let that stop." He exhaled, sat on the step and crossed his arms over his chest.

Jewell looked at him. He was so handsome. Virile. And he wanted her. She started to take a step to go to him but he spoke before she did, saving her the embarrassment. The mistake.

"Sit."

She stared at him a moment, not because his tone was harsh or demanding but because she wasn't sure what he was telling her.

"Please."

She sat on the step below him and a safe distance away.

"I know we should talk about what wild pressure valve just went off between us, but," he groaned, "I don't want to. I can't. Not enough will power." He inhaled deeply. "We can never talk about it, Boots. Not unless we intend to finish it." He rubbed his hands on his thighs. "So, tell me. Why Sugar Mill? Why didn't you pick some other plantation to look for Twinnie?"

"Mignon saw it in a movie. She saw it painted pink and announced that was where she and Twinnie used to play."

"That's it?" He shook his head, unfolded his arms and leaned back against the step behind him. "Did you show her pictures of other plantations?"

She frowned. "Of course I did. That's the obvious thing to do." His eyebrows shot up, looking half amused by her annoyance with his question. "She had no reaction to the others. Just more stories about Twinnie. Then, I showed her a photo of Sugar Mill, not painted pink like in the movie. Like this, white with dark green shutters and beautiful." She waved her hand toward the front of the plantation. "She didn't say that Sugar Mill was her home or that it was a place she and Twinnie played, until yesterday."

"That was convenient." He sat up and looked deeply into her eyes. She knew he was trying to read her...to determine if she was telling the truth. God, she hated having her integrity questioned. It happened much too often lately.

"Maybe it was a coincidence." She averted her eyes from his, pretending to study the wood on the steps near her feet. "Look, I didn't really believe much of the whole Twinnie story, Beau. I planned to investigate it, anyway. Then, she opened that hidden nook..." Jewell knew she didn't have to finish the sentence.

"I don't buy this story, Jewell." He gently lifted her chin for her to look at him.

"So you've said before."

"You could find out about hidden nooks in architectural drawings in your research." He dropped his hands to his knees.

"You're implying I'm lying, then."

"It's a theory."

Jewell wanted to slap him. Her cheeks burned. She clasped her hands together. "I have integrity. My work is based on truth finding and the factual documenting and retelling of those finds. If I don't honor the truth then I have fiction. Fantasy. That's not where I live." She closed her eyes. That is where her mother lived. She shook her head. What more could she tell him to make him understand? She didn't intend to beg him to believe her. "I will never compromise the truth."

"The District Attorney of Orleans Parish seems to disagree. What happened with the Monroes?"

"That is none of your damn business. That has nothing to do with me being here."

He shrugged. "A non-related coincidence?"

"A non-related complication." She ground her teeth.

"I'll tell you what may or may not be a coincidence but certainly is complicated," he said, his voice deep and low. "You kiss me with enough heat to melt the flesh off my bones and your body is sexy enough to do the same. Hell, that kiss brings me back to convenient or maybe even calculated."

"You said we wouldn't talk about what happened." Her answer had been swift, automatic, then his words sunk in. *He'd said calculated.* What was he implying by that? Did he think she purposely kissed him to sway his decision?

"Yeah, well, retract what I just said, strike it from the record," he replied. "Pretend I never said it."

"Yeah, like that ever happens." She said, half engaged in the conversation now. She was still trying to figure out what to make of what he'd said earlier. *Calculated?*

"Sure it does, Boots. I forgot about it already."

She looked at him, his pupils were still dilated, his breathing unsteady. "You do know that what happened between us has absolutely nothing to do with Mimi and our conversation? Nothing."

One of his brows, arched. "Then what in the hell was it about?"

"A mistake."

"The hell it was."

"Again, I thought we weren't going to talk about it."

He stood and began to pace.

"What is it you're so afraid of, Beau? Why do I threaten you? What is it that you think I'll do that will hurt your family?"

He stopped pacing and looked at her. He just stared at her for a long minute. His expression was unreadable but she knew he was running his answers through his head trying to figure out the best response to give her. Then, he sat on the step even with her. "Nothing, because I won't let you."

"Then we don't have a problem." She sighed. "I will finish the job for Elli and Ben and I will do a little investigating to see if I can figure out if Sugar Mill, or any other plantation around this area, has a connection to Mimi and a lady named Twinnie."

Beau didn't answer right away. Once again, he obviously was considering what she said. She gave him his mental space to think it through knowing whatever he said wouldn't change what she intended to do. He could make it difficult though.

"Okay. Fine," he said and extended his hand to her. "But you will not do any investigating unless I'm at your side. Like I said, I don't buy this story. I need to see you pull every little evidential document and clue from whatever dusty, spider-web wrapped crevice it comes from so I know it's legit. If you try to claim you found something allegedly relevant when I wasn't present, I won't allow it as evidence in whatever case you're trying to make."

"Case?" Jewell started to protest but realized very quickly by his tight body language that he was not going to negotiate. "I may need a sitter to help with Mimi, but I certainly don't need a sitter to stalk me. It's a pretty solitary job that I do." Beau waved good-bye and started to get up to leave. "However," she continued, "if this is the deal, it's the deal. I accept." She extended her hand to shake. He took her hand in his and covered it with his other hand. He ran his thumb over her knuckles.

"Deal." He grinned a sexy, crooked grin. "And I can help with that sitter for Mimi." When she started to protest he lifted his finger to her lips. "Shhh. Don't blow this. You're getting what you asked for, Boots." She closed her mouth. "Tante Izzy and Ruby will be Mimi's sitters."

Chapter

8

I had expected that coming to this plantation, my plantation, would help my memories return. At least, some of them. And, I hoped it would help me find...what is her name? Oh, no! I can't remember it. I do remember her and her pretty shiny face and blonde hair.

So, you see, the plantation hasn't helped me remember things afterall.

It hasn't sharpened my thoughts or given me any insight into my distant past or even into yesterday. In fact, I think with all of the new faces, new sights and new excitements in my life, my world may have gotten a little fuzzier. Words seem to be getting more difficult to find. The names are jumbled into a gumbo of letters. The faces are so blended that one person's features looks the same as another. Yet, as confused as I feel much of the time now, I am enjoying the emotions that fill the space around me with laughter, happiness and love.

It's good.

I wonder if Jewell feels it, too. I will have to talk to her about it...if only I can remember to do so when we are alone. I want her to understand that this is what family is supposed to be like.

Twinnie. Her name is Twinnie. I remember...for now.

***

Beau had gone over the impromptu porch step meeting with Jewell a hundred times and he still didn't feel his family was in any better position in dealing with her and her unpredictable grandmother. If he didn't know how to deal with Dr. Jewell Duet, who was accused of felony theft, he didn't know how to protect his family. He needed more information on the crime she was charged with to help him change that situation. That was the reason he called in a favor with his well-connected friend, Stewart Smith, to arrange a meeting with the Monroe's estate attorney for that same evening.

Beau checked in with the front desk security and rode the elevator up to the top, the twenty-sixth floor, to the elegant legal offices of Henry, Ladeaux, Frasier and Zimmerman. He was meeting with Frederick Henry, a short but fit, balding man in his sixties.

"Come in," said Frederick, once Beau was led into the large corner office with two walls of floor-to-ceiling glass windows. Frederick wasn't alone. There were two other men there.

Frederick, who wore a light blue suit, walked around from where he was sitting behind an oversized mahogany desk to shake hands with Beau. He introduced himself and then the other two men. "This is Claude Monroe," he said, indicating the brown-eyed, blond man who appeared to be in his mid-twenties. He was dressed in expensive jeans, a sports coat, and designer shoes. He was young, but he already had the look of old money.

"Nice to meet you," Beau said, shaking his hand. He was glad he had decided to go with a more professional look of black slacks and a tan sports coat since the three men were dressed for a business meeting.

"Likewise," Claude answered in an easy, no-hurry New Orleans accent.

"And this is the family's longtime business manager, Ralph Bergeron." Frederick said, motioning to a tall, thin man in his seventies, who was extending his hand to Beau. They shook hands and nodded to one another.

Ralph Bergeron ran his hand over his wavy gray hair even though there wasn't a hair out of place. Then, he nervously pushed up the wire-rimmed glasses higher on the bridge of his nose.

"Please sit down," Frederick motioned to the three dark brown leather chairs in front of his desk. Beau chose the one closest to the door. As he waited for the men to settle in their seats, he glanced out the top floor windows at the spectacular evening view of the New Orleans city lights, Mississippi River bridges and the dark, winding Mississippi River beneath.

"Thank you for seeing me on such short notice," Beau said, feeling as comfortable here in the opulence of the traditional dark woods, masculine leathers and Turkish rugs as he did in the plantation kitchen. This office, as did the attorney behind the huge desk, screamed wealth and success.

"No problem," Frederick said. "I have a dinner engagement at seven thirty. I had a little time to kill. Ralph and Claude were available, too. I asked them to join us." He looked at his mobile phone sitting on the desk. "We have fifteen minutes before I have to leave. So, our mutual friend Steven tells me you have an interest in the Monroe theft case."

"Yes, I do." Beau appreciated his not wasting time and getting right to business. "I'm actually most interested in knowing more specific details of what Dr. Jewell Duet is actually being charged with."

"She's charged with felony theft," Ralph snapped, his voice deep, his New Orleans Garden District accent heavy. "She stole from the family."

"Yes, I have that information," Beau said, keeping his voice even. "What I want to know is how she stole from your family."

"Don't you know there is a gag order on the case?" Ralph stated, sounding annoyed. "The judge has closed the proceeding."

"You have to excuse Ralph," Frederick began, resting his elbows on his desk. "He's very protective of the

Monroe family. He worked for them for nearly forty years." He glanced at Claude, nodded. "Ralph hired Dr. Duet and was in the house with her when the theft occurred."

"She's a common thief." Ralph pushed up his glasses again. "I thought she was a trusted expert. Honest. Ethical. The best in her field of antiquities. History." Ralph looked at Claude. "I'm sorry, Claude. I should've done better than to bring this woman into the family. And while you were mourning the loss of your grandmother."

"You couldn't have done any more than you did," the young man answered, his voice kind. "Beau, we hired her to do a job. In the end, we were robbed. I think that anything else you want to know about what happened isn't really important. Besides, I don't want to risk saying something that would result in our not getting a conviction. We can't tell you anything that isn't already known. Isn't that right, Frederick?"

"That's right." Frederick sat back, rubbing his hands on the arms of his chair. "The case is pending. It's scheduled to go to trial in less than two weeks."

"Without speaking of the case, can you assuage my curiosity as to why you requested a closed proceeding? It's highly unusual to have a gag order for a felony theft case."

"Mrs. Monroe and her late husband, Bertrand, and even her two sons, God rest their souls, did a lot of good work in the city." Ralph said, then made the sign of the cross and kissed his thumb on his fisted hand. "I didn't..." he hesitated, looked at Claude. "We didn't want their legacy of philanthropy and good citizenship for this great city to be remembered with the tagline that after Mrs. Monroe died, some lowlife professor pretending to be an antiques expert robbed her." He shook his head. "Damn shame to be remembered that way. Don't you think? Why should Claude have fingers pointed at him the rest of his life from people who say, 'Poor thing, he was robbed when his good grandmother wasn't even cold in her grave'."

Beau nodded. He understood what it was like to never be able to shake off the town gossip or a label that was attached to you. No matter how far he and his brother—who had just retired with honors from the Navy—had risen from his dishonorable, abusive parents, it still followed them around. It was probably a big reason why his brother Jackson hadn't returned to live in Cane after retiring. Beau, on the other hand, had just learned to live with it. He even accepted it as a badge of pride that he'd turned his life around from that time. He supposed he understood how someone who loved and took care of the Monroe family for nearly forty years would feel protective of their reputation and legacy.

"We have a question for you, Beau," Ralph said, frowning. "Why is the Monroe family theft so important to a country lawyer from Cane?"

"I'm like you, Ralph. I'm just trying to protect the family I'm charged with protecting. My family." Beau looked at Claude. He was the only one there besides himself who wasn't an employee of the Monroes. He was the lone heir to the Monroe family. He would be the one who might be willing to give him the information he needed to know. "I don't want to know about the theft for any other reason than to protect my family from being in the situation you are in now." He looked at the sole surviving Monroe. "Claude, it has been reported that Jewell...um, Dr. Duet, had stolen family heirlooms, pearls, an engagement ring, some coins. Did she steal anything else? How did she steal it?"

Claude didn't turn to his attorney or business manager for advice as Beau had hoped he wouldn't. He kept his intelligent eyes locked on Beau. "I wish I could tell you." He shook his head. "I won't jeopardize our case for only one reason. I want her to return what she stole from me, Beau. I'm willing to drop the charges..."

"No. Don't." Ralph interrupted. "She needs to go to jail for what she did. Even if you recover what she stole.

We'll be guilty of letting a thief go free to do it again to some other poor, unsuspecting person."

Claude ignored Ralph. Beau knew he was wiser than his young face indicated. "I want what she took. I need it. I told Dr. Duet what I just told you. Return what you stole and I will drop the charges. Don't return it and you will rot in jail."

Ralph's face reddened. "We took the woman into the family confidence and into their St. Charles Avenue mansion, and she stole from us...um...them. How despicable can a person get?"

"How do you know she actually stole from the estate if you've never recovered the stolen items?" Beau asked Claude. Ralph pointed his finger at Beau.

"Hell, man," Ralph said, his voice sharp. His nostrils flared. "Who else could have done it? I know for a fact no one else had opportunity. I was there. I'm the one that called the police when..."

"Don't say any more," Frederick warned, holding up his hand, an easy smile on his lips. "I'm sorry, Beau. As a courtesy to our mutual friend, I've agreed to have this meeting. Specifics on the case, we can't share with you." He shook his head. "We can tell you she was in our employment as contract labor when the theft occurred. You know why she was there."

Beau nodded, stood. He'd learned more than he knew before, such as Claude was willing to drop the charges if she returned the family jewelry she had stolen.

Allegedly stolen, Beau thought, hearing Elli's voice in his head. *Innocent until proven guilty*. Hell, these men sure believed she was guilty.

Beau wished he could've learned more, especially how she'd allegedly stolen the family property. "If you have any information that I should know that might help me in any way to make sure this same crime isn't repeated with my family, I would appreciate your telling me. You can advise me, without giving me specifics to your case."

Frederick and Ralph stood. Claude remained in his seat.

"My advice? Don't let her into your home," Ralph spit out. "I hired her on the excellent recommendation of a friend. She had very impressive credentials." He frowned and his light brows furrowed. "I only hire the very best for young Claude, as I did for his grandmother and his father. She conned me."

"She conned you?"

Frederick walked around the desk and stepped in. "I must go now. I'm glad to have met you. You have an excellent reputation as a litigator, Beau. Not to mention our friend, Stewart, thinks the world of you." He shook his hand and patted him on the back, turning him toward the door to leave.

"Thank you for meeting with me." He turned to Ralph and Claude. "Thank you, both. I'm sorry for your loss. I heard that Mrs. Monroe was a remarkable lady. The community will certainly miss her."

Beau left the offices. On his way down in the elevator, he knew that even with what little he learned, Elli still wouldn't fire Jewell. So nothing had changed except his suspicions were higher. He'd stay the course—continue to watch Jewell closely. Mignon's ridiculous claims about living on the plantation and Jewell's so-called investigation into it would give him cause to hound her like one of Ben's hunting dogs chasing down a rabbit.

If he really needed a reason.

Protecting his family was reason enough.

***

Beau had gone straight to bed when he returned home from New Orleans after the meeting the night before. He knew Ben and Elli would already be asleep, and he would have to wait until the morning to tell them what he'd learned. He'd talk to them in person. Ben hated to talk on the phone. Besides, he knew Elli wouldn't see the new information as reason to boot Jewell off Sugar Mill

Plantation. Nothing changed her position that a person was innocent until proven guilty. Frankly, on many levels he didn't really blame her. That didn't mean Dr. Duet didn't need watching. It only meant it was up to him to keep a focused eye on the Professor, as he'd already planned to do.

The morning dew hadn't dried off the grass when Beau drove up to Sugar Mill, yet already there were a half-dozen vehicles parked in the driveway, including *T-Bob's Haulin' As You Wish* moving trailer. He knew Elli had hired T-Bob to move a few of their personal furnishings, including Ben and Joey's favorite recliners, to the refurbished old slave cottages at the kennel. They'd be staying there when they returned from their beach vacation next week. The advance movie crew would arrive before then to prepare for the filming at the barn and the big house.

Tante Izzy's vintage, nearly neon pink pickup truck and Ruby's red Caddie were parked in the mix. Those ladies were definitely taking their job as sitters very seriously. They had promised Beau they'd arrive for breakfast, and it looked like they had with the way the camper was bouncing around from a lot of movement inside. It probably hadn't occurred to them to take their ward into the big house to prepare breakfast, Beau thought with a smile. Man, he sure would've liked to have been a fly on the wall to see Jewell managing those two pushy, well-meaning women in her tiny Airstream camper. Especially when they had arrived with their arms laden with enough food to feed the entire Bienvenu clan. Beau knew they had done that since they had told him they would. The food was the reason he suspected there were several other cars he recognized in the driveway. His reason for being there had more to do with the meeting the night before in New Orleans than a delicious breakfast. He had to keep his eye on the woman who the three men he met with believed was a thief and who had conned the Monroe family.

He glanced at his cell phone, both out of habit and necessity. He was always careful managing his time. Time was money in his busy workday. It was eight thirty, and he'd already had an early meeting with a client and rescheduled a deposition because another client had gotten a virus. Since it was Tuesday, he'd surprised his office staff by telling them they could go home after lunch. He had the rest of the day off, if he chose not to spend it catching up on paperwork. Of course, dealing with Jewell was work too.

Beau knocked on the closed camper door and Ruby answered it right away. The sweet and smoky scents of breakfast breads and bacon greeted him before Ruby did.

"Hello, Beau," she smiled, fluffing her poof of collar-length red hair.

He adored Ruby. She might be a bit of a gossipy pain in the neck sometimes, but she had a heart as big as her eighties-styled hair and a personality as bright as the canary yellow knit top and pants she wore. No doubt about it, with her spiky heels that made her middle-aged body waddle unsteadily and her obvious questions about his clients and love life, she was someone he usually avoided...unless he was in the mood to have a little fun with her.

Teasing Ruby was a sport for Ben and him. Even though she was ten years older than they were, it had been that way since they were young boys. They could lead her on with some tall tale for an hour before one of them cracked. Usually him. She had a great sense of humor about it, too, and Beau wondered if she played along with their games as much as she fell victim to them.

Beau leaned in and gave Ruby a friendly kiss on the cheek, sneaking a peek inside the camper as he did. Yep, just as he figured. There were eight, or maybe ten people, casually squeezed into the very tight quarters. He didn't see Jewell among them.

"You want to come in?" Ruby looked behind her and narrowed her eyes. "I think there's room in the back bedroom area if you sit on the corner of one of the single beds. Maybe on the left one where Steve is finishing his *pain perdu.*" She laughed. "Oh, wait, I think there's room on the floor next to Jewell's desk. We can put a cushion down for you there."

Beau's stomach grumbled. He loved *pain perdu* or, as most everyone else in the world called it, French toast. He just didn't love being packed in like a sardine to eat. "How about you pass me a plate. I'll eat out here."

She nodded. "Okay, I figured you'd say that." As she moved away from the door, Tante Izzy and Mignon were directly in his line of sight. They waved to him, but kept talking in French, as they pushed needles through white tube socks with red thread. Jewell's socks? Did anyone really wear tube socks anymore other than little old men with brown dress shoes and plaid Bermuda shorts? It amused him to imagine her wearing them inside of those expressive rubber boots of hers.

"Here you go." Ruby handed him a white dinner plate with some sort of blue detail hidden beneath a two-inch high stack of *pain perdu,* covered with cane syrup and confectioners' sugar. A mound of crisp, still sizzling bacon and several slices of dark pink watermelon made finding a handhold tricky. "Is that enough?" she asked with all sincerity.

Enough to feed him and the Cane High School football team's defensive line, he thought, accepting the plate. "Thanks, darlin'. It's perfect."

He turned to leave, but Ruby stopped him. "Oh, wait, Beau. I need you to return something to the plantation kitchen." Beau nodded. Ruby reached into a purse on a side table not far from the door and retrieved a pair of salt and pepper shakers. She handed them to him. "These belong on the kitchen table. Mignon took them." She raised her eyebrows and shook her head. "She sure seems fond of them."

"That she does." He smiled. "Thanks for breakfast." He took his meal into the quiet plantation and placed the salt and pepper shakers on the table in their usual spot. He poured himself a glass of organic milk and sat at the kitchen table to enjoy his food alone. That was how he usually had breakfast and dinner. The way he preferred it. Lunch was either surrounded by paper work in his office, which he enjoyed, or with a client, which he tolerated. He loved being with his Bienvenu family and he enjoyed working and meeting new clients, yet he was most content eating alone. He didn't need a shrink to tell him that it was a byproduct of going off alone during his domestically violent childhood and finding a small measure of peace.

As he savored the meal, he recalled his childhood and how his brother Jackson would fight him for the last strip of bacon. Reaching for his milk, he glanced up, and down the hallway saw Jewell heading toward the stairs to the second floor. Even though it was daylight and the house was filled with a lot of natural light, she had her head lamp turned on. The light, coupled with her tool belt strapped around her slender waist told Beau she was ready for work. He wasn't sure what her pumpkin orange rubber boots said or even what was painted on them. He did note, however, that her jeans were tucked inside the boots and she wore her usual blue logoed work shirt. Her hair was in the usual single ponytail, too.

A surge of irrational anger filled him. *What in the hell is she doing in the house?* Her job was out in the barn. Not wandering around the main house unsupervised. And even though he doubted there was room to slide a pilfered piece of paper into the pocket of those tight jeans, he didn't trust her any further than he could throw her.

Damn it, she'd just ruined a perfectly enjoyable breakfast and moment of peace. He pushed aside the *pain perdu*, shoved the last piece of bacon into his mouth and followed her upstairs.

He didn't see her anywhere.

He walked through the guest bedroom floor-to-ceiling window that served as doors to the upper *galerie*. Then, he walked around the three sides of the *galerie* and still didn't see her.

"Are you a ghost with sticky fingers, Boots?" he whispered, turning to walk back to the guest bedroom. That's when he spotted the closed double-wide doors along the exterior wall. In all the years he'd played and hung out on that balcony, he'd never noticed the doors before. He supposed that's because they always had their backs toward the wall where it was located as they dropped things over the side railing or tossed them into the yard toward the bayou. These hidden doors were faced with the same siding as the house, and had tiny wooden doorknobs painted white, so they blended into the wall. He pulled on the door to the right, having to give it a hard jerk to get it open. Stairs led up directly in front of him.

Now this was a surprise. A secret passage? Wouldn't this have been fun for him to know about as a boy playing hide and seek? He guessed Ben must not have known about it back then, either, or he would've told him.

Beau leaned in further and heard the faint sound of singing. Not that he'd call the barely recognizable, off-key rendition of Sheryl Crow's tune, "If It Makes You Happy," singing.

Climbing the extra wide, thick, unpainted cypress stairs two at a time, he realized the hidden staircase had been designed to haul large items into the attic. Clever architecture. The singing got louder as he neared the top. When he reached the landing his eyes scanned the huge attic, which covered the entire width and length of the house. A fluorescent light illuminated the center of the large space, leaving the corners dully lit by the natural light of the dormer windows. Jewell was in the paler light toward the right corner, swinging her hips and dancing. She kept beat with the song she was belting out at the top of her lungs, clearly not worried about disturbing anyone in the house from way up here. Wearing white cotton gloves, she smiled at the faded blue bonnet she was holding.

"I thought we had a deal," he said, containing the anger that had started to build when he first saw her in the house. She didn't respond. She kept dancing and shaking her pretty derrière. He walked up behind her and repeated what he said. As she began the second chorus and bent over to reach into the chest in front of her, her bottom bumped against his thigh. He was already aroused, seeing her dancing like smooth sex and singing like a sick duck. Having her making physical contact pretty much sent him over the top.

She jumped forward, gasped and turned, one gloved hand to her throat like a Victorian maiden. "God! What are you doing here?" Her voice came out in a breathy rush. Forget the smooth sex; with a voice and body like that, there would be nothing smooth about it.

"I was just about to ask you the same thing." She shook her head, pulled off her ear buds. The music was blaring loud enough for him to hear Sheryl Crow singing as the song should be sung. "Since I know there are better places for karaoke and dance clubs, I think you're up in this hot attic for reasons other than that. Reasons, I thought we agreed you would not explore without me."

She sighed, rubbed the back of her neck. "I hate having to explain everything I do to you as if I'm a common criminal," she looked at him, "which I'm not." She lowered the volume on her iPhone. "Elli and I were talking over breakfast in the camper about the barn and what still needed to be done and one thing led to another. Next thing I knew we were discussing the plantation attic." She shrugged. "We came to take a look together. She said there wasn't much here but, oh, Beau, what's here is magnificent."

She turned to the four chests and three boxes in front of her. "Each of these chests is French, dating back to the late 1700s. They probably came over to the plantation with the original owner. The wooden boxes? I don't know what's inside all of them." She squatted in front of the chest nearest her. "But this one has baby clothes in it."

With the clean, pristine white gloves covering her hands, she lifted a thin, faded white cotton baby bonnet from the open chest and ran her hand lovingly over it. It looked like an old, dull handkerchief to Beau, but by the radiant look on her face, what she held was something special to Jewell.

He wondered if she ever looked at a man that way. Oh, hell, he hated that he thought such a ridiculous thing.

"All of that's well and good," he said, looking at the bonnet again. Hell, he'd tossed out dress shirts in better condition than that old thing. "But you weren't supposed to go near any of this stuff without me." He squatted next to her and closed the chest. He looked at her. "You've contaminated the evidence."

"Evidence? Is this a crime scene? Are we going to court? What are you talking about contaminating evidence?" She stood, bumped him as she walked away toward the stairs. Before going down, she turned, looked at the boxes, the chests, then him. He could see she was torn with distancing herself from him or staying with the old crap behind him. "For the record, Counselor, while I'm going through inventory, I would never, ever, contaminate history."

She took a few steps back into the room, and the natural light through the dormer shone on her hair, capturing strands of red and gold.

"I preserve it. I record it. I honor it." She glared at him.

If looks could manifest, he'd be in a broken heap at the foot of the stairs by now. Nope, she was definitely not a Victorian maiden. More like a bare-knuckle brawler. That image made him smile. Her eyebrows furrowed. She stomped her boot hard on the unstained wooden floor.

"I'm a historian, damn it."

Fleurs-de-lis. Gold and brown and green *fleurs-de-lis.* That's what was on her orange rubber boots today. He stood and walked up to her. "Such passion, Boots. Or is it?" Shit. He wanted to believe her. He wanted to believe the theft at the Monroe home was a mistake, a misunderstanding. It would make his life less complicated. Besides all that, hell, she was so damn believable. In a hot, sexy way. Crap. That's what made her so unbelievable. Was it his lust thinking? Not logic. Confidence games worked because the people who conducted them were believable. They played on the victims' weaknesses. Was she becoming his? Ridiculous.

He'd be damned if he allowed her indignation or her annoyance to sway him. She'd agreed to his terms. Now she had to abide by them. "We look together. That's the deal."

"I'm not used to checking in with someone every time I move from one space to the next." She shook her head. Then, as he'd seen her do earlier, rubbed the back of her neck.

Did she pull a muscle? Was she feeling tension there? Not his concern, he reminded himself.

"It's very annoying," she said, her voice even, but there was no mistaking her annoyance with him. "It's a waste of time. It's unnecessary. Besides, I'm sure you have to go to court or do whatever lawyering it is that you do."

"I have the rest of the day off." He crossed his arms over his chest, widened his stance and stood his ground.

She exhaled, looked up, then away. "Yeah, I get it. You don't trust me." She faced him again. "We look together. That's the deal." She sounded resigned but not dejected. She threw back her shoulders, stiffened her spine. "I want to look here, now." She waved in a large sweeping movement indicating the attic. "Elli hired a moving crew to group the furniture in the barn for me, to save time. They have stronger backs and the right equipment to move the heavy pieces so I can actually get to them. I have to stay out of their way." She stuffed her hands in her back pockets. "I tagged each piece in the barn with colored labels earlier this morning. They're placing each item into the corresponding color-coded squares I taped on the floor."

"With Elli and Ben off in the marsh to train the St. Bernards for water patrol rescue, you don't think you need to supervise the moving crew?"

"I learned to delegate what I could long ago. I know when to be there and when I'll get in the way and slow things down. Slowing things down will cost Elli more since she's paying the workers by the hour."

She waved a hand so he'd move out of her way. Beau stepped aside to let her pass. He smelled soap, shampoo and warm woman. He also smelled that unique, smoky lightly sweet fragrance he would forever associate with her. She went back to kneel in front of the open chest. "Besides, I just checked on them. T-Bob is amazing. He's so careful handling the furniture, he has everyone wearing gloves. He's smart."

So, that was where she was coming from when he saw her walk by the kitchen. "Of course he's smart. He's a Bienvenu."

She laughed softly. "You all say that as if it a mark of honor, a title. Like a Lord or Duchess of...whatever. T-Bob the Bienvenu of Cane and Lord of Haulin' As..." she laughed. "He told me to leave off the rest of his business name, *As You Wish*. He only added the rest of it to make Tante Izzy happy."

Beau bit back on a smile and ran his hand through his hair. How in the hell did she do that? Make him angry one moment and want to laugh with her the next. He sure as hell wouldn't fall into her charming web. He knew a thing or two about using a smile and friendly quip to win someone over. Hell, he was infamous in Cane for it. He did it because he liked the people he was messing around with, having fun with them. He would never tease nor charm them with ill or evil intent. That, he suspected, was exactly what Madame Historian was doing.

"Well, Tante Izzy wields a lot of power in the family," he said, kneeling in front of the chest beside her.

"You should kneel on a cloth or the top from one of the cardboard boxes so you don't get dust on your dress slacks from the dirty floor." She started to get up to get it for him. Even if she was scheming against him and his family, he knew in this instance, she had acted spontaneously. Jewell was used to taking caring of her grandmother.

"No need." He touched her arm to stop her and looked at the years of grime all around them and shrugged. "So, it's just children's clothes in that chest?"

"Yes." She reached into her tool belt and took out a second pair of white cotton gloves and handed it to him. "Put these on so your hands don't contaminate the evidence I've already contaminated."

"Funny girl." He slipped on the gloves, but they didn't quite fit his long, slim fingers and large palms. "I feel like OJ Simpson. Got another size?"

"No. I keep this extra pair for me in case I soil one pair and need the spare." She shrugged. "If you want to work with me, you'll have to buy your own. Only touch the items with the parts of your fingers that are covered."

He picked up the bonnet, using his index finger and thumb like tweezers. It looked like coffee stains were on the edges. "Once again, this looks like dirty old junk to me."

Jewell sucked in a breath. "How can you say that?" She took it from him and pointed to the hand stitching. "You see this detail? The way the stitches are crossed and looped? It dates the garment. It was a popular stitching of a certain date." She wet her full lips. "The ladies of the day would have embroidery and hand sewing socials. They would show each other special techniques that usually were only done in a particular region or time period."

"Kind of like Tante Izzy's quilting club, huh?"

She smiled. "Exactly. The quilts they're producing will be studied and dated by some future historian."

Beau couldn't believe it, but she actually sighed. Damn, if he didn't know better, if he wasn't on to her scam, he'd believe she actually was really loving this stuff. Hell, maybe she did and she was still running a scam.

"These items were created by grandmothers, aunts and mothers-in-waiting," she smiled a Mona Lisa smile— not at him, but in her reverie. "These ladies would've made this bonnet or this receiving blanket," she lifted a pale blue, cotton blanket from the chest and gently unfolded it, "while waiting for the baby to be born."

She carefully ran her hand over the top like a whisper, the tips of her fingers fluttering like a lover's stroke. Beau's heart began to pound harder. His mouth went dry. He all but felt her fingers whisper soft on his naked chest. She looked up at him, her eyelids heavy, her eyes dark sable beneath them.

"In the twilight of the ending day, the wives would gather in the ladies' parlor in front of the warm fireplace, hand sewing each tiny stitch as their young toddlers played on the floor near them. They would tell stories of the household staff, their children, their husbands...who would be in the next room discussing the politics of the day, the price of sugarcane and sharing an amber-colored whiskey."

Beau sat on the floor next to her. This was interesting, but not enough mental and physical activity for him. Oh, hell, his brain went right to an activity he would enjoy doing right now with sexy Little Miss Historian near him.

She looked at him, rubbed the back of her neck again. "Sorry. I didn't mean to bore you. I get lost in thinking about these...treasures."

"Bore is a strong word." He smiled. "So is treasure." He frowned. "Your neck hurts? You keep rubbing it? I saw you do that yesterday, too."

"Nah. I just slept in an odd position. It's fine..." She placed the receiving blanket in the open lid. "It's in really great shape." She pulled out a smocked dress from the chest. "Another blue item. Probably for Ben's father. The clothes in the chest are either blue or boy styles."

"Looks like dresses to me."

She laughed, a soft honest laugh that had him thinking of feathered pillows, cool smooth sheets and...oh, hell.

"Yeah, well," she continued, obviously unaware what her laugh did to him. "The young boys wore dresses back then."

He winced. "I guess it's better than when I was a baby and didn't have on anything more than a stained T-shirt or no shirt at all when I crawled around unsupervised in my diapers while my parents were passed out drunk. At least that's what I was told by a number of people who used to see Jackson and me like that when we were babies. Yeah, a dress would've been better than dirty shirts and diapers."

"I don't think it was the stained T-shirts and diapers that were the problem," she said, her voice no more than a whisper.

He'd heard it loud and clear. There was no criticism in her tone. She wasn't judging. She'd made an observation. Yet when Jewell's eyes settled on him, there was sympathy, concern and maybe even empathy in their depths. His heart constricted in his chest. He sucked in a breath and immediately was embarrassed. Damn. She saw too much. Why in the hell had he told her even that little bit about his pathetic childhood? She had distracted him with that damn laugh of hers. This was all insane. He was too idle. Too much in his head. Too much in her space. He needed to move. He needed to do something other than sit around listening to her melodic voice and laughter while surrounded by her intoxicating scent.

"Some of us aren't fortunate enough to get the elegant plantation mothers and fathers, are we?" She asked but it was intended to be more of a statement. "But some of us still manage to be blessed with people who love us like our parents are supposed to." She exhaled and he saw it in her expression that she knew more about him than what he'd told her.

"Us? Or me? You are talking about my life, aren't you, Jewell?" It was damn uncomfortable thinking the expert and formidable historian looked into his history, uninvited. "I don't like you digging into my personal history. How did you find out about me?"

"It's not that difficult," she admitted. There was no apology in her voice. "I told you I researched the Bienvenu family history when I knew I was coming for this job. You're in this family." She paused and he nodded for her to continue. "I just did a simple search. Read some newspaper articles, birth announcements, obituaries. I saw no birth announcements for Ronald and Bernice, your parents, yet when Bernice passed away, the obituary had her survived by her two sons, Beauregard and Jackson." She shrugged. "I put two and two together. It's what I do."

"So much for private adoptions." He didn't like this one bit.

"Nothing is private or secret." She sighed. "Almost nothing." She looked away and changed the subject. "I think we're just about finished with this chest once I take some photos of the items and catalog them."

She paused before snapping her first photo to glance at him. It was obvious that she realized he'd noticed her staring at him. Her cheeks colored a pretty pink. In his experience, Beau had never known a woman to fake blushing.

He sat quietly, thinking about how if she found out information on him, she certainly could have found information on Martine. "What other private or secret information did you discover about my family?"

"I don't think there was anything else," she said, her voice distant as she took photos and typed each item into her iPad, all the while patting and loving each piece. "I didn't have much time to look too deeply. I searched for what I thought I might need for the job interview, the job and for my search for Twinnie."

"And did you find anything that helped?"

"No. Yes. No."

Beau looked at her a moment and realized she answered in order of his questions. No, it didn't help with her job interview. Yes, it helped with her job. No, it didn't help with her search for Twinnie. Interesting. Was she telling the truth? Half-truths? Lies?

He mulled that around awhile, until he came around to thoughts of how Dr. Jewell Duet had revealed a little about herself when she offered an understanding of how not all parents were elegant plantation mothers and fathers. It wasn't only a revelation about him. He'd definitely check more into her past, not only Mignon's.

"How much longer?" he asked, growing anxious again now that he had a plan of action. Her scent, her body, her sideways glance and those loving pats with the items in the chest were too intoxicating to a man who was aroused by her smooth dancing a little while ago. "Do you have any games I can play on your iPad?" She looked at him as if he'd grown two heads. "I need some stimulation." Wrong word. His body immediately responded.

"I'm stimulated enough for both of us." Her response was quick, automatic. He wondered if she was as distracted as she looked, typing into her iPad, or had her words been purposefully intended?

"Are you now?" His voice had lowered and his accent deepened, noticeable even to his own ears.

Her eyes widened, then she looked down the bridge of her nose at him. "How and why do you do that?"

He sat back. "Do what?"

"Disrespect, belittle and hate on me and then flirt with me and give me that look like you want to jump my bones?"

He leaned back on his hands, extended his legs and crossed his ankles. "Because I do want to jump your bones."

Chapter 9

"You want to what?" Jewell asked, not sure why she had. She'd heard him the first time. He'd said he wanted to jump her bones, but his posture, as he remained leaning back, was so relaxed and comfy that it said he didn't want to jump anything. His dark, hooded eyes rimmed with only a sliver of bold green gave away his desire, however. That, there was no mistaking.

"Jump your bones," he answered, looking like he was enjoying the bantering too much in his smoldering way. It was so disconcerting to hear him say it again and to see him looking so self-assured...and ridiculously sexy.

She looked at him a long minute, trying to act every bit as carefree as he was, but her heart was beating so hard in her chest, she was afraid she would start hyperventilating. "I want to call you a liar," she began, making sure her voice was smooth, even. "The logical thing would be to say, you can't possibly want to have sex with someone whom you loathe and mistrust." She shrugged. "But, logic isn't always a guidepost. Obviously, you do want to have sex with me. I can see it in your eyes. The way the muscle in your jaw is straining and the cords in your neck are pulled tight."

He sat up. Rubbed his jaw with one hand. "I thought I wasn't being obvious." He smiled easily, and her shoulders tensed. His eyes moved over her face, settled on her lips. Oh, yeah. He knew exactly what he was doing. He was totally toying with her. If she wasn't struggling to keep her breathing steady, she would've laughed. He leaned in toward her.

She held up her hand to stop him from advancing. "I know a man doesn't need to trust or have any feelings of good intent toward a woman to have sex with her." She shook her head. "I've studied biological anthropology."

"Biological anthropology, huh?"

"Yes, and I've observed human behavior my entire life." She frowned. Damn, he was good at this seduction game. She was onto him. Still, it didn't mean he didn't affect her on some primal level. He was a good-looking man, and she was human, after all. Still, she knew what he was doing. She'd seen her mother do this to men. If she knew what was happening, then why wasn't it easy to brush off the attraction? "Your playful, charming game doesn't affect me one bit," she said, knowing he wasn't buying it by the way he lifted one brow. "Save it for someone you'll have a better outcome with."

He leaned in, inches from her lips. He kept his eyes locked on hers. "Are you challenging me, Boots?"

She felt his breath on her mouth. Smelled its sweet scent. She shook her head and her lips brushed against his. Her eyes widened in surprise. He eased in a little closer.

***

"Oh, *chère,* that was sweet," Beau whispered, just above her lips. Was that look of surprise part of her game to play the unwilling partner? To make him want the forbidden? He wanted her. His tongue slid and tasted, moistening her full dry lips. He ran his thumb along the inside of her wrist, felt her racing pulse. "Your body's telling me it desires. Did you learn anything about that in your anthropology classes?"

Even if she'd perfected the scam, the tease, she couldn't fake her body's response, could she? She shifted. He held her arms to keep her close.

"Do you really want to go, Boots? Or do you want this?"

He kissed her. He moved his lips over hers, feeling the soft flesh of their fullness, of her womanliness. She was soft where he was hard. She didn't kiss him back, but she didn't stop him from ravishing her, from caressing her neck to feel her pulse there. It was as strong as his own. She whimpered then. It was contained. A woman trying not to give in to what she wanted. Not to be vulnerable. It made him want her even more.

He lifted her into his arms and sat on the floor with her. He kissed her again, pulling her on top of him. She moved to get off him, but then stopped, sighed.

And kissed him.

"Oh, hell," he said, deepening the kiss.

Heat trickled over him like warm rain. He slid his hands down her back, felt the ridges of her spine and the curve of the small of her back. He ran a finger inside the waistband of her jeans. He wanted to feel her flesh. Wanted her to touch his. He yanked the soft knit shirt from her pants, touched her velvety back, and she arched. Long silky strands of hair slipped from her ponytail, brushing his cheek. There was so much to feel. Her heat against him, her soft flesh beneath his hands, her cool silky hair on his face.

"Sweet. You're sweet and desirable as that forbidden praline you wanted to withhold from me."

Jewell jerked away.

She cupped his face with her hands, her elbows braced on his shoulders as she held him at a distance and stared into his eyes. Searching. But what was she searching for? Her pupils were black and dilated and aroused. She inhaled deeply and exhaled. Damn. The moment was gone.

He was both relieved and annoyed as hell. He wanted her. But he didn't want to want her.

If she hadn't stopped them, they would have...What?

She moved off of him. Sat up, pulling her knees to her chest. "That was..."

"Just physical," he said, completing her sentence. "Biological anthropology stuff, just like you said, Professor." He sat up, took her hands into his. "Don't read any more than that into what happened. It changes nothing between us."

She laughed without humor. "Of course it doesn't." She dropped her head onto her knees and said something in French about a praline. Then she spoke to him in English. "You, sir, have won that challenge. You're good at seducing a woman. Now that I have seen you in action, it will not happen again. Not with me."

"I don't feel like I won anything." He let go of her hands. "And, for the record, you're the one who's been seducing me since we first met."

Her head popped up. "What? Are you crazy?" She shook her head. "Typical male."

"You've been giving me those vulnerable sideways looks, and walking with that sexy swagger. And you talk about stimulation and..."

She stood. "I am just being who I am, Beau. You're the one who has an overactive libido and ego. Those things were never directed to seduce you. Get over yourself."

He stood. Damn. She was right. He'd had an overactive libido the instant she walked into Sugar Mill. Never had he gone from 0 to 100 in two seconds over a woman before. "It's your scent. It must be a voodoo scent," he shouted, pointing at her. "What in the hell is that bewitching scent you wear?"

"Bug repellent," she snapped back.

She walked to the chest, turning her back to him. Again, she mumbled something in French. *Cul* was the only word he understood. *Ass.*

Bug repellent? That couldn't be. Was he that drunk in wanting her that he thought a lousy bug repellent was some kind of aphrodisiac fragrance? His ears burned with anger at himself. And, at her. He'd better not say another damn word until he got himself unaroused and his temper under control.

"I want to clear the air." She fisted her hands at her sides and faced him. "So you don't misinterpret my bug repellent or my regular gait as an act of seduction." She lifted her hand and ticked off her fingers as she spoke. "One, I don't like you. Two, I'm not interested in you. Three, I definitely don't want to have sex with you. Four, I don't want to share my workspace or investigative time with you." She slammed her fist onto her waist. *"Comprends?"*

"Yes, I understand, Boots." He ran his hand through his hair. "I deserved some of that anger. But tonight, when you climb into bed and turn out the lights and think about us on this hard attic floor, you're going to realize that you kissed me as much as I kissed you."

She blew out a breath, turned toward the chest, and spoke in rapid-fire French again. She rambled on as she kneeled, her words slowing and her tone softening as she secured the chest. Work seemed to ease her temper and calm her; he watched her close the lid of the chest. She inhaled deeply, rubbed the top of the chest, and began to push it toward the wall. Beau looked away. He didn't want to see her in those tight jeans anymore. He wanted the hell out of the stifling hot attic and back to his office. Back to normalcy.

"I've had enough of this today. Let's get out of here," he growled. She didn't respond or move. Was she ignoring him? He waited a few beats, controlled tempered his tone and spoke more calmly. "Let's go."

"Uh, Beau. You'll want to see this," she said, speaking English. He turned to look, not sure if she was going to continue this cat and mouse thing they had going or if she had moved on to something else. "I don't want to be accused of contaminating evidence by finding new old things in the attic."

Beau walked over, grabbed the gloves off the floor and using them like a dishrag, picked up what she was pointing to. "It's a wooden spool. So what?"

"It's a *fezzo*, a *bobbin*," she corrected, using a heavy French accent. "A childhood toy. *Fezzos* were used in races down the halls of the house by the plantation children or tied together to make doll legs or spun with a string and stick like a top. If a child could think of a way to play with it, they did."

Beau held it up to the light. "I remember my brother, Jackson, had found some in an old tackle box one time." He paused realizing she already knew that Jackson was his brother from the obituary she read. "We used them as corks for fishing." He flipped it over. "There are two letters carved into the top. W and W. Or M and M."

"What?" Jewell stood, removing a magnifying glass from her tool belt. She slid on her head lamp and turned it on. "May I?" Beau handed it to her. "These initials are M's; see how there is a faint line beneath the open side of the letters, like it's sitting on the line?" She pointed to the markings. "It looks like the initials were burned in." She studied the rest of it, reading the manufacturer's writing along the side. "I'll have to date these serial numbers, but my guess is that it's from 1910 to the 1940s. I'm familiar with the company stamped there," she indicated the name on the side of the spool. "New Orleans Spool and Thread went out of business in 1946."

"And the M's? I guess one could stand for Martine. She was the daughter of Aguste, Ben's great-grandfather." He frowned, thinking of how she had researched him and his family. "You know that, of course."

"I saw her name in my research." She looked at him. "You don't have to be so annoyed by it. It's my job. If I know the ancestors when going through the family heirlooms, I can put the pieces and family history together." She held up the spool.

Beau conceded that made sense. The research may have led her to family secrets that he didn't want her to know about, though. He had to sort that one out. "Well, I'm guessing the M is for Martine," he said. "I don't know of any other person with the initial M who lived here. What I don't understand is why they didn't put MB, her full initials?"

"I don't know. Maybe the child asked for her initial to be placed there twice. Not that I'm familiar with the thinking of children, but it seems to me they aren't logical thinkers. I didn't see any death records on Martine. Is she alive? We can ask her. She may know."

"The family lost track of her over the years." No. Beau didn't like her digging too close to Martine one bit.

"Oh, that's so sad. Have you considered hiring a private detective?"

"Several times."

"How long ago did the family lose track of her? And what does that mean?"

"A long time ago," he said answering the first question and choosing to believe the second question was rhetorical.

"You're being so vague."

"You're being so nosy."

She looked down her nose at him. "At least I'm not being rude."

He laughed. She had him on that one. "Sorry."

"What's up with Martine that has you so defensive?"

"Did I ever tell you how much I liked that nightgown you wore when you raced into the kitchen?"

She looked down her nose at him again and stared at him. "Oh, you definitely are being defensive and evasive over Martine. Why is that?" He shrugged. "You know, if you won't tell me, Elli or Tante Izzy will."

"Crap." She was right. At least if he told her about Martine, he could control what he wanted her to know. If she presented any other information to him, then he'd know she had another source. Hell, she probably knew about Martine already and was just pretending she didn't. "Martine has been missing since she was three years old."

"Oh, my God," she said, sounding sincerely shocked. "How?"

"We don't know. When the nanny went to wake her one morning, she was gone. That was it."

"How awful. The family must've been devastated. Her father..."

"Never got over losing her. He hired private detectives until he died. He looked for her himself. She was never found."

"Could she have wondered out at night, fallen into the bayou?" she asked, her voice soft.

"The family doesn't believe so. The doors to the house were locked. And, even as young as she was, she knew how to swim."

Her eyes were wide and they looked so sad, he nearly gathered her into his arms.

"Is she presumed dead, Beau?"

"No." He stopped himself before he told her that the family would never give up hope until she was too old to still be alive. Jewell's big, beautiful, mesmerizing, eyes almost had him saying more.

She nodded, then walked to the second cypress chest that looked just like the first one a few feet away and opened it. Her hand went to her throat. "Perhaps there were two little girls with the letter M in their names who lived here that weren't family?" She lifted two rag dolls that were lying on top of the folded items in the chest.

"Too easy. Nope." He shook his head.

"Well, then maybe Martine liked having two of everything to play with."

Beau walked to the chest and looked inside. There were two matching tan dresses with the same tiny flowers stitched on each of the collars. "This doesn't make sense."

Jewell lifted the dresses and held them up together. They were the same size.

"Maybe one is for Martine and one is for her twin sister, Mignon."

He wasn't all that surprised to hear her make the connection. "I would've given that idea more than two seconds of consideration, Jewell, if I hadn't seen all of the family documents associated with Martine and the Bienvenu family. She didn't have a twin. In fact, there were never any twins in the family. Ever."

Jewell lifted two more identical dresses from the chest. "What documents, Beau? There couldn't have been many documents from that generation. Did you see a birth certificate or a midwife's book proving that? Family letters announcing the birth of a daughter? Plantation records that indicated a single baby had been born here and certain purchases had to be made as a result? Or did you see it written in the family bible?"

"No, none of those." He ran his hand through his hair. She would know exactly what kind of evidence could be found to corroborate facts of birth. How much did she already know? How much should he tell her? "I've seen the legal and binding last will and testament of Martine's father," he offered, deciding she wouldn't stop asking or looking until she had answers. "He sure as hell would've known if he had twin daughters."

She nodded, appearing to be satisfied with his answer. Remaining silent, she gently placed the dresses back into the chest with the rag dolls and lifted her iPad to take photos of the items. "I'd like to look at that will."

"I'm sure you would." He shook his head. "Private family papers, Boots. It is none of your business."

"Are you absolutely sure of that?" Was she planning to twist this story of the twins to eventually bring it around to claim that Mignon was the long-lost Martine? Was that her scam? Or did she believe there actually were twins? There hadn't been enough time or opportunities for her to plant the double items in the chest.

"Yes, Boots, I'm sure." He nodded once. "A couple of matching dresses, dolls, and *fezzos* do not point to Martine having a twin. Circumstantial at best. It can certainly be explained in other ways. Maybe she was a messy eater and needed extra clothes. Maybe she had a habit of misplacing her toys and to keep their princess happy, they always had a spare handy." He folded his arms over his chest.

"In my research coming here I had a good idea of the family lineage but I saw nothing of the mistakes." Jewell said, her voice low, even. "Were there illegitimate children? Maybe Martine had an illegitimate sister who was very close in age."

Jewell never made eye contact with Beau; her attention was on the task of snapping a few more photos of the inside of the open chest. She then added a notation to the inventory in her iPad before taking out a single item and repeating the tedious process of photographing and cataloging it. When she was finished, she returned everything as she'd found it. The process took twenty minutes, before she closed the chest and shoved her magnifying glass into her tool belt.

"An illegitimate sibling isn't a stretch, is it?" she asked, as if there hadn't been a long pause in their conversation. She placed the wooden spool with the initials on it onto the floor and took a series of photos of it at various angles. When she finished, she turned off her head lamp. "That was a common occurrence in a closed plantation community. It's not the same as what we've come to learn of the slave girl–plantation owner affairs in the generations before Martine, but men have been having affairs with the help throughout history."

"So you're saying Mignon is the illegitimate heir of Aguste Bienvenu?" He laughed a short laugh. "Come on, Professor, you can come up with a better story."

"I'm not saying Mignon is the illegitimate heir." She kept her voice even, but Beau heard the impatience in her tone. "I'm not saying she is the legitimate heir. I'm not saying she's one of the M's on the wooden spool or the little girl who wore one of those matching dresses. I'm certainly not saying she is actually Martine." She hesitated, looking like she was gathering her thoughts before continuing. "What I am saying, Counselor, is that she *might* be one of those things. I will investigate this until I figure it out." She paused. "Why—isn't that what you want, too? Why do you prefer to just dismiss an old lady's claims that she lived around here rather than see if there's any legitimacy to them? Does she threaten you?"

"Hell, no. Not her. You. You threaten me."

Jewell looked at him, her mouth open, but no response came.

"It's lunchtime," he said, not wanting to continue that conversation. He looked at the time on the phone. 11:00. So it was an early lunch. "Let's take a break, get a sandwich..."

"Then come back to work," she said, finishing his sentence. It wasn't what he would've said, though. He would've said they should call it a day and go their separate ways.

An hour later, they had finished lunch, checked on the progress of the work being done in the barn and returned to the attic to catalog the items in the second chest. While Jewell worked, Beau sat on the floor, leaning against the wall, reading an old book taken from one of the chests. The book was a faded sable brown, the pages yellowed and brittle. The subject was outdated and entertaining as hell. "Uh-oh. I'm in violation."

"What?" Jewell looked up from the small box of buttons she had on the floor in front of her. "What's wrong?"

"It's bad, Boots." He sighed hugely. "According to the *Ladies and Gentlemen's Pocket Companion on Etiquette and Manners*, I have made a huge faux pas." He shook his head in exaggerated movements. "Here it is, in black and white...er, black and yellow." He lifted his brows playfully. "Yellowed pages." Then, he pointed to the book. ""It clearly states that—*At family dinners where the common household bread is used, it should never be cut less than an inch and a half thick. There is nothing more plebeian than thin bread at dinner.*" He looked at Jewell, eyes wide. "I'm plebeian." His brows furrowed. "What does 'plebeian' mean?"

She smiled. "A commoner. From the Roman times, the lower, common class of people were referred to as the plebeian class."

"Well, there it is." He slapped his forehead. "I've served bread only an inch and a quarter thick, so I must be plebian."

She laughed easily and it warmed him the like sun did when he sat on his back porch to watch the sunrise.

"Who knew?" She said, walking to where he was sitting. Her alluring, earthy fragrance slid over him as she sat next to him and looked at the book. He never seemed to be prepared for the sensual assault of her unique scent. He closed his eyes a moment to both allow himself to enjoy it and to fortify himself against it. Then, he shifted the book so they both could read it.

"I've seen this book before," she said, her voice soft and light. "But I didn't realize how personally revealing it could be."

"Yes, indeed." He flipped a few pages. "Revealing and full of useful advice. Read this." He pointed to the sentence that he wanted her to read.

Jewell shifted closer to Beau to better see the passage. Her shoulder pressed against his, sending a slow heat through his body.

"'*The less your mind dwells upon lovers and matrimony,*' says Mrs. Farren in her address to young women, '*the more agreeable and profitable will be your intercourse with gentlemen.*'" She looked up at Beau. "Ha, ha. Very funny. You aren't plebian. You're mischievous." She rolled her eyes. "Now what do you think this *really* means?"

He held up one hand in surrender. "I didn't say I thought it meant anything." He wagged his brows and smiled. "You have a dirty mind, Dr. Duet."

She inhaled, looked up toward the ceiling and shook her head. "I'm sure there were a lot more interesting and historically significant passages you could've selected for me." She tapped the book.

"Well, there was something in the book about how ladies' minds are less occupied with important concerns, so they are better observers of propriety or impropriety."

"Less important concerns, huh?"

"Hey, I didn't write it." He closed the book and placed it on his lap. "I think deciding on the luncheon menu and what dress to wear to the ball are very important concerns."

Jewell punched him in the arm. "Chauvinist."

"Hey, be careful. You aren't being agreeable for your intercourse with gentlemen."

She laughed, started to get up. "Well, at least I'm not with this gentleman." He extended her hand to point to him and he grabbed it and tugged her back down. She landed on his lap. "Hey."

"I've never said I was a gentleman." He rubbed the silky strand of hair that had fallen around her face between his finger and thumb. Her mouth fell open, her lips softened, as if in invitation. Nothing else seemed to exist around him, except those lips and the sound of her breath sliding over them. Plump, soft, wet. He slowly moved in, his eyes focusing only on her mouth as everything else around them seemed to disappear in a fuzzy cloud. He angled his head, moistened his lips...and was jolted from the magical haze by Jewell jumping back.

What the hell happened?

Then he heard her phone. It was playing the verse, *Jambalaya, crawfish pie, filé gumbo*, complete with fiddles, accordions and rubboard.

"That's the ringtone for Tante Izzy," she said, sounding both breathless and worried. She answered her phone.

"Hello." She looked at him, her eyes wide. "It's Tante Izzy. She says we've spent enough time in the plantation attic."

"I agree." He folded his arms over his chest.

Jewell rolled her eyes at him. "Yes, ma'am. Okay. We'll meet you there." She ended the call. "Beau, I think I was just extorted, and my Mimi is being held for ransom." She smiled. "Tante Izzy said she has been patiently waiting for me to go to her house to clear out her old stuff. But she 'isn't patient no more.' She's taking Mimi to her house now, and if I want my Mimi, I have to get her there...but only after I do what she hired me to do." She looked at Beau, humor in her eyes. "Should I call the FBI and report a kidnapping?"

"Hah. Forget the FBI. You'll need the Marines, Air Force and Navy Seals."

***

Jewell reached the parking area near the camper and walked toward her old beat-up truck. "Let's take my car," Beau said, pointing to a black, late model BMW that had the white fluffy clouds from the sky reflected on its shiny hood and doors.

"I'd prefer taking mine." Jewell opened the driver's door and climbed in. "You can take your car if you want," she said, hoping he'd ride separately. She wanted to mull over the recent finds and see if she could make sense of it all. Having Beau around muddled her thinking. She had to be careful that she didn't say something wrong that could jeopardize her job here. When he was around, she felt on edge and defensive. It was exhausting to always have to be on her "A" game around him.

By the time she closed the door and reached into the ashtray where she kept the keys, Beau was climbing into the cab. "I really don't mind if we drive separately," she said, trying again.

He pushed aside a pile of work papers and a brown wicker basket filled with pricing labels. "I hope to God I'm caught up on my tetanus shots." He kicked aside a plastic grocery bag filled with dirty rags.

"Ha, ha. Very funny." She started the truck and drove toward the entrance gate near the kennel.

"I have no idea where I'm going," she told him. "Since you're here, you'll save me the trouble of figuring it out. I can get to the main road, but after that, you'll have to direct me."

"Good thing I came with you." He adjusted the air conditioner vent, but when he realized no air was flowing through it, he reached for the AC controls. "Do you mind if I get some air circulating in here?"

"I do not," she said. "You'll have to roll down the window to do so, though."

He stared at her a minute. "You don't have air conditioning in your vehicle and you've lived in south Louisiana your whole life? I thought it was as much a necessity for everyone who lives here as a strawberry snowball in the afternoon, an ice cold beer at sunset, and a swim in the bayou or Lake Pontchartrain when the mood struck you."

"I used to think that too." She frowned. "But not all of us have fancy cars with functioning cooling systems." She rolled down her window and immediately rolled it back up when dust started swirling in from the dry road. "Some of us choose to use their funds to reinvest in their business." *And to pay for the expensive care and keeping of a dear grand-mère.* "For the record, I do splurge on a strawberry snowball or cold Abita beer on occasion."

He didn't respond and she was glad. Enough had been said on the subject as far as she was concerned. He didn't need to know how desperate her financial situation actually was, although she suspected he probably knew.

"You know, I could figure my way to Tante Izzy's if you want to stay behind or drive there in your air conditioned car later." She shrugged, hit a bump without slowing down, and negotiated a curve too fast. "I'm resourceful. I have a cell phone, Tante Izzy's phone number, Google, GPS and a good sense of direction." She reached the closed gate to exit the property. She looked at the gate, then Beau. "Why isn't it opening automatically? Don't electronic gates simply allow a vehicle to exit when they approach?

"Oh, hell." He shook his head. "Not the ones that are designed to keep runaway dogs from escaping onto the highway or thieves from easily escaping with the valuable dogs."

"That makes sense. A motion sensor would open when an animal approached, too. It must drive the UPS and delivery guys crazy." She laughed. "I guess the gate can be opened from the kennel like you opened it from the house when you thought I was the pizza delivery guy, huh?"

"Yes, and with the remote or code Ben gave to those of us who come to Sugar Mill often." As much as she hated to admit it, now she was glad Beau was with her to get her through the gates. But, wait, he wasn't making a move to get out of the truck to open it and he was frowning. "What did you mean by, 'Oh, hell?' Can't you get us through the gates?"

He rolled down the window and sucked in some warm, humid air.

"Turn the truck around and go back to my car, Jewell," he said, his voice even, controlled. "The remote for the gate is in my car. I don't have the code. Ben changed it last week and I didn't put it in my phone. Hell, I didn't even look at the paper with the code written on it or I would know it."

She shook her head. "Why didn't you say so right away?" She turned the truck around and headed back toward the plantation.

"You didn't ask for my help, Boots. You said you could take care of it all yourself, remember? You're resourceful." He rolled up the window. "I suspect you don't ask for help often. Not that I want you to ask me for help."

She hated that he was right. She didn't like to ask anyone to help her, so she didn't. It was part of the reason she'd gotten into trouble with the law and had lost her job at the university.

She glanced out of her window, noticing tall, bright green sugarcane blades jutting from beige stalks alongside the road. "The sugarcane is pretty," she whispered.

Beau looked out of the window. "Yes. It is. It'll be harvested soon."

Jewell smiled. "Mimi said the same thing, but I don't know how she would possibly know that. She's a city girl."

"Interesting."

"That it is." She drove past acres of thick, healthy stalks, lined in neat, straight rows that created the illusion of it undulating back and forth as she passed by. It reminded her of an image she'd seen too many times as a child living near Bourbon Street in the French Quarter...that of a slowly swaying dancer in silhouette behind a sheer curtain.

She shook her head to clear the image. "When does harvesting begin?"

"It actually begins in October," he answered easily. "So, it's underway. It continues until all of the crops are cut and brought to the sugar mill in December. The farmers try to get it all done before Christmas."

"When I researched this area, I saw that Sugar Mill once had a mill on the property, and there are still a few around the area."

"That's true. The closest mill is up the bayou about fifteen miles away. There are five others around the area. I'm sure if you've driven on the roads around here while working for the Simoneauxs, you've encountered a few of the cane-hauling trucks."

"Yeah. I've been slowed to a crawl behind many of them," Jewell told him, glad to have something—anything—to talk about that wasn't adversarial. "I love that the cane sugar industry is still as relevant today as it was hundreds of years ago. It's so wonderful when we can have the same experiences our ancestors did. We smell the same earthy scents of the fresh cane being cut and the fields' soil being turned by the plows, just as the people of the middle and late 1800s did." She smiled. "I imagine once some of the plantation mills started to close, the people of the region had to negotiate their horse and buggies around carts laden with cane stalks being hauled to the other mills for grinding, like we do around the tractors and trucks hauling the cane today."

"Cane trucks, burning fields, steam coming from the sugar mills... It's just what we expect here in the fall," Beau said.

"Cooler weather, football games, Halloween, All Saints and All Souls Day, festivals. That's what we think of in the fall in New Orleans. Not cane season."

"Those things are fall to us too." Beau turned a little in his seat. "It feels like you're circling around something here, Jewell. What are you really talking about?"

"Oh, I don't know. I'm just trying to put some pieces together." She gripped the wheel tighter again. "Mimi seems to have some real sensory memories with the earth, the crop and maybe even the processing of sugarcane." He groaned. "Hey, I'm not making the connection with that and the double items in the chest, so don't you go thinking I am."

"Sure. I won't think you're thinking I'm thinking that, Boots." He ran his hand through his hair, clearly annoyed with her. She was surprised at how calm he sounded when he spoke again just a few seconds later.

"Sugarcane has a very distinctive smell in each of the stages," he offered. "But it's not something uniquely known to the people who live around here or the grinding mills." He folded his arms over his chest. "We took tours of the sugarcane farms and processing plants as schoolchildren. You know, from the farm to the factory sort of thing. Anyway, there were always groups from New Orleans or Baton Rouge there too. School kids, Rotarians, conventioneers, others. Maybe Mignon took a tour at some point in her life."

"Maybe before I was born or was old enough to remember her doing that." Jewell drove up to his car.

"Park the truck and let's take my car. I want to drive."

She looked at him. She knew her truck didn't take the bumps well and she suspected he wasn't pleased with her handling of the sharp curves either. And then there was the lack of air conditioning on top of that. "Fine." She parked the truck, put the keys in the ashtray and got out.

"That was the easiest thing we've agreed on," he said, climbing into his car and closing the door with an expansive slam. "A sign of progress."

"Progress?" She laughed, closing her door. The car smelled clean, new and expensive. "Nah. I wouldn't go that far and call it that. I'm just cheap and your gas is free."

"Yes, my gas is free, but more importantly, I have the remote to get us out of Sugar Mill," Beau told Jewell with a crooked grin and eyes full of humor.

He opened his ashtray and pulled out what she knew was his car key. He waved it between them.

"So it's not progress, but would you agree that brilliant minds think alike?" His eyes crinkled as his smile broadened. "Would you go so far as to say that?" He dropped the key back into the ashtray, pressed the starter button that only required the key to be in the general vicinity of the ignition, and drove off.

Jewell laughed and he glanced at her with his light, intelligent eyes as he turned the air conditioner on high. The wind blew the silky dark waves of Beau's hair, mussing it up just enough to make him look sexy and ruggedly handsome, even in his neat clothes and fancy car.

"Brilliant? Hmm...Some would say we are plain ol' dumb for putting our keys in a place where a thief could easily steal them." She was surprised that he actually kept his keys in the ashtray. He seemed like the kind of guy who would have them carefully protected somewhere he could keep an eye on them. He didn't seem like he'd trust his possessions where someone could steal them.

"Not in Cane." He negotiated the curve on the dust and shell road with ease. "We don't have much crime here, especially not car theft."

"Well, I keep putting my keys in the ashtray and keep my insurance paid up in hopes someone will steal mine." That wasn't exactly true, but it was the story she always told when she was questioned about her habit of putting the truck keys in such a vulnerable place.

He laughed. "My guess is that's a white lie, Boots." He approached the front gate, lifted the remote from a slot in his door, and pressed it. He barely slowed down as the gate opened and they drove through. "I know keeping your tools at hand is important for you. I see the way you keep your tool belt organized. I think your truck is part of your tools. You need it to do your job, hauling stuff around."

She shifted in her seat. She didn't like that he had observed and assessed her so accurately. It felt uncomfortable. Would he use what he learned against her? If not this, something else?

"I think," he continued, scratching his chin, "you keep the keys in the ashtray because you don't want Mignon to have easy access to them when you aren't around. Although I think it wouldn't be hard for her to get them from there."

"Not as easy as you think." She sighed. "If she finds the keys in the house, she gets very agitated about not being allowed to drive. Mostly, she thinks they're her keys to her car. She remembers what her car looks like and will try to find it parked on the street as it had been for most of her life. We sold her car a long time ago, but she doesn't always remember that." She shook her head. "If she sees the keys in the truck when I get them out of the ashtray to drive, she doesn't say a word about it. She knows it's mine. She just accepts it."

"Couldn't you hide it in your purse or in your tool belt or belongings?"

"There's no distinction between what's mine and hers. She has a hard time telling our things apart. She'll grab my purse just as often as hers. Labeling things mostly doesn't help. I've adjusted. I have ways to keep the things I can't have her accessing away from her." She shrugged.

They drove a little farther in silence, each to their own thoughts. "I'm sorry, Jewell," he said, breaking the silence. "It must be difficult having to be the 24-7 caregiver for your grand-mère." She nodded. "What about your mother? Does she help at all?" Jewell stiffened. She rubbed her hands on her thighs. Beau looked at her and his eyebrows furrowed. "Sensitive subject?"

"Very. I don't want to talk about my mother."

"You know, that makes me want to know about her even more."

"Figures."

"I like the forbidden and off-limits stuff, me," he said, his Cajun accent heavy. "I'm bad like that. Very, very bad."

"A regular rebel in your starched, button-down shirt and groomed European sports car."

"You'd be surprised what I'm really made of, Boots." He smiled a devastating smile that made her heart knock against her chest. "Tell me about your mother."

"No. She has nothing to do with our situation and nothing to do with Sugar Mill. Never will. Leave her out of it." She turned to face him. "Please."

The muscles in his jaw tightened. He leaned farther back into his seat, looking more relaxed than ever. If it wasn't for the muscle twitching in his jaw, she would think he was unaffected by her plea. A plea she was totally embarrassed that she'd made.

He pointed to the right side of the car. "Look familiar?"

Yes. The Simoneauxs' estate. She looked at the house and the dark, hollowed area beneath it and shivered. She was a tough woman. If she could belly crawl under that old house in foul-smelling, wet, slimy mud with snakes and raccoons and God knew what, she could deal with whatever her mother's life and reputation dragged into hers. Only she'd prefer to crawl in that godforsaken pit and avoid the latter.

"Rumor is the Simoneauxs are still on the fence about whether or not it was worth hiring you for the estate sale."

"I'm not surprised." They had valued their family possessions a lot more than the rest of the world.

Jewell stared out the window at the low-hanging branches of the old oaks, heavy with gray moss and thick leaves. A white wooden swing hung from a sturdy A-frame under a majestic tree and swayed in the gentle breeze, much like the swing did under the old oak near the bayou at Sugar Mill Plantation. She pictured snuggling on it with an old worn soft quilt.

"Stop. Stop the car," she shouted a second later. Beau slammed on his brakes.

"What the hell?" He looked around the car. "Did I hit an animal or something? I didn't feel anything."

"No. Back up." She strained to look behind her. "We have time, don't we? Tante Izzy won't mind if we're five minutes later, right?" She didn't wait for Beau to answer. "Oh. Just pull over here. No cars are coming. I won't be long." She opened the car door and got out. "You're mostly off the road, this is good."

"What the hell is going on?"

"I need to take a look at something." She smiled, realizing she'd said need instead of want. When it came to looking for something wonderful in a pile of junk, it felt more like a need than a want. She'd spotted an old desk at the edge of the road with a pile of branches and other cast-aside furniture. She loved this kind of treasure hunt and the feeling of being so hyper-focused that everything else in the world slipped away. More often than not, she actually forgot her real body's needs, like food and water, overtaken by her spiritual need to rescue a part of history that was about to be destroyed.

She heard him running behind her as she reached the desk she wanted to look at. "I wish I had my tool belt." She looked at him for a brief second.

"What the hell, Jewell?" He shook his head. "Are you kidding me? I thought we were running to an accident. I was actually reviewing how to do CPR and administer first aid to a severed limb."

"I hope not at the same time. That can't be good for the victim...chest compressions and a tourniquet."

"Very funny." He glanced at the pile of discards tossed to the side of the road. "I can't believe this, Boots. You had me leave half the rubber from my tires on the road when I slammed on my brakes for this pile of junk?"

She gave him a hard look. "This might look like junk to you, but to me it looks like an adventure maze with a possible treasure in the middle of it."

"Yeah, it's rainbows and fairy dust." He was still shaking his head. "You're either crazy, blind, irrational, have a romantic soul or are brilliant. I don't think going through moldy tree limbs, termite-infested logs and old furniture is so brilliant."

She pushed aside a large branch and tugged on the desk that was half covered by it. "Are you going to just stand there and whine?"

"I'm not touching that crap. There's poison ivy in there."

She stopped, looked at the tree limb and kicked it away with her rubber boot. A skinny brown spider jumped from a small branch onto her boot. Jewell yipped. Beau quietly scooted it away with the tip of his leather shoes. "I got that big, ol' bad spider for you, *chère*."

Jewell immediately went back to kicking the limbs away from the desk. "Damn, Boots, you are determined." He picked up a broken yellow broom handle at the bottom of the pile and shoved the poison ivy-infested limbs aside. Once he had pushed enough of the branches away, Jewell reached to get ahold of the battered desk. Beau grabbed her shoulder and nudged her to the side. "I'll get it." He blew out a breath. "I can't believe you have me digging in other people's garbage to get a skinny old desk with three legs." He placed it at her feet right along the hard surface of the highway. "And a missing seat."

"I can fix all of that." She looked down the highway from where she was now standing partially in one of the lanes. "No one is coming. No one ever seems to be traveling on this road." She smiled and walked around the desk. "Isn't it beautiful! It's an antique lyre-harp writing desk-chair combo. I knew it. I was sure I had seen the lyre shape when we passed." She jogged in place and threw her hand in the air to Beau.

He high-fived her. "Let's write a note on it saying that we'll be coming back for it," he said, not sounding as enthusiastic as she felt. "We'll put it over there away from the trash."

"We can't leave it, Beau." She started carefully digging through the pile of rubble using the broomstick, looking for the missing leg. "Someone else might take it."

"I hardly think that will happen." He looked at the desk with his hands on his hips. "I'm certain of it. Besides, you don't think we're going to put that thing in my car, do you?"

"It's a lyre harp writing desk-chair combo. And yes. It'll fit. It's not that big."

He looked down the road. She knew he was hoping a big truck would drive by and roll over the desk. She wanted to smile at his obvious thoughts. Jewell looked at him, but was immediately distracted at the sound of a truck coming down the road, shifting gears. She looked behind her. "Oh, no! Truck."

"Cane truck," he shouted, grabbing the desk with one hand and her around the waist with the other and stepping off the road, half stumbling and half falling over the pile of limbs. The truck whooshed by, gears grinding just as they landed hard in the dry ditch. "You okay?"

She rubbed the back of her head where she'd hit it on the desk. "Yeah." He stood, climbed out of the ditch, and extended his hand to her. "Let's get out of here."

"Thank you for saving my desk...and me," she said, still standing in the ditch. Then she reached for his hand, but just before she took it, she started to laugh. "Look what I found." She picked up the missing desk leg. It was completely covered in mud and hardly recognizable.

"You like digging in trash and mud way too much," Beau said, his smile giving away his good humor about her junk-pile diving. "Give me your hand. No. Your clean hand."

She tossed the muddy desk leg onto the road, grabbed the desk by one of the legs and dragged it out as Beau pulled her up the short incline. "I think we cracked the drawer." She noticed the gash in the front panel that hadn't been there earlier. "I can fix that."

"Why you would want to, is beyond my understanding." He shook his head, lifted the desk and carried it toward his car. Jewell rubbed off as much mud as she could in the roadside grass before following him. "If you're as tenacious and stubborn as you are with this piece of crap desk when you're trying to find Mimi's Twinnie, I think you'll drive me absolutely insane."

"So you understand why I need to look for Twinnie?" She hated that she wanted him to say yes. Hated feeling such a strong need to have someone, anyone, validate her determination to research Mimi's claims. "You believe that it is possible she exists?"

He left the desk at the back of the car, then opened the driver's door and unlocked the trunk before answering her. "I didn't say that." He put the desk and the dirty leg into his clean and completely empty trunk. Jewell had never seen a trunk completely empty before. "I'm not sure what the hell I believe. I just know what I won't let happen. I won't let anyone hurt my family. I think I've made that clear."

"One thing I can say about you." She held up two fingers. "Actually, two. You are consistent. And, you are either freaky neat with your car trunk or you are a mass murderer who needs to keep it squeaky clean to hide the evidence from carrying the bodies in there." She closed the trunk and climbed into the car. "Maybe Mimi was right about you."

He closed his door and started the car with a push of a button. "Did she say I was handsome, smart and extremely kind to crazy women who like to dig in the garbage like a rabid coon?"

"No." She bit back a smile. "She said she thought you were a mass murderer."

Beau and Jewell turned onto the road leading to Tante Izzy's. If they hadn't made the stop for the desk, it would have taken them less than fifteen minutes, instead of the forty minutes it had taken to get there from Sugar Mill. Jewell, always paying attention to details, noticed that the road consisted of the same shell and dirt bedding as the one at Sugar Mill. She also noted that while the house wasn't near the road, it wasn't set as far back as the plantation, and the large two-story Acadian style farmhouse quickly came into view.

"Oh...my...it's pink," she gasped, rubbing her eyes to make sure something hadn't malfunctioned with them. "Did she really paint this beautiful old home the color of cotton candy?"

"You can thank Elli for that." He parked the car near the front door. "It's the same color Elli had to paint Sugar Mill for the first movie she brought there."

"I saw it. I thought it was done with special effects." She looked at the rose bushes near the front porch, where the pretty pink blooms were lost in the color of the house. "I guess it was just wishful thinking."

"Word of advice. Keep that opinion to yourself."

"Well, 'bout time," Tante Izzy shouted from the front porch. Like the roses, she was lost in the color of the house too because she was wearing a long, pink shift dress and matching pink fuzzy bunny slippers.

"Yeah, 'bout time," Mimi echoed.

"Oh, for heaven's sake." She was camouflaged in the same shade of pink and similar style dress as Tante Izzy. Both of the ladies had gone to the beauty parlor that morning and had a similar haircut, a low teased style with the same pale strawberry blonde hair color. Jewell looked at Beau, who was biting his lower lip to keep from laughing.

"Hello, gorgeous. Hello, beautiful. You two look like the Susan Hayward twins with your new hairdos," Beau said easily, giving each of the ladies a kiss on the cheek. He carefully avoided their bright bubble-gum pink lipstick when they tried to kiss him in return. Jewell, on the other hand, didn't have his maneuvering skills. She knew without seeing it, that petite Tante Izzy had left her thin lip print on the right side of her neck where she'd kissed her in greeting, while Mimi had smeared her lipstick in a sticky mess on Jewell's left cheek.

"Don't Mimi look pretty wit' da Fanci-Full rinse in her hairs from Margie's Beauty Shop? And me too?" Tante Izzy added.

Jewell nodded. "It's a nice color."

"I can make you an appointment if you want? Margie does fine work."

"Not *ma sucrée*," Mimi said, saving Jewell from answering. "She doesn't wants to change nuttin'." Her accent sounded more Cajun than Parisian. "In fact, I tried encouraging her to get a tattoo, and she refused."

"I want a tattoo." Tante Izzy nodded. "Somethin' pink. Maybe a pink crown. I like being queen. Maybe you and me can go get ourselves tiaras."

Beau leaned against one of the wooden square house columns and crossed his arms over his chest, grinning. He was enjoying the conversation and did nothing to dissuade them from what they were planning.

"Don't get youself too comfortable, Beauregard Bienvenu," Tante Izzy said, walking to her front door and abandoning talk about a tattoo. "You might be all handsome lookin' like Rhett Butler from *Gone wit' da Wind,* but we got work to do." Then she whispered something in his ear. He shook his head and frowned.

"You should've talked to me first," he said.

"You would've said no, so why would I talk to you?"

"We got lots of work to do." Mimi said, interrupting their conversation, again speaking with the same accent as Tante Izzy. Jewell forgot about the cryptic conversation between Beau and his aunt and laughed. Mimi was adorable. She'd spent one day with Tante Izzy and had picked up her Cajun accent.

Tante Izzy waved them inside. "You come too, Beauregard."

"Just for a little while. I have work to do."

"I thought you said that you had the rest of the afternoon off." Jewell smiled a fake smile.

"So happy you enjoy my company so much that you want me around, *chère,*" he whispered in her ear. His warm breath lingered on her ear and neck like the memory of their earlier kiss.

"Glad you has time for your poor aunt wit' da very rich oil well." She smiled. "What we has to do will take all afternoon."

"She got a lot of stuff, *ma sucrée,*" Mimi said, grabbing Beau's arm to walk inside. She looked up at him. "Now, who are you again?"

"I'm the man who's crushin' on the very attractive strawberry blonde on my arm."

Mimi smiled. "Oh. That's right. You'll have to fight my man for me, you know?" She batted her eyes at him. "He's really tall." She looked up at him. "Like you. Only he used to play professional football, so he's got more bulk. And his skin is a really pretty dark color. Now, he's a big NFL front office man, you know?" She paused, looked away like she was searching for a memory. "Or he was..."

"Sounds like I'll have quite a challenge then." Beau smiled.

Jewell had no idea who Mimi was talking about. She had never mentioned dating a former NFL player before. Maybe she would ask her more about it tonight. It could be one of her imaginings, or it could be a happening from her past that she never thought was appropriate to share with her granddaughter. If it was the latter, Jewell wanted to hear the story. It was part of her Mimi's history. Her history. It was one of the life events, grand or small, that made her grand-mère the woman she had become, the one who had passed her values on to the young girl she raised.

Jewell walked into the house with the others. Thank God, the inside wasn't decorated as brightly and out of character for the era as the exterior. The front parlor was filled with antique walnut furniture and local craftsmen accents. Local art hung on cream plastered walls. Soft, well-worn floral cushions rested on just about every seat, while doilies draped every armrest. There were red and royal purple silk roses in glass vases and statues of the Catholic saints on tabletops. And there were about a dozen photo collages framed in dark wood hanging on the wall. The photos appeared to be mostly of children in their school uniforms, probably given each year they were taken to their favorite aunt.

If the large number of family photos around on the walls and tabletops didn't hint at the age of the homeowner, Jewell thought, the scent of the room would. It smelled of old-fashioned face powder and that special flowery perfume she always associated with elderly ladies. This was definitely the home she would've imagined Tante Izzy living in. There were even a few stuffed animals to complete the picture.

"The pink poodle is so adorable." Jewell walked over to the fluffy toys positioned in the center of the large red velvet mission style sofa. "But this soft, cuddly, furry raccoon and the huggable crocodile are incredibly sweet.

I've never seen anything like them before. Wherever did you find them all in pink?"

"I didn't," Tante Izzy said. "Beauregard did." She pointed to him. "He gets them for my birthday every year. He knows I collects them. I have more upstairs, but these are my favorites."

"She said I can have the raccoon," Mimi told Jewell in French.

Tante Izzy looked at her, eyes wide. She walked over to Jewell, "I did not tell her dat," she whispered in French. "She lies a lot. I don't like it. I like *her,* but I don't like her lies. Must be da old-timer's."

Jewell felt her throat tighten with emotion. She nodded. She felt she should respond, but what could she say? *You are right. She lies, but not because she has ill intent. It's because my Mimi's mind is slipping away and I can't do anything to stop it.* Jewell swallowed hard. Beau's hand settled on her shoulder. She felt his strength in the simple touch, in his body standing so near to her. She wanted to lean back into him, let him hold her and kiss her until the reality of her world slipped away as it had earlier, when they had kissed in the attic.

Foolishness. It was something her mother would think...hope for...do. And look what kind of person she was.

Jewell moved away, pretending to look at the stitching on a hand-sewn linen napkin that was draped over the back of a burgundy Queen Anne chair in the corner.

"If you like dat," Tante Izzy said, motioning toward the adjoining room, "you will like my momma's needlepoint."

She led Jewell, Beau and Mimi into the dining room, where a large framed tapestry of hand-stitched needlepoint was featured on the center wall. Mimi sat on a dining room chair, uninterested in the needlepoint artwork. Jewell wasn't certain if that was because Mimi didn't notice it or because it didn't look familiar to her. Either way, Jewell wanted a better look.

She moved in as close as she could to look at the types of stitches that were used, but a tall buffet prevented her from getting too close. Besides that, the piece was under glass, and without her magnifying glass or the right lighting, it was hard to make out the details. She could tell the flowers were created from the same pattern as the flowers on the footstool Mimi had taken from the nook.

"It's beautiful," Jewell told her. "Did you help your mother make it?"

"Mais non." She frowned. "She gave it to me when I made sixteen. It was for my hope chest. She was disappointed I never got me a man to marry, but I used my pretty t'ings anyway." She nodded. "I done gave a lot of it away as weddin' or grad'ation gifts. I even gave my Beau a pretty paintin' my momma gave me." She looked at Beau. "It was a house warmin' gift when he bought hisself a house. Right, Beau?"

"Yes, indeed."

"It got his great-grand-pépère, Emile, in it. He's standin' with his brother, my grand-pépère, François Bienvenu. You know him?"

"I know of him." She stepped back to look at the needlework as a single piece of art. The pink, gold and green colors in the piece were still vivid. "François, whose full name is Aguste François, was the man who came from Toulouse, France, in his twenties and built Sugar Mill Plantation soon afterward." She looked at Tante Izzy. "I haven't seen any documentation to confirm it and maybe you have family stories passed down that do, but that was around the time of so much political unrest in France. I suspect he came to America as most immigrants had, for a better life. He must've made money or inherited it to be able to come and establish a plantation in Louisiana when France was so economically depressed. That was in the years following Napoleon and just before the Franco-Prussian war."

"The war is what convinced my great-grand-pépère to follow his younger brother to America," Beau added. "He didn't see it as a noble thing to stay and fight for an emperor he did not support."

"My momma said da bad feelings for da Germans from da Franco-Prussian war continued for a long time," Tante Izzy added. "It was a hard life in France and a sad one in America."

Jewell remembered seeing the death date for François's wife and his six children listed as being the same day. "François lost his wife and six children on the same day, didn't he?" Jewell asked.

"It was a fire in New Orleans. At a fancy hotel. Dey had gone to a party at a friend's home earlier. It was Epiphany, January 6, 1886. Dey had been dere to celebrate da kickoff to da Mardi Gras season on All Kings' Day."

"How did François survive?" She touched her chest, her heart aching for the horror that he'd had to endure. "To lose your entire family in one single event. That's awful." Tante Izzy made the sign of the cross.

"François's wife, Marie Brigitte Bissette, had taken all six of their children to a Mardi Gras party at a friend's home," Beau said. His voice was even, but Jewell could see how much the tragedy moved him. "The family story, Jewell, is that Aguste was scheduled to attend, too, but the temperature had dropped into the teens. It was unusually cold and he feared severe problems at the plantation. He stayed behind to oversee the preparations."

Jewell felt a lump form in her throat. She looked at Tante Izzy and Beau. If Aguste had not survived that night, they wouldn't be standing in the dining room with her right now. Would his life or death have affected her grand-mère's life and, in turn, her own? She looked at Mimi. Her chin was resting on her chest. She was sound asleep.

"Huh, it must be nap time," Tante Izzy said, looking at Mimi too. "But you cain't take a nap. You got to work."

She pointed her crooked finger at Jewell. "Down here is da good stuff. I don't go upstairs anymore. My family t'inks it's a bad idea since I live alone and don't need to. Dey afraid I will fall and cry like da lady in da commercial. *I've fallen and I cain't get up. Help.'*"

"At least she let her family get the emergency call button for her," Beau said. "And she wears it around her neck." He looked at Jewell. "She's agreed to restrict her movements to the first floor. She has a bedroom and everything she needs on this one floor," he added. "The upstairs is mostly storage."

"What exactly do you want me to do, Tante Izzy?" Jewell asked.

"I want you to clean my upstairs and have a garage sale."

"I'll take a look now, but you do know I have to finish Elli's job first." Tante Izzy frowned. "I'm sorry. I have a contract with Elli, and she has a tight deadline before she needs the barn finished."

"I have a tight deadline too."

So did Jewell. She pulled out her phone to look at her calendar, but she didn't need to see it to know what was on it. The trial was still scheduled for the end of the following week. Whatever the decision, she'd be in the news and then be a pariah again. The fact that it was going to be a closed hearing only made the case more mysterious and appealing to the public. Whatever she was to accomplish, it had to come before the trial began.

"I'll show you the upstairs," Beau said, placing his palm on the small of her back and gently urging her toward the stairs.

"We'll be down here," Tante Izzy said. "Mignon's finished her nap. She's awake now, so we gonna watch Ellen."

"We like to dance with Ellen," Mimi added, settling into a different chair and shoving a needlepoint pillow in the small of her back.

Beau escorted her upstairs, but her heart and emotions had turned so heavy at where her thoughts had gone that each step felt like she was walking with cement blocks on her feet. She couldn't pull herself out of the fog shrouding her enough to notice the special architecture or photos that were certainly along the way. When they reached the top floor, he turned her to face him. "I'm not getting involved with your problems and those sad eyes," he said, anger in his voice. "Hell, I don't even know if I believe you're really sad, except that it is seeping through your pores and over your pretty skin. Damn it, Jewell. I don't know what to do with you."

"Don't do anything." She shoved him away. "I don't need your help. I don't want to involve you and your family in my problems. Those problems have nothing to do with my work for Elli or for Tante Izzy. Nothing. I don't know any other way to say it. Why can't you just believe what I'm telling you? If you don't believe me, fine. I just need for you to not get in my way." She turned her back to him. "Let me do my job."

He grabbed her shoulders from behind, but he didn't turn her to face him. "I want you to do your job. Just not here."

Tears slipped quietly down her cheeks. She felt his struggle. She hated that she understood it and his loyalty to his family. It mirrored hers for Mimi. She swallowed back the pain and worry. Her problems with the criminal trial against her, with what to do with Mimi if she went to jail, with losing Mimi to dementia, with just getting through the next day...would not be resolved now in the upstairs of an eccentric, kind old lady's home. She heard Mimi's voice wafting up to the second floor from where she and Tante Izzy were watching television.

"My daughter's a celebrity like Ellen," Mimi said, causing Jewell to flinch.

She inhaled deeply. "I'll start with the first room here on the right." She walked away from Beau's heat, his strength, to go into the room alone.

"Yeah, I know," Beau said, walking into the room behind her, flipping on the light switch. "You don't want to talk about your mother. Your celebrity mother. Or was that fantasy and confusion from Mignon's dementia?"

Jewell turned to face him, prepared to lie as she had her entire life. But she couldn't. She couldn't utter another deflecting tale or half-truth to hide the embarrassing reality of who her mother was. She'd suddenly and inexplicably reached her lifetime limit on lies about her mother.

"No. It isn't fantasy." She looked directly into Beau's beautiful eyes. Eyes that saw things in only black and white. Her tainted life fell mostly into the gray area. The darkest of grays. "My mother is very famous in New Orleans, Beau. Legendary. For the last thirty-plus years, she's danced on dimly lit, seedy Bourbon Street stages wearing nothing but a G-string and tassels." She paused, swallowed hard. "She's Miss Praline of the Crescent City Lantern Club."

***

Holy crap.

Beau knew exactly who Jewell was talking about. Everyone in the state of Louisiana or men who traveled to the infamous Bourbon Street had heard of her. In fact, most of the men in the state and tens of thousands beyond had made pilgrimages to see her as a rite of passage when they turned twenty-one.

Including himself.

In fact, besides his going to see Miss Praline's show a number of times when he turned twenty-one, he'd been back to see her for several of his friends' birthdays and bachelor parties over the years.

Holy crap.

Yeah, he knew who she was all right, and the resemblance between Jewell and her exotic and beautiful mother was unmistakable.

Holy crap.

"Miss Praline is your mother?"

She nodded. "Not that she ever acted like one. Mimi was more of a mother to me." She looked at her hands. "She never allowed me to call her Mother. She had me call her by her stage name, Praline." She blew out a breath. "I've accepted the situation. I did long ago. I just don't go around telling everyone that my fifty-one-year-old mother struts around in a G-string and tassels on a dimly lit stage on Bourbon Street in kinky six-inch heels. Not good for my business. It doesn't attract the right clientele. And as you can imagine, it can cause other problems with people who make assumptions about me being like my mother or those wanting a personal introduction to her."

"Like you said earlier, not all of us get the picture-perfect, well-behaved plantation mothers and fathers we've grown to think are ideal." He stuffed his hands in his pockets to keep from gathering the miserable woman in front of him in his arms. He wanted to. God knew he wanted to. She looked so damn vulnerable, like a woman who needed a hug...and reassurance.

Damn. When had he turned into such a nice, charitable guy who wanted to soothe a woman who very well might be his enemy? Hell, maybe he didn't really care about her feelings. Maybe he was the one who needed the reassurance? He'd let his guard down enough with Jewell that some old emotions—long believed to be resolved—from bad childhood memories had resurfaced to bite him on the ass. Maybe he'd been so busy watching out for the family that he'd forgotten to watch out for himself.

Nah, that felt like a damn lie.

He did care about her. He shouldn't, but he did. His humanity was damn inconvenient. Her intellect, passion for her work, love for her grand-mère, vulnerability and her sassy independence made her likable. It also made her dangerous. She had all of the attributes to run a scam—intelligence, access to information on much of the family history and knowledge of how to use it or spin it to create the scenario to gain trust so she could accomplish her goal. That left him in a tight, dark crack. He liked her as a person but did he trust her? He had to answer that, once and for all, with complete confidence. Did he believe her claims that she was ethically beyond reproach and only cared about protecting and recording history? Or, did he believe that she was capable of scamming him and his family? Her legal troubles warned him to distrust her.

If that wasn't enough, he should take Tante Izzy's concerns about Mignon into account. Tante Izzy had whispered to him on the front porch that she couldn't stop thinking about the way Mignon was claiming that Sugar Mill was her home. His unpredictable old aunt had gone so far as to arrange for the manicurist, a Bienvenu relative, to give her Mignon's cleaned fingernail clippings she collected during her manicure at the beauty parlor. She then mailed it to the lab that was used by the GENE ID Foundation that she was involved with. Tante Izzy was going to have a DNA analysis run on Mignon Duet to see if she was related to the Bienvenus. It was a shocking and not so legal thing to do, but an efficient way to get at the truth.

A truth that had nothing to do with Jewell's mother being the celebrity stripper, Miss Praline.

"Okay. Now you know," she continued. "I just ask that you keep it to yourself. Can you do that?"

He thought about it for a moment before answering. "As long as it doesn't affect Elli and Ben or the rest of my family, I won't bring up your mother." He sure as hell hoped he wouldn't think about it too much either. The idea that the buttoned-up, brilliant professor of Louisiana history in the quirky rubber boots was the daughter of the luscious, buxom queen of Bourbon Street was a dichotomy that played with a man's mind. Was she the way she was today because of her mother's behavior and choices? Of course she was. "I'm not sure your grandmother will be so discreet."

Jewell shrugged, her eyes counteracting the casual gesture. Her mother's onstage persona troubled her a great deal. Beau wondered which had hurt her more...a mother who was a stripper or a mother who clearly was not maternal. He knew it was the latter. "That can't be helped."

"You know, I get why you don't want to be associated with Miss Praline of the Crescent City Lantern Club. I'm sure it was especially tough when you were a teenager." He ran a hand through his hair. "My mother wasn't Betty Crocker, either." She looked at him, her eyes bright with an emotion that he could only label as hopeful. Hopeful of what, though? Hopeful that he would be understanding? That he was falling into her scam? "Yeah, well, having an alcoholic mother or a stripper mother..."

"The most infamous stripper in Louisiana history, who refused to age out of the business when she was well beyond the age when most girls in her profession did," she corrected.

"Yeah, well, I get why that can suck, but it could've been worse." Her eyes widened. He leaned against the wall and crossed his ankles.

"Don't try to put this into a pretty, shiny pink box when it belongs in a tattered, smudged one, Beauregard Bienvenu."

"I won't." Damn that urge to take her in his arms. "What I was going to say was that you didn't get the dream mother or father as a kid, but you were lucky to get a wonderful grandmother who loves you."

"Yes. Thank God." Jewell sucked in a ragged breath. "I can never repay her for what she's done for me."

Was this really what her life had become, a mission to pay back her grandmother for rescuing her from the influence of her mother's wanton world? Or was it a scam to pretend it was her quest? Maybe it was both. And how did the possible criminal charges pending against her play into this?

It certainly made sense that the motivation for a scam to get at Martine's trust could be for Jewell to give back to Mignon what she couldn't give her on her own.

"I feel your pain," he said, purposely looking as though he felt no pain at all. Just trying to project an image of apathy, skepticism. "I'm an empathetic guy." He folded his arms over his chest. "But don't expect me to feel too much, Boots. I won't let this sad tale of a less than ideal mother weaken my resolve to protect my family. I won't let it lessen my defenses. Whether or not that was your intention."

"Whether or not it was my intention?" She closed her eyes for a brief moment, obviously trying to control the anger that made the tips of her ears turn red. "Well, we're even on that point, Guardian of the Bienvenu world. I won't let your zealous, gladiator attitude stop me from attaining my goals either."

She turned away from him, taking her cell phone out of her pocket. She began to snap photos of the dark walnut antique four-poster bed and the faded lace-trimmed canopy draped over the top. She moved around the room, snapping photos of the other well-preserved furniture pieces, old porcelain dolls and stack of folded quilts. When she finished in the first room, she moved to the next room and the next, doing the same thing. Her movements were as brisk and unemotional as the few necessary questions she had to ask him while in each of the dusty, stale, warm rooms. When she finished with her photos she headed down the creaky wooden stairs without a backward glance.

***

Tante Izzy, Ruby and two other women she didn't recognize waited for her at the foot of the stairs. They all smiled at her, looking as sweet as each of the different heavy fragrant perfumes they wore. "I tole them not to bodder you," Tante Izzy said. "But they wouldn't take *'go and leave my house'* as an answer."

The three women began speaking at the same time. With their heavy Cajun accents, and fast-talking excited voices speaking over one another, it sounded like they were underwater. It was muddled, loud and almost incomprehensible.

"I'll wait for you and Mignon in my car outside," Beau said in an even voice that she somehow heard clearly over the jumble of noise in front of her.

"Coward." She frowned at him.

"No. I'm just smart, me," he said, his Cajun accent heavy and smooth. He grinned, looking so ridiculously sexy and charming that despite her wanting to remain unmoved by this man whom she knew viewed her as the enemy, Jewell's body reacted. Her insides warmed, making her feel flushed. Then, in easy movements that looked like an agile dance, he kissed Tante Izzy on the cheek, avoided her bright lips that tried to return his affection, flirted and wooed the chaos of women with a wave, wink and a look, then sauntered out of the house.

"Wow. He's good." The room had gone silent a millisecond before she spoke and her words sat in the room like an early morning fog.

"I think she's sweet on our Beau," said the tall, fifty-plus-year-old woman standing next to Ruby with the short brown hair, wearing the blue maxi dress.

"Are they dating?" The other woman whom Jewell didn't know and who appeared to be in her middle sixties looked at Ruby for an answer to her question.

"Of course not. Don't be silly. He's just hanging out with her for other reasons," Ruby answered. It shouldn't matter, but her response hurt. The ladies seemed satisfied with Ruby's answer and began speaking at the same time again. This time Jewell understood some of what they were saying. They were there to hire her to purge their houses, attics and garages. They wanted to have garage sales, too.

She held up her hand. "Ladies." Their voices lowered. "Ladies," she repeated and they quieted. "I would love to discuss working for the three of you. Please call me, so we can make an appointment to discuss your jobs."

"Me first," Ruby said. "You know I asked first, Jewell."

Five minutes later she was in Beau's car without Mimi. Tante Izzy, Ruby, and the other two ladies she now knew were Pearl and Beth, were taking Mimi with them to the St. Anthony's bible study and the late afternoon potluck social afterward.

"How did you get out of going to bible study?" Beau asked, driving away from the house.

"If you had hung around and not hid in the kitchen, you'd know that I told them that if I went with them, I would never have time to get to their jobs." She smiled. "They practically pushed me out of the house."

He laughed. "Good one."

"I'm smart like dat, me," she said, mimicking the Cajun accent he'd laid on her earlier.

"Dat you are, *chère*."

She rested her head against the back of the seat. When they were joking with one another like this, she really enjoyed his company. It was nice to be with someone her age...some who had a good sense of humor and quick wit.

"I got an idea when I was talking to your cousins, Pearl, Beth and Ruby about bible study," she said, closing the vent blasting cold air on her. "I had mentioned it earlier in the attic as one of our research options. I think it should be a priority. I need to look for the original Bienvenu family bible. The one that Martine's name is in."

"How do you know Aguste had the family bible, and that Martine's name is in it?" He lowered the fan speed on the car air conditioning. The man didn't miss anything. He observed her every movement and he stayed focus on the conversation. It was both admirable and disconcerting.

"I don't know for sure," she responded, looking at the acres of sugar cane fields along the roadside. "I'm hypothesizing based on what was usual and customary for the French people who lived on Louisiana plantations of that time." This felt right. This felt comfortable. This was what she understood. "Even most nonreligious families owned a family bible. That's because the major selling pitch by door-to-door bible salesmen was that it could be used for the "records" or "register" section, which is usually located in the center or between the Old and New Testaments."

"Good marketing by the publishers."

"Yes, it sold a lot of bibles, but it actually did serve a need. When the bibles were purchased or received as a gift, these special pages were blank. It represented such hope and anticipation for young families who couldn't wait to use pen and ink to fill the lines with names, dates of births, marriages and even deaths. It recorded their lives. Some family record keepers put in other notations of important family events or included slips of papers or noteworthy certificates."

"If our family has one, it hasn't been pulled out with the old photos of holiday gatherings. I've never seen, nor heard, about a Bienvenu family bible. Which makes me think it doesn't exist."

"Well, I've heard of some families displaying their bibles or sharing it at family gatherings, but mostly I heard of the modern families securing it in safety deposit boxes or special places. It depends on the family or who actually has possession of it."

"That is the question for the Bienvenus, I guess." He smiled. "I'll call around and ask if anyone has Aguste François Bienvenu's bible. That will create a stir in the family, no doubt." She laughed softly. "What does this bible look like?"

"I would guess it'd be pretty typical of the ones I've seen, since the publishers didn't produce a big variety of bibles. It would be a large, heavy, black leather-covered book. Have you seen something that looks like that around the plantation?

He shook his head. "I think I would remember seeing that. There are a few possibilities as to who has it if it wasn't thrown out with the trash by Elli's Aunt Rosa or someone who lived in the plantation and didn't realize the value of it."

Jewell shivered. "God, I hope not."

"It could be packed away somewhere in the plantation, maybe been given to a family member who asked Ben's father for it, or maybe Ben's mother, Helen, has it." He sat silently a moment. "Of course, maybe the obvious person has it. Maybe Aguste's youngest child has it."

"Tante Izzy."

Beau slammed on the brakes. "No time like the present to find out." Before the dust had settled around the car, they were turned around heading back to the house, and Tante Izzy's bright pink pickup truck appeared on the road in front of them.

"Oh, good. There she is." Jewell smiled, clasping her hands. Her excitement quickly faded. She didn't look like she was slowing down. Her heart began to race. "She's traveling awfully fast." The truck hit a bump, lifted and came back down with the bottom hitting the road. She kept coming head-on toward them. "Beau. I don't think she sees us." He blew his horn. She blew hers back at him. She didn't slow down. He moved to the side of the road and stopped just as she whizzed past him without a glance in their direction.

"Crazy old woman," Beau mumbled, his face pinched and his cheeks red.

"Oh, my God, her eyes are barely above the top of the steering wheel," Jewell said, looking behind them where she had driven past them. "Can she even see to drive? She's like a child-size adult." She looked at Beau. His jaw was clenched, the muscle straining. "Your family seriously needs to evaluate your aunt's driving privileges." Her mouth fell open. "*Mon Dieu*, Mimi is in that speed demon's truck. Go stop them!" she shouted in French.

"I don't know what the hell you said," he shouted back, turning the car around and heading back to the main road. "Relax. She doesn't drive that way on the main roads. Just on her own property."

"That does not make me feel any better. There's a huge ditch on the side of this road." She looked at him. "You don't look like that excuse makes you feel any better either."

"Not a ditch. A bayou."

"That is not a bayou. It's too small and dry to be a bayou."

"That's Little Bayou Avril. It has water in it in April. The spring. I'm not going to argue about this with you now." Beau turned onto the highway. He hit the gas pedal and the sports car went from 0 to 70 in seconds, feeling as smooth and gradual as if they were just on a leisurely Sunday drive. "See. There she is. She's driving much slower."

"She's stopped at a red light!" She opened her door and started to get out, but the light changed and Tante Izzy took off in a jerky acceleration. "Go. Go. Go." Jewell shouted to Beau, closing her door.

"I'm going. Calm down."

Jewell strained to look inside the truck, past the gun rack in the rear window. "Your family should consider evaluating her gun privileges, too. Oh, my word. Is that Mimi trying to take the rifle out of the rack?"

"Looks like Ruby's stopping her. Oh, wait. That's cousin Pearl. I see her blue dress and dark hair."

Tante Izzy reached the next red traffic light and slammed on the brake, stopping in the middle of the intersection. Jewell jumped out and raced to the truck. She knocked on the driver's window and opened the door. "Mimi, leave that gun alone," she said in French. Then she began speaking in English. "Ruby, would you mind climbing into the backseat with her and sitting on Mimi's hands?"

Ruby answered 'yes' in Cajun French, opened the passenger door and got into the backseat, shoving and pushing on the other ladies who were protesting how tight it was. Pearl climbed out of the truck and walked to Beau's car and climbed in. Beau got out of his car and walked toward the truck.

"Tante Izzy, put this truck in park...Please." Jewell continued in French. "I'm driving."

"You sound upset. Do you need a ride? Did Beau kick you out his car?" Tante Izzy looked out the window at Beau, who was approaching her truck. "He looks upset too."

"I think it's because you were driving like a wild woman," Ruby said from the backseat. "You scared me to death."

Tante Izzy harrumphed. "You don't look dead to me." She put the truck in park. "I just didn't want to be late for bible study, dat's all."

"I think you should let Jewell drive," Ruby said, looking at Beau, who was standing next to Jewell. "Tell her, Beau. She'll listen to you. All women do."

"My Jewell is a good driver," Mignon interrupted. "She never had a wreck a day in her life."

"You can't say the same thing, Tante Izzy," said Beth.

"Jewell, you drive my car," Beau said, patting Tante Izzy on the shoulder. "You don't mind if I drive your truck and let these ladies calm down a bit."

"I can't sit on her hands, Jewell," Ruby shouted. "Her big ol' rings are cutting into my derrière. It hurts. I'll be so embarrassed if I have to go the ER and get stitches in my *fesse*."

"Stitches?" Jewell laughed, and lowered her voice. "Just don't let her touch the rifle. She can't be trusted with firearms." She looked at Beau. "Thanks for offering to drive Tante Izzy's truck but I think I should stay with Mimi."

Beau ran his hand through his hair, looked at Mimi staring at the rifle in the rack. "Take her into my car, away from the temptation."

"If she goes in you car, Beau, I go, too. I'm takin' care of her. She is my responsibility." Tante Izzy insisted.

"Okay. *Allons*." Jewell motioned for them to get out of the truck. Tante Izzy, Ruby and Mimi slid, grunted, waddled, and pushed their way out of the truck into the middle of the intersection.

Beau jumped into action, directing what little traffic that came by safely around them. He joked with the people in the cars, too, diffusing what definitely could've been a really dangerous and embarrassing situation, especially when Mimi and Tante Izzy started arguing in French over who would sit in the front seat. While they argued, Beau moved Tante Izzy's truck to the side of the road next to his car. When he walked back to his car, Pearl had settled the argument over riding "shotgun" by telling them that she was not getting out of the front seat of the fancy two-door car. She just wasn't doing it.

Pearl leaned her tall body forward and folded her long legs up against the dashboard as Beau tilted the seat as far forward as he could so Tante Izzy could climb into the back. It wasn't working. Tante Izzy was small but not agile enough to maneuver into the small space.

"This isn't going to work," Jewell said, looking at the pink truck and Beth, who was texting inside of it. No doubt she was already telling all of Cane what a scene they created in the middle of the highway.

"I've got this, Boots." Beau grinned his sexy grin, put down the convertible top, and lifted his petite aunt into his arms, carefully tucking her pink cotton dress tightly against her legs. "How you doing, darlin'?"

"I feel like a young bride," she laughed, as he placed her into the backseat.

Jewell looked at Mimi. At nearly 180 pounds, she was going to have to get her in the car another way. "We really need to let Mimi sit in the front," Jewell said to Pearl, who immediately blew out a heavy breath and got out of the car. But when Jewell turned to help her grand-mère into the car, she had her arms lifted up to Beau. He bent over, picked her up, his arms beneath her knees and shoulders, and placed her in the backseat like she was a young child.

"There you go, princess. You're in your chariot." Jewell's heart swelled seeing how kind he was to her grand-mère.

"Now that we got this all settled," Pearl said, sliding into the front seat of the BMW, "can we get to our bible study?"

"Be careful drivin' my truck," Tante Izzy called to Beau as he started to walk away. "Don't you drive too fast or take a turn too sharp. I got some bouillé in a pot on da floor up front. It's my turn to bring dessert for da potluck."

Tante Izzy touched Jewell on the shoulder once she got in the car and started it. She glanced at her.

"I don't understand," she said. "Why did you stop me in da middle of da highway?"

Jewell pulled behind Beau as he led the way to the church. "I, uh..." She didn't want to tell her that she'd stopped her because she was scared out of her mind by the way she was driving. She'd had that awful conversation with Mimi, the one that involved telling her she didn't have the ability to drive safely any longer. She would let Tante Izzy's family have that heart-to-heart with her when they felt the time was right...which would probably be soon. She could tell her the truth, though, about why they started to go after her in the first place. "I wanted to ask you about the Bienvenu family bible. The one that your mother and father had."

"Oh, you mean da one I have in da truck?" She pointed to her pink pickup truck. "I use it for bible study."

"That's great! Are the family births recorded in it?"

"Births, marriages, deaths...my grand-pépère François gave it to my papa and his first wife when dey got married. My momma found it a few months after she married my papa. She was da one who recorded his first wife's death in da bible and every birth and death after dat until she died."

"We have a family bible from our mother," Pearl said. "My sister, Beth, has it."

"Are you a Bienvenu?" Jewell asked, wondering where in the generations Pearl's bible began. Did she copy the earlier dates and record it in her bible as many families did?

"Yes and no. Beth and I are Cheramies. We married Bienvenu brothers."

"Sisters married brothers," Tante Izzy clarified. "Dere husbands' grandfather was Aguste's second cousin. He came to America to work on the plantation. He came before I was born, but died when I was a little girl. He had t'ree sons. Dey are not all in my family bible. My brothers are and some of the children."

There were so many Bienvenu heirs today, but she knew from her research there were only Tante Izzy and the families of Ben and Beau that were from the same branch as the original plantation owner.

And Martine.

Jewell was anxious to look at the recorded births to see if there was another name or notation that might have been overlooked or not noted anywhere else in her research.

"My momma has a family bible, *ma sucrée*," Mimi said.

"You never mentioned it before when I was doing research on our family history and couldn't find anything. I had even asked you if you had any documentation, including a bible." Jewell wasn't sure if Mimi was claiming to have a bible now because she wanted to be part of the conversation or if there was truth in her statement. It was plausible there was a family bible, but why had she told her there wasn't one all those years ago? "Where is it?"

"Momma keeps it in the chest at the foot of her bed."

Was it an old memory or a memory of someone else's discussion? "What color was the bible?"

"Black leather with purple velvet."

"Unusual." Not something someone of their class would've had, if it was even manufactured. A custom-made cover could have those details. "I would love to see it." Jewell would have to question her more about it later, before trying to formulate some conclusions.

"I want to see it too," Tante Izzy said.

"Me too," Mimi repeated.

"Don't you have it?" Tante Izzy looked at Mimi.

Jewell glanced at her grand-mère in the rearview mirror, trying to gauge if she was truly present in their conversation. Her eyes looked bright, clear, and focused. "I gave it to Praline."

Why in the world had she done that? Her mother would never appreciate the sentimental and historical value of the family bible.

"Who is Praline?"

"My mother."

Pearl looked at Jewell. "Your grandmother named her daughter after a famous stripper?"

"*Mais, non,*" Mimi answered, not giving Jewell a chance to deflect the question. "Praline is my daughter."

Pearl smiled. "My momma had dementia, too. I know how confused it makes them."

Jewell sighed. She couldn't falsely blame Mimi to save herself embarrassment. "Mimi isn't confused," she said, making sure her voice held no apology or excuses. "Praline, the famous stripper, is my mother."

Pearl's eyes widened. She gasped, but immediately closed her mouth.

"Son of a gun," Tante Izzy shouted. "Do you t'ink she'll teach me how to pole dance? I always wants to learn dat."

"Oh, for God's sake, Tante Izzy," Pearl gasped. "Look, there's the church."

The blinker started flashing on Tante Izzy's truck in front of them, saving Jewell from answering Tante Izzy, who was now chattering how she could use Mimi's steady cane to learn to pole dance instead of a real fireman's type pole because it was more her height. She only paused in her excited description to make the customary Catholic sign of the cross as they passed in front of St. Anthony's Church to turn into the shell parking lot next to it. Mimi and Pearl had also automatically crossed themselves without thought.

Jewell parked behind Beau and immediately got out of the car and away from the pole-dancing conversation. Beau climbed out of the truck that looked an impossible neon pink in the bright afternoon sunlight. Masculine and totally comfortable in his own skin, he could have been exiting a black monster truck, the way he walked with confidence and ease, she thought, watching him close the door behind Ruby before walking over to their car.

"Enjoy the smooth drive in my hot ride?" he asked, grinning.

"Jewell's stripper momma is goin' to teach me to pole dance," Tante Izzy announced to him as he helped her out of the car. "You wants to learn too, Mignon?"

She nodded. "Yes, I do." She looked up at Beau, who was now helping her out of the car. "You're a nice man."

"Your momma is a stripper?" Ruby asked from where she'd walked up near the car.

"Not just any stripper," Pearl said, coming around the car, anxious to share what she knew. "She's the infamous Miss Praline from Bourbon Street."

"She still has her figure," Beth added. "How does she look like a twenty-six-year-old?"

"Must be plastic surgery," Pearl chimed in, not sounding mean-spirited. "Maybe she'll share the doctor's name with us. I'd like to look twenty-six again."

"He'd have to be God to get you looking twenty-six, Pearl," Beth told her. "Maybe you can look fifty-six."

"Do you think Praline would come to Cane for a benefit to raise money for the church?" Ruby asked Jewell. "I don't think Father Mark will mind that she's a stripper, being she's so famous and all."

"Sister Isabelle will," Pearl said, *tsking*. "That's for sure."

"Oh, *mon Dieu*." Tante Izzy rolled her eyes. "You always trying to get a celebrity for some kind of benefit, Ruby." She turned to Jewell. "She almost got George Clooney to come one time. But Elli didn't know him."

"She knew his stylist," Ruby added, as if that explained what the heck they were talking about. Jewell was getting dizzy trying to follow the conversation. She was just glad it had moved off her mother.

"Do you think Miss Praline would come judge the quilt contest at the Downtown Cane City Festival?" Ruby asked. So much for moving off her mother. Jewell shrugged.

"Tell your mother that if she wants to convert, she is more than welcome at our bible study," Pearl offered.

"Convert to what?" Tante Izzy asked. "She's Catholic like you and Mignon, right? Or is she Hindu or somet'in'? Hmm." She thumped the side of her chin with her thin, bent arthritic fingers. "Come to think of it. I did saw her in a TV ad one time doin' yoga." She looked at Pearl. "Yoga ain't as good for the leg muscles as pole dancin'. Right, Jewell? Pole dancin' is better."

Jewell looked at Beau for guidance in how to answer his aunt or what to say to his cousins, whose conversation had run amok. He was laughing. He was actually laughing.

While she was sinking in red-faced misery, he was having a grand time. She shoved his arm hard. He stumbled a step.

"You see Mignon and these ladies safely inside. I'm going back to work at the barn." Where she could make sense of the world.

She jumped in his car, ready to make a quick exit, but saw Mimi frowning at her.

"Do you want to come with me, Mimi?" she asked in French.

"No, *ma sucrée*. I'm having the time of my life. I'm going to learn to pole dance at bible study," she answered speaking French.

Jewell's mouth fell open. Never a dull moment...

As she turned to tell Ruby to call her when she was ready for her to pick up Mimi, she saw Ruby and Pearl flank each side of her grand-mère and help her walk toward the church. She heard Pearl speaking to her, offering her a walker to use. She'd done it in a way that wouldn't bruise Mimi's pride. Jewell felt a rush of emotion and relief. Maybe these women could finally convince her that it was time to give up the cane and use the walker.

"It's one of those royal blue fashion models with a pretty sky blue seat. That chair is really special, Mignon. You'll feel like you have your very own personal chair with you whenever you need it."

"And it has a nice basket," Ruby added. "It's perfect for shopping at the estate sales you go to with Jewell. Think about how many more pretty things you can buy if you have that basket." She leaned forward and looked at Pearl. "I think I want one, too. You don't happen to have a second one at your house for me, do you?"

"No, just the one," Pearl said.

"Well, you can't have mine," Mimi snapped.

Jewell's throat was tight with emotion as she waited for Ruby to finish speaking to Beau.

"Go on," she said to him. "We're fine. I called my better half to come get us. Big John is happy to do it."

"Thanks, Ruby." Beau climbed into Tante Izzy's truck.

Jewell started the car and took in a deep fortifying breath. It was going to be okay. Mimi was making progress. She would get around better with a walker. She enjoyed socializing.

"You see that work, work, work ethic," Jewell heard Mimi tell the ladies escorting her. "She gets that from me and her momma."

"What about her daddy?" Ruby asked. "Was he a hard worker too?" Instead of driving off, Jewell hesitated to hear what Mimi would say.

"No, he was a lazy good-for-nothing," she began, speaking loud and clear. "He was a rich son of a bitch who never worked a day in his life."

Pain shot into Jewell's chest and her knees turned to rubber. Mimi *had* known who her biological father was when she'd sworn to her over the years that she did not.

Mimi had lied to her.

Jewell knew that as certainly as she knew the cloudless sky above her was blue. Mimi's admission hadn't been the statement of a confused woman. There was too much heat behind her words, emotion. Reality. If anything, it was the unguarded words of a woman whose dementia had stolen her ability to keep secrets.

Mimi had lied to her, all these years.

When Jewell was five, Mimi told her she didn't know who he was. She repeated the same thing again when Jewell had asked her directly about his identity when she was thirteen and again while researching their family ancestry in grad school. Other than those three times, they had never spoken of him.

Although it didn't feel true, Jewell wondered if Mimi had actually discovered her biological father's identity later. Maybe she hadn't lied at the time of their heart-baring conversations.

No. Dear God, no. Mimi knew. She'd always known. It hurt so much to learn that the one person whom she'd thought had always been honest and truthful with her was not.

Jewell gasped, trying to find her next breath. Her world had just tilted.

Her foot slipped off the brake, onto the gas pedal, and she jerked forward in a screeching acceleration. She pounded hard on the brake, but it was too late. Beau's beautiful, clean, sleek, expensive, once-perfect sports car was perfect no more as she rear-ended Tante Izzy's solid old neon pink truck.

Chapter

11

"Da car is on fire!" Tante Izzy shouted from somewhere not too far away from where Jewell remained in the wrecked car.

Oh, my God. Fire.

Smoke filled the cab. Jewell shoved at the deflated airbag. She twisted to unbuckle the seatbelt. It was locked so tight across her chest she could hardly move.

"There's so much smoke, I can't see Jewell!" Pearl screamed from outside the car. Jewell knew she had to get out right away, but her hands shook. Fear made her fingers clumsy. *Hurry. Hurry. Hurry.* The red tab on the seatbelt was right there, but she couldn't depress the button to release the belt.

"Someone call nine-one-one! Get out of the car, Jewell!" She heard Ruby scream. "Hurry!"

The driver-side door flew open; a heavy arm reached across her body and unfastened the seat belt. With watery eyes Jewell looked up through the smoke. "Beau." She wrapped her arms around his neck. "Fire. Help."

"No fire, *chère*. It's not smoke. It's the powder from the airbag deploying. Relax. I got you."

She rested her head against his chest, smelling his clean, warm scent. Even though she was shaking all over, she felt safe in his arms. Tears welled, blurring her vision. She cried for the loss of her perfect, honest, grand-mère. She felt she'd discovered that there was no Santa Claus all over again. And she'd crashed into this sad place using Beau's beautiful car.

"Your car," she said, her voice barely a whisper. She'd thought she'd hit the dry, empty bottom of her financial barrel and was now finally starting to refill it. But God had a wicked sense of humor. She'd have to sell her organs to pay for this damage. "I'm sorry. Oh, God. I'm sorry. I wrecked your beautiful car."

"It's okay." She tried to get out of the car but he stopped her. "Hang on. Relax." He eased back, squatted next to her. "Are you hurt?" His voice was calm, but his eyes were intense, studying her eyes before examining her body.

"I'm fine." Except for the emotion clogging her throat and making it hard to breathe. "I've got to tell Mimi I'm not hurt." Still she thought of her frail grand-mère. She couldn't be angry with her. Disappointed. Hurt. Yes, those things, but Mimi was too childlike for Jewell to be angry. "She'll be frantic."

"She knows you're okay. Ruby is with her." He stared hard into her eyes as she shifted to try to get out again. He shook his head. "I know you want out, but we need to wait for the paramedics to make sure you're okay before you move around. It's safer to stay still and in place." His eyes softened. "And since you know there is definitely not a fire and the airbag powder is settling, it's all good."

"All good? Really? Have you seen your car?" Her voice caught. She realized she needed to see his car. She tried to get out once more, but Beau stopped her. "I'm okay." The damage must be bad for him to be so concerned about her injuries, she realized. Oh, God. She started to speak, but had to clear her throat to get the words past the tightness in her throat. "I'm really sorry, Beau."

He shrugged. "Are you sure you're not hurting anywhere? Any pains in your chest from the seatbelt or airbag?" He stood, looked her over, running his hands over her arms. "Any pain at all?" He touched both sides of her ribs.

She lifted her hands to his face. His neck. "Are you hurt? How do you feel?"

"I was in Izzy's truck, remember? It's built like a steel tank." He covered her hand with his, and then removed it. She felt his warmth one moment, a chill the next.

"Thank God, the ladies got out of both vehicles before the accident." She bit her bottom lip, trying to keep herself from crying. "I'm sorry, Beau."

"Jewell, you didn't answer me," he said, sounding concerned. "Do you feel any pain anywhere? Is your vision blurred? Answer me, damn it."

She pressed her hand to her chest. "A little sore here, but nothing much. Just what you'd expect. Nothing feels broken." She lifted her hand to her left cheek. "This hurts here a little." He lifted her chin and studied her face, eyes serious.

"Looks like you have a bruise forming on your cheekbone. Probably where the airbag hit you when it deployed." He ran his thumb gently over it. "How bad does it hurt? Nothing looks broken. It's not swollen. Just discolored a little. We still need to get you checked out."

She touched the spot. Shook her head. Getting it checked sounded expensive. Unnecessary. "It's not broken," she didn't think it was anyway. Besides, Jewell wondered a little hysterically, what could be done for a broken face? A cheek splint?

Beau squatted next to her, again. He patted her reassuringly on the thigh as he looked at her with a tenderness she'd never before seen in his eyes. Was she that transparent? God, she hated looking exactly as she felt—weak, overwhelmed and upset. So she smiled, stiffened her spine and tried to sit straighter.

"I'm uninjured," she said, firming up her voice and looking into his beautiful green eyes. "I'm fit as a fiddle. See?" She did a few bicep curls. He grinned. "I get that waiting for the paramedics is textbook...but not necessary. Really. I want to get out of the car." She shoved hard against his shoulder, throwing him off balance, and he had to stand to keep from falling. She took the opportunity to climb out of the car. The full force of the sunlight in the cloudless day hit her in the eyes after being in the shade of the interior of the car. Black dots danced through her vision as her knees buckled. She reached for the door, trying to find her equilibrium, but Beau grabbed her around the waist before her hands found the door. He lifted her and cradled her in his arms.

"Stubborn woman."

"I'm fine, Beau." She blinked, and then shaded her eyes with her hand. The spots were still there. "Really. I can walk."

"Yeah. I know. Fit as a fiddle." He was frowning. He was stubborn too. She didn't want to make a scene and argue with him in the middle of the parking lot when she knew he would win this battle. Besides, she wasn't entirely certain her shaky legs could hold her, not yet. Not that she'd admit that to him.

He carried her toward the church. Jewell tried to look at the damage to the car as they passed the front of it, but people were gathered around it and she couldn't see past them. She smelled oil, or something like it. Did some mechanical fluid leak from the car?

Dear Lord, how bad was it? Bad enough for people to gawk? And what about Tante Izzy's truck? He said it was built like a tank, but there had to be damages, right? She'd have to pay for the damage to that too.

She only had the minimal required state liability insurance. It wouldn't pay for this. Even if it would, filing a claim would raise her rates. She couldn't afford that. This would have to come out of pocket.

Beau placed her on a bench under an oak tree that was positioned along the walkway near the parking lot. The shade from the tree made it a few degrees cooler, but that certainly had nothing to do with why she was trembling. The realization of what she'd done and the ramifications of it made her a physical wreck. They weren't very far from the church entrance, and she considered running inside and prostrating herself before the Holy Tabernacle, begging God for mercy.

She didn't have time to make the dash inside because she spotted Mimi. She was standing six feet away, holding onto Ruby, crying. "Mimi," she called to her, waving her over.

"Ma sucrée" she sniffed, her eyes red-rimmed and wet with tears. Her lined mouth was in a deep frown. "Are you hurt?" she asked when she neared her.

Jewell's heart broke. Mimi must've been so worried, frightened. Ruby was kind and attentive to her, but she obviously wasn't able to console her. Jewell understood why. Mimi might be confused about a lot of things, but she was always aware of how much she depended on her. To think something bad had happened to the one person who took care of her, that saw to her needs, that was her companion, had to be terrifying.

"I'm fine, Mimi. I'm not hurt at all." She smiled, tried to get up to go to her, but Beau squeezed both of her shoulders to keep her seated. He shook his head.

"Come sit next to her, Mignon," he said, before Jewell could tell him where to get off. Then, to her surprise, he repeated for Mimi to come sit in Cajun French. *"Assez-vous s'il vous plait."* His voice was calm, kind. He looked at Jewell. "Don't worry, Boots. I don't speak French. That's one of the few phrases I know. Besides the cuss words."

"You heard him?" Mimi asked Jewell. "He *vous'ed* me instead of *tu'ing* me. He's so respectful and nice. He must really like me. "

"I do," Beau said without hesitation. "How can I not?"

Ruby helped Mimi sit next to Jewell who grabbed her hand. Mimi rested her head on Jewell's shoulder, receiving as much comfort as she gave. Mimi's familiar scent, compounded with her favorite drugstore face powder and hairspray, reminded Jewell of home and family. It no longer mattered that Mimi had known who her father was. Her not telling her or denying knowing must've been done because she was trying to protect her from a father who hadn't cared. He and his family hadn't wanted to bring his child into their fold. Mimi brought her daughter's illegitimate child into hers, though. That was reason enough to deny knowing her jerk sperm donor.

"I thought you were dead," Mimi said, tears rolling silently down her cheek. "I don't know what I'd do without you."

Jewell sucked in a harsh breath. Fought back the tears. "It's just a fender-bender, Mimi." She stroked her hand, hoping what she said was true. "I'm good. I'm..."

"Fit as a fiddle," Beau said, interrupting Jewell and making her laugh. Despite not knowing how she'd pay for the damages to Beau's car and having her distraught Mimi clinging to her, she actually was laughing a real genuine, heartfelt laugh. A laugh she was certain bordered on hysteria, judging from the odd breaths mixed in.

"*Mais*, is she laughin' or havin' a seizure?" Tante Izzy said, walking up to the bench. "I t'ink she got a brain injury."

Mimi looked up at her and smiled. "She's not having a seizure, Izzy. That's how my Jewell laughs when she's happy."

Happy? Oh, dear, Lord. Do my happy and hysterical laughs sound the same? She patted Mimi on the hand. She was smiling now.

Beau knelt in front of her. He ran his hands over her knees and lower limbs again. She knew he was looking for injuries, since she'd collapsed on her shaky knees. She moved her legs out of his reach, but he remained kneeling near her.

"Beau. Is she really all right?" Ruby asked, bending over his shoulder.

"Seems like it." He shrugged, looking at Jewell for confirmation.

She nodded. "I'm good." Mimi rested her head on her shoulder again.

"You look okay, Jewell." Ruby added, still looking worried. "Thank God, you don't have no twisted limbs. Oh, my, you do have a nice shiner on your cheek." She squeezed Beau's shoulder. "The paramedics will tell us for sure. They should be here any minute. We called the ambulance, right away."

"And the fire department when we saw the smoke," Pearl said, looking over Ruby's shoulder. "But then Beth told us that the airbag did that."

"We called the po-lice too." Tante Izzy squeezed in closer to Jewell by using Beau's shoulder as ballast. "And Beth called Father Mark out of the rectory, in case you needed last rites."

A man with a black golf shirt, black slacks, gray hair, and light eyes waved as he walked up to the cluster of Bienvenus encircling Jewell. She finger-waved to him and he waved back.

"Father, no matter what Ruby says about bringing in Miss Praline for a benefit, don't do it," Jewell told him. His brows lifted, but to his credit, he didn't ask her what in the world she was talking about. He probably thought she had a brain injury too.

"I called Jesus, Mary and Joseph," Mimi said, looking up at her. "I called them to protect you in the fire and carry you to safety. Only it was Beau who carried you to safety." She looked at Beau and smiled. She took one of the last three rings off her finger and gave it to him. "Thank you, for saving my grandbaby." Now, Tante Izzy, Ruby and Beau each had one of her special rings.

Ruby sniffed, wiped the tears off her cheek with her sleeve. "That's so sweet...it's enough to send a menopausal woman into sobs," she cried.

Beau accepted the ring with a smile. "She's safe and unharmed now, darlin'." He put the ring on his right pinky. It fit just past the first knuckle. Jewell's heart suddenly felt lighter in her chest as warmth flooded into every pore inside her body.

She looked at Beau, who was listening to her grand-mère talk about the ring, telling him some ridiculous story of how she'd gotten it from a boyfriend who was a New Orleans Saints coach. He was grinning and nodding. Beau was such a nice, kind man. A caring man who respected and loved his family and respected and showed kindness to hers. If only...

If only what, she thought, uncertain where her thoughts were headed, but certain they weren't based in reality. They were based in gratitude, maybe. And only gratitude for a few acts of kindness he'd shown to them. She had to not let her judgment be distorted by how he treated Mimi when he'd just recently accused her and Mimi of scamming his family. Yes, Jewell had to be wise in remembering she had to think as a researcher, using only the facts. The last time she'd let her emotions corrupt her judgment, it left her in big trouble...life changing trouble.

"Tante Izzy says I should call your mother too." Ruby said, whispering to Jewell. "She says she'd want to know her daughter was in a car crash. I tried to discourage her. I told her you're a grown woman who can call her momma if she wants to. It's not like you're incapacitated or in need of a blood transfusion."

Jewell went on full alert. "No. Don't call her. This incident is over. It's not serious." She stood. She had to get away from any more discussion of a mother she'd spoken to only once in five years. She didn't want to explain why she didn't want to call her or hear them try to talk her into contacting her. Beau stood too.

"Where are you going, Boots?" He slipped his arm around her waist. She felt the cool, smooth metal of Mimi's ring on her side. "You should just hang out here for a little bit."

"I need to walk." She looked at Mimi. "You're okay?"

"Yes. I'm fine." Mimi said. "Because you're fine. And Beau will protect you."

Beau gave her side a squeeze.

"Don't let her comment swell that already overindulged ego of yours, Beauregard." Jewell shook her head, feeling both annoyance and relief that he was at her side.

Father Mark, who'd been in a private conversation with Pearl, spoke to Jewell for the first time. "We'll take Mignon into the church hall to have refreshments," he said, sounding friendly, with a heavy Southern, non-Cajun, drawl. The deep lines in his cheeks attested to his being a man who smiled easily, as he was doing now. "I'm glad you're well, Jewell. Nice meeting you." He shook her hand.

"Nice meeting you, too."

"And I'm very grateful that I didn't have to meet you while I was performing your last rites, as Pearl had claimed you needed." He glanced at Pearl with humor in his eyes.

"Well." Pearl threw up her arms. "Better safe than sorry. I didn't want her to spend eternity in purgatory or worse."

"*Ma sucrée* is going straight to heaven." Mimi pointed a crooked finger at Pearl. "She's a good girl. Besides that, I've offered my month of first Friday masses for her—three times—to make sure of it."

Father Mark's smile deepened. "Let's go have some punch and cookies now."

"And my cake and bouillé," Tante Izzy added. "Beth, you got it out my truck like I tole you, right?"

"Yes, ma'am, I did."

"I want some refreshments too," Ruby added, helping Mimi up from the bench. "We'll just have a little bit, though. We don't want to spoil our appetite for the potluck afterward."

"I'm goin' to wait here," Tante Izzy said. "I need to talk to Captain Naquin. He always come to accident scenes in da Hook and Ladder truck. I'll meet y'all right after."

"Beth, stop texting for half a minute," Pearl said as they walked away. "I don't want to pick you up off the ground like I did at the Piggly Wiggly because you're not watching where you're going. I swear, I think you have a texting addiction."

"More likes a gossipin' addiction." Tante Izzy harrumphed, sitting on the bench as Father Mark escorted the other ladies toward the church hall.

"Shall I expect that everyone in Cane will know what an idiot I am for rear-ending a bright pink tank of a truck that you can spot miles down the road?" Jewell motioned to Beth.

"I'd say what happened passed into the Bayou grapevine thirty seconds after the accident." Beau looked toward the street as sirens approached. "Even without the town texter, the cavalry charging in with full sirens blaring would've alerted everyone." A fire truck and ambulance were racing down the highway toward them.

She sighed and he turned her face toward him. He looked like he wanted to say something, but had second thoughts. Her mind couldn't wrap around what it might've been. All she could think about was how she'd crushed his beautiful car. At least she thought she did. Maybe, if she was lucky, the damage was minimal. She'd heard airbags deployed with minimal damage sometimes, right? Her optimism felt thin, though. Might as well take a look at Beau's car and either put herself out of her misery or plunge further into it.

Jewell walked to the front of the car, as the sirens neared. Beau still had his hand around her waist as she saw the damage from the wreck for the first time. The bumper looked like a crumpled sheet of paper. "Oh, God." She looked up at Beau, who was staring at the mangled bumper of his car. He didn't say it, but she could see that it hurt for him to look at his once beautiful sports car. "I'm sorry. So very sorry."

He shrugged. "It's only a car, Jewell. At least Tante Izzy's tank didn't receive one little scratch."

A fire truck pulled up and five firemen rushed toward the car. Tante Izzy raced toward them. The only thing Jewell heard from the distance was her asking if their fire pole was available to rent for someone who was taking pole-dancing lessons.

When the paramedics got out of the ambulance, Beau waved to let them know that Jewell was with him. "Let's let them check you out."

Jewell glanced back at his smashed car as the paramedics came up to her with a stretcher. "I can walk," she said. They allowed her to walk with them to the back of the ambulance, where they had her sit on the stretcher for them to examine her. Jewell answered their questions about aches and pains as Beau stood nearby, leaning on the ambulance's open rear door.

"Don't forget to check her cheek," he told them, sounding annoyed when they seemed more focused on a rash forming on her neck and arms from what they said looked like the typical reaction from the airbag's powder and chemicals.

"We can take you in to get some x-rays and let the doctor in the ER examine you," the dark-haired paramedic who seemed to be in charge said. "Is that okay with you, Miss Duet?"

She and Beau answered at the same time.

"No."

"Yes."

She looked at Beau. "I'm fine. If I feel like my condition gets worse, I'll go in to get medical attention. I'm not stupid, Beau. I'm fully aware that Mimi depends on me, and I will be careful. I appreciate your concern, but this is my decision. Not yours."

Beau shoved his hands in his pockets.

Jewell looked at the car. It was her fault and she was responsible. *Dear God. I will find a way to pay for the repairs and make it right.* Her stomach tightened. How in the world was she going to do that? She was broke, and it was going to cost a fortune to fix his expensive foreign car. Her insurance wouldn't cover it. She had to find a way. Her fault. Her responsibility. No one was loaning her money these days. She couldn't mortgage her house or workshop again. She'd have to take those garage sale jobs the Bienvenus were offering her. She'd clean their attics, their closets, their floors...whatever it took.

Her heart sank further. She'd forget about repairing her former reputation and business. What difference did it really make anyway? With the legal problems still hanging over her head, and the media chomping to report on them, finding work in what she loved and was trained to do was just a dream. She had to be practical. She had to survive...for Mimi. Just get a paycheck. Pay the bills. Stay out of trouble. Take care of Mimi.

"Sure don't make cars like dey used to." Tante Izzy came to the back of the ambulance where Jewell had just been handed a clipboard with a form to sign indicating her refusal to be taken to the hospital. "Looks like you car is totaled, Beau."

He winced. The muscles in his jaw tightened.

"Oh, God. Do you think so?" Jewell sucked in a breath, putting the clipboard down on the stretcher unsigned.

"Probably not," he said. "Depends what damage is behind the bumper. Under the car. The stuff we can't see." He looked at her. She knew she had to be pale. She felt like the blood had drained from her face. "I'm sure it's not that bad. You weren't traveling that fast."

"No, she wasn't." Tante Izzy patted her on the shoulder. "Runnin' into my truck was like hittin' a cement wall, dat's all." She worked her mouth a moment. "I know how much da car meant to you since it was da first time you could afford to pay for one you really liked." She patted him on the hand. "First brand new car you..."

"It's okay, Tante Izzy," he said. His voice a little rough. "I'll get another one. Maybe I'll get a truck like yours next time." He looked at Jewell, and she knew he did so to remind his aunt that she was sitting right there.

"Oh, *mon Dieu.*" She shook her head. "I'm sorry. I didn't t'ink before I talked. I know you feel bad, *ma sucrée.*" She clasped Jewell's hand. "It was just an accident. I didn't mean to make you feel worse."

Jewell nodded. "I know." Tante Izzy kissed her on her bruised cheek.

"You're a good girl." She patted her hand and walked away. "I might talk to da *traiteur* for you."

"What is she talking about?"

"Boots, it's best you learn not to ask or try to figure out everything Tante Izzy says or does." He frowned when she flinched as the paramedic put an icepack on her cheek. "When you know things, she'll pull you in deeper than you want to go."

"Well, I got to get to bible study. Ruby says we are goin' to say a rosary for you at da end, so you won't be too sore tomorrow."

Beau looked at Jewell, then Tante Izzy, before he spoke. "Okay. I'll bite. Why don't you want her to be too sore tomorrow?"

"Well...um...we're hopin' tomorrow you'll take us to meet you momma to see about those pole-dancing lessons and celebrity appearances." She walked away toward the firemen standing at the front of Beau's car.

Jewell looked at Beau and rolled her eyes. "Didn't you just tell me not to ask? That it was better not to know everything that she was up to?"

He walked up to the stretcher, picked up the clipboard to read the form. "Did I say that?" He shrugged. "Okay. I admit it. I'm a sucker for little old ladies."

"So I noticed." She lightly touched the ring still on his pinky. "Thank you for being so kind to Mimi." He looked up from reading the clipboard. "And, me...especially after I killed your car." Tears welled in her eyes. "I'm grateful."

He touched the undamaged side of her face and let his fingers linger in the hair that had come free from her ponytail. "Ah, Boots." He looked at the clipboard. Ripped the page out and tore it up. "Prove to me how grateful you are. Go to the hospital and let a real doctor examine you. Let's make sure you don't have internal injuries from the airbag and seatbelt."

"Beau...I can't. I don't have health insurance." God, she hated admitting that aloud.

"I have insurance. I'll take care of it."

She shook her head. "I can't take..."

"Do it for Mimi if you won't do it for me."

"You go for the jugular." She frowned.

A police officer walked up to them and started asking questions about the accident. When she started to answer, Beau spoke over her. "Hi, Greg. Thanks for stopping by to check on things, but it's all settled. We're all in accordance with state law. There's no *at fault dispute* here. I'll file a self-claim report with my insurance company." His voice was firm but easy. He was not only a man taking charge, he was a lawyer directing things to happen as he wanted it to. "The accident occurred on private property," he began. "Both parties involved have settled amicably. It's me and Tante Izzy. No conflicts there. We don't want an incident report to be filed with the state and put in the system and on our records. Who the hell wants this little thing attached to their license, right? "

"That's fine, Beau, if Tante Izzy says it's okay," he said, looking to where she was talking to the two young firemen.

"Fair enough."

Greg nodded to Jewell and walked toward Tante Izzy.

"Thank you. Once again." Jewell watched Tante Izzy point her crooked finger at Greg and then shoo him away. "I wouldn't have thought to ask the police not to write an accident report."

"An incident report," he corrected. "It's different than an accident report since it's on private property. If the accident occurred on the highway, he wouldn't have had a choice." He smiled. "You're welcome. Now let's get you checked out. I'll drive you to the hospital in Tante Izzy's truck, save you a ride in the ambulance."

***

Jewell and Beau returned to his car from the hospital just over an hour later. She had been surprised that the regional hospital ER in Cane had been able to examine, x-ray, declare she was uninjured and release her so quickly. It wasn't what she was used to in her visits to the busy New Orleans hospitals when she had to bring Mignon in after a fall.

Now, they just had to wait for the wrecker. Beau had offered to call someone to give her a ride back to Sugar Mill so she could rest, but she insisted on staying with him until everything that could be done was done. Beau appreciated her stand-up gesture, but he honestly would've preferred to wait alone so he could take his time to examine the damage and mourn over it. He just couldn't do that in front of Jewell. She looked so damn miserable. Her normally beautiful silky caramel complexion was pale and absent of color, except for the dark circles under her eyes and the purple sand-dollar-sized bruise on her cheek. Her eyes were haunted and tired. Even her usual prideful, yet graceful, posture looked deflated, despite her trying to appear otherwise.

"It's almost three-thirty. Do you think they're just about finished with bible study?"

"I'm sure they're at the post-bible study potluck, now." He grinned. "I need to clear out my car," he told her as he opened the driver's side door. She walked to the passenger side and climbed in, ignoring the white airbag residue that had settled on the seat and all of the surfaces. He started to gather his phone charger, spare sunglasses, and remote to the Sugar Mill gate. "Look inside the glove box and take out everything except the insurance card and car manual."

"I'm surprised you don't have a cousin who could've towed your car to the dealership in New Orleans." Her voice was nonchalant, but he knew what she was really saying. Didn't he have someone who could tow his car for free?

"It needs a special tow truck because of the design of the car. Besides that, I need to follow the warranty documents or I'll negate the warranty on the parts that weren't damaged."

She nodded. "I hate to have to ask you this." She handed him the unused fast food napkins, flashlight, and two pens she'd taken from the glove box. "Insurance isn't the only thing I don't have." She cleared her throat. "I don't have the money to pay for the damages upfront. I intend to pay it, though." She refastened her ponytail. "This is really embarrassing." She looked out the side window, away from him. He felt her humiliation at having to admit that she was less than she wanted to be. He'd been there before. "I've used all my savings on lawyers, reestablishing my business, and day-to-day living. My income is inconsistent, but if things go well, it will be steadier in the near future. I'll have some money then..."

He waited for her to explain further, but she just let the sentence die. He couldn't help wonder if she believed this future income she was counting on would come from Martine's trust. He could ask her where the money would come from, but what good would it do? She wouldn't admit to him that she planned on taking the trust that he was determined to protect. She was too smart for that. He'd just let her talk, give her more rope, see what she'd say and if she hung herself in the process.

She shook her head. "Anyway, I'm only telling you all of this because you have a right to know why I need to set up a payment plan. Are you okay with doing that?" She looked at him, her big brown doe eyes bright and intently waiting for an answer.

"Jewell, I have insurance." He grabbed her hand and squeezed it. It felt cold, thin. Hell, she might not be going after the trust. She might be an innocent who was as desperate as her disarming eyes indicated. He nodded, deciding to trust his instincts for the moment. "I've got this."

"No. It's my fault your car is wrecked. "

"We'll figure it out." He let go of her hand, sensing that he needed to not make a big deal about this when he wanted to insist that she drop the whole thing about paying him anything. He reached into his middle console for his electric razor. "I won't be able to come over tomorrow. I have court." He looked at her bruise. "You need to rest, recover. You're going to be sore."

"No, I won't. The ladies are saying a rosary for me." She smiled. "I'm fine. You heard the ER doctor." She frowned. "I can't spare the time."

"You need to take care of yourself." He blew out a breath, knowing she wouldn't do that. "I'm sorry. I know you want to work in the barn. It can't be avoided. I have court."

"Okay. We have a deal. I'll research the pieces I have cataloged and price them. See if anyone is searching for what we have."

He liked how adaptable she was. He leaned over to look deeper into the center console. The sweet, earthy alluring scent she wore wrapped around him like a sensual dream. She'd said it was bug repellent. Ridiculous. "I think I have everything."

"We don't have everything. We need to get the desk out of the trunk." She smiled when he groaned. "We can put it in the back of Tante Izzy's truck."

"Or in the dumpster." He motioned to the gated area on the other side of the parking lot.

"You're a funny man, Beau Bienvenu."

"I'm a lot of other things, too, *chère*." He smiled and her eyes turned soft and dewy. Her gaze dropped to his mouth. He knew that look. He leaned closer to her. "I'm also a man who's about to kiss a woman with pretty, luscious lips." He moved in but took a moment to enjoy the warmth of her sweet breath on his mouth...and the heady feeling of anticipation.

She wet her lips with a slow slide of her tongue and closed her eyes. She was enjoying the moment of anticipation too. He brushed a light, feather kiss on her lips. Then he sucked on her full bottom lip. She smiled.

"You like that?" He sucked on her bottom lip again, then released it to press his lips fully to hers. He placed a gentle kiss on each corner of her mouth. Her eyes fluttered open, looked at him. Scam artist or not, Beau felt her passion and desire in that long, telling look. He grabbed the back of her neck and claimed her mouth with his.

It was hunger and satiation. It was desire and satisfaction, bare moments apart. Jewell's mouth and tongue moved with his in a harmony that left him knowing that he had to have her. She might be in Cane to take what wasn't hers from his family, but he'd have this woman who turned his blood to liquid fire. He'd have her...and still protect his family.

Jewell pulled away first, laughed softly. "Do you realize we're making out in a wrecked car with a deflated airbag hanging from a busted steering wheel, white powder smeared everywhere around us, in front of a church filled with a dozen bible-studying, rosary-praying parishioners?"

"And the problem is what, Boots?"

She grabbed the front of his shirt and pulled him toward her. "Nothing." She kissed him.

Beau pulled her against him until he felt her large round breasts against his chest.

"Why don't you just confess right now, Mignon Duet? Admit it. You took da salt and pepper shakers from da plantation." Beau heard Tante Izzy's voice and eased away from Jewell. "You sure surprised me when you pulled dem out when we were eatin' after da rosary."

Jewell touched her lips and retied the ponytail that he'd loosened only moments before. She climbed out of the car. Beau opened the trunk and walked to the back of the car.

"She took da salt and pepper shaker from da plantation again," Tante Izzy told Jewell when she was near. "Why does she keep doin' dat?"

Mignon looked angry. "I told you," she said, speaking fast and loud. "Momma wants me to take care of them. It's my job. The shakers are special."

"Yes, but deyz ain't yous," Tante Izzy insisted.

Mignon looked at Jewell, then turned to Tante Izzy. "Neither is this church yours, but you help take care of it."

Tante Izzy frowned. "Harrumph."

Dementia or not, Mignon had made a solid argument for herself.

Beau removed the desk and carried it to the truck. "Is it okay if we put this...desk...in the back of your truck until we can drop it off at Jewell's camper?"

"*Mais,* of course it's okay." She looked at the desk. "Dat looks like trash. If you like dat, Jewell, you're goin' to love da t'ings in my house."

Jewell smiled one of her sexy, closed mouth Mona Lisa smiles and Beau's heart skipped a beat. He rubbed his chest, not sure what in the hell that was about.

"Big John's here to give us a ride," Ruby said, waving to her husband who turned into the parking lot from the highway in his king cab truck. "Pearl and Beth got another ride home, so it's just the three of us riding with Big John. If that's okay with you, Jewell. We're going to go hang out at Tante Izzy's and watch some mindless late afternoon television and rest. We'll bring her home later. Not too late."

Jewell spoke to Mignon on the side to ask her what she wanted to do. When they returned, she told Ruby that her grandmother wanted to stay with them. "Mimi said she's having fun with y'all."

"Great," Ruby said, clapping her hands. She turned to Beau. "Take this." She handed him Tante Izzy's rifle. "Tante Izzy took it from her truck before we went inside because she didn't want the law to give her a hard time about having it in the vehicle."

Beau shook his head. "It's legal. It's not concealed."

"I've got a concealed carry license, anyway," Tante Izzy said, her voice loud and clear.

"Me, too," Mignon said, working her mouth. Beau looked at Jewell for verification.

"She does, but she doesn't have a weapon. I took it from her when we arrived at Sugar Mill."

"You're kidding? She came to Sugar Mill armed?"

"I didn't know she'd found a gun and slipped it in her purse." Jewell said it like it was a reasonable explanation, which it wasn't. "She didn't have any bullets."

"I feel so much better." His sarcasm had all of the gun-toting women rolling their eyes. "And I suppose you have a concealed carry license, too?"

"Of course, silly man."

Ruby threw up her hands and looked at her husband. "Well, I want a concealed carry license too. Why am I the last to get one?" She jammed her hands on her straight hips, making the long canary yellow knit top bunch under her fists. "Let's go, ladies. Climb into Big John's truck."

"Don't worry about your truck, Tante Izzy," Beau called to her as Jewell started to help her and Mignon into Ruby's husband's truck. "I'll get it home to you later."

"Keep it as long as you needs it," she said with a wave of her hand. "I can get rides from da family."

Big John waved to Beau and shouted to him before climbing into the driver's seat. "I'm sorry about your car," he said.

"Thanks." He nodded. "Glad you could come to get the ladies."

Jewell closed the door, folded her arms to her chest, and stepped back as Ruby's husband drove away. Once the truck pulled onto the highway, she turned. Tears were streaming down her cheeks.

Beau rushed over to her. "Jewell? It's okay. Please don't worry about the wreck. I've got it covered."

She shook her head. "It's not that." Her voice was barely a whisper. "Happy tears, Beau. These are happy tears. Look."

She unfolded her arms and handed him the black book she'd been hugging. "Bible," he read on the old, worn leather cover.

"Yes." She clapped her hands, then wiped away a tear, her excitement palpable. "It's the original Aguste François Bienvenu's bible. The man everyone in your family referred to as François. The founder of Sugar Mill Plantation. Tante Izzy just gave it to me."

Chapter

12

Mimi's name wasn't included in the Bienvenu family bible.

Neither was Beau's.

Jewell felt a disappointment for one and a sadness for the other. She hadn't really expected her grand-mère's name to be there, since Mignon Duet hadn't shown up in any Bienvenu family documentation during her research. She did expect to see Beauregard Bienvenu's name. She supposed that was just fanciful optimism. She'd hoped François's brother Emile's branch would've been included all the way until present day.

It was a mild fall day. The sugarcane fields lining the highway stood a dark green, tall and shining in the sunlight. The sounds of the breeze rustling the cane flowed through the open windows and harmonized with the rock music Beau played on his phone. Tante Izzy's truck was so old that her radio only played AM stations in mono. Beau wore dark, designer aviator sunglasses and tapped his hand on the steering wheel to the beat of his music. He looked handsome, masculine, expensive and comfortable in his own skin. He didn't look any better in a fancy European sports car riding with the top down than he did in the old Pepto-Bismol colored truck with the loaded gun rack in the rear window.

Enjoying the feel of the wind blowing in from the windows, she spent the fifteen minutes it took to drive back to Sugar Mill reading through the names and corresponding birthdates listed on the family tree. It began with the man who was born in France and built

Sugar Mill Plantation at the unbelievably young age of twenty-six. His first wife, Marie Brigitte Bissette and their six children were listed next, followed by his second wife, Caroline Cecile Giroux. They had one child together, a boy, who had the same name as his father, Aguste François Bienvenu.

When Jewell came across a separate sheet of paper that had the family tree of Emile, she was excited. Her earlier hopes for him and his descendants to be included were realized. Well, at least partially. Emile's family tree had been handwritten on old thick parchment paper and pasted into the bible. Emile and his wife, Marthe, had a very large family of eight boys and three girls. Ruby, Ronald and their spouses were named in that lineage as were other Bienvenu family members she hadn't met.

She shouldn't have felt so badly that Beau's name wasn't in the bible, since there were others whom she'd recently met that weren't listed either. But she did. She couldn't help but wonder if his name wasn't included because he was adopted and not a blood-related Bienvenu. Somehow, that just didn't ring true. Even though Beau was closer to the root than other cousins who weren't included on the offshoot branches, the omission of his name must've been simply a result of the bible not being updated in a couple of decades...except for the addition of Ben's son Joey, and Elli, when she'd married Ben.

Jewell didn't share that during their drive back to the plantation. She didn't have any new facts to discuss. There weren't any new findings in the bible. As far as she could tell from first glance, the birthdates, marriages, and deaths were the same as she'd discovered in her research of the Bienvenu family.

"I assume by your silence that Mignon isn't listed in the bible," Beau said as he parked in front of her camper and lowered the volume on the music. He looked at her, and she could feel his intense eyes on her, even though she couldn't see them through his dark sunglasses.

"You assume correctly." She opened the door, but didn't get out. "It looks like it hasn't been updated in a long time. If Tante Izzy will allow me, I can do that for her."

"In your spare time, since you have so much of it." Then, he nodded and his expression softened. "I'll talk to her about it. I'm sure she'll be happy for you to do it."

"I'll need her help in gathering the names of the family members. If she doesn't have their birth and marriage dates, I can get that information from public records or from the Catholic diocese."

"I have them."

"All of them? For the whole family?"

He patted the phone in his pants pocket. "Yes. I have them all."

Jewell found that incredibly endearing. "That's remarkable, Beau." She looked closer at him. A faint flush of pink formed on his cheeks, just under the rim of his sunglasses. Was he embarrassed that she knew he cared enough to keep track of his family's births, deaths and marriages?

"Somebody has to remind everyone of important dates. Not everybody is on Facebook."

He grinned, and it made Jewel's stomach do a little flippy thing. It wasn't often she was around a man as good-looking as Beau. Those were the men her mother hung around with. Still, she couldn't help but appreciate what an appealing picture he made with his white teeth, dark hair, angled features, and fashion-magazine sunglasses. Hell, if she could've gotten to her phone without any fuss, she would have considered taking a picture of him.

"I'll e-mail the list to you."

"Great." She climbed out of the truck, holding the bible. "Don't forget to include your birthdate and your brother's." She started to close the door but hesitated. "What's your brother's name?"

"Jackson. Jackson Landon Bienvenu."

"Got it." She tapped the side of her head with her finger. "Memory like a steel trap." She blew out a breath. "And Beau, I'm truly sorry about your car. I feel terrible about it. I hate you having to file your insurance for the damages when it's my fault. Paying your deductible doesn't seem enough. Your rates will go up."

"Jewell, it was an accident. Don't beat yourself up over it. You're the one who is insisting on paying something. I've told you, I've got this covered."

"I'll pay you back. I insist." She closed the door and leaned in the open passenger window.

"Whatever, Jewell."

"Thank you." She didn't move. She felt like saying *thank you* just wasn't enough, but she didn't know what else to say that didn't make her sound so desperate...which of course she was.

She was relieved that he said she didn't need to pay even though she intended to do so. His generosity gave her the extra time she needed. To pay now would've been an additional financial burden that would effectively put her out of business. She had no idea what kind of job she could've gotten to cover expenses and allow her to take care of Mimi, too. The thought was depressing.

His phone dinged with a text. He slipped it from his pocket, slipped off his sunglasses, and looked at it. He frowned, and his eyes seemed to darken.

"Problem?"

"Yeah, you can say that. It's a client whom I'd rather not deal with. He's self-destructing and I can't stop him." He held up his hand. "Hang on a moment. I have to answer him." He put his sunglasses on the seat next to him, then typed a short message. When he was finished, he returned his attention to her. "What's your next move with your investigation?"

"I want to see if I can find the name of the midwife or midwives from around the time when Twinnie was supposed to have been born...and Mimi. I think Tante Izzy or maybe a peer of hers from the community may have that information."

"Even if you do get the name of the midwife who was delivering babies almost ninety years ago, she wouldn't still be alive for you to interview."

"Of course not." Jewell laughed lightly, talking to him through the open passenger window. She glanced over her shoulder toward the beautiful plantation. It stood so stately and quiet on the lush lawn, surrounded by mature green waxy-leaf camellia bushes. The plantation looked so lonely with no one around. Jewell knew that next week, it would be a lively center of activity with the film crew moving around it.

"I'll be looking for the midwives' books," Jewell said, "They often maintained a book or ledger where they kept detailed notes about the births they facilitated for their own record-keeping, education and legacy. I'm sure there were other reasons too. Anyway, it's probably in the possession of a family member."

"Sounds like a long shot to me. Finding a needle in a haystack."

"Yeah. I guess it could be." He was right. She'd come across a few over the years and had studied some in a class she'd taken on plantation life. "No stone unturned. I have to exhaust all potential sources to find information." He nodded. "But first, I have to get going to complete my job for Elli and Ben."

"Speaking of..." Beau smiled, turned off Tante Izzy's truck and opened his door just in time to greet a darling young boy in a Cub Scout uniform running toward him. Ben, Elli, three of their dogs and a boxer puppy she hadn't seen before were racing alongside of him. Jewell figured that as he had the same dark hair and beautiful green eyes as his father and many of the Bienvenus, the thin, handsome boy had to be Joey. "Hey, little dude." Beau tossed the seven-year-old boy over his shoulder and turned in a quick, tight circle.

"Uncle Beau," he giggled. The dogs jumped, tails wagging, as they pawed at Beau's legs. "You're making me dizzy," he laughed. "I like it."

"Of course you do." Beau's grin was huge and infectious. Jewell's bruised cheek hurt from smiling, but she couldn't stop herself.

"So," Beau said, putting him down. "You're leaving for the beach tomorrow?"

"Orange Beach, Alabama." The excited dogs tugged on Joey's pants leg.. "We're going to The Little Zoo That Could to pet the lemurs. And we're going to see the Blue Angels and their planes in Pensacola. It's close." His sentences were running one into the other. "And the fort that's at the beach. I forgot the name. It's old."

"Fort Morgan," Jewell said, smiling. "It's over one hundred and eighty years old. There are several cannons, a dry moat and other things you can explore."

Joey looked at her and smiled, his eyes curious. "Are you my momma's friend from New Orleans?"

Jewell couldn't say why, but hearing him refer to her as Elli's friend touched her. It made her throat feel thick, but not in a bad way. It felt good. Really good.

"Yes, she is," Elli said, filling the silence. "Joey, this is my friend and the best historian in the state of Louisiana, Dr. Jewell Duet." She moved closer to Jewell and lowered her voice. "Are you okay? I heard about the accident?"

Jewell nodded, touching her cheek automatically. "Yes. I'm fine." She wasn't surprised that Elli had already heard of her wrecking Beau's car. She was surprised by the genuine concern in expression. For the second time in minutes, she was touched by Elli's warmth and friendship.

Joey extended his hand to her. "Pleased to meet you."

Jewell's eyes filled with happy tears. "I'm so pleased to meet you, young man."

"Are you a doctor who takes care of sick people or the kind who goes to school a long, long time?" Joey asked. "We just learned about that kind of doctor in school."

"The kind that goes to school for a very long time."

"Did you study forts?"

"Yes. And a lot of other things."

Beau bent down to pet the puppy and take a stick the dog had picked up off the ground. He tossed it out into the yard and all four dogs chased after it. He grinned.

"Time for you to get a dog," Ben told him. Beau's answer was to shake his head and laugh. He tossed a stick that the bloodhound named Doe brought back to him. It wasn't the same stick the puppy had earlier. The Lab mix named Jenny had that one. The adult beagle, which Jewell knew was called BJ, trotted up to Beau dragging a very long, thin, dead branch about as big as she was. It was covered with dried leaves. Beau threw his head back and laughed.

"You've been to Fort Morgan?" Joey asked.

"Yes. I actually excavated a site there and wrote a long report on the artifacts we found. Some are on display at the Fort museum. Others are in a museum in Mobile, Alabama."

"Wow!" He looked at Beau, who was fighting BJ for the ridiculously long branch. "She must be smart like you, Uncle Beau." Joey's eyes widened and his head jerked to his mother and father. "And y'all, too, Mommy and Daddy. Y'all are smart too."

Beau roughed up Joey's hair and laughed. "Yes, indeed. You're a diplomat for sure."

"I don't want to be a dip-lo-ma...I want to be a dog trainer like my dad, Uncle Beau. You know that." He looked at Jewell. The beagle had given up on playing with Beau and had brought the dead tree limb to her. The other dogs decided it was a good idea and joined her. Joey ignored them. This game of theirs must've been commonplace, Jewell figured. The sweet little boy was more interested in the conversation. "Or I want to work dogs for movies."

"Very interesting and honorable professions." She smiled, grabbing an abandoned stick and waving it in front of the pack. When she had their attention, she tossed it into the yard. All of the dogs took off running, leaving the sticks and limbs they had found so important a moment ago.

"Maybe I should be a doctor of dogs. The school kind. Not a vet kind," Joey said, his eyes shining. He moved closer to Jewell and looked at her boots. "I have boots like that, only mine are white shrimp boots with my name written on them with black marker. That way I can tell mine apart from my dad's. We use them to work the dogs on the muddy field."

God, she loved this kid. He was so sweet. Engaging. And it was so endearing how he clearly seemed to like her. She was never around children. She should spend more time with them. Most of the time she was around old ladies, cerebral professors or either eager or apathetic college students. Children were so spirited. Refreshing, really. What a pleasure to be around such unencumbered, curious happiness. It was like breathing fresh air after being closed off in an airless, stuffy room.

"That's an excellent way to tell them apart," she replied, after tossing the stick Doe retrieved, followed by the other three on the ground. "I'll have to remember that trick."

"Well, we better get going before Jewell wears these dogs out and they're too exhausted to walk on their own," Ben smiled. "I don't think Beau and Elli want to carry them to the kennel."

"Ha, ha." Elli swatted her hand at Ben. "I'm ready." She looked at Jewell. "We need to run the rescue dogs through their evening training exercises, finish packing, and get to bed for an early start tomorrow. If you need anything, call me." She touched her own cheek in the spot Jewell's cheek had been bruised, giving her her support without words. "Anything." She looked at Beau. "Make sure our friend recovers from the day," she told him. He nodded. "And, thank you for taking care of Nancy while we're gone. I know the kennel staff could do it, but I think she needs extra love and attention. She's a baby and hasn't been away from her momma that long."

Beau shrugged. "I will *not* be her substitute momma." He laughed. "But I'll take good care of her." He looked at Ben. "She's housebroken, right?"

"I told you she was." He shook his head, picked up the boxer puppy and handed her to Beau. "Her food, bowl, leash and bed are all in a duffle on my desk at the kennel. There's a carrier there too. I recommend if you have to leave her for a little while, you put her in it."

The puppy gave Beau a sweet lick under his chin. He looked at the friendly animal who was staring at him with such adoration with her big brown button eyes. "Yeah, I know, you're cute, but I'm not a pushover."

Elli started laughing. "That's a funny one."

"Hey..." He frowned, and Jewell thought he actually sounded offended.

"Let's go." Ben whistled for the dogs to heel. "Jewell, if you need anything with the project in the barn, Beau will help you." He looked at Beau and waited for him to nod. "Good luck."

Elli hugged Beau. "Thank you for taking care of the movie crew and...Jewell."

"We'll get back a few days after the crew arrives," she told Jewell. "I appreciate your help." She hugged her so tightly that Jewell felt the sincerity and heart of it in her bones.

Jewell held on to her a few seconds longer when Elli let go to leave. "Thank you for everything."

Suddenly, both women were hit around the legs, causing them to stumble. Thin, small arms wrapped around them. "Group hug," Joey shouted, giggling. "Come on, Uncle Beau. Daddy. It's a group hug." Beau and Ben mumbled something Jewell couldn't understand, but they soon had moved into the hug. Ben stood behind his wife, giving her a kiss on the back of her neck. Beau carried Nancy into the group hug with him as he moved to stand behind Jewell. His clean, earthy scent enveloped her as his warm, hard body leaned against her back. She felt strength in the ridges of his muscles as one of his arms came around her shoulders with a tenderness she'd felt earlier, in the attic. He rested his cheek against hers, turning his face a little to take in a deep breath.

"You smell so damn good, *chère,*" he whispered for only her to hear, his breath raising goose bumps on her flesh. "You cannot possibly smell like flippin' bug spray."

"Uncle Beau, your phone is dinging."

Beau reached into his pants to grab the phone, but remained standing solid and close to Jewell. Joey moved out of the group hug first. Jewell wanted to scoop Joey back into the fold, but Ben and Elli were already moving on, his arm still around his wife's waist. Elli waved good-bye to Jewell and called Joey to come along with them.

Joey picked up the puppy after Beau put her down, and handed her to Jewell before he rushed off, moving as children do, much like the dogs, in quick, awkward movements. He tripped over an oyster shell, laughed, and regained his balance by grabbing hold of the tall brown bloodhound. Then, without missing a step in what looked like an orchestrated dance, he shouted over his shoulder. "Bye, Nancy. Bye, Dr. Jewell. Bye, Uncle Beau."

Jewell waved good-bye.

She watched until Ben drove away. The dogs, with their tongues hanging out of the sides of their mouths, sat contentedly in the bed of the truck. Jewell looked down at her hand and smiled. What a silly person she was. She'd been waving to the dogs. Nancy licked her hand.

Beau took a step back, texting on his phone. Jewell turned to face him. When he hit send, he glanced at her and exhaled. He reached over and scratched Nancy behind the ears. "Sorry. Had to answer a persistent client." He lightly touched her bruised cheek. "You should ice that."

"I left the icepack the ER nurse gave me in Izzy's truck." She reached for her cheek to see if it felt like it had swollen more; he looked so concerned. He reached for her cheek at the same time and their hands touched. Electricity jolted through Jewell straight to her heart, making it race as if she'd been hit with defibrillator paddles. She dared to look at him. Had he felt the same fast, unexpected current race through his body?

"I really don't know what the hell is going on between us," he said, his voice deeper than she'd ever heard it before. His light eyes had darkened to a very sexy jade.

So he had felt it too.

"I've been attracted to women before, but, damn, there is something preternatural between us." He lifted her chin, stared into her eyes. "What kind of voodoo is this, Jewell? It's like I have no say in this. Another force seems to control my body when I'm near you." He leaned in closer to her. Nancy rested her head on his chest but remained in Jewell's arms. "It seems to be getting stronger the more time I spend with you. I think there's only one way to stop it."

"Spend less time together," she whispered, because speaking was too hard with the way she was struggling to breathe.

"No, Boots, just the opposite. In fact..." He kissed her.

Where she felt an electric bolt before, she now felt bone-melting heat. She had to grab hold of his shoulder to keep from slipping into a hot puddle at his feet. She could only use one hand because she held a now sleeping puppy with the other. Beau was right. There was something preternatural between them. This wasn't normal. Never had she been kissed so deeply, passionately, completely that she couldn't stand on her own two feet.

"Damn it," he said, lifting his mouth from hers. She heard his phone signal a text as it had earlier. "I've got a client who's determined to meet. I'm sure it's him again."

He shook his head, but when she thought he was going to turn away, he took Nancy from her, leaned over, and kissed her again. She kissed him back, sliding her hands around his neck, pulling him more firmly against her mouth. She knew somewhere in the part of her brain that was still functioning that she should resist him, push him away, but her pull to him felt like a moth to flame. His soft, smooth lips felt so good on hers. His tongue was so intoxicating, moving in a slow rhythm against hers. His scent was carnal and masculine and potent. Then he ended the kiss and cursed again. Jewell was both grateful and disappointed.

He yanked his phone from his pocket and looked at the text. "Sometimes I hate my job." He read the text. "I wish I had different work ethics. I'd ignore him, shut my phone off, and finish what we started." He looked at Jewell. "I *do* intend to finish what we started."

She shook her head. "We can't. It would be a mistake."

"Damn right it will." He grabbed her arm. "But it will be so mind-blowingly incredible." He blew out a breath. "Right now, I've got to deal with this anxious client who thinks he can break the law and not have to face the same consequences as the rest of civilization."

He gave her a quick peck on the lips. "Remember, rest tomorrow while I'm in court. No working in the barn or attic." He kissed her to silence her when she started to protest. "I'll come over later. I'll pick you up at seven tomorrow night. Dinner and dancing." He walked away, climbed into Tante Izzy's truck with the puppy and closed the door. He started the engine and leaned out of the open window of the bright pink truck in all of his sexy masculinity. It was a picture that made Jewell smile. "And Boots, wear something nice...like you actually like the guy who's taking you out.

"But I don't," she shouted back, knowing that was a lie. "If I go at all, I'll wear my mourning weeds. That would be appropriate."

Oh, geez. She did like him...most of the time, when he wasn't harassing her or accusing her of misconduct. She liked the way he cared about his family. She liked the way he showed tenderness to Mimi and Tante Izzy. She even liked how committed and loyal he was to his clients and work. But none of that really mattered. There was something more elemental between them that transcended like, hate or indifference. There was a physical pull that was unreasonable and unexplainable.

She walked toward the barn, feeling emotionally drained and a little sore from getting slammed with the airbag. It had been an awful day. It had also been a good day—she'd been given the family bible and she'd discovered that Beau wasn't just being a bully with her under the guise of trying to protect his family.

Finding out he kept all of the birthdates and anniversaries of his family members told her he really did care about them deeply. It made no logical sense, and it certainly wasn't tied to her guilt over the car accident or the bone-melting kiss they'd just shared, but Jewell knew that she'd make sure his life was linked with the Bienvenu family that he cared so much about. The first name she'd inscribe in the bible when she updated it would be that of her adversary, Beauregard James Bienvenu.

Chapter

13

Jewell's chest muscles had ached most of the morning from where the airbag had struck her and the seatbelt had locked across her body in the crash the day before. It was probably why she had slept so fitfully the night before and risen before the sun did. Then, again, her mind was such a jumble of thoughts and worries that it probably had more to do with that than her aches. Work always helped focus her mind and settle her anxiety.

While Mimi slept, Jewell worked on her computer, taking care of the research necessary to price Elli's furniture and incidentals. Mimi had slept later than usual, to almost ten-thirty. She had been exhausted from the activities of the day before. But, she woke up happy and chatty, talking in fragmented sentences about the two girls who she played with at the church the day before. She never mentioned the accident. She didn't seem to remember it.

Ruby had picked up Mimi after lunch to go the movies with her and Tante Izzy, so Jewell had taken advantage of the break and went for a walk in the sugarcane fields. On her way back, she decided to go into the barn to check on some details she needed for her inventory sheet. She knew Beau wouldn't be happy about that, but time was tight and she had no choice if she was going to meet the deadline.

Jewell had only been in the attic for fifteen minutes when she heard Elli call her name from downstairs.

"I'm up here," she answered and Elli immediately climbed the narrow, ladder-rung stairs to meet her.

"Hello, there," Elli said, stepping fully into the attic. She was such a striking beauty, the kind of woman other women noticed and wanted to look like, even while wearing simple gray yoga pants, a soft pink long-sleeve exercise top, and running shoes. She took four long strides and hugged Jewell. "We had to delay our departure. Ben had to make a morning house call for a desperate client threatening to bring his dog to the shelter." She shivered. "He still hasn't gotten back yet. " She shrugged. "Joey's in the house getting a favorite book he wanted to bring to the beach. I figured I'd come by to see how you're feeling." She looked down. "Cute boots. I love all of your boots."

Jewell laughed and looked down. "Thanks. Part of my work uniform. And, I am working." She waved her hand behind her. "I'm feeling fine."

Elli walked further into the attic and smiled. "You certainly are making progress." She ran her hand over the top of a dresser, then picked up a heavy metal candelabra on top of it. "This is pretty."

"It's an eighteenth century French gilded bronze." Jewell pointed to the base of the candelabra. "This foliage motif is very desirable. With this good condition, which is unusual for its age, more than two hundred years old, you should get a couple of thousand for it. If we had the pair, you'd get much more."

"Wow. We had a two-thousand-dollar candelabra hidden away in this musty old barn. It seems like a crime." Elli smiled. "I'm so glad you're here to not only clean out the barn, but to give all of these things another life. I love knowing that someone will enjoy having them as part of their lives."

"Yes," Jewell said, clapping her hands. "I feel that way too."

"I understand the family has been standing in line for you to take a look at their stored treasures." She laughed when Jewell nodded repeatedly. "They can be very intimidating and persistent, but their intentions are honest and true."

"I sensed that." She took her iPad from her mailbag. "They're just so competitive about who will get their treasures looked at first."

"Ha. I understand Tante Izzy has earned that honor."

Jewell laughed. "No. You have."

"For that I am very grateful." She picked up a small crystal ashtray.

"That's worth about twenty dollars."

"I think I might keep it. I can put it in my bathroom to hold my jewelry when I wash my hands."

"That brings up something I wanted to talk about." Jewell turned on her iPad. "We don't have much time to move this inventory from the barn before the deadline. We need to determine what you want to do with it."

"I hate having to move it twice." Jewell nodded in agreement. "What do you suggest?"

Jewell lifted her iPad for her to see. "This is the list. Most of the items have prices assigned to them. I have to verify it, of course, and give values to about six pieces I'm not familiar with."

Elli pointed to the bottom line. "That's a nice total value."

"I assume you'll want to keep some of the pieces and sell others."

"Yes. Can you e-mail this to me? Ben and I will discuss it on the drive to the Beach. I want to execute the option in your contract for you to be hired as the sales agent to sell the rest of the items."

Heck yeah! Jewell wanted to shout, but she remained poised, professional. She needed the money she'd earn from sales commissions for a number of things including fixing Beau's car and her upcoming trial. She hadn't heard from her attorney who said he'd call her this week to confirm if the trial was still set to begin next Tuesday. Whether it was next week or next month, she had to pay her legal bills. She hadn't been able to hire the most desired attorney in New Orleans, but she hired the best one she could find for what she could afford. And she really couldn't afford him anymore. He'd been paid with her savings. His billable hours must already be adding up again as be prepared for trial.

While she wouldn't earn nearly enough from this job to pay both her business and personal expenses, she at least had a back-up plan to take care of what was most important—make sure Mimi was set up in an excellent facility if she went to jail. She would sell their house, the warehouse and all of their assets to accomplish that. It was so freaking overwhelming.

"I'd love to continue to work for you," Jewell said. "Once you and Ben decide which items you want to keep, we need to move the rest somewhere buyers can access them—or where we can ship the pieces to buyers."

"You can call T-Bob for the moving part."

"Great." Jewell looked around the room. She had another income-generating place where the furniture could be stored. "I can rent you space to store the inventory in my New Orleans warehouse. It's a nontraditional-looking warehouse, but it serves its purpose." She smiled, thinking of the old building that was abandoned and left in dire condition for years after Katrina. "I bought an old fire station four years ago and rehabbed it to suit my needs. It's adjacent to Mimi's house, so I can be close to her or easily bring her over while I work."

"A fire station. That's so cool. I love repurposed buildings. I'd love to see it one day."

"I'd be happy to show it to you." She really loved the old three-story building that had once held two fire engines, offices, and the firemen's living quarters. "It hasn't been used as a fire station for twenty years but the city had used it as a community center before it was flooded by Katrina and abandoned. It's not fancy, but totally functional."

"That's wonderful. I love having our business so close to our home," she confided. "It makes it nice for Joey to pop in after school and for me to drop in and see my husband when I'm missing him." She smiled. "Which I do the second he walks out the door in the morning." She laughed. "I had no idea I'd be so crazy in love with somebody that I'd want to spend all of my day, every day, with him."

"That's really lovely, Elli." Jewell meant it. She couldn't imagine that kind of relationship for herself. Her time was so centered on Mimi and work. No man would be interested in entering that world, especially now that she had the added legal threat of being locked up in jail. She was definitely not a desirable partner. "You're blessed to have that."

"I hear the subtext in your voice." She patted her back. "*I'm* blessed to have it, but *you* never will...I don't believe that. You're a very special, loving person. I see how you care for and respect your grandmother. Someone who does that, especially when it isn't easy to do so, is definitely a person that a good man could be loyal to and love unconditionally."

"You're kind." She turned off her iPad, uncomfortable with the conversation and not wanting to get into all of the reasons she didn't really believe that was enough to form a lasting relationship. "So..." she began, ready to change the subject.

"So..." Elli replied, and smiled in a way that told Jewell without words that she understood the conversation of her personal love life was over. "So I had a lightbulb moment I wanted to run by you. The other reason for this impromptu visit." She picked up the crystal ashtray and turned it in her hand. "I was writing my to-do list, you know, bring sand shovels for the beach, bring sunscreen, do this, do that, tell Jewell to sell the items we don't want, et cetera, et cetera." She laughed. "Then I thought about Tante Izzy's stuff that she'll be wanting to sell...and the other family members. They'll need a plan to facilitate that as well."

Jewell nodded. "I probably have room for all of their stuff."

"Yes, that's good, but I was just talking to my friend Abby in LA. That's Los Angeles L-A, not Louisiana L-A. Anyway, we were discussing a fundraiser idea for the GENE ID Foundation we're involved in to help people trying to get genetic testing for the BRCA breast cancer gene." Elli smiled, clearly proud of her involvement. "In fact, it has reached to other areas besides California now— Texas, Montana, and I heard that Tante Izzy just sent something in to the genetic testing center to be tested from right here in Cane."

She waved her hand with the ashtray in it.

"Sorry, I'm rambling," Elli laughed. "It's just exciting to have family working with me for the foundation. More than just working. Tante Izzy is on the board of directors."

Jewell wasn't sure what all of that had to do with the inventory. She nodded for Elli to continue.

"Well, the Abby conversation led to another about helping women here in Cane and the surrounding areas with additional issues they're struggling with. Unemployment, abuse, anything that can help lift women up." She waved her hands in a movement to indicate that one thing flowed into another. "We discussed providing quality secondhand clothes to help dress these women for job interviews, for work...or selling the clothes and using the money for their other needs."

"That's a wonderful idea," Jewell said. "Churches do it all the time in varying degrees. I've seen private groups hold flea markets or events for charities, too."

"Exactly." Elli's eyes were sparkling. Her enthusiasm was palpable. "We could open a consignment store here in Cane to sell clothes we procure from LA celebrities and others."

"I see where you're going with this. You can include furniture and home décor too."

"Exactly." She pointed to Jewell, then herself. "Like minds. What do you think?"

"Love the idea!" Jewell knew she was smiling. She felt her insides smiling too. She thought of all the items in her warehouse that hadn't sold for one reason or another. Many were solid, good pieces that weren't antique, but finds that she'd loved and restored. Much more affordable. "It has legs. People love to shop for bargains and interesting items. Having high-end clothes, vintage clothes, jewelry, furniture and home décor items all in one location would be wonderful, Elli."

"I really love this idea, too." She moved toward Jewell and hugged her, the ashtray still in her hand. "I want to talk to Abby about it some more." She backed away, preparing to leave. "Let's plan for the three of us to discuss this next week when I get back. I'll e-mail you a meeting date and time."

The idea of a storefront location to facilitate sales was very exciting...and for charity! If she could just get her finances straight and be in a position to do this...she could at least advise Elli in her efforts, right? Even from prison.

Oh, God. She didn't want her mind to drift to negative thoughts of prison. Not yet. She sighed. Maybe it was time.

Elli looked at her a moment, studying her face but didn't comment when she had obviously hearing her sigh.

"I'll put some ideas in writing to bring to the meeting."

"Awesome," Elli said. "I trust you and Beau to take care of everything while we're gone." She started to jog toward the stairs, stopped and turned. Her laughter was instant and Jewell started laughing with her, without knowing why. How could she not? She was feeling light-headed and excited not only about helping with the consignment store, but with Elli wanting her to be involved with it. It felt like they were old friends, sharing in a joke, a happy moment. Yet, they had been strangers just four days ago. They were two very different-looking women; one very tall, blonde, and lean, and the other tall, brunette, and curvy, both laughing, enjoying a moment together in the middle of a dim, dusty, spider web-laced attic. Jewell hadn't expected that this would be one of the treasures she'd find in the attic.

"I like you, Doc," Elli said. "It's why I have to give you a heads-up about Tante Izzy. She is well intentioned, but I heard through the family gossip-line that she was talking matchmaking for you."

"Oh, dear God." Her cheeks flushed with heat. "Does that gossip-line work in reverse? Can you send messages back so Tante Izzy hears that I don't want a match with anyone?"

"Not even Beau?"

Jewell's head jerked up.

"Oops. Did I say that out loud?"

"Do I really have to answer that? It was a joke, right?"

"Um..." Elli shrugged. Looked at her watch. "I have to go. The beach awaits."

They said their good-byes, and once Elli left with her new treasured ashtray, the dim light of the barn attic seemed dimmer. Some people just had a natural light within them that lit up a room.

Jewell put the matchmaking Grand Bienvenu Madame out of her thoughts and let the idea of the consignment store in Cane fill her head. She had a sweet rattan rocker and painted wrought iron table and chairs that would be perfect for the store. The items had been in her inventory for some time, and she hadn't been able to sell them. They were great finds, but she hadn't found the right buyer for them. She could part with them. She just wished she was in a financial situation that allowed her to give the store more of her inventory. It would be fun to give homes to her finds. If only everything worked out with her court case and she cleared her name. Then she might soon be financially solid again.

She had to call her attorney. Her life was in a complicated, troubled holding pattern until her legal problems were resolved, one way or another. She would ask him if he'd gotten confirmation on the trial date.

Jewell pulled her phone from her back pocket, called her attorney, then sat on the floor. "Hello, this is Jewell Duet. I'd like to speak to Rick Neal, please." Her cheek began to throb where the phone rested on the swelling. It was tender; she knew it had to look like a plum.

"Hold on, please."

She didn't have to wait long before she was connected. "Hello, this is Mary Powers, may I help you?"

"Yes, Mary. I'd like to speak to Mr. Neal."

"He's unavailable." Jewell heard the hollow clicking sound of someone typing on a computer. "May I help you? I'm his law clerk. I assist him with his cases. I know we haven't met. I'm new to the firm, but I'm very familiar with your case."

"No. Thank you. I want to speak to Mr. Neal. He's my attorney."

"He's not available. He's got a huge case that's consuming a lot of his time right now. So I'm helping out with some of the other cases." She sighed. "I really can help you. I'm very familiar with your case. If I can't answer your questions, I'll consult with him. I promise."

"So he's not actually handling my case?"

"Uh, well, I mean, he is, but I am..." Her voice started sounding younger and younger to Jewell. She'd probably taught students her age. "Let me explain, Miss Duet..."

"Dr. Duet," she corrected, feeling abandoned, annoyed, scared. "No, let me explain. If I'm not getting the full attention of the attorney I hired, I expect my bill to reflect that." Jewell hated that the financial concerns were as crushing as her worries that she wasn't getting good representation. The lack of both could send her right into jail. "I'm sure you are a very intelligent and capable law clerk, but if I get billed Mr. Neal's fee when you're doing his work, that is unacceptable. I expect to be refunded the overcharges." Mary tried interrupting a few times, but Jewell was not having any of that. "Tell *your* very busy Mr. Neal that for me, okay? And, tell him that his lack of attention to my trial is totally unacceptable."

"Wait. Miss...I mean, Dr. Duet," the clerk stammered, searching for the right words to repair what damage had been done. If Jewell wasn't so upset over her lack of representation, she might have felt sorry for young Mary.

She felt sorry for herself more. At the end of the day, Mary would be reprimanded for how she'd handled her, but she'd still be employed. Jewell, on the other hand, might be in jail and Mimi in a nursing home because she didn't get the experienced legal help she required.

"I didn't mean to imply you're not being fairly represented by our firm. I don't want you to think that..."

"That the attorney I hired has passed off his contractual responsibilities to someone who is fresh out of law school and new to his firm?" Jewell closed her eyes, took a calming breath. "Reduce my bill, Mary, and have Mr. Neal call me with the confirmation of my court date. Good day." She hung up the phone.

Dear Lord, what was she going to do now? Force an attorney who was already marginal to begin with—and was now too distracted with another case—to pay attention to her? That didn't seem like it would help her in any way. She'd get a half-hearted effort from him at best. She certainly couldn't just hope that young Mary-the-law-clerk-with-no-experience was capable enough to keep her from going to jail. She had to give this all some thought. She had to quickly figure out what she was going to do with her day in court scheduled for early next week. She also had to finish the job for Elli and Ben.

Jewell was good at organizing, categorizing, analyzing. She had to do that with her problems. She'd do that tonight after Mimi went to sleep. Dinner and dancing with Beau could not happen. Heck, it couldn't happen for many reasons. She lay back on the hard, dusty wooden floor, looking up at the ceiling rafters. She had to stay focused on getting this job done and staying out of jail. Jewell typed a text to Beau.

Sorry. No dinner and dancing.

He responded immediately. *I'm sorry. I didn't receive your text. Something must be wrong with my phone. See you at seven.*

She typed: *Seriously...No.*

I can't hear you.

"Ugh." Jewell groaned in frustration. Then, she started to laugh. "Your phone isn't working? My eye."

Her phone began to ring. "I'm serious, Beau, I can't go to dinner with you."

"Um, okay." It was Ruby, not Beau. She definitely had to give Ruby her own ringtone.

"I'm sorry, Ruby. I thought you were Beau."

"Yeah, I got that." She laughed. "You should go to dinner with him. He's fun and a terrific man."

"Can't." She sat up. "I'm still in the barn, but I can pick up Mimi in thirty minutes. Is that okay?"

"Actually, she and Tante Izzy are napping right now," Ruby said. "I'm not sure why. They slept through the whole movie, too. As soon as the lights went out they both started snoring." She laughed. "Those two are really something. You'd think they were sisters with the way they argue over everything, then love on one another like they hadn't disagreed the moment before. I'm enjoying spending time with them." She rushed on. "Big John and I want to take them to the American Legion bingo tonight at six. It's our turn to call Lucky-7, Four Corners and Blackout." She laughed. "I love to call Bingo. We have so much fun. Anyway, I've cooked a shrimp stew and fixed a green salad while they were sleeping, so we'll eat first and head right over afterwards."

"Mimi loves bingo, but she'll need help."

"I've got it covered. Pearl's coming with us. Between her and me, we'll help her watch her cards." Ruby mumbled something, then spoke up. "It's really a good setup. The lighting's good and the sound system's good too. And you know, when Mimi heard us talking about bingo, she told us how much she enjoyed playing with the nuns she used to work for at the convent. She also told us," Ruby snickered, "that the nuns used to cheat."

Jewell laughed. She'd heard that story a thousand times. "Oh, Ruby, I just don't know if she should go," she said, feeling torn. She'd been having almost daily episodes with sundowning and the resulting anxiety that went along with it. "I hate for her not to go since she really loves bingo. She hasn't played in a long time. But..."

"Don't you worry. We really want to do this." Her voice was soft and sincere, her Cajun accent rhythmic. "Jewell, take advantage of having good help you can trust and your Mimi likes. I bet you don't get that very often."

Never. Jewell sighed.

"Mignon is very social, as you know. She enjoys spending time with people close to her age and she likes knowing she's not a burden to you."

"Oh, Ruby, she's not a burden." God, she never wanted Mimi to think that.

"She knows that you love her." Jewell could hear the smile in Ruby's voice. "No guilt, now. No worries. I have this. With pleasure."

Mimi did need to spend more time socializing with her peers and other caregivers. If the trial went badly, she would be thrown into a life with strangers, without any preparations. Jewell's chest hurt. God, she hoped if she was found guilty, the appeals process would be lengthy enough for Mimi not to be forced into that situation.

"Okay," Jewell finally said, "but call if you need anything. Don't hesitate for any reason. I know I've explained to you about her sundowning before, so I won't repeat myself, but just be aware it could be a problem. Oh, and Ruby, if she is left alone, she may get a panic attack when she doesn't recognize anyone around her. Also—"

"We've got this." Her voice was gentle, reassuring. "I will love on her and care for her as if she was my own mother." Ruby started talking to someone else, telling them that Jewelie said it would be okay for Mignon to go to Bingo. She'd never had anyone call her that nickname before. It made her smile. A very deep male voice answered, but Jewell didn't understand what he said. "Big John's here. He's got a big ol' grin on his face. He thoroughly enjoyed the ride from the church to Tante Izzy's yesterday. It was his idea to take the ladies with us tonight."

"You're a dear woman." Jewell meant it. She really liked Ruby. Everyone she'd met in Cane had been wonderful, really.

"Oh, you're making me *honte,*" Ruby said, using the Cajun expression for embarrassed. "Now, get ready for dinner with Beau. Wear something pretty. We'll bring Mignon home to the camper around nine-thirty. I'll get her settled in bed and stay with her until you get home. Take your time. Big John and I stay up late all the time. We'll bring a movie with us."

"That won't be necessary."

"*Alors pas,*" she laughed, again using a favorite Cajun expression, which she repeated in English. "Of course not. Stay out until the sun comes up if you want. Big John and I have the entire morning free. We only have to go shopping later in the day for the tailgate party on Thursday." Ruby paused. "Oh. Oh, Jewelie. Did anyone tell you that Steve is planning on tailgating under the family oak at Sugar Mill? There's a special televised late Thursday afternoon LSU game. We'll kick things off around two in the afternoon. Steve's making a chicken and sausage jambalaya. My daughter, Rachel, you haven't met her yet, is planning to bring a whole bunch of trout and redfish she and some of her cousins will catch at the camp down the bayou tomorrow. We're going to fry it up. There'll be a gumbo, potato salad, cracklin', barbeque grillades and a bunch of desserts." She laughed. "Tante Izzy and your Mimi plan to make some *pain perdu* and other desserts tomorrow."

"Sounds like a feast." Jewell laughed, feeling Ruby's infectious joy.

"We love to gather the family under the big oak behind the big house. It's tradition for us to meet there." Jewell heard the pride in Ruby's voice. "Oh, we've got an extra TV coming so Mimi can watch something else. We won't subject a Tulane fan to watch the Tigers."

Jewell was touched by how easily the family included them into their fold. She would be lying to herself if she didn't admit that she was a little bit envious of how close the Bienvenu family was. The love and loyalty was remarkable. And, to think it was en masse. They were special people to open their lives to her and Mimi, especially when many of them knew that Mimi was claiming to have once lived at Sugar Mill, and they really didn't believe that was true. No one seemed threatened by her.

No one except for Beau.

"The invitation, the extra TV...it's all so generous."

"I'll take that as a yes." Her voice was rushed, now. Her Cajun accent was heavier because of it. "Oh, I've got to go, Jewelie. The ladies are waking. It's five, and they'll want their supper."

Ruby didn't wait for Jewell to say good-bye. She hung up.

"Thank you, Ruby and Big John. I have the evening free...to work, now." She looked at her dusty jeans, the dirt on her arms. She shrugged and picked up her iPad. She'd start by researching the items that needed pricing. The iPad didn't power up, although it was plugged into her second portable power pack. She'd have to do the research on her laptop in the camper.

"All good," she thought. It would be nice to shower, get in comfy clothes, fix a sandwich and hot tea, and spend an evening doing what she loved. If her research went well, she might finish the inventory pricing tonight.

***

Beau drove up to the camper and parked in front. He still had Tante Izzy's truck, but his insurance company had arranged for him to pick up his rental car in the morning. The interior light of the camper was glowing through the tiny windows and shining on the bright silver exterior. He took the light being on as a good sign. Maybe, just maybe, she was ready to go to dinner with him.

Beau really wanted time alone with Jewell, away from her work, away from his family, away from Mignon. Away from the distractions. He wanted to see if he could assess once and for all if she was the scam artist he feared or just a woman down on her luck with a grandmother who thought she had ties to Sugar Mill. He hated that he wished for it to be one more than the other. He was losing his objectivity. Her sharp intelligence, tender sensitivity, quick humor and womanly curves softened his hard edge.

Heart racing and feeling as nervous as he once did picking up his high-school prom date, Beau climbed out of the truck and knocked at the camper door. Jewell didn't answer. He knocked again. Still, no answer. He turned the doorknob and opened the door just enough to call inside. "Jewell?"

No answer. He opened the door all the way and looked inside. Jewell, wearing a creamy, yellow satin robe sat Indian style in front of her computer. Her beautiful caramel legs were partially exposed where the robe didn't cover her knees and thighs. Earbuds were in her ears. Her head was bobbing to the beat of whatever music she was listening to as the towel that was turbaned over her hair tilted precariously with each movement. And she was barefoot. No rubber boots to cover her pretty, slender feet.

Beau smiled.

He walked up behind her and looked over her shoulder at an image of an armoire she had on the computer screen. His senses went on high alert. She smelled of old-fashioned soap, fresh floral shampoo, and best of all, her unique, earthy scent that heated his body faster than extra spicy Tabasco sauce.

"Hi there, Boots," he said, near her ear. She jumped, her hand flew around, knocking over a hot cup of tea and punching Beau hard in the cheek. He stepped back. "Damn. You've got a great left cross, Doc." He laughed, rubbing his cheek.

"Beau! You scared me to death." She stood and hastily closed her robe, but not before he got a tantalizing glimpse of her smooth, flat belly and full cleavage. *And maybe a tattoo.* Oh, hell, did she have a tiny tattoo low on her hip where it would've been hidden by her panties if she'd been wearing them? Damn. His breath caught. Was she completely naked beneath the robe? What in the hell was the tattoo of? He stuffed his hands in his pockets. He was tempted to find out. "I could've shot you!" She slid open the desk drawer to reveal a 9 millimeter handgun. "It's loaded."

He closed the drawer. "What is it with you women in Cane and your weapons?"

"Only a problem for the person who breaks in and enters my home." She picked up the teacup from the floor, grabbed a paper towel from the kitchenette counter and wiped up the spill—holding the robe tightly closed the entire time.

"For the record, I knocked three times and announced myself before entering."

"Oh, that must've been why I knew you were here." She tossed the paper in the trash and motioned to the sofa. "Have a seat."

"It doesn't look like you're ready for dinner," he said, sinking into the soft '50s-style mustard brown foam sofa. He noticed there was an untouched sandwich on a plate next to her laptop.

"Beau, I told you I couldn't go with you."

"Couldn't or won't?"

"Same thing."

"Jewell, it's just dinner and conversation. I think we need to talk without the distraction of our families. We need to resolve some issues, figure out how we're going to move forward."

She lifted a brow and crossed her arms over her chest, causing the fabric of the thin robe to tighten so Beau could see the outline of her breasts. He shifted in his seat and forced himself to glance away. He looked down at an antiques magazine on a side table. It was much less interesting than Jewell in a robe that barely covered her breasts. Dammit.

"Move forward?" She sighed. "Are we talking about what has been happening between us personally or professionally?"

"Yes," he said right away. "I won't push on the personal part. That, frankly, isn't something I really like to chat about anyway. It's chick conversation." She nodded. "The work stuff, we need a plan of action and some organization. I need to know where you're heading with your expanding work with other family members and with your investigation."

She paused for a minute, her eyes giving the telltale look that meant she was analyzing what he said. "Okay. Not that I think most of it is any of your business. I agree we need to discuss work here. I'm at a point where some decisions need to be made about moving the inventory, and Elli said to work it out with you." She shook her head, a little humor in her eyes. "No chick conversation, though."

"Okay. Go get dressed. Please."

***

Thirty minutes later, Jewell and Beau were seated in a cozy red faux-leather booth next to a large picture window, facing the parking lot of the Do Drop Inn restaurant. It pleased Beau that she'd chosen a dress instead of her usual jeans and work shirt, which he'd half-expected her to do. The dress material was like one of his favorite denim shirts. It was soft, faded, but totally comfy. On her the color and fabric looked like high-end designer fashion. It may have been because it fit her like a glove. Or it may have been because when set against her skin and hair, the pale blue made her look very natural and sexy. He was surprised to find this look so appealing when he'd thought he preferred a more tailored, sophisticated, put-together style. In fact, he especially liked the way she'd left a few of the top buttons undone to reveal just a bit of the swell of her full breasts. He liked the way the buttons were left undone from just above her ankle to well above her knee to let the dress split open with each step she took, showing her shapely legs and the funky rubber boots that were shaped like cowboy boots and painted like red bandanas. As great as she looked in her dress and even in her crazy boots, his mind kept going back to that damn tattoo low on her hip and her crazy sexy feet.

Those images he couldn't get out of his head.

"What would you like to drink?" he asked when the waitress approached the table to take their order.

She looked toward the long, walnut-stained bar in front of them. "I'll take whatever local beer you have on tap," she said, pleasing him yet again. He liked a lot of the finer things in life, expensive cars, clothes, but he enjoyed a good cold beer and local food.

"I'll have the same. And bring us a dozen oysters, half raw and half charbroiled." He looked at her. "Is that okay? They have good, cold, salty oysters here."

"Yes. Sounds great. It's a month ending in R, so we should have oysters, right?"

"Yes, indeed," he smiled.

The band took the stage with guitars, fiddle, rubboard, and accordion. Jewell looked at them and smiled.

"I know you love music. I think you'll enjoy Nonc Noon and the Bon Amis."

She laughed easily. "Uncle Noon and Good Friends. I haven't heard of them. It's always nice discovering new bands, though."

"The man on the rubboard." —Beau motioned with his head toward the stage— "That's Jude. He's my third cousin. His momma is a Bienvenu. He'll be bringing the rubboard to the tailgating Thursday. Big John will bring his accordion and his daughter Rachel will bring her git-tar," he said, purposely mispronouncing guitar.

"Mimi will love it."

"And you? Will you love it?"

She shrugged. "I have to work, Beau. I'll pop in to be polite."

He shook his head. "I guess that means you'll make me miss it too." He frowned and pointed a finger at her and then to himself. "No culling through the attic or barn or anywhere on this property without me, remember?"

She rolled her eyes. "With you always breathing down my neck, how could I?" she murmured. Then, she spoke louder. "I remember. It's our agreement."

"Yes, it is."

The waitress put the beers on the table in tall sweaty glasses with just a bit of foam at the top. Beau lifted his glass and held it out to her. She tapped hers to his, making a heavy clanging sound.

"To making money on old junk," he said.

She laughed. "To finding loving homes for historic treasures." She took a sip. "And making money doing it."

Jewell looked at her menu. "Just so we don't have that awkward moment at the end of dinner when the bill comes, I want to clarify now that we're going Dutch."

Argue now or argue at the end of the meal. He decided to wait until the end of the meal. Beau took a sip of his beer, noticed how the amber light from the single bowling ball-sized bulb hanging above them made her skin glow in what looked like the soft focus he'd seen used on movie stars in films. Her skin was flawless, except for the bruise on her cheek.

"You been icing your face?" He reached across the table and gently touched her cheek. She tucked her chin, looking shy, but not pulling away. "It's not as swollen as it was earlier today."

"No. I just heal quickly. And I put on a little makeup to cover it so everyone in the restaurant wouldn't think you beat me up." She lifted her cold beer and rested it against her cheek.

"Ah, so considerate, Boots." He laughed. "I hate to bust your bubble, but I'd guess most everyone in the restaurant knows about you running into Tante Izzy's truck. She's our resident celebrity, so to speak. If something happens to her or her stuff, everyone is talking about it. Since you're the new person of interest in town, the combination of you and Tante Izzy is just too tempting not to gossip about."

"I hate being the subject of gossip."

"You say that like it's happened before." He knew it had. It seemed like a good opportunity to open the subject he wanted to talk to her about. Her legal problems. He really needed to see if he could get a good feel for her guilt or innocence.

She shrugged. "You know who my mother is."

He nodded. "Yeah, but you look like you're talking about something more than that."

The waitress put the oysters on the table, but Jewell didn't reach for them. She was looking at him in that thoughtful way she did when she was trying to figure out what she wanted to do. Beau slid a few raw and charbroiled oysters on a plate and handed the plate to Jewell. "Eat up." Then he smiled and repeated it in French, *"Mange."*

She added a little horseradish, ketchup and hot sauce on the side of the plate and mixed it together to make a cocktail sauce in the same way all locals did.

Beau was formulating his opening question when the band started to play. The first song of their set was one he'd heard on the radio for the first time the day his mom, Bernice, and his dad, Ronald, rescued Jackson and him from the hellhole where they lived. He'd loved the Cleveland Crochet's Cajun Zydeco song, "Sugar Bee," ever since. The questions could wait. The night was young. He stood and extended his hand to Jewell.

"Let's dance, *chère*. We both need to have a little fun."

She shrugged. "More than you know." She nodded. "Besides, I can use the exercise." She took his hand and walked with him to the dance floor. Five other couples were already dancing. Three of them were doing the traditional Cajun two-step.

"I know you've got moves, Boots, I've seen your solo dance in the attic," he teased, spinning her to face him. "Do you know the Cajun jitterbug?'

"No, but if you can lead, I can follow."

"Oh, I can lead." Beau started moving her across the dance floor, keeping the steps Bernice had taught him simple and in time to the beat of the music. "You're a natural," he said, meaning it, twirling her under his arm as they moved in easy grace across the wooden floor.

"Not a natural," she laughed. "Dance lessons. Lots of them since I was three. My mother insisted. She had some crazy, twisted idea that I'd go into the business with her or into the entertainment industry and I'd need to know how to dance. She didn't care if I made an A on my history exam, but she cared if I earned the solo for the dance recital."

"Ouch." Beau twirled her one way and then reversed the direction. She smiled and followed, keeping time with the music and him.

Beau pulled her tighter against him, her dress wrapping around his legs. He enjoyed the feel of her body moving in rhythm with his. The way her back and hip muscles tightened and eased under his hands as she dipped and swayed was so damn sensual. There were no awkward moments of new partners trying to figure out what the other would do. They just flowed easily with one another as if they'd been dancing together for years.

Beau lost track of how many songs they danced to as their eyes met and held. The happy Cajun beat simply flowed through them.

Then the music stopped. Jewell looked up at him, bit her bottom lip, and made a silly face. "If the band insists on taking a break, I guess we should too." She brushed aside a few strands of hair that had slipped from her braid onto her cheeks.

"That was fun." He guided her back to their booth. "I like to dance, and I can see you do too." He kissed her on the cheek. "Thank you. I enjoyed that. You're a very good dancer."

"Only because you are."

He held up two fingers to the waitress to bring two more beers. "Are you hungry?"

She nodded. "What do you recommend?"

Beau tucked a stray strand of her long, dark hair behind her ear. "I think you'd like..." His voice trailed off as something, or more accurately—someone—caught his attention from outside the window. *What in the hell was he doing here?* Beau jumped out of his seat. "Jewell, stay right here. I'll be back." He ran outside.

Chapter

Beau had spotted his client, Stanley Boudreaux, as he drove up to the Do Drop Inn restaurant in a brand new fire-engine-red BMW. It was the same model as the one Jewell had wrecked just the day before. Dealership stickers were still on the rear window. He'd driven it with a suspended driver's license after his third DWI. Beau was furious.

"Hey, Beau," Stanley said, staggering toward the front door that Beau had just exited. He was dressed in the same clothes he'd worn at their meeting that afternoon. Khaki slacks and camouflage golf shirt with his seafood processing business logo embroidered above the left breast pocket. "Long time, no see." He laughed, smoothing his thinning salt and pepper hair. Damn it, he smelled of heavy alcohol and self-destruction.

"Are you kidding me? You're driving intoxicated with a suspended license." Beau couldn't believe how stupid this guy was. He grabbed him by his thick biceps and pulled him off to the side, away from the door and the curious onlookers. Stanley protested, cursed being manhandled. Although in his late fifties, Stanley was fit and muscular from working out at the gym every day. Being drunk made him uncoordinated, though.

"What the hell are you doing?" he asked, stumbling over his words.

"Trying to keep you from being thrown back in jail." Beau let go of his arm and faced him.

"I'm sorry to hear about your Beamer." Stanley looked at the car he'd just illegally driven. His comment was meant to be a slam. He wasn't sorry at all. "Should've told you earlier. You know, once you've wrecked your first car, it doesn't hurt as much for the next one."

"I didn't wreck it," Beau said, knowing if he'd heard of the wreck, he'd heard the story of Jewell rear-ending Tante Izzy's truck. "Stanley, you can't drive. You don't have a license. We went over all of this today. I thought you understood." Beau knew he was wasting his breath talking to a drunken man. He knew it much too well.

"And I explained to you that the DA and I are fishing buddies." He looked toward the door as someone exited. He tried to whistle. Beau turned. It was Jewell. He motioned to her to stay where she was.

"Hey, look at me. I'm talking to you." He jabbed his finger at Stanley's chest. "Your fishing buddy's hands are tied. The fact that he couldn't get you out of your mandatory two-day jail sentence for refusing a Breathalyzer and blood test should tell you something." He didn't turn around, but he sensed that Jewell had walked closer to them. It annoyed him, and he was already annoyed that she hadn't listened to him and had come outside.

"Stanley, you've known the law since your first DWI. It's why you refused the test. There are new laws. I've explained them to you. Louisiana's *implied consent law* states very clearly that if you're arrested for probable cause for driving while intoxicated, then you must consent to taking a chemical test of your blood, breath or urine to determine your blood alcohol content. If you refuse, which you did because you knew you'd fail it, there is an automatic two-day jail sentence and suspension of your license." Stanley made a snapping hand gesture indicating that he thought Beau was talking too much.

Yeah, what did he expect trying to reason with a drunk? He should've known better than to do that.

"Hello, beautiful," Stanley said to Jewell, ignoring Beau. Beau's ears burned from his anger, first for his flirting attention to Jewell, and second for not taking his DWI seriously. "You're even prettier than what people are saying and they're saying you are movie star pretty."

"Damn it, Stan. We're talking here."

"I spoke to the DA after I left your office."

Beau stood in silence for a moment. He needed to calm down and deal with his defiant client professionally. "Bad move," he told him, keeping his voice even. "I'm your attorney. Let me handle this. Ex parte conversations will cause more damage than good."

"The DA and I go way back," Stanley snorted. "Why wouldn't I chat with an old pal?" He looked at Jewell and stood taller. Stanley was married with children, but he was posturing to impress her. "I'm a multimillionaire," he said, speaking more loudly for her to hear. "I have power." He stumbled over his words.

When Stanley started to make excuses for his behavior the night he got caught driving drunk leaving the Lucky Cajun Bar, Beau raised his hand to signal him to stop talking. "You were caught red-handed. The charges will hold. This is your third DWI. The law and judicial system are uncompromising on the three-strikes-and-you're-out policy."

"I'm not going to jail or picking up litter on the side of the road in an orange jumpsuit." He made a fist and punched it into the air. Beau moved so his body was fully between Stanley and Jewell. He wanted her to get the hell away from Stanley's volatility. His temper was escalating. Beau recognized the look of it in the eyes before it manifested any other way. He wanted to tell Jewell to go inside, but his client was shouting now about how he'd paid taxes in the parish and had rights. He was dangerous, and anything could send him from a verbal tirade into a physical one—including hearing him sending Jewell away. "Stan, let's talk about this tomorrow." Beau tried to use his voice to calm him.

Stanley continued ranting. "Talk to this," he shouted, showing him his hand and laughing as though it was extremely funny.

Beau shook his head, tried to reach behind him to urge Jewell to leave. "Go inside, Jewell."

"Are you chasing my girlfriend away?" Stanley shouted. "I want her to stay. Tell her how my employees need me. And I can get a good deal because of it. You want to hear that, right, honey?"

"We'll talk tomorrow, Stanley." Beau kept his eyes on his client. "You have an audience." He motioned toward the bar windows where the patrons were gathered, watching to see what would happen.

"I don't give a crap about them." Stanley bowed toward the window. "They can't hear us anyway. Talk now. What's the deal?"

Beau hesitated but knew not telling him the deal would only agitate him more. If Jewell wasn't there, he wouldn't give a damn about that. Since she was, he did care about keeping her safe from the hot-headed drunken fool.

"I can negotiate a deal for community service, no jail time, and probation if you agree to enter an inpatient alcohol treatment facility."

Stanley started cursing, throwing up his hands. "I don't need no jerk-off alcohol treatment. I'm not an alcoholic."

Beau stole a glance over his shoulder to Jewell. Her eyes were wide, worried. "Get the hell out of here, Jewell." She didn't move. She took her phone out of her pocket. *Damn stubborn woman.* He looked at Stanley. "Take the deal. Go to rehab. Hell, go to rehab somewhere expensive with a pretty beach."

Stanley looked at Beau, two bloodshot orbs under tired lids. "I don't think you tried hard enough to fight this," he said, his voice a low growl. "It's because your parents were the town drunks. Your dad served time for taking advantage of people. You want them to go to rehab, not me. You had a miserable life living down the bayou in a stinking shack because of them. I'm not a lowlife drunk like them..."

Beau's hands balled in fists. "It's the booze talking now, you ass." He spoke through clenched teeth. "The smell of it is oozing from your pores. It's a smell I've known my whole life. Just like your kids now know. Stop the damn madness for them. You're ruining your kids' lives every bit as much as my parents did mine. Yeah, I wanted them to get sober, to go to rehab. That ship has passed. My mom is dead—she drank herself to death and my father's in prison. You want that? Any of it?" He didn't give Stanley a chance to answer, he had more to say. "I'm not transferring my crap with them to you, you idiot. Get your act together before you kill yourself or worse, before you kill someone else and really destroy your family."

"Screw you." Stanley stomped forward, stood toe to toe. "I want a new lawyer. You're fired." He jabbed his finger into Beau's chest.

"Thank God." No sooner had the words left Beau's mouth than Stanley's fist landed hard and solid right across his eye. Pain, sharp and hot, exploded. Beau ignored it, for Stanley was swinging his beefy fist again. Beau blocked his arm, grabbed his wrist and twisted it behind the other man's back. Beau immediately reached into Stanley's pocket and pulled out the keys to the BMW. The smell of booze on his heaving breath mixed with the scent of his own blood now dripping down his cheek from under his eye, turned his stomach.

He looked up. Jewell had moved in closer. Her hands were fisted, one cocked back. She was ready to jump into battle with him. "Call a cab for him." Beau told her.

"I'm driving. I've got a car...give me the damn keys." Stan shook his shoulder to free himself, slipped and fell to his knees.

"Not your car," Beau said, releasing his arm. Anger burned his chest, but he was surprised how even and controlled his voice was. "If you bought it, the dealer would've removed the stickers when they delivered it." Stanley stumbled as he tried to stand. "For the life of me, I don't even know how you got possession of it without a license."

"I know people, asshole. Give me the damn keys." His voice sounded wet, greasy, and too familiar. For the second time, Beau's stomach turned.

"I'm liable if I knowingly let you drive the dealer's car drunk, with no license, and you wreck it. It's unacceptable and frankly, I'm insulted that you'd put that on me."

Stanley cursed using a string of words in both English and Cajun French that were meant to intimidate and get Beau to do what he wanted. It was his dysfunctional MO, one he used when he was sober. It worked for him with his employees and his family because he usually sweetened it with kind words and bonuses afterward. Beau was immune to that kind of abusive behavior. His hide had been thickened with scars formed each time his biological father had spit a cruel, ugly word or smacked him and his brother.

Beau asked Jewell for her phone. She handed it to him. "She called a cab," he said, noting that the cab number had been dialed. "I can call the sheriff's office. My real father will be more than glad to send a deputy. Which will it be?"

"Screw you...and *my* girlfriend."

He walked away, purposely knocking into Beau and stopping in front of Jewell, staring her down with a nasty slide of his eyes over her body. Beau saw red. His gut twisted in a violent knot. He rushed to him, afraid Stanley would strike her. In the seconds it took him to reach him, Jewell had stiff-armed Stanley, causing him to stumble.

"Back off, jerk," she said, her voice firm, fearless. "Get a backbone and break this stupid, spineless, downward spiral. Frankly, it's pathetic. Have some pride, Stanley. You sound like a man who cares about his image. Listen to Beau before you become the town joke."

"Mind your own business..."

Beau grabbed him by his shirtfront and shoved him away from Jewell. "She's my business." He held up her cell phone. "Cab or sheriff?"

"Go to hell." Stanley walked away, into the parking lot. When Beau saw the glow of Stanley's cell phone from a safe distance, he turned to Jewell.

"Are you okay? Did he hurt you?" Anger still burned hot in his gut. He ran his hand down her arms, knowing his voice was rough. "What in the hell were you thinking coming out here? Are you crazy?"

She jerked away from him, walked inside the restaurant.

"What the hell?" He couldn't believe it. She just walked away and didn't say a word. Then, she came through door. A small plastic bag with ice in one hand and a stack of napkins in the other.

She wiped the blood off his cheek with the napkin. She wasn't trying to be gentle. She was angry. "To answer your question," she began, patting the cut under his eye. "I came out here because I knew you were in trouble the second everyone in the restaurant rushed to the windows."

"So you threw yourself in the middle of the trouble?" Was she kidding him? He looked into the parking lot at Stanley who was still on the phone. "For a smart woman that was a dumb move."

She looked at him, grabbed his wrist and turned his hand palm up. She dropped the ice bag into his hand. "So was coming to dinner with you. Put that on your eye." She folded her arms over her chest. "And to think I thought we'd turned a corner and actually could have an amicable discussion...relationship."

Beau put the ice on his eye. "Amicable discussion?" Was she flippin' kidding him? "You're worried about polite conversation when you could've been hurt by a dangerous drunk?" His voice was deep, loud, yet it seemed muffled in his ears. Damn. It reminded him of when he was a child and he'd squeeze his old foam pillow over his head to drown out the sound of his father's voice when he was on a drunken rage in the next room. No, the anger in his voice wasn't as out-of-control nor were his words as frightening, but that hollow sound in his ears was every bit as real as if his father was the cause of it.

Beau tossed the ice pack into a garbage can near the building. He ran his hands through his hair. He felt the weight of the memory on his shoulders and rolled them to try to physically remove the memory from his body. Not many things reminded him of the nightmares of his childhood. Dealing with Stanley did. And, in a way, so did dealing with Jewell...Stanley because he was an irrational, violent drunk like his father. And Jewell could possibly be an immoral con artist like his father who was also damn good at pretending to be a decent human being.

"Don't direct your anger with that despicable man at me." Her voice was firm, yet it held no heat. "You have every right to be angry with your client's behavior. He was out of line and self-destructive." She glanced at Stanley in the parking lot talking on the phone before returning her gaze to Beau. "I even respect the way you tried to bring him in line when he went right for your jugular and...your heart." Her voice softened. "Don't direct your anger from your childhood experiences with a drunk at me, either."

"Oh, hell." He ran his hand through his hair. She was right. And she was wrong. He was filled with anger for Stanley, but anger wasn't what he felt toward Jewell. It was fear. He was afraid for her. "You could've been hurt. He could've hit you. I've seen it happen when a man drinks too much and gets violent. Stanley had that look in his eyes, Jewell."

She nodded. "I saw it. It's why I reacted as I did. I'm not an idiot. I surprised him by standing up to his intimidation. It gave him pause. I know it could've backfired on me." She shrugged. "I've had my experiences with violent drunks too."

"What?" *God, No. Not Jewell.* He felt sick knowing she might've been treated as he and Jackson had been.

"My mother had a boyfriend once who was like that." She took a step closer to him. "She probably had others. I don't know. But the one I encountered was a bartender she brought home when I was about five. He went on a destructive rage. Mimi came home from work and put a stop to it. She hit him over the head with a frying pan. Knocked him out cold."

"Did he hurt you?"

She shrugged. "He slapped me a few times, said I was a brat. My mother stepped between us to stop him. He hit her a few times before Mimi arrived." She shook her head. "It was awful. I can't imagine how you survived living through that kind of horror over and over again, Beau. You not only survived it, you've come out a good, honorable, strong man in spite of it." Her eyes softened. "I had my share of crazy family incidents, but Mimi taught me the meaning of being a tough lady. To defend myself." She touched Beau where Stanley had hit him near his eye. Her concern for him, when she had to still be frightened from the violent scene, touched him. "I also learned not to buy into that kind of crazy, dysfunctional kind of thinking about love that my mother had. Mimi shielded me from my mother's illogical thinking with men."

She looked at the parking lot again. Beau heard her brave words. Understood them. Still, he saw the hint of fear in her eyes with Stanley so near, shouting something they couldn't make out into his phone.

She brushed his hair off his forehead. "You stopped him. He knew you wouldn't let him hurt me." She looked at the cut under his eye. "You've stopped bleeding."

"Let's get out of here." He felt calmer, but the urge to beat the crap out of Stanley was still strong, especially after hearing how another man had hurt Jewell when she was so young and vulnerable. He led her to Tante Izzy's truck and opened the passenger door. He helped her climb in and closed the door. He wanted to make sure she was safely inside, in case Stanley decided to return.

"I've got to call the Do Drop Inn," he said after he drove onto the dark, two-lane state highway. He pulled over, found the number quickly, and called. "Hey Sylvia, this is Beau. I'm sorry I had to leave in a hurry. I'll come by tomorrow to settle my bill."

"We saw dat fight with you and dat fool Stanley Boudreaux, *ça c'est un couillon*," she repeated, calling Stanley a fool in Cajun French. "If you need a witness, Beau, I'll stand for you," she offered. "He's been out of control for some time. He comes here and gets *chockayed* all da time. He's a drunk. Hey," she laughed lightly. "One of my customers videoed him when he went after dat pretty junk dealer. We just looked at it. His eyes were like big gumbo bowls when she got in his face and told him off. What did she say, Beau? We have bets on it. I said, she told him she knew where da best junk yards are to bury his body where nobody would find him. Am I right?"

He simply shrugged, then looked at Jewell, the tension easing as he saw her sitting so calmly next to him.

"I knew you wouldn't tell us," Sylvia complained. "Man, oh, man. There were bets on that, too." She raised her voice so Jewell would hear her. Beau leaned closer to Jewell so they could share the phone. "Hey, pretty lady, are you goin' to tell us what you tole Stanley?"

She smiled. "No point in it. It's over. Let it rest."

Sylvia grumbled under her breath. "Well, I guess I can respect dat. You're not lookin' to make a mountain out of an ant hill."

"All anyone needs to know is that Jewell handled him perfectly," Beau added. "Pass the word that I don't want to see that video on YouTube or on any social media."

"Looks like you handled it perfectly," Sylvia said, the noise level increasing in the background. "Oh, lookie dere, Beau. His wife is pickin' him up in da parkin' lot and Marty's cab pulled in behind her. I'd love to be a mouse in da backseat of her car and hear what she has to say when she sees his bloody lip."

"I bet you would."

"Oh, and Beau. Sorry about YouTube. It's already been posted." She hung up.

"It'll go viral, you know." Jewell said and smiled her sweet half-smile. His chest got warm.

"Hungry?" he asked, pulling back onto the road.

She nodded, then looked at her watch. "I have a couple of hours before Mimi returns to the camper from Bingo. Do you know a restaurant where none of your troubled clients will show up?"

"Yes." He squeezed her hand. "I have the perfect place. Quiet. No chance of us ending up on Facebook." She looked out of the window. All humor disappeared from her eyes. "I'm sorry you were dragged into that drama. Next time, when I tell you to stay put, stay put."

"Next time? Do you often have fights with drunk clients in parking lots?"

"No. Thank God." He chuckled, then his laughter faded, as he heard his words echo in his head.

Next time.

Those were words that indicated there would be future outings with Jewell. Hell, if he was really honest with himself, he realized that was exactly what he wanted.

"Beau, do you want to talk about the big elephant in the truck?" Her question had him wondering if she read his thoughts. Did she sense he was thinking about moving their relationship into another category, as foolish as that was? The "one-night-stand to get her out of my system" category was one thing, but the *"next time"* category was something entirely different.

Damn, who was he really fooling? He never, ever had more than a two-week relationship with any woman, so why was he even mentally worrying over this now? Something just felt different with Jewell. Something off, something weird, and something—whatever that something was—told him that two weeks wouldn't be long enough.

Mon Dieu.

"Beau?" She shifted in her seat to look at him. "Do you need to talk about what happened? Debrief?"

Ah, the elephant. She was talking about what happened with Stanley. He felt relief. "No. Stanley and I are finished. He fired me."

"I heard." She curled both knees onto the front bench seat, tucked her dress modestly around her legs. "It had to stir painful memories, dealing with him in his current state. I know you called Ronald and Bernice your real parents when you spoke to your client, but..." she sucked in a breath. It sounded like she'd felt some kind of pain. "I don't know. I've moved on past my mother, but something will pop up and bam. My feelings are raw, fresh. I'm just saying...I don't know what I'm saying. Forget about it."

Beau touched her hand again. "I know what you're saying." He looked ahead on the dark, familiar road he'd driven thousands of times in his life. This would be the drive he'd remember. "Yes. You're right. Stanley stirred memories and feelings I thought were gone. Or at least I wanted to believe were gone."

She nodded. "If you don't want to talk about it, it's okay. I just thought you might need to cleanse a bit. Not let what happened fester emotionally. You know, get it said, sorted and dealt with so you can move on."

If it had been anyone other than Jewell, he would've said that was a ridiculous thing to do, but she understood the ingrained emotions of the child of abusive parents in a way most people did not. "I want to tell you to mind your own business, you know."

She laughed softly. "But..."

"But you're right. I need to talk this through." He glanced at her. Her eyes were set on his, her expression nonjudgmental. There was no pity in them either. Just understanding. "Yes, Stanley reminded me of my father. My father never achieved the level of success that Stanley has, but he had the potential for it at one point in his life. A point I never saw, but heard about from people in Cane when they saw bruises on me and tried to be kind to me."

She nodded, but didn't say a word. She gave him the time and space to tell her what was on his mind. So he did. He couldn't say exactly why, but he felt safe doing it.

"Tonight, I thought about the day I confronted my father. The day I told him I wouldn't take his abuse any longer."

"How old were you?"

"Thirteen." He blew out a breath, turned safely off the highway onto a dirt road in a sugarcane field and parked. He wasn't ready to go to his house, where he wanted to take her.

Not just yet.

He didn't want this conversation to be the first memory they had there together. The headlights pointed into the dark abyss of the thick, seemingly endless cane fields and night. He turned off the engine. The lights.

"I don't know why I waited so long." Hell, yes, he did. "I did evasive maneuvers for years. You know, hid in the woods with my brother. Hid in my room away from him. Hid at Ben's house." He turned to face Jewell, played with her long braid that now hung over her shoulder. "Tonight, I felt the same kind of anger and uselessness I haven't felt since I was thirteen and confronted my father."

He looked out the front window, lost in the memory.

He continued. "Jackson and I were already living with Ronald and Bernice for about a year as foster kids. My father often showed up drunk at their house, making one demand or another of them. Usually money. I remember it was a really cold day outside. We couldn't go outside to play. My dad, Ronald, had to work with the record cold causing busted pipes and wreaking havoc around town. Momma Bernice had gone to town for bread." He laughed a nervous laugh. "She was always having to run to the store for something because we were hungry growing boys always emptying her pantry. Anyway, it was around Christmas. Hmm. I remember that, I think it must've been the day after or close to it because Jackson and I were playing a Super Mario video game we'd gotten as a present. It was the first video game we ever owned." He looked at her and she smiled, sharing that nice memory.

"That was when he showed up." Her smile faded. "He needed money. He always needed money. Sometimes he sent my mother over to ask for it. When he was desperate, he came himself. Since Bernice and Ronald weren't there, it really ticked him off, especially seeing us in the nice clean house, wearing new clothes, and playing a brand new game on a new TV."

He shook his head. "He was furious. One thing led to another, and he started breaking things in the house; the TV and video game were first. Then he turned his anger on Jackson. Typical. The weakest person there." He closed his eyes. "That's why I just knew Stanley would go after you." He looked at her, took her hand into his and held it gently. "He'd try to hurt you. He'd hurt you to hurt me. It's what happened with Jackson that day. Or started to. I couldn't let him do it. I charged him. I was so angry. All of the rage built up in me from the years of his being cruel and my mother standing by and letting him—it all exploded in that moment. I knocked him over, jumped on top of him and beat the crap out of him until he was bloody and unconscious.

"Jackson pulled me off him. Then we both dragged him outside and dumped him in the yard. I called Ronald and told him, 'I killed the son of a bitch. Come arrest me.'" Beau laughed a sad laugh. "He wasn't dead. Hell, he's still alive today, living off the government in the same dumpy house...alone. His wife, my biological mother, died ten years ago. I went to her funeral, paid for it. He didn't show up."

Jewell shifted closer to him. "You know, I'm not a child," she said. "I'm a tough lady. You're not a child. You're a strong man. People like your father and Stanley can't hurt us. Not really. Bruises heal. We're smart enough to know the emotional hurt they inflict is their sickness. Their issues. We've done nothing wrong. We don't deserve that treatment."

"Yes, indeed." He nodded as he kissed her on top of the head. "I think I've always understood that, because I was blessed enough to see how good people behaved and treated their families." He put his arm around Jewell's shoulder and hugged her. Holding her felt right. Her warmth and light weight against his side felt comfortable. "Ben was like a cousin or even a brother to me well before Ronald and Bernice took me in. Tante Izzy was always like my grandmother."

"We were both saved by strong people who protected us." She looked up at him. "They gave us second chances. We were smart enough to take it."

He nodded.

"It's why I'll do anything and everything to make Mimi's life better. For her giving me a second chance and simply because I love her."

Beau liked hearing her say the words "I love." His heart pounded hard in his chest. In that moment he wanted her to say them about him, and it scared the crap out of him. Was he feeling so vulnerable and emotional talking about his childhood after dealing with a drunken irrational client, that it made him wishy-washy in the brain? Hell, this was not something he should try to figure out now when his feelings were raw.

"I'm hungry," he said, starting the car and turning on the lights. He was ready to take her to his house now. It was weird how nervous he felt about it. How important it became to him that she would like it. "I want to show you something."

She slid to her side of the seat, as though she sensed that he'd put a wall between them. When he looked at her in the dark cab, he could see, even with only the dim light cast by the full harvest moon shining through the truck windows, that she looked relieved.

He drove slowly down the bumpy side road. She'd been right that they'd been given a second chance. He thought of what her life must've been like as a child, with a famous mother in a wanton profession on decadent Bourbon Street. How had her mother's behavior, and the lifestyle associated with her profession, affect Jewell? Based on the story of the abusive jerk boyfriend, Beau figured Praline probably hadn't shielded Jewell from it, or Mignon wouldn't have raised her.

What scars had it left that surfaced in the solid, respectable adult life she'd created? *Oh, hell. This isn't my problem.* He didn't want to empathize with her. It clouded the solid boundaries that he'd established to protect the family that saved him and Jackson.

Boundaries?

What a joke. He'd crossed those boundaries to hold her in his arms. To kiss her. To desire her like he'd desired no one else. Who was he kidding? Now he wondered if he could reestablish those boundaries. This was new territory for him. Seemed logical, though, that if he'd just get her out of his system, give his body what it craved, then he'd crave it no more.

The other part of the fix he realized was to get Jewell to finish the job for Elli, finish her investigation on Mignon's Twinnie and get her the hell out of Cane. Only then would his life be back to normal again.

But not tonight.

***

"We're only about two miles from Sugar Mill, right?" Jewell asked, trying to get her bearings by looking for landmarks she wasn't sure were actually there.

"A little more than that," Beau answered as he turned off the main highway into the first marked driveway past Sugar Mill Plantation. She looked into the silvery night, making out the silhouette of the sugarcane fields around them. "It feels creepy and beautiful at the same time."

"Feeling spooked?" His light eyes glowed bright, looking mystical.

"If I didn't trust you and my ability to defend myself, I'd be totally spooked."

"I should be the one who is spooked. I saw how you defended yourself earlier." He gave an exaggerated fake shiver. "Besides that, I know you like to pack heat."

"Ha, ha. Well, rest easy. I left my weapon hidden in the camper...Where are you taking me, Beau? Some backwater restaurant?" When he didn't answer right away, she realized where he was taking her. "Is this the way to your house, Beau?"

"Yes, I wanted to show you my work in progress and grab a quick meal where we won't run into any more drama."

"I don't know..." She looked up at the line of sixteen ancient oaks, eight on each side of the drive that created a dramatic canopy over the well-maintained road. "Wow," her voice sounded breathy to her own ears. "The moonlight shining through the stately oaks makes this all look so magical. Not spooky at all. Oh, Beau, this is stunning." She looked at him; his face was smooth, expressionless. Yet, something in his eyes hinted that he was nervous. "Is this why you wanted me to see this? It's amazing."

She rolled down her window, tilted her head out and inhaled deeply. The air was cool, damp.

"It smells so fresh. Clean." She touched his arm. "Could you stop a moment? Just a moment."

He braked. "See something?"

"I want to listen." The sound of the truck's old engine seemed to bounce off the branches of the trees. "Can you please turn off the engine?"

He turned off the rumbling engine and instantly the night sounds of the crickets, owls and distant gators filled the space around them. The fragrance of moist trees and grass, and of Beau's masculine clean, earthy scent floated on the air. It felt like a dream.

"This is what it sounded and smelled and felt like two hundred years ago," she whispered. "Maybe there would've been a horse and buggy clomping nearby with a gentleman and his wife riding side by side, dressed in their evening finery. They might be headed to a special dinner or social gathering where the sounds of laughter, music and clinking glasses would greet them through the open windows as they arrived."

Beau stretched his arms over the back of the seat and rested his head on the seat. Jewell felt his eyes on her. "You're hidden in the night shadows, but your dress is glowing an almost ghostly kind of blue in the moonlight." He pinched a bit of her dress fabric between his finger and thumb and rubbed it. "You really like to transport yourself into the past, don't you?"

"Yes, I do. I like to imagine being there." She closed her eyes. "I don't like all of the political and social struggles of the time. It was awful. I'm sure I would've been deep into the fight to right the injustices, but I would've loved being part of the rise of the beautiful architecture and the introduction of the new traditions and cultures into the area. I would love to have observed the growth of a new community. That era seems so much simpler in many ways. Not easier, but clearer."

He turned to face her, tucking a long curl behind her ear. His light touch on the tender flesh of her ear made her shiver. She rubbed the chill from her arms.

"Is life so terrible for you today, beautiful Jewell?"

She looked at him. How much should she reveal to this man who had carried her in a fairy tale-like dance on the cypress plank floor, who had tried to protect her from a violent man who stirred to life awful demons from his childhood, and who now made her feel like he both wanted her near and far from him at the same time? "I don't know how to answer that honestly." Her eyes filled with tears she didn't know were so close to the surface. She looked away, hating that she felt so confused and vulnerable with Beau. It frightened her.

He gently clasped her chin and turned her to face him. "Your eyes speak of loneliness, *chère*. They speak of your battle and your doubt. They tell me you are tired." He kissed the first tear that fell onto her cheek. "Don't be sad."

"I don't mean to be." She rested her head on his shoulder, allowing him to gather her in his arms. She sighed.

Beau felt her sigh rumble through the marrow of his bones. It was cold and achy. He understood instinctively that it was the feeling of utter and complete loneliness. It felt awful. Even in his worst time with his parents in the sagging shack, he wasn't alone. He had his brother who loved him...who had his back. He knew that Jackson would be there if he needed him. Later, he also had Bernice, Ronald, Ben, Tante Izzy and the rest of the Bienvenu clan. Once her Mimi was gone, Jewell would have no one. Hell, with her grand-mère's advanced dementia, she *really* didn't even have anyone now. His breath caught as he tried to speak. He cleared his throat.

"Do you have friends in New Orleans, *chère*?"

He felt her shrug. "They were fair-weather friends. Not real friends. When my life got complicated, they didn't want to complicate their lives. I have a few old college buddies in other states. The kind you forever have a tender spot for in your heart, but who are too distant and busy for visits or many calls." She sat quietly. The only movement was from her breathing. "It's a pathetic thing to admit, but I guess Mimi is my best friend."

"That's endearing. It also must break your heart to see your best friend slipping away." He thought of how difficult it had been to lose Bernice, only a few years after she'd become such a wonderful mother for him and his brother.

She sucked in a soft, gasping breath as if she'd been stabbed. The tears were flowing now.

"Sweet Jewell. You're in mourning. You probably have been for some time."

"What?" She looked at him, her lashes wet, her heart exposed in her dark, dark eyes. She continued to stare at him for what seemed like minutes. Her intelligent gaze assessing what he'd said. "Yes. I guess I am. I hadn't realized it. But I am. That's exactly how I feel." Her breath was ragged, her voice weak. "Oh, God. How will I live without her?" She grabbed his shirt, her fingers digging into his chest. Her raw emotion was thick, palpable, in the interior of the old truck. "What will I do, Beau? Oh, God. I can't breathe. I can't breathe." Her chest was heaving up and down, up and down. "My heart hurts. It hurts, Beau."

He wrapped his arms around her narrow waist, rubbed his hands over her back and let her cry. He whispered words of encouragement, told her how brave she was. How good a granddaughter she was. What wonderful memories she'd created and would always have. "And you still have time to create more."

She nodded. "She's leaving me alone while she's still here. It's tearing me apart."

Her pain tore into his heart.

"Oh, God. I don't want her to leave me." Her fingers dug into his arms. "She's my nucleus. Who will love me unconditionally? Who will even know that I exist? Who will know my history? Oh, God, Beau, I could die in my home and no one would know or care." She sucked in a breath. "Do you know that Mimi didn't recognize me last week? She woke up in the middle of the night, calling for "Twinnie." When I went to her, she looked at me with the most god-awful blank look on her face. She wasn't there, and I couldn't be there for her." She clutched her chest.

"I'm sorry, Jewell." He kissed her on the top of her head again. "You know all anyone has is this moment. Elli taught me that. We have to live in this very moment. Take every single thing life has to offer us this second. I saw it from Elli's perspective as a person who nearly died fighting breast cancer." He stroked her hair, feeling the silken strands against his palm. "I see how it makes sense for all of us, in all times of our lives. Life reminds us how precious the moments are." He thought about that before continuing. "Elli says we need to live like those crazy dogs. They don't worry about tomorrow or yesterday or the next second." He twirled a long lock of her hair around his finger, smelling the clean scent of her floral shampoo and the sweet earthy scent of her damn bug repellent. "I don't know about all that, but if we just appreciate what we have right now, we can be happier for right now. It won't take away the sadness and pain of what is to come."

She nodded.

"When I was a kid, all I could think about was the future. I imagined wearing clean, nice clothes. Living in a house without empty beer cans littering it. Where food was eaten hot at the kitchen or dining room table without fear that a hand would come out of nowhere and knock me to the floor." Her tears were still flowing quietly down her cheeks. "I spent so much time worrying about getting that, hating my life, that I lost my childhood and the moments that I could've enjoyed." He stroked her hair. "I don't want to lose another day to bad stuff." He swallowed hard. "I was rescued..."

"You rescued yourself. You made a decision to move forward and not let that terrible time define you."

"Yes, *chère*. I did it because my dad, Ronald, and my mom, Bernice, gave me a second chance. They were my true parents."

"Mimi is my true parent." She sniffed. Her fingers gently stroked the side of his face. "We were so blessed that people cared about us."

He grabbed her hand and kissed her palm. "Not everyone has that, Boots." He kissed the inside of her wrist, the inside of her elbow. She sighed.

"I'm so tired of my heart hurting."

He kissed the tips of each of her fingers, took each one into his mouth and enjoyed the feel of it sliding over his tongue. Her breathing changed as she slid closer to him on the front seat of the old truck. She wrapped her arms around his neck.

She kissed his cheek, whispered in his ear. "Thank you for listening." She nibbled on his ear. Now his breathing changed. He sucked in the warm, humid air around them. "I want to forget for a little while. I want to live in this moment." She kissed him, not holding back her passion and desire. The roots of his hair tingled.

"Oh, *chère*." He deepened the kiss, pulled her on top of him, and lay back on the seat. His hands slid down her back, over her derrière. He felt the edge of her underwear. Her thong. "Holy damn. You do wear a thong..." He squeezed her firm round bottom and pulled her tighter against his arousal. She groaned. Her erotic sound was more beautiful than the crickets' song under the harvest moon.

Her hands were as anxious as his, as she pulled the bottom of his shirt from his pants. She slipped her hand under the shirt, touching his heated flesh. His muscles bunched under her hands. He sucked in a breath, her unique, special scent filling his lungs, making him want her impossibly more.

"Tell me what you want me to do, Beau. Tell me." She lifted his shirt and kissed his chest, her tongue and lips leaving a path to his nipples.

"You're doing just fine. Better than fine," he managed to say, as he grabbed her perfect bottom and pulled her tighter on top of him. She shifted, opened her legs to sit astride. He reached up, grabbed her breasts and gently ran his flat palms over them, feeling the hard points of her nipples. He lifted his head up, closed his mouth over her right nipple, through thin fabric and bra.

She threw her head back and moaned. "That feels good."

He tried to move, but his knee hit the steering wheel, limiting him. He tried to open the buttons of her dress, but they were so small, his fingers so clumsy he couldn't do it; he took her hands off him and pressed them to her chest. "Buttons." She smiled a wicked smile and started to unbutton her dress. Beau didn't waste a moment, he was too needy to be patient. He pulled the fabric of her dress free from the tangle of their bodies, lifted it and ran his hand up her thigh. It was firm and smooth and so damn hot. She was hot everywhere. He was hot. Perspiration made them both slick, and it was damn sexy. He groaned.

He ran his hand along the tiny triangle of fabric over her center. She lifted a little to give him full access as her dress fell open. Then he saw it. The tiny fleur-de-lis tattoo low on her hipbone. It was partly covered by the single narrow strap of her white lacy thong. Beau outlined the small design with his finger, knowing he'd have to do the same with his mouth later. Then, he'd have the lights on. He'd be able to see what images were drawn on each of the three arching flower petals of the fleur-de-lis and on its center.

He sucked in a breath, looked up at her as she shifted and moved in the most erotic dance against him.

"I like this, *chère*," he whispered, running his finger over her tattoo, then letting his finger slide over her hip along the edge of her thong's thin strip of lace—until his fingers dipped to where their bodies met so intimately.

She smiled that sexy half smile of hers, and he thought he'd explode into a million pieces right there beneath her. He lifted his body to kiss her. He had to kiss her, feel her hot, lush lips on his. She lowered her mouth to meet him.

When their lips met, Beau saw bright white light, felt the white heat too. She moaned with her pleasure as he did with his, as their tongues and bodies moved in a rhythm that brought them to an erotic place Beau hadn't known existed.

She was beautiful. As she rose above him, sliding over him, her lush, glistening body was exposed for him to see. Her breasts were full, spilling out of her bra. Her waist was tiny and narrow, her legs, long and lean.

"Beau. This feels so good. I want you to feel this good."

"Oh, *chère,* I do." He touched her breasts, sat up and unfastened her bra. He tossed it, and it flew out the window.

"Oops." He smiled. "We'll get that later."

She laughed. "If a raccoon doesn't get it first."

"Nah, not her size." He shifted on his side. "Come a little closer, darlin'. I'm getting lonely." He pulled her alongside of him. "You're so magnificent. Perfection." His large hands eased down to dip inside the lace between her legs. She was wet heat. And so damn ready. He'd been wanting her for days. Wanting her more than he'd ever wanted anyone. Now he'd get her out of his system. They'd get out of each other's systems. And they'd do it with the best sex of his life.

He shifted his weight awkwardly on the narrow seat, crashing into the steering wheel again. "Out," he shouted. "We need to get out of here. Need more room."

Jewell leaned over him and opened the door. Instead of climbing out, she eased her body down on him, kissed him deeply, passionately. "I can't move off you," she said. "Don't want to."

"Then don't." He reached down, unbuttoned his jeans. She kneeled over him, hooked her hand over the waistband of his jeans and underwear and with a lot of effort and laughing from both of them in the tight quarters, slid both down, freeing him.

"Tell me what to do," she pleaded.

"Wallet. Back pocket," he managed.

Reaching in, Jewell pulled out his wallet, found the condom and handed it to him. Tearing it open with his teeth, he slid it on quickly, distracted as he watched her slip out of her thong. Gripping her hips, he slid her down onto him. They both sucked in a breath. Looked at each other. Her orgasm started seconds before his.

Chapter 15

There's a peace when you stop fighting, when you know you have no power. God had decided my mind should relax and rest. I decided I should do the same. Then I found the grace I didn't expect...or at least I don't think I expected, since I can't remember if I expected it or not. The thing is this. You think that because you can't remember very much of anything anymore, that each day you will have to wake up and have to learn peace and acceptance all over again...but you don't. That's the grace...the gift. You do it once, and it is done.

I just wish that my granddaughter will learn acceptance and peace enough to welcome true love into her heart so she doesn't have to wake up each day, over and over again, not knowing that gift.

***

Beau parked in the front of his home. It was country dark. There were no lights from neighboring homes or subdivision streets to brighten the night. Only the amber glow of the full moon and the headlights from Tante Izzy's truck hinted that there was a very large home hidden within in a grove of majestic oak trees. He tapped an icon on his mobile phone and the house was hidden no more. It appeared that every light inside and outside of the modern glass and steel home instantly turned on.

"Wow," she gasped. "It's stunning. And, exactly as I would expect your home to be." New. Modern. Sleek. Expensive.

"I know it's not like the plantation and old homes you like," he began, with a shrug. "But it's home."

Jewell found it endearing that he seemed to be both proud and apologetic for his modern home. "It's lovely, Beau. Beautiful. It looks like a piece of art."

She meant it. Her tastes always had been to the historical homes. Rarely did she find pleasure in the clean lines of a contemporary home, but she had to admit, Beau's home looked right nestled in the ancient trees and set along the bayou side. Its peaks, curves and angles blended harmoniously with the peaks of the adjacent ancient cypresses and oaks, the curves of the slow moving bayou and the angles of meadows and fields nearby.

"I'm glad you like it." He slid his arm over the back of the seat and drew her tighter against his side. He turned to look at his house, and Jewell took the moment to steal a lover's glance at him.

He was a beautiful, disheveled sexy mess. His hair was tousled where her eager fingers had raked through the silken waves. His shirt was untucked, half unbuttoned, and wrinkled from her tugging on it so she could get to the hard muscle and smooth flesh of his back and abdomen. His dark, tight jeans were still unbuttoned, the fly folded open to reveal his gray boxer briefs that rode provocatively low. This man who was devastatingly handsome in his tidy classic clothes was even more so half undressed in the front seat of an old truck.

"You know," he began, sounding a little less sure of himself than he usually did. "I can't say why, but I wanted you to like my house." He looked at her, making a dismissive, carefree expression. "Hell, maybe..." he hesitated, his eyes looking young, vulnerable. "I may have been a little nervous about you seeing it." Then he laughed, his accent got heavier, his tone lighter. "I figured maybe you'd give me an opinion if my home was going to be as good as an antique plantation two hundred years from now." He was joking, but Jewell wasn't fooled by the dodge. This confident, self-assured man's eyes didn't hide that he really cared what she thought about his home.

Jewell reached up, kissing him gently on his cheek.

He sucked in his breath as if her kiss had touched him in some profound way. Tears filled her eyes, but she fought to keep them contained. "We have to make sure you have a grand title for your home so when it is on the historic register, it will be quite the thing." Her heart beat a little faster knowing her opinion mattered that much to him. It felt important. Like his tender words and understanding had to her in the truck earlier before they had made love.

Or maybe she was just imagining it.

Was she just acting like her mother did with men? Transferring her hopes and thoughts and applying it to the situation when all they really had was great sex, a physical connection that left her feeling so wonderful because of endorphins? God, she was losing it, thinking it was more than that. She suddenly felt pathetic. Vulnerable.

She slid to her side of the truck and opened the door. "Are you going to feed me or not?" she said, laughing on the surface while she was crying on the inside.

"I have a home-cooked, spectacular meal planned for you that will knock you off your feet and into my bed, *chère*." He grinned. "You know, we're going to do it right next time."

Jewell had thought it was pretty darn right the first time.

"First, Nancy needs to get out of her carrier and go outside," he said, taking her hand and leading her toward the front entrance. He gave her a construction lesson along the way. "The house was built with steel and concrete, but you mostly see the stonework and glass," he told her pointing to the gray and brown tones of the exterior house beams and frame. "It's low maintenance. And, the hurricane glass and the other materials are more resistant to mold, termites and all of the things that we have to deal with down here."

"The colors mimic nature beautifully," she said, appreciating the artistic beauty of the house. "All those windows let you see this beautiful land." In the daytime, she imagined, his views would be exceptional. "Now I understand why you were so good at cleaning the barn windows that first day I was working in there," she laughed. "Lots of practice."

He laughed. "Nah. I have a window washing system on the house. "

They walked up three short levels of stairs over three separate terraces, to reach the first floor, which actually was on the second floor. Beau again said that extra elevation was the practical thing to do when hurricane season was half the year and you lived close to the gulf coast. Jewell understood after living though Katrina.

Beau unlocked the front door with another tap on his phone and opened the huge steel door. They entered and were greeted by a grandiose hall and the wood treads and glass rail of the winding staircase leading to the open living and kitchen area with panoramic windows from floor to ceiling facing the bayou at the rear of the house. Moths and other insects flew in and out of the beams of the outside lights that shone on the path leading to the bayou behind the house.

Jewell turned in a circle in the main living room, slipping a little on the blond maple floors. "This is incredible. There's so much volume in this room with the soaring ceilings...and the barnwood beams are so huge. I feel so tiny in here."

"I think once I have it furnished, it'll feel less like a shopping mall." He smiled. "I just have the sofa and chair." He pointed toward the floor-to-ceiling fireplace on the far end of the room where a deep-seated white leather sofa and chair rested. For the third time, he tapped on his phone. This time the fireplace ignited with a soft whoosh and glowing flame.

"Let me look at that," she teased, reaching for his phone. He hid it behind his back. "What else can it do? It's like a magic wand."

He lifted a brow and grinned. "Oh, I have some extra special features on this thing that I can show you in my bedroom. Want to see?"

She laughed. "I think we need to let Nancy out of her carrier."

"So that means we can play with my apps afterwards?"

Her stomach did the same flippy thing that it had done when she first met him. She was saved from answering him as he grabbed her hand and led her through the maple wood and white kitchen to the mudroom behind it. Nancy was barking her sweet high-pitched puppy bark, excited to see them. They let her out of her crate, and she greeted them with happy tail wagging and enthusiastic jumping. Beau swept her into his arms. He settled the sweet, anxious boxer puppy as he carried her outside where Jewell joined him. Nancy took care of business quickly and returned to Beau for praise and loving.

When they returned inside, they walked into the mudroom-slash-laundry room where they tossed their shoes off. When Beau noticed she was wearing the white tube socks Mimi had been darning, he laughed, knelt in front of her and slipped them off.

"I never, ever thought that white tube socks could be as sexy as they are right now." He stroked the tops of her feet, stood and kissed her so deeply and passionately that she didn't think they'd make it to the bedroom to play with his phone. When Nancy started to whine and scratch Beau's leg for her usual post-potty treat, he took Jewell's hand and they walked into the kitchen, barefoot, with him constantly sneaking looks at her feet. It excited Jewell to see that he could be so aroused by something as simple as her long, skinny feet.

Beau refused to let her go into the rest of the house until they had eaten, saying if she did, she'd be too distracted to eat, and he'd be too distracted by her to care about eating too.

They sat at an old round walnut table that looked like it was a hand-me-down. It wasn't modern at all, but the lines were simple enough to work in the space. It gave Jewell some ideas about some of the pieces of found furniture she had in New Orleans.

"You know, Beau, I'm not sure how you plan to decorate your home, but you may consider an eclectic style. Mixed pieces. Older, warmer pieces that are restored but with clean lines." She picked up Nancy and cuddled her.

"Honestly, I'm not good at decorating," he admitted. "I knew what kind of home I wanted, but the pieces to put it in it..." he shrugged. "I don't know. I figured, I'd know it when I see it."

"I have the perfect table for your dining room area," she said. "It's in my warehouse. I'd love for you to see it." She walked into the space imagining it there. "It's a beautiful antique Danish dining table. Beautiful. It's quite unusual in that it seats fourteen. Maybe a couple more if you want to squeeze in a bit for those big family dinners." She smiled, thinking of Big John having to scoot over closer to Ruby and eat with his elbows tucked in. "It would suit this house. You. It's elegant, but not fanciful. It's formal but not stuffy." She looked at him. "I'm sorry. I don't mean to try to furnish your house."

He came up to her, lifted her chin and gave her a gentle, simple, but what felt like an intentioned kiss. "The dining table sounds like exactly what I envisioned for the room." He tapped his index finger on her nose, took Nancy from her and cradled her so her head rested in the bend of his elbow.

"I'm going to look through my inventory and see if there are other pieces you may like. I'll show you pictures of what I find." The pleasure she felt thinking about finding furniture to place in his modern home was fleeting, however, when she realized she had no business planning things in the future. Not when she had an upcoming trial that could erase her future. Jewell's stomach suddenly tightened into a knot of stress and worry. She tried to think of happier things to replace the fear of a guilty verdict and what that would mean in her life. It didn't work.

"I'd like to see what you recommend, Jewell. Thank you," he said, as he opened a bottle of chilled Chardonnay for their dinner. She accepted a glass, pretending all was right with the world.

The wine turned out to be much finer than their meal, but not as endearing. His spectacular home-cooked dinner consisted of scrambled eggs that were highly seasoned with Louisiana Hot Sauce, undercooked turkey bacon, and burned multigrain toast. Once finished, Jewell jumped up and walked down a wide hallway on the same level, not waiting for his permission. When she opened the first door on her left, she found a fairly large half bath. It was unadorned, but had a very nice, oversized marble sink and tall arcing faucets. "I have a great turquoise Turkish rug that would be great in there," she said, as she was closing the door and heading to the only other room down the hall.

She glanced at Beau over her shoulder. He was smiling at her, holding Nancy and leaning against the wall. She opened the door, waved to him and stepped inside the room. She gasped. It was a glass room. Floor-to-ceiling walls of glass on two sides of the room and most of the ceiling above it. "This is spectacular." She moved so close to the glass that she saw her breath fog into a small spot on it.

Jewell saw Beau's reflection in the glass as he came into the room and sat on the corner of the bed. "This is incredible, Beau. Incredible." She spoke staring out into the dark night, beyond where the outside lights illuminated the yard and bayou side. "Good thing you don't have neighbors, or you wouldn't have any privacy."

"I own all the land around here."

"Small town lawyers do well, then."

"Good ones who invest well do." He put Nancy on the ground and she trotted to Jewell, the tags on her collar jingling as she did. Jewell bent down and petted her.

"I'm happy for you. " She looked at him. "You know, you really don't need much furniture in here. It's so beautiful. Why clutter it?"

"I've got a king-sized bed so my feet don't hang off the end." He laughed, waving to the bed that looked a full size smaller because of the enormous space of the room. "A good, comfortable mattress. A smart TV. What else do I need?"

Jewell looked around. "You're all set. You even painted the room a soft ecru, making it nice and tranquil."

"Is ecru beige?"

Jewell laughed. "Yes."

"I thought I had painted it white, until Ruby said it was off-white. Tante Izzy said it was cream. That's when I thought it might be beige." He shrugged. "I told you, I'm not a decorator."

She laughed. "That was a conversation I would've enjoyed hearing." He might not be a decorator, but he had style. She'd seen it in his clothes, cars, sunglasses and now in his home.

He patted the bed next to him. "Have a seat."

Jewell's stomach did a somersault that had nothing to do with bad thoughts of her legal mess and everything to do with the sexy man inviting her in his bed. Wanting a man to invite her to his bed as much as she did now was a brand new experience for her.

She walked to him with her heart racing and sat a little away from him, feeling nervous and shy. His earthy, clean, sensual scent wrapped around her as much as his unique style signature did in his home. Masculine. Sophisticated. Complicated. Yet simple.

Nancy trotted to a black and gray woven pillow at the foot of his bed, where after making three circles on it, she went to sleep. Beau leaned back onto his elbows.

"You smell good," she said, her voice timid, awkward. It embarrassed her that it was.

Beau didn't smile. His pupils dilated. His eyelids seemed to get heavy. "It's not from bug repellent, I can assure you," he joked.

She smiled, looked toward one of the nightstands next to his bed. There was a TV remote there, an iPad, a charger cord for his phone, a chrome lamp and four-inch stack of files. His personal things were all on the left side. His side. She didn't have a side. Her bed was too small for sides.

Knowing which side of the bed he preferred seemed so intimate. Not that having sex with him wasn't. Both things were confusing to Jewell since he'd established himself as the tyrant border guard with her not so very long ago. He probably still felt that way, even though they'd physically crossed the formidable barricade. He'd let her over to his side, but she had to remember that he would toss her back and shut the barricade again.

Still, right now, in this special domain of his, she was allowed to see who he really was. She saw it as much as when he was laughing and advising and loving his family. Dare she allow herself to just accept this visit to his side? Savor it? Or should she not set herself up for the pain she might feel when she was locked out again?

Or locked up if her trial went badly and she was convicted?

If she understood this night for what it was, why should there be any pain at all? She was logical. Reasonable. She didn't have to be emotional. Why shouldn't she capture a really solid, wonderful memory to take with her? Wasn't it better to have the amazing memory of a real experience than to regret never having it?

"Is that the painting of Emile, François and his son that Tante Izzy spoke of?" she asked, pointing to the large, colorful oil painting hanging on the wall near the door. Jewell got up and went to examine it. She recognized the older man as François from photos she'd seen of him in her research. He was standing in the center. The other older man on the right must've been his brother Emile, and the younger man on the left had to be François's only surviving child, Aguste. The boy he had with his second wife, Caroline Cecile. All three men had their arms hanging loosely over each other's shoulders in a friendly, jovial pose. Their grins were huge, eyes twinkling. They looked happy under the huge oak with its moss-draped branches. The plantation was in the background behind them.

The men in the painting could've been Beau with the men he was closest to...Jackson and Ben, she thought. She let herself enjoy that idea, blurring all of the details of the painting she hadn't yet examined.

"Yes. She gave it to me as a housewarming gift," Beau answered, now standing next to her. She hadn't heard him approach. He leaned against the wall next to the painting, his eyes focused on her. She'd seen him look just like this so many times before. Seemingly relaxed, carefree, with his arms folded over his chest. Not a care in the world, although his eyes told a different story. He seemed like a man ready to pounce. To protect or take what he wanted. The dangerous tiger.

She was his prey.

Only she didn't have the fear of the hunted as she walked back to the bed, on the very edge near the head. So why had she moved as far away from him as possible, she wondered as her palm sank into the one of the four white, down king pillows at the head of the bed. It was soft, comfy, perfect for a long night of sleep after exhausting sensual play. She blushed at having the thought, but she also felt oddly safe having it. Sexual contemplations never, ever, felt safe before. Not because of the sex itself, but because of how it made her afraid that she had these thoughts because she was more like her mother than she ever wanted to be.

She looked at Beau, still watching her from across the room, his eyes dark, his hot expression unchanged. Could she really just be herself, explore her sexuality with a man who she felt safe with and not be like her mother? Of course she could. Her studies in human behavior taught her that, but she'd never related it to herself...until now. She'd never really wanted to.

Jewell tamped down what little nervousness she felt. She closed her eyes and just allowed her body and mind to slide into the sensual feelings of the moment. She had no experience with seduction, but when she looked at Beau, saw his dark, aroused, hungry look, she knew she didn't need it. She slid her fingers lightly, slowly...over the white duvet covering the bed and the dark gray chenille throw tossed without a care on top of it. He looked down at her hand, sucked in his breath, then glanced at her bare feet.

Hmm, maybe she'd been wrong. Maybe she wasn't the hunted prey.

He was.

That felt like power to her.

Jewell rested her hands on her lap for a moment, not sure what to do next. She closed her eyes, relaxed her shoulders and her mind, and just let herself exist in the room. She felt the cool air from the whir of the huge no-frills fan above her. She felt the shift of the fabric of her dress brush against her skin as she took in each breath. Her hands went up to her buttons at the waist of her dress. There were no thoughts or plans of sequence. She simply did what she felt like doing. It was liberating.

She opened her eyes when she heard Beau breathing harder. His eyes were on her hands. His lips parted. This seduction, this hunting, was intoxicating.

Arousing.

Emboldened by his reaction and her fearlessness, she moved her hands up to the top buttons near her breasts. They were already undone. She didn't have a bra on. It still remained on the side of the road where Beau had inadvertently tossed it out of the window. Jewell would remind him that she was there without a bra. She let her hands slide over her breasts. Her nipples hardened.

Beau didn't move from the wall. He just leaned and watched and breathed heavier and heavier. She shifted a little, feeling need and desire build between her legs; then she released her braid, shook out her hair, and let it fall down her back.

She thought she heard him groan, but she wasn't sure. He remained where he was. She reached for the top button that held her dress together. It was low, the swell of her breasts showing, her heavy breath making them rise and tease him even more. She released the first button, then the next one. And the next. She let the top material fall open until her left breast was exposed, with just a hint of her aroused nipple showing.

She slid her hand into the top of her dress. Touched her nipple with one hand and slid her other between her legs on top of the dress. *Who is this woman doing this?* The thought slipped through her desire, threatened to stop this new exploration of her awakened sexuality. She closed her eyes again. *No.* She let her head fall back. *Not tonight. Not now.* She may never have another chance where she felt safe, desired and where she desired in turn.

The bed shifted. Jewell felt Beau's heat over her before she looked up and saw him staring at her with his catlike green eyes. His warm breath brushed across the exposed flesh of her neck as he moved closer to her, supporting his weight on his hands, placed on either side of her shoulders.

His mouth was on her, gently, slowly and erotically. His teeth scraped along the long line of her neck. The stubble from his chin roused her sensitive skin. His mouth sealed over her nipple. His groan vibrated over her breast.

Need, hot and instant, consumed her. She fell back onto the bed, sucking for air, grabbing his head with her hands, holding him tighter against her.

"Oh, *chère*." He groaned again, shifting to kneel between her legs. "I want you."

She lifted for him, dragging his head to her mouth. He grabbed the bottom of her dress, clumsily, but he lifted it up, and she raised her arms up overhead to help him. She was naked now, except for her lacy thong.

He got off the bed, stood. Stepped back. Looked down at her with hooded eyes. He smiled. "Beautiful." He slipped off his pants and boxers together and removed his shirt over his head. He stood before her, with a flat, six-pack abdomen, wide shoulders, narrow hips and totally aroused. He climbed on the bed next to her, hugging her naked body to his. The feeling of skin against skin was awakening. She moved to let her heated flesh slide against his.

He kissed her. His lips were gentle, careful, like a man who was handling precious, fragile glass. His fingers moved so lightly over her neck, down her chest, and over her breasts, she felt a whispered plea on her lips. "I want more." Never had she felt such incredible need as she did now. She grabbed his biceps, felt his hard muscles tense beneath her firm grip. She rolled over on top of him, sitting astride. She looked down at him.

He didn't move, held her hips in a tight grip. She could see by the straining cords in his neck that he wanted to take her then. But there was something controlled and tender in his expression. She wanted him to get out of his head, out of his own way, and be as lost in them as she was. She moved over him. He dug his fingers into her hips more tightly.

"You keep that up and I won't have the willpower to go the distance." He grinned. Flipping her over. He was on top of her. "You make me crazy."

She smiled at him and he groaned. "Just that...just that damn smile, and I am so undone. What is your voodoo?"

She kissed him, her mouth and tongue as tender and caring as his as he taught her new sensual explorations, and she gave it back to him, and more. When she took his hand and placed it on her center, he groaned.

"I think we're going to have to do this a lot, Boots. I'm not going to get you out of my system any time soon."

He rolled onto his side on the bed, taking her with him, so she faced him, then he moved down her body, touching, kissing and exploring her curves. His fingers traced the outline of her small fleur-de-lis tattoo just above her thong and he smiled, looking pleased to see it. "Sexy," he murmured, inching down her body with a trail of kisses until he reached the small flares of the design. She liked seeing his soft, peach lips and tongue slide over the blended blue, pink, and yellow colors of her tattoo. Her heart pounded harder. Dang. She really, really liked it. A lot.

His mouth found the top edge of the white lace of her thong along her hip. His fingers ran on the inside of it, following the narrow lace to her bottom and back. He groaned again, sliding her thong down and following the tiny strip of material over her legs with the scrape of his teeth, a bite, and then a tender kiss. She moved. Restless, anxious, and needy with each touch, each kiss. She rolled onto her back, felt the cool, smooth sheets on her skin. It was another sensual stroke, escalating her need. Desire. Wanting what her body was building toward. She looked in his eyes.

"Beau. I need you."

He took a condom from the bedside dresser and quickly slid it on. He eased on top of her, and slowly slipped just a little bit inside of her. She sucked in a breath. Lifted her hips to him. Moved. "More." He slid in a little more. "More."

His face was straining, tight. So handsome. She lifted her hips higher, grabbed his firm buttocks and took him the rest of the way. "Is this what you want, *chère?*" he said, teeth clenched.

"Yes. Yes."

"Me. Too. Oh...me too."

They moved in rhythm, never taking their eyes off of one another. The hunter and the prey...no longer.

"More," she whispered.

"More will never be enough."

He flipped her so she was on top. She moved, in a perfect dance of abandon and sensation with a fearlessness she didn't know existed, until she cried out. Beau looked up at her and smiled, then found his release.

***

Beau held her in his arms. She was on his side of the bed, her leg tossed over him, her arm holding on to the arm securing her to his chest. Her pretty, narrow, bare feet with their surprisingly pale coral painted toenails were wedged between his calves, one on top and one on the bottom.

He'd never actually *slept* with a woman before. He'd tried it a couple of times, but within five minutes it was like crawling through *piquantes* or, as the English called them, cockleburs. Hmm. Not this time.

This felt pretty good.

Having this curvy yet lean woman wrapped around him like he was a Christmas present felt pretty damn good. His lids fluttered shut. "I'll just rest my eyes a moment, Boots, before we leave."

***

An hour later, Jewell's alarm sounded on her phone, jarring him awake. "What the...?" Nancy barked a tired half bark from where she slept on a pillow near Beau's head.

Jewell rested her arms on his chest and looked down at him. "Sorry. I should've warned you. I set the alarm to allow forty-five minutes to get back to Mimi no later than eleven, the time I told Ruby I'd be there in case dinner or our conversation ran long at the restaurant." She shrugged again, lifting her brows and smiling a silly smile. "Never planned on this."

"I like your spontaneity. A lot." He thought of her seducing him on his bed. He would never walk into his room without thinking of her lying here, with her hair like silk ribbons fanned out on the pillow and her dress fallen open to reveal her full, round breasts and dark nipples.

She laughed. "Spontaneous? Not usually." She shook her head, rubbed the back of her neck, and lifted her shoulders. "Being the caregiver of a very tenacious and demanding old lady while running a business doesn't typically allow for it." She tried to get up again, but he held her. "I have to go, Beau. I'll just take Tante Izzy's truck, and you can go back to sleep. If I remember correctly from your conversation with your insurance agent, your rental should be here in the morning, right?"

She kissed him tenderly on his bruised eye and touched it lightly.

"I'm sorry you were hurt." She held the duvet to her chest and sat up. He pulled her back on top of him.

"You're not getting away that easy, Boots." He patted her on her bare bottom, liked the warm, smooth feel of it beneath his hand. He was instantly aroused. By the way her eyes widened, he knew she noticed.

She made a funny face at Nancy, who was staring at her from her comfy pillow. She scratched her under the chin and the pup placed her paw on top of Jewell's hand for her not to stop. "You're a sweetheart, aren't you?"

"I'd like to think so," he teased, earning him a gentle tug of his hair.

"Funny boy." She smiled, tilted her head, right, then left. Did her neck hurt? She seemed to be doing that a lot lately. "I really do have to go." She shrugged, her hair cascading over her shoulders. He reached up and brushed it back off her face.

"I don't want you to go just yet, Jewell," he told her and immediately regretted that he did. Saying he wanted her and needed her in the throes of heated lovemaking was a slip he could explain away, but saying it now in the calm after the sensual storm was another thing. It wasn't a good position for the family advocate to have with a woman he still wasn't sure wasn't trying to scam them.

Oh, hell.

She smiled at him, clearly liking what he'd said about not wanting her to leave. Then she kissed him gently on both of his cheeks.

"That's really sweet, Boots."

"I like when you call me Jewell or even *chère*."

He blew out a breath. *"Chère, Jewell,"* he murmured. Who was he kidding? He was actually sure that she wasn't scamming the family. She'd been fair and inclusive in sharing the information of her investigation of Twinnie. And Mignon clearly wasn't the fraud he thought she might be. She really was a sweet old lady who was suffering from advanced dementia. Jewell had had plenty of opportunities to push Mignon as Martine, but she hadn't. Sure, she'd brought it up as a possibility, but she never tried to close the argument on that idea.

No, Jewell wasn't running a scam. He'd actually come to that conclusion before she'd knocked the wind out of him with the best sex of his life.

Still, he needed proof. Just because his gut and heart said Jewell had absolutely no ill intent toward his family, it wasn't fair for him to move forward making that assumption for everyone. He couldn't expose them in that way. It wasn't what their advocate should do. He needed proof to verify his sexual desire wasn't skewing his decision-making ability. He needed to help her prove her innocence of the criminal felony charges, and he needed to help her prove or disprove that Mignon was Martine.

"We have time for a shower," he said, making circles with his finger on her shoulder, thinking of how much he wanted to really help her now. "Sugar Mill is only about ten minutes, door to door, from here."

"I'll go first," she said, sliding to the edge of bed with the duvet, hiding her body. This time, he didn't stop her. He was looking forward to watching her walk to the bathroom without a stitch of clothes on.

She had other thoughts, though. Still covered mostly with the duvet, she retrieved the throw that had fallen on the floor and tossed it over her shoulders like a long shawl. He was out of the bed, standing in front of her in two seconds flat.

"You know how to break a man's heart, Boots." He grabbed the ends of the throw and pulled her toward him.

"What?" she looked at him, her expression one of total confusion.

"No need to hide that delicious body from me, *chère*." He smiled, enjoying the play of the lamplight on her disheveled hair that was half tucked under the throw. "I plan to join you in the shower and run my soapy hands over every inch of you. I'm going to massage that tender neck of yours, too." Her eyes widened. "Yes, I can see it hurts you."

Then she bit her bottom lip and smiled. "I guess that might be okay."

"I intend to have a nice look at the little fleur-de-lis tattoo your Mimi doesn't know about, too." He grinned playfully. "And if you don't behave yourself, I just might tell her about it."

"Don't you dare." She punched him lightly on the arm. "I think I can find many ways to make you suffer for that devious deed, Mr. Beauregard." She stepped away from him. Walked toward the bathroom door. Without missing a step, she looked over her shoulder and let the throw drop to the floor.

"Oh, I sure as hell hope you do."

As he followed her to the shower, something he couldn't identify felt like it grabbed him by the throat and pulled him away. He turned to the Emile and François painting.

He had to look at it. He had to look at it now.

There it was. He'd never noticed before. Standing off to the side behind the younger Aguste stood a slender woman, holding the hands of two young girls. They had the same golden blonde hair and exact same sky blue dresses and black ankle boots. They also looked to be exactly the same age.

Lord, could it be? Was this Jewell's grandmother and her Twinnie? Had proof of her grandmother's claim been hanging in his house all this time?

Beau and Jewell shined their flashlights toward the tall wheat-colored grass that lined the side of the drive. Nancy happily bounced around, chasing the light beams.

"Are you sure this is where we parked?" she asked, kicking at the grass to get a closer look. Beau moved behind her and wrapped his arms around her waist, kissing her on the side of the neck.

"Mmm. You smell like my shampoo and you." He grinned. "I like it. I like it a lot. And to think I thought it was the bug repellent that was drawing me in like a Venus flytrap!"

She turned in his arms, ran her hands through his still damp hair and kissed him. Her body tingled from head to toe, as it had the first time their lips met tonight.

He squeezed her bottom and then patted it, before breaking the kiss. They didn't move away from one another, though, remaining in each other's arms, as if they were each afraid that this magic would be gone if they did.

"Do you ever ride a bike with a wire basket on it to carry your papers to work, Beau?" His smile made his eyes crinkle in the corner. "Or do you wear glasses with duct tape on them because you can't take the time to get them fixed?"

Her ideal man. So she'd always thought.

He threw his head back and laughed. "What do you think?"

"Nope," she smiled. "Definitely not your style."

"Why do you ask such a silly thing?" He kissed the tip of her nose and resumed his search. She shrugged. "Is it because that's the type of guy you've been attracted to?" He moved closer to her and ran his hands down her arms. Her body tingled with his gentle touch. "And now you're attracted to a stud like me?"

She rolled her eyes. "Who said you're a stud, and who said I'm attracted to you?"

He wrapped his arm around her waist and pulled her tightly against him. She wet her lips, anticipating his kiss. "Oh, you like me."

"It seems as if you're the one who can't keep his hands off me."

He ran his fingers lightly down her spine. "Guilty as charged."

She liked being desired. She just wouldn't let herself be fooled into thinking it was anything more than a physical attraction between them. He was a good man. He was also an honest, sensitive, ambitious, intelligent man who cared for his family. She just wasn't sure he really cared for her. That knowledge hurt when it shouldn't. She'd gone to him with her eyes wide open, knowing their attraction was strong. Knowing she might be in jail next week or that he might tire of her before then.

"Why the sad look in your eyes, *chère*?" He lifted her chin to gaze deeper in her eyes. "Remember, we need to live in the moment, and I think this moment is pretty damn good." He gave her a tender kiss on her lips. "Let's not let worries of other things intrude just yet. Okay?" She nodded. "The moon is full. The air is cool. Our bodies are feeling pretty amazing from the best lovemaking of our lives. Well, my life anyway." He lifted her and turned her around. "It doesn't get any better than this."

She laughed, let herself feel the cool air against her cheeks, his warm breath on her neck, and the dizzying sensation of being in her lover's arms. He was right. Why ruin it with *what ifs*?

Nancy trotted up to them and barked once. "Get your own friend," Beau told her, but Jewell had leaned over to look at the dog.

She laughed out loud. "Good girl. "Nancy seems to likes pretty undies. I think a trip to the lingerie boutique may be in your future, sweet girl."

Beau looked down and started laughing too.

Nancy sat near their feet, her pointy brown tail sweeping the dirt road. Jewell's white lace bra was clamped in her mouth.

***

It was after eleven and Jewell had called Ruby and told her that she was going to be a little late. She and Beau were as tidy as they could make themselves after the shower and riding in an old truck with the windows down. Of course, Beau looked neater and more put together than Jewell. He had a natural fashion sense and ability to look fresh and vibrant, where she always seemed a little bit disheveled, with her silky hair always sliding out of the ponytail holder.

As they drove up to the camper, Jewell noticed there was a police car parked in front, next to Ruby's Cadillac. Her heart stopped. A police car couldn't mean anything good. She leapt from the truck before Beau fully parked. Racing into the camper, she stopped dead, her heart in her throat. Tante Izzy was sitting in her office chair with her back to the desk. Ruby was next to her. Big John was sitting on her sofa, filling up the small space. A tall, thin man in his mid-sixties, wearing a baseball cap and sheriff's uniform, stood near the kitchenette. "What's wrong?" she asked everyone there, searching the room for Mimi.

Ruby stood.

"Where's Mimi? Is she okay?"

Tante Izzy waved a dismissive hand to her. "*Mais,* calm down, child. Everyone's fine. Nobody's hurt."

Jewell couldn't calm down. Not until she saw for herself that Mimi was okay. She rushed to the sleeping area in the back of the camper. The privacy accordion doors were closed.

Beau walked into the camper, extended his hand. "Hi, Dad."

"Hi son." They gripped hands and hugged with back slaps and a handshake.

Jewell opened the door and peeked inside. She leaned against the doorjamb and sighed with relief. Mimi was lying on her back, her chin jutting upward, her mouth open. The quilt was pulled to her neck. Her bare feet and cotton candy-colored toenails were uncovered. No doubt Tante Izzy's doing. She looked old and pale, but she was sleeping in the same position she'd preferred her entire life. Then, as if sensing someone was looking at her, her eyes fluttered open.

"Can you rock me to sleep?" she asked, speaking French in a childlike voice.

Jewell nodded, sat on the edge of the bed and gathered her in her arms and began to sing a soft lullaby in French. Mimi's favorite. Mimi reached up and brushed at the loose tendrils of Jewell's hair and sighed. "I love you."

"I love you, Mimi."

Beau walked into the shadows of the tiny space, then leaned against the doorjamb and watched them. It was such an intimate private moment, one she shared with Mimi every night, yet, she didn't mind Beau witnessing it. There was a level of trust she felt with him now that he wouldn't cause harm or hurt knowing of their vulnerabilities.

"She's okay," he said, his voice quiet. "My dad's here because Tante Izzy called him for a ride home." Jewell nodded, kissed Mimi on the top of the head and gently eased Mimi's heavy, sleeping weight back onto the bed. Jewell immediately rubbed the back of her own neck.

Beau's hands were on her neck instantly, massaging. "So that's why your neck hurts, *chère*. Sitting with her in that very tiny bed that way, holding her...what, for hours sometimes?"

Jewell looked at him, her eyes filled with tears. She nodded. "I put her to sleep this way most nights. Other nights she wakes, in tears...even hysterics sometimes. She just needs to be held. Consoled."

Beau gathered her in his arms. Rubbed her arms. "She is lucky to have you."

"I've always been blessed to have her."

The voices in the other room intruded on the moment and Beau took a step back. That step was a clear signal that they'd entered a different place with his family nearby. It was a different place for their relationship. She got it. What they had shared just now and earlier was just for those moments. Nothing more. She had understood that all along.

Still, it hurt.

And, that was such a ridiculous thing since she should've expected the behavior. It wasn't complicated. It was just men and women's biosocial behavior as it related to biological anthropology.

Jewell closed the door, moved around Beau, careful not to touch him, and went to the sheriff. "We haven't been introduced." She extended her hand to him. "I'm Jewell Duet."

He put Nancy on the ground and she started bustling around the camper, sniffing the floor. Ronald shook Jewell's hand firmly and smiled. "It's a real pleasure to meet you, Jewell. That's a pretty name." He looked at Beau. "I heard you and Jewell got into a scuffle with your client, Stanley Boudreaux, outside the Do Drop Inn." He pointed to the bruise under Beau's eye.

Beau touched where his father was looking. "Not my client anymore."

Tante Izzy frowned. "I didn't hear nuttin' 'bout that. How come I didn't hear nuttin', Ruby?"

"Guess we were too busy playing bingo," Ruby said.

"I won Blackout," she announced. "*Ma sucrée,* you grand-mère won Four Corners. *Mais,* she was so excited, she jumped up and forgot da word to scream out. She yelled, 'T'row me somet'in', Mista'."

"It was so darling," Ruby said, laughing. "After that, every time someone won, they shouted, 'Throw me something, Mista'. We had a good time. In fact, Jewelie, they asked Mignon to come back next week to call a game. They're going to make it a Mardi Gras theme."

"Harrumph. Dey never asked me to call bingo." Tante Izzy shrugged and looked at Jewell. Her lips were pursed as her eyes slid over her from head to toe. Then she nodded, scratched her head and nodded some more.

"What are you scheming?" Beau asked his aunt, narrowing his eyes at her. "Whatever it is, forget about it."

Ronald and Big John began to laugh. "Asking her to forget about scheming is about as useful as using an outhouse for a coon dog," Ronald said, patting Beau on the back.

Big John jumped into the teasing. "Asking her to forget about her scheming makes about as much sense as a screen door on a *pirogue*." His laugh was as big as he was. "Get it. The small boat would sink with all those screen holes on it."

Ruby rolled her eyes. "Honey, if you have to explain a joke, it's not funny." Big John looked wounded. "You sure were cute saying it, though." She smiled at him as she sat next to him on the sofa and rested her head on his thick shoulder.

Big John kissed Ruby on the top of her head and she grinned at Beau. "I sure love my man." She winked at Tante Izzy, still wearing her tight grin. She looked like the orange cat that ate the canary, sitting there in her orange jeans and matching orange cardigan over a crisp white T-shirt with *Bingo* spelled in metallic gold. Ruby turned to her husband and kissed him squarely on the lips.

She and Tante Izzy were definitely up to something.

"Harrumph, looks like there's a lot of hanky-panky going on tonight..." Tante Izzy rolled her eyes, looking at Ruby, then Beau.

Jewell felt her face heat. *Dear Lord, was it that obvious what she and Beau did?* She didn't dare look at Beau.

Tante Izzy got up from her seat near the computer and sat at the kitchen banquette. "Beau. Dis is fer your own good. Listen to me. It's time you settle down. You got a nice house. A good job. You own a city block of real estate downtown where you have an office. Now you need a wife to share it all."

"Tante Izzy, I love you," he began, sitting across from her at the table. "But that is none of your business."

"Yes, it is. My family is my business." She reached into her dress pocket and handed him a vial. "Pick someone and drink dis."

Jewell recognized the type of vial she'd given him. It was like some of the ones she'd come across from the traditional healers who used herbs, potions and prayers to cure any number of illnesses as well as emotional and lifestyle issues. The healers who most often served as midwives too.

"Is that a *traiteur's* vial?" she asked, walking to the table. She picked up the vial to study it.

"Sure is. It's a love potion," Tante Izzy told her, sitting taller. "You want to drink it?"

"Oh, for God's sake," Beau groaned, folding his arms over his chest. He frowned at his dad, who was laughing. "There's nothing funny about any of this."

"Heck, no, I don't want to drink it," Jewell told Tante Izzy. She shook her head, turned the vial in her hands. It was small enough to fit in her palm and had a tiny metal screw top to keep the brownish-green contents inside of it.

There were no words or labels indicating what the liquid was. "Who's your *traiteur*?"

Tante Izzy looked at her, eyes narrowed. "Why you wants to know? You got da *mal de tête*?"

"No, I don't have a headache." Jewell handed Tante Izzy the vial. She handed it to Beau, who immediately put it on the table like it was some kind of poison. "I just want to meet her. For my research." Jewell looked at Beau. She could see in his expression that he remembered that she wanted to talk to the local *traiteur* about the possibility of having a midwife record book for the plantation.

Tante Izzy nodded. "I can ask her if she wants to talk to you. I'll order me some body butter and bat' salts while I got her on da phone." She lifted her chin. "You wants some so you can smell pretty like me?"

"The *traiteur* has body butter and bath salts? That's unusual. I thought they only made special potions with herbs and said healing prayers."

"My *traiteur* has scented candles and holiday soaps, too. Her niece, Teal, makes it." She extended her thin forearm for Jewell to smell. "Dat's lavender I'm wearing, but I like Mardi Gras Mambo best. Mardi Gras Mambo drives da mens crazy."

Beau grinned, shaking his head. "I have to beat them off her with my *pirogue* paddle."

"You're a good nephew," Jewell laughed. "Tante Izzy, did your *traiteur* learn her craft from her grandmother, aunt, or another family member?"

Tante Izzy rolled her eyes. "*Mais,* of course. Her name is Eleanor. She just done had a birthday. Ninetieth. Started learnin' to be a healer since she was seven. She's teachin' Teal to take over when da time comes.

"Perfect." Jewell said. "I'd like to meet Eleanor tomorrow. Will you take me?"

"I will," Beau said, not giving Tante Izzy a chance to answer. "I'll pick you up at nine. My rental car will be delivered to my office around eight thirty."

"Y'all bring me back some Mardi Gras Mambo body butter."

"I'll take the lavender body butter and bath salts," Ruby shouted to Jewell from where she sat on the floor next to her husband.

"Happy to do it." Jewell looked at Beau. "Mimi and I will be ready for nine, then."

"Um, Jewelie," Ruby said, shaking her head. "With the tailgate party on Thursday, I promised to take Mimi and Little Miss Matchmaker there to get manicures tomorrow before they cook up the desserts. I hope you don't mind. The only appointment available for the three of us was at ten."

"I heard dat. Y'all talkin' about me like it's my funeral and I'm not here." Tante Izzy snorted. "We gettin' shellac on our nails."

"You won't be going anywhere if you don't get your beauty sleep," Ronald said, moving toward the door. "Are you ready?"

Tante Izzy stood and walked to the door. When she got near the kitchenette, she stopped, looked at the counter next to the sink. "Oh, *bon Dieu*. Not again." She picked up the now familiar crystal salt and pepper shakers. "What's goin' on wit dis?" She looked at Jewell.

"I wish I knew," Jewell said.

"It's her old-timer's." Tante Izzy frowned. "You know, today she called me Pauline."

"That's Praline's real name," Jewell said, frowning. "I'm sorry."

"Hmm. Not me," Tante Izzy raised her head. "If she t'inks I look like pretty Miss Praline from Bourbon Street, dat's fine by me."

"Miss Praline?" Big John and Ronald said at the same time.

Jewell looked at Beau, her eyes wide and pleading for him to make sure they didn't tell anyone.

"I'm goin' to get me some pole-dancin' lessons wit her," Tante Izzy announced with a flourish.

Both Big John and Ronald made dismissive gestures and smiled. They hadn't believed for a minute that she knew New Orleans' most famous stripper, much less that she was getting pole-dancing lessons from her. Beau winked at Jewell. She knew, however, that it was only a matter of time until the truth would come out and stick.

Ruby, who was now standing next to Jewell, patted her on the hand. "You know, the salt and pepper shakers are really important to her," she said, slipping her purse on her arm as she prepared to leave. Big John handed Nancy to Beau. "She was pretty quiet today. She didn't say much. She seemed content with listening. Once, when she did speak, she told me that it was her job to keep the kitchen table in order for her momma. She said Twinnie helped. She also said they were really good at picking up all of the little pieces of thread off the floor." She linked her arm with Jewell. "You know, when she talks and she and Tante Izzy aren't fussing about some nonsense, she mentions Twinnie a lot." She lifted her shoulders. "I believe that Twinnie is a real person. A person she loves and misses a great deal."

"Harrumph. She also says Sugar Mill is her home." Tante Izzy's voice was a little harsh. "Do you believe dat too?" She didn't give Ruby a chance to answer. "*Mais*, no. I can tole you one thing, she's not a Bienvenu. I'll prove it for sure in about a week." She took the salt and pepper shakers, turned to leave, then stopped at the door.

"Are you really certain that she's not a Bienvenu?" Beau asked, surprising Jewell.

"*Alors pas,*" Tante Izzy put the shakers back on the counter. "Of course not," she repeated in English. "Not dat I'd mind. She's growin' on me. If she just wouldn't tell stories and steal...um...er, borrow stuff." She frowned. "You can't make it true just because you wants it be dat way." Tante Izzy opened the door and walked out of the camper. "Put somet'in' on that bruise on you cheek, *ma sucrée,*" she called from outside. "It's really red tonight. Like you done got a brush burn on it." Ruby, Big John and Ronald followed her out.

Everyone said good night.

Jewell moved to the small, round mirror hanging near the door. "Beauregard Bienvenu, why didn't you tell me I have a beard burn on my face?"

He shrugged and stepped closer to her. His finger dropped to her chest, right between her breasts. "I guess you wanted me to tell you that you're missing two buttons here, too."

"Oh, no!" She pulled the fabric at the top of her dress together. "What else are you not telling me?" she asked as a joke. Beau's face became serious and he answered without hesitation.

"There are two girls that look to be the same age as each other in my painting of Emile, François and his son." Beau's voice was even. Calm. "They're holding the hands of a young woman in the background." "What?" Jewell felt like she had to play catch-up. Why hadn't he mentioned this before? Why didn't I notice them when I looked at the painting?"

"You were distracted." He kissed her on the side of the neck. "You had other things on your mind." He handed her his phone with a photograph of the painting on it. "I took this right after our shower, just before we left." He enlarged the image to see the two little girls and the woman.

"They're in silhouette but look to be toddlers. No distinctive features. Just the same wheat, blonde hair. The same pale blue dress," she said, moving the photo image around. "E-mail it to me. We can blow it up and look at it on my computer."

He did, and a few minutes later she had her laptop on the banquet table and they were seated next to each other looking at the photo.

"It's possible the girls weren't actually wearing the same color dress and the artist just painted it that way," she said, considering all of the possibilities.

"With that thinking, he may have just painted two little girls the same height and size, not really replicating them true to life."

Jewell nodded. "That's a possibility." She moved her cursor over the image, enhancing it. "It's still out of focus but it's clearer. Do you see an initial on each of the girl's dresses?" She pointed to the yoke of the dress. "Right here."

"I don't know. Enlarging it only makes it blurrier." Jewell got up, opened the chest with the printer, and got her tool belt. She brought it to the table.

"Is this better?" She and Beau looked through her magnifying glass at the computer screen. "I think I see an M, very faint, but it appears to be there in a yellowish-cream-colored paint, one on each of the dresses."

"I can't be sure." He sat back. "Let's assume there is an initial M on each dress and the girls are about the same age. What does that prove?"

Jewell shook her head. "Nothing. It gives us more possibilities and fewer dead ends."

"I'll concede that." Beau leaned his elbows on the table and pulled the picture to normal view. "Who is this woman? Is that Aguste's first wife, Louise Olivie, or his second wife, Claudette Isaure Joubert?"

"I don't know. There aren't very many years' difference between the two women. If one of those little girls is Martine, then it is definitely not the first wife. She died during childbirth." Jewell got up again, opened the drawer to her small desk, and took out the original Bienvenu family bible. She opened the page to the family tree and handed it to Beau. She zoomed out to see the full painting. "I think François and his brother look to be in their seventies. They're older men here. Grandfathers."

"Both men have gray hair, wrinkles." Beau pointed to the group of people standing off in the background behind Emile. "Do you think those are Emile's children and grandchildren?"

Jewell counted heads. "If you count the ones in silhouette in the background near the table on his side, there are fifteen people, not counting the servants putting food on the table." Beau turned a few pages until he found Emile's family tree. "He had nine children. I think that number is probably too low, considering they would've been adults with children of their own."

"Maybe that was all who could show up for the painting that day."

Beau looked at her and nodded. "We can't correlate Martine's age based on the others in the painting, especially since they are all in silhouette."

"What I feel comfortable concluding is that the two little girls in the photo are both wearing identical dresses with the initial M on them. And they're holding hands with a young woman. Last, if they have been painted to correlate with their true ages and sizes, I conclude that the girls are the same size and age. I'd guess around two or a little older if they are petite."

Beau pointed to the bible entry for Aguste François. "François, Martine's grandfather, died just before she turned four." He lifted her hand and began to play with her fingers. "Who is that other little girl in the painting?"

Jewell looked at him. Was he starting to think that Martine was Mimi's Twinnie? If she was, how were they related? Sisters, friends, cousins? And was Beau prepared to believe it?

"We need to get the midwife's birth book, Beau," Jewell said, closing her computer. "That could hold the answer to the mystery of who that other little girl in the painting is."

He nodded twice. "Tomorrow, if we're lucky, the *traiteur* will have it for us to examine."

She glanced at the computer monitor and sucked in a breath. *"Mon Dieu."*

He leaned in over her shoulder, his breath whispering over her hair. "What is it, *chère*?"

"I hadn't noticed it earlier, Beau. I was so focused on the people in the painting, I didn't really look at the plantation." She looked at him. "Do you see it?"

He shook his head. "No. What?"

"The cistern. There's a cistern near the house. Here." She pointed to what looked like a cypress cistern off to the side of the plantation. "Remember when we first came to Sugar Mill, Mimi asked you what you did with her cistern. Here it is."

"Yes, indeed. It sure as hell is there."

Chapter  17

It took Jewell and Beau thirty-five minutes to ride down the bayou Thursday morning to get to the *traiteur's* home to continue their investigation on Twinnie. During their drive, she reflected on how in the short time they had known each other, Beau had learned much of her intimate feelings. He'd seen her in her most vulnerable time with her grand-mère in the quiet darkness of the night as she held her. He'd seen her heartfelt tears as she cried with the ache and fears of losing Mimi. It was uncomfortable to have someone know that much about her personally when she'd guarded it her entire life. Yet, there was also a feeling of peace and safety having Beau know about it, too.

She tucked away her thoughts and after a steep climb up sturdy treated lumber stairs, they were finally inside the beige trailer on stilts located along the bayou's edge. Eleanor and Teal graciously offered them a steaming cup of fresh-brewed coffee as they sat comfortably at the table in the pleasant smelling kitchen where Teal was mixing a batch of her signature fleur-de-lis embossed lavender soap.

"I understand your family treated six generations of Bienvenus," Jewell asked, excited to interview Eleanor.

"Our family is very proud to have worked for Beau's family," Teal said, with a flirtatious grin. She was in her late twenties and didn't hide her interest in Cane's most eligible bachelor. In fact, Jewell had seen her unbutton the top three buttons on her blouse when they had arrived. She'd bet the observant attorney had noticed it too.

Jewell ignored the tossing of her long dark hair and come-hither looks as she explained to the ladies *what* she was looking for. She didn't say *why*.

"Nothing was written down or recorded until almost 1930," Teal said, speaking for her frail aunt, as she poured the floral but sophisticated scented liquid into the soap molds.

Jewell glanced at Eleanor, who she ascertained must have been hard of hearing based on the volume of the introductions when they arrived. Eleanor also appeared to be very sleepy. She seemed to nod in and out of sleep from her rocking chair near the table. Or, she pretended to. When she was awake, her black eyes darted between Jewell, Beau and her pretty niece.

"All information, potions and traditions have been passed down orally, right, Auntie?" Eleanor didn't respond with a gesture or word. Teal continued. "Healers in our family, most families of that time, didn't learn to write until around the mid-thirties. The *traiteurs* left any written accounts of babies born or family health issues to the people to whom it mattered the most."

Jewell thought about what Teal said. Oral traditions were how they taught the next generation. Did they also pass on stories of the people they helped? If they did, the older woman had to have heard stories from her mother or aunts when she was a young girl.

"*Madame,*" Jewell said, speaking loudly and addressing the older woman in French. She stopped rocking and looked at her.

"*Oui.*"

"Do you remember hearing of twins being born to any Bienvenu descendants of Aguste Bienvenu?" Jewell asked, knowing that Beau had told her there had never been any twins in the family and that the bible didn't have any recorded. Still, she had to confirm that was true.

She started to rock again. Teal looked at Jewell, her expression questioning. "What did you ask her?" She obviously didn't understand French.

Jewell didn't answer. She continued to address the older, woman. "They would've been born around the same time you were."

Eleanor reached into an ashtray on a side table and retrieved an antique cypress carved pipe. She took a moment to light the tobacco in the bowl. It smelled light and sweet. "The first time I remember going to the plantation was with my momma," she said speaking Cajun French. Her voice was a gravelly smoker's voice. "We brought herbs for the missus to make a tea to help carry her baby to term. I went before, but I was too young to remember."

"Were there twin girls living at the plantation when you went there?"

"*Mais,* no." She puffed her pipe. "Only the baby boy. Benjamin." Ben's grandfather. The old woman looked deep into Jewell's eyes. "Momma said the missus was going to have a baby girl. She did."

"Tante Izzy?"

She nodded, puffed on her pipe.

"Did your momma speak of any other girl babies born there before then or the woman who died in childbirth?" Jewell persisted.

She shook her head. "I know the first wife died, but momma didn't tell me. I just always knew it. Momma didn't speak the names of the ones she helped. It's not our tradition. We speak only of the prayers and herbs as we teach the next generation."

Jewell tried a few more times, but the woman didn't say anything more.

After saying their goodbyes, they left with Ruby and Tante Izzy's requested body butters. When they descended to the bottom two steps, Teal called out to them to wait. She raced down the stairs, her loose wavy hair flying prettily behind her. When she reached them, she pressed a small white paper bag into Beau's hands.

"This is for you. It's a special shaving cream I created. It leaves your cheeks as smooth as a baby's behind." She kissed him on the cheek, blushed. "Call me sometime."

"Thank you, Teal." He smiled his *I'm a lady-killer smile* and Jewell all but heard Teal's heart sigh.

As they walked away Jewell shook her head. "You're shameless."

"What? What did I do?" He held out his hands in surrender.

"Oh, you know very well what you did." She laughed.

"So, what's next?" Beau asked as they drove north, heading back toward Cane. It was an overcast morning with light showers, but the day didn't look like it would be a total wash.

"The movie crew will start arriving tomorrow night or the next morning," she said, disappointed that the *traiteur* and her niece hadn't been able to add anything new to the information she already had. "They'll be setting up their tents and work areas so they can begin work on Monday. I need to go to New Orleans to organize my warehouse so I have enough room when the inventory from the barn is brought over." She turned the air conditioning vent so it wouldn't blow on her face. She preferred fresh outside air, especially this time of year. She rolled down her window a couple of inches, not wanting to let the light rain into the car. "Do you mind?"

He turned off the air conditioner. "Of course not. It looks like the rain is stopping." He rolled down his window fully; air flowed through the clean black SUV that had been provided by the insurance company. The air smelled fresh from the cleansing rain, with the undercurrent of the heavy sweet scent of the freshly cut sugarcane mixed in. She thought of Mimi talking about the smell of the cane on their first day at Sugar Mill. She now understood the distinctive fragrance she spoke of.

"You're wearing your bug repellent again," he said, grinning in the sexy way he did that made her insides turn to mush. Apparently, he had powers to zoom in on her special fragrance and not notice the scent of the cut cane.

"You never know when the mosquitoes will come out in South Louisiana."

"Come on, *chère*. Be straight with me." He grinned again and she knew she'd tell or do anything he asked. "It's hocus-pocus New Orleans voodoo stuff, right? It has to be. It absolutely drives me insane. Better than anything I smelled in the *traiteur's* trailer or at the mall." He inhaled deeply and faked a shiver. "It lingers when you leave a room." He took her hand and kissed the tips of her fingers. "Your scent was on my pillows." He groaned. "The dreams I had about you, last night..."

"It's natural amber oil," she blurted out, fanning herself with her hand, feeling hot and flushed. "Geez, Beau. I've worn it for years and no one has said it affected them like that."

"This rich, warm, exotic aroma is amber?"

"Yes. A totally natural amber oil that I have blended with a few other natural essential oils... And, oddly, as good as it smells, bugs hate it. In my line of work that's important."

"I still say there's hocus-pocus voodoo with it." He laughed. "Hey, what do you say we skip tailgating. Make it a power workday. Take care of business. Let's go to the warehouse right now."

She needed to go to the warehouse, but she hadn't planned to go with Beau. Why did the idea of him coming into her workspace feel so scary? It felt like she was exposing herself in some way. Hadn't she already done that by letting him see her weaker moments with Mimi? To him, her warehouse was just a building, a workplace. He wouldn't know it was where she spent hours crafting her dreams.

Ridiculous.

"I'll call Ruby to make sure that it's okay for her to watch Mimi for a few more hours. I hate to impose."

She made the call and was assured that Mimi was enjoying herself. "You know, while we're in New Orleans," Jewell said as she disconnected the phone with Ruby. "I think we should swing by the Monastery of St. Teresa." She folded her arms over her chest, leaned her head back against the soft, expensive leather seat. "Ruby said Mimi's been talking a lot about the nuns making her and Twinnie clip their fingernails really short and keeping them exceptionally clean."

"Do you think her manicure today sparked a memory?"

Jewell shook her head. "I don't know. I just think we need to follow any thread we have, even if it doesn't seem to make sense."

"You doing okay?" he asked, gently gathering her ponytail and letting it slide through his fingers.

She inhaled deeply. Her heart felt heavy. Her body, too. Grief was so physical. Painful. "Not really." A tear slipped onto her cheek. "Having Mimi leave me like this is hard. I want to be at her side now, but...I feel I have to still try to see if I can find Twinnie for her before it's too late. If it isn't already." She wiped the tears with the heel of her hands. "I guess there can't be any easy way to deal with losing someone you love."

He ran his fingers gently over her cheek, and Jewell rested her face in his palm for a moment, drawing strength from his nearness. It was odd that he was offering her comfort now, when just the night before he'd stepped away from her. What had changed? After a moment she sat upright again, and he returned his hand to the steering wheel. "I want to find Twinnie for her, to give her something when she has one of those windows of awareness."

"I want that for you and her too."

The wind from the open window lifted and played with his hair and laid it back down neatly in place. "Will you be able to accept it if that doesn't happen?"

"I won't have a choice, will I?" She closed her eyes, turned her body until she was curled sideways, facing him on the seat.

"I guess not." He didn't say anything for a few moments. "You're a brave lady."

"I'm so tired. My body aches."

"Rest." He pulled down the armrest between them and patted it. She rested her head on it. He stroked her hair, massaged her neck. Her breathing was steady, but she wasn't sleeping. The silent tears burned her cheeks and kept her awake.

"Beau." She didn't move as she spoke.

"Yes."

"Thank you for being supportive. I know you have your family and practice to take care of." She thought of her attorney who had handed her case off to his law clerk because he was so busy. She knew Beau would never do that. "I hope you still don't have any doubts about me harming your family. I promise you, I'd never do anything to harm them...or you."

"I know that, Boots." He twirled her ponytail around his finger. "I guess I've known it since I saw you holding those stained baby clothes in the plantation attic. Someone who cared so damn much for old pieces of musty clothes, thin from age and wear from people who lived hundreds of years before she was born, had to have different priorities than I was worried she'd have."

***

An hour and a half later, they stood just inside the thick, weathered oak side door of the St. Teresa monastery in a small receiving room. The space was actually more of a walk-through, large enough to fit only an old church pew and umbrella stand. It was obvious the Carmelite cloistered nuns' French Quarter monastery hadn't been designed to receive visitors.

"We've been here for twenty minutes, and I have yet to see a live person. Or nun," Beau said, finding the hard pew too low for his long legs. He finally gave up on getting comfortable and stood.

"They're probably trying to find the sisters who are allowed to have contact with people from the outside world," Jewell explained. "The nuns still live a cloistered life here, but there are a few nuns who are allowed to leave the grounds and interact with people to conduct business so they can maintain their monastic life." She smiled as he began to pace. "They still use that revolving door I pointed out to you at the front of the building, so the nuns can receive goods or deliver them without being seen."

Beau took two steps forward, reached a wall and turned to take two steps back. "This place smells old. Moldy."

"What historic French Quarter building doesn't?" Jewell smiled.

"Could use paint on the walls. A little sanding. The plaster is peeling." He studied it a moment. "Maybe Ben, Big John and I could do that sometime." He shrugged and shook his head like he was surprised his thoughts had gone in that direction.

"Y'all could. I've seen your house. You've got skills." She pointed to the ancient stained glass skylight depicting Jesus with the children gathered around him. "Look at the details in that. Magnificent, isn't it?" She smiled. "I taught a class for a few semesters on the influences of the Catholic church on art, architecture and traditions in south Louisiana. We visited a few religious edifices, including this cloistered monastery. It was founded around 1878."

"Did you say your great-grand-mère and your Mimi lived here? That doesn't make sense."

Jewell laughed at how big and out of place he looked in the tight quarters. "It really doesn't. But Mimi said she and her mother lived here when the nuns rescued them. They were destitute. No husband to help support them. Her mother was in demand for her skills as a seamstress. According to Mimi, her talent was exceptional. She and Mimi were brought to live with the nuns until they could get on their feet. They helped with the ecclesiastical embroidery and the making of church vestments as repayment for their room and board."

"Living with the cloistered nuns...raising your child here..." He stopped pacing and looked up at the stained glass. "I don't know. Something feels off. Even creepy."

"Ah, could be that you're sensing what that room right there was used for." She pointed to the plain, unadorned door less than six feet from where he stood.

"What about it?"

"That's the room where New Orleans's Catholic exorcisms were conducted."

He made the sign of the cross. "You're kidding, right?"

She laughed. "Nope. Would a historian joke about something like that?"

Just then, the door to that room opened and Beau took a step to the side to protectively stand in front of Jewell. She looked around him. A nun in full brown and black habit, with a long, thick, brown rosary hanging around her waist walked up to Jewell. Two other nuns, heads lowered, followed her into the small vestibule and walked down the hall, disappearing through another door.

She extended her hand to Jewell. "I'm Sister Monica," she smiled. She looked to be in her fifties. Her skin was smooth and fair. Her white coif and wimple were sealed tightly around her head and face, not revealing any hair, but her light eyebrows and eyelashes told Jewell she was a blonde.

She turned to Beau and introduced herself. After he told her his name, he nodded to the room she'd exited. "Everything okay in there?"

She laughed and looked at Jewell. "You both heard that it was the exorcism room?" They nodded. "Not any longer. It's a small prayer chapel now."

"I hope that's because business is slow for exorcisms in the city."

Sister Monica laughed. She seemed to laugh easily as she guided them through the dark monastery, speaking of the history of the Carmelites, the vegetables grown in the gardens, and what they were having for dinner that night. When they reached a small wood-paneled office back inside the old monastery buildings, she invited them to sit on two plastic chairs across from her desk. "How can I help you?"

"We're here on behalf of my grand-mère, who lived here at St. Teresa with her mother for four or five years in the early 1920s."

Jewell gave Sister Monica the details of how Mimi and her mother had come to live at the monastery. She added that both women had helped with the seamstress work even after they left the monastery to live on their own.

"Of course I know Mignon," Sister Monica said with a fond smile. "She continued sewing for us and the Cathedral until, what about five years ago?"

Jewell's heart grew heavy. "Four. I used to drop off the garments she'd sewn, in the revolving door in front, when she couldn't do it herself anymore."

Sister Monica nodded. "Yes. In years past, she would come in on occasion to have a cup of coffee. That's how I met her. How is she?"

Jewell shook her head. "She's aging. She's in her end-of-life years. You know..."

"I'll pray for her. And you."

"Thank you." Jewell smiled. "We're here, Sister Monica, because we're hoping we can examine any files or

documents involving them from when they first came to
live here and in the following years. Since the sisters were
well educated and the Catholic Church is very dedicated to
detailed record-keeping, I assume you have files?"

"Oh, yes. Quite a bit. We've just recently copied all
those records to the computer." She shifted, and the
vintage office chair she sat in squeaked. "We spent two
years scanning all of the old documents. We've sent copies
to the Vatican so they can be preserved there. Let's see if
we have the files that you're looking for first." She started
typing on the keyboard on the desk. "Here is something."

"Oh, this is wonderful." Jewell said, turning to Beau.

"I feel a 'but' coming," Beau said, resting his elbows on
his knees.

"I found it, but I can't give it to you," Sister Monica
said. "I'm sorry. I cannot give you personal information on
Mignon if she hasn't given you permission to do so. In
writing."

Beau looked at Jewell. "Do you have power of attorney
for her?"

"Yes." She opened the small cross-body purse she
carried and pulled the paper from her wallet. She handed
it to Sister Monica

"Oh, good. I hated having to turn you away." Sister
Monica made a copy of it on the scanner that she slid out
from a bottom drawer in her desk and returned the power
of attorney letter to Jewell. Swiveling around in her
squeaky desk chair, she opened the doors of a recently
constructed and painted cabinet behind her. Two huge,
thin monitors were turned on with screen savers of cute
kittens running through different bible story scenes.

Beau and Jewell looked at each other and smiled.

The kindly nun typed on her keyboard for a few
minutes, moving from one section to another, then
clapped her hands. "Here you go." She looked over her
shoulder "Come. Come." She waved to them. Jewell and
Beau hurried to stand behind her.

"Wow." Jewell couldn't believe what she was seeing. At the top of the page were three black and white photographs. The first was of her great-grandmother, whose birthdate was listed under her name, Adelise Tassé Duet. The next photo was of three-year-old Mignon Tassé Duet. The third photo was of another little girl who had the same light hair and light eyes as Mimi. "Rosary Tassé Duet," Beau read. He looked at Jewell. "Could that be Martine? Or could Mignon be Martine?"

Sister Monica spoke. "Adelise claimed to have had the twin girls before coming to America," she said, translating the French document unnecessarily for Jewell, who had already read that section. "She said her husband died on the ship during the journey from France. She had tried to make her way in the new world, but came to the monastery in need of help."

"The girls look healthy, well fed and cared for," Jewell said. "Their clothes look clean and the fabric, although the photo isn't that clear, appears to be more of the fabrics the wealthy children of that era would wear. I've seen photos of many who were poor. Their clothes were usually sewn of rags, broadcloth. Not fine wool."

She looked at Beau, who was studying the photos. "These girls definitely don't look like the poor children from the port or docks that I've seen in many historical papers."

Sister Monica continued reading silently for a few moments, then spoke again. "This is odd." She looked at Jewell. "It says Adelise was poor and had no family, but here," she pointed to the monitor, "she had a wealthy benefactor who visited her three times a year. The benefactor would make a generous donation to the monastery upon her visit."

"Did it name the benefactor?" Beau asked.

Sister Monica shook her head. "No."

"Would there be other documents that might list who made charitable donations to the monastery at that time?" Jewell asked.

"I can research that, but it will take some time." She clicked to continue to the next page. "Oh. No." She looked at Jewell.

"Yes. I see it." Jewell turned to Beau. She shook her head. "Oh, Beau. It says that one of the children died of influenza at the age of five while still living at the monastery."

"Who was it?"

"Mignon."

***

They hadn't said much to one another since leaving the monastery. Jewell understood that Beau, like her, needed time to sort what they had learned in their own way. When they arrived at her fire station warehouse they were ready to speak about what Sister Monica had shared with them.

"Have you had time to digest the revelations about Rosary and Mignon?" Beau asked, as Jewell unlocked the fire station door and flipped on the light switch.

"I have more questions. A lot more questions."

"Me too." As they entered the downstairs bay, where the fire trucks had once been parked, the room lit up. Beau walked into the space and looked around. He whistled. "Impressive."

She locked the door behind them.

Beau leaned against the eighteenth century Dutch marquetry armoire she had covered with a drop cloth. "Do you think the girls exchanged names? Did someone write the wrong name in the document of the child that passed?"

"Both possibilities." Jewell folded her arms and sat on what looked like a sofa covered by another tan drop cloth. "We didn't actually see a death certificate."

"Do you believe they were twins or did Adelise Tassé Duet lie about that? If she lied, why?"

"I have no proof that Mimi was a twin. I've seen her French birth certificate." Jewell blew out a breath. "Or, rather, the birth certificate of *one* of the girls if Mimi isn't Mignon." She shook her head, swallowed past the emotion tightening her throat. "And, Beau, on that birth certificate the box that should be checked for multiple births was blank."

"Indicating she wasn't born a twin."

"Yes." She rubbed the back of her neck. "And, Jean Duet's name was listed as her father."

"Do you doubt he was her father?"

"To tell you the truth, I wondered if maybe Aguste had returned home from fighting in Europe after World War I with a baby he'd fathered there...and her mother. Maybe he tried to pass the baby off as the twin of the baby his wife had nine months later."

Beau's eyes widened. He ran his hands through his hair. "I hadn't considered that." He sat thinking about it a minute. "If he did that, he would've had documents to back up that story. Not that anyone would believe it." He shook his head. "I've seen all of the family documents and the letters that Aguste sent home to his father while he was off at war. There was nothing in the documents that said he had a second daughter until Tante Izzy was born. And, there was never any mention of him fathering a baby while off at war."

Jewell shook her head. "That's not something you'd write home about."

"I think it was." Beau sat in silence a moment. "The man who wrote the letters I read believed in family honor. He was passionate about it. It was a vocation for him. Hell, it dictated his actions." His voice grew stronger, like he was giving closing arguments in court. "Jewell, the letters and the family story told over the years are consistent and corroborate who Aguste, the man, was."

Beau stood and began to pace as he spoke.

"The family story is that Aguste enlisted in World War I. He hated the Germans because he was raised on his father, François's, terrible tales of his experiences living in France. He lived there during the Franco-Prussian war, a tough time when France endured ruthless dictators." Beau sat next to Jewell again. "So when the war broke out between the United States and Germany, Aguste felt a family obligation to fight the Germans. He fought them for his father. He fought them to protect his family from ever having to endure what his father had." He turned to face her. "No, Jewell. Aguste wouldn't have hidden his child. And if he tried to protect her by pretending she was one of his twin daughters, there would've been documentation supporting that."

Jewell nodded. What he said made sense. It wasn't the right thing for a researcher and historian to do, but she accepted what he said as fact without seeing the evidence to prove it herself. He'd seen the papers and she trusted what he said was true.

"Okay, then. Martine is Aguste's child. Mignon is Jean and Adelise's? Who is Rosary? If Mignon died, who is my Mimi...really? Who am I? It's all so confusing?"

"Complicated," Beau corrected, squeezing her hand. "Let's try to make sense of this. Let's deal in the facts. What do we know for sure?" He held up his fingers and started to fold one for each point he made. "One, we saw the photographs of the two girls. They were at that monastery and lived there until one died when she was five years old."

"Two," Jewell said, taking her turn. "Two girls of the same age and coloring, like in the photographs, were pictured in the painting in your room of a Bienvenu family scene at Sugar Mill. That places the two girls with a young woman holding their hands there. Whether those girls are the same girls in the monastery, we don't know for certain."

"Three." Beau said, his voice even. All business. "Your grand-mère claims to have a twin or a sister or someone she calls Twinnie that she was close to and whom she claims to have lived with on a plantation. Most recently, she claimed it was Sugar Mill plantation."

Jewell nodded, blew out a breath. "Mimi has knowledge of a hidden nook at Sugar Mill. She also has knowledge of a cistern that once existed at the plantation when she would've been a very young girl."

"Four," Beau continued without hesitation. "Sister Monica confirmed that Mignon's mother, or the woman who claimed to be her mother, was an excellent seamstress and embroiderer. Mignon claimed it was her mother who did the beautiful needlepoint on the footstool that she'd taken from the nook at Sugar Mill."

Beau paused to give Jewell a chance to jump in with the next point. When she didn't, he spoke.

"Five." He looked at her, angling his head as if questioning Jewell. "Do you have a five?" He sat next to her on the sofa. It groaned under his weight.

"Five is what Mimi said today to Ruby about the nuns insisting that she and Twinnie keep their nails clipped and clean. That places her at the monastery with Twinnie."

Beau nodded. "The photos in point number one do that."

He slid his arm over the back of the sofa, then cupped his hand on Jewell's shoulder.

"I think we can conclude that Mignon was at Sugar Mill when she was a little girl," Beau said. "Knowing of the hidden nook, the footstool and the cistern makes that fact indisputable." He leaned forward to look into her eyes. "Because Mignon and Martine are the same age, I think it's safe to assume they were both at Sugar Mill at the same time..."

"Despite Adelise claiming she'd just come from France with her twin daughters," Jewell added. She rested her head on Beau's shoulder. Emotion made her weary. "Who are you, Mimi?" she whispered.

Beau stroked her hair. "I know you've considered this, Jewell. Your grand-mère could be Rosary."

"Or Mimi could be who she is, Mignon, and Mignon actually didn't die and Rosary did. They may have switched the girls' names for reasons we don't know. But who is *they*?"

Beau shrugged. "Wouldn't a three-year-old child know her name and protest a change or not go along with it? Certainly the girls wouldn't have kept the secret."

"We only know what we know of the girls from written documents," Jewell said, turning to face Beau. "And my guess is that they were pretty much cloistered like the nuns. We don't have accounts of what stories Adelise told the nuns or...."

"Or who the benefactor paid off," Beau said, interrupting Jewell. "Money is a powerful silencer."

"Fear is too." Jewell rested her head on his shoulder again. "Who wanted to keep them silent? Who wanted to keep Martine hidden away?"

Beau tapped her on the side of the head. "That's the question that will give us the answer to the mystery, smart lady." He kissed her on the top of the head, stood and began to pace again. "Who had the most to gain with Martine gone?"

Jewell sighed. "I wish I had the bible with the family tree with us. I know the answer to that is right there."

He stopped pacing and looked at her. "We can put our heads together and remember what's in it, Jewell. You and I both have done enough research on the family to know the players."

She stood. "Let's go to my office. I have a blackboard up there that was left from when the upstairs was used as community classrooms."

Jewell led him up the spiral metal stairs she'd reclaimed from a demolished building uptown. They passed through a hodgepodge of small paneled offices and halls, turning on lights as she led the way. Finally, they reached a large room at the back of a narrow hall and walked inside. On one side of the room was a wall of mirrors and a ballet bar. The other side had floor-to-ceiling blackboards. A long, full, modern black leather sofa sat alone on the third wall. An air conditioner in a high rectangular window, with an old dented metal desk beneath it, filled the fourth wall.

Beau smiled. "This is a multipurpose room from the community center, I presume." She nodded. "And these furnishings are treasures you found on the side of the road?"

"The desk and desk chair are. The sofa was Mimi's. She was tossing it out to buy another."

Jewell picked up a piece of chalk from a narrow shelf along the floor under the blackboard and wrote the name Martine at the top of the board. She drew a line down from her name.

"Who didn't want her at the plantation?"

"The wicked stepmom?" Beau shook his head as Jewell wrote *Stepmom Claudette Isaure Joubert.* "You know, I hate that we automatically assume it's the stepmom," Beau said, picking up a piece of chalk. "My experience is that the stepmom is pretty damn wonderful."

Jewell smiled. "Following the stepmom thread, as wrong as it may be...Why didn't she want Martine on the plantation? She was just a precious toddler."

Beau rubbed his hands together to wipe the chalk residue off them. "Hell if I know." He smiled and crossed his arms over his chest. "Let's see if we can find an answer from the family stories, as Tante Izzy tells it. Louise Olivie, the first wife, was left behind to live at Sugar Mill. She had to hear of her father in law, François's, anxiety that his son wouldn't return from war and produce an heir. Day in. Day out. François obsessed about it." He frowned. "He only had the one son to produce an heir, to carry his name forward." He continued. "As Tante Izzy says, Louise Olivie grew *malade,* sick with worry. By the time her husband returned from war, she insisted on having a child right away. Despite being frail."

"She died in childbirth. Martine survived."

Beau nodded.

"She wasn't the heir the patriarch wanted. Martine was a girl, after all."

Beau nodded, again. "Aguste was distraught. He was so in love with his wife. He was filled with guilt. Still, he had a sense of obligation. He was, after all, the son who went to fight the Germans to avenge France for his father and his family." Beau looked at the board. "He eventually remarried." He underlined Claudette's name. "They had more children. Tante Izzy and the male heir, Ben's grandfather."

"Yes, but not before Claudette had two miscarriages. Both girls." She rolled the chalk in her hand. "No babies at first from her husband, who clearly loved his first wife and was still pining over her death. According to the bible inscriptions, the babies she miscarried were girls. She had to wonder if she would ever have a boy and carry him to term." She thought about the anguish this woman must've felt. "She may have also thought that if she could just have a boy, she could make her husband happy. Stop him from mourning for the first wife. Make him love her."

"Do you think she could really think so illogically?" Beau asked. "If she thought that way, do you think she also thought that if she got rid of the child from the first marriage that she would get rid of the constant reminder of her husband's role in his first wife's death?"

"I absolutely do think she had considered that."

"Tante Izzy speaks of her mother as a loving and good woman, though, Jewell. I don't know." He circled Claudette's name on the board.

"She was desperate," Jewell sighed. "Desperate women and men don't think rationally. She didn't kill Martine. We know that. She just wanted to get her out of her house so she could have a better life with her husband." She looked at Beau. "She had to be in mourning herself from the miscarriages. Oh, Beau, I feel sorry for her. I don't excuse her sending Martine away, if she indeed did that." She shook her head. "She had to be so sad. She'd lost two precious babies she wanted so badly. She probably had loved them from the moment she knew they were growing inside of her."

Beau walked up to her, lifted her chin and looked into her eyes. "You seem to understand her."

"Mimi once told me that the very instant she knew she had life growing within her, she loved her baby. It was hers. She wasn't alone. She'd never known a love like that before." Jewell's voice caught. "I know it was Claudette. She had the financial means to make Martine disappear. That home must've been seeped in sadness, stress. She wanted to bring life and joy to it. Her not being able to have children, especially a male heir, must have made her feel like a failure...a disappointment to her husband. Martine had to be a constant reminder of the first wife and his life before war, before the disillusionment. Only one of those things was in her control to change or remove."

"So, she sent Martine away."

Beau walked to the board. He wrote three questions on it.

Is Martine alive?

Did she die as a child and someone switched her name with Mignon's?

Who brought Martine to New Orleans?

Chapter

18

It didn't take Jewell long to decide where she'd place the furniture from the Sugar Mill barn. That pleased Beau. He was anxious to get back to Cane and talk with Tante Izzy to see if she had any information that might help answer the three remaining questions surrounding Martine's disappearance. He had to wait for Jewell to check on Mimi's house first.

She led him through the narrow adjoining backyards between the fire station and her grand-mère's home to get to the back door of the house. He enjoyed seeing her efficient movements as she walked into the old bungalow house, flipping on light switches along the way.

It was an average-sized home, bright, with tall ceilings and simple architecture. A large kitchen and family room spanned the back. Three bedrooms were adjacent to the family room. A hall led to the front door. That was it. It had some age to it, but it was clean and functional. He thought it looked like a homey house for Jewell to grow up in and that pleased him.

"Which bedroom is yours?" Beau asked, but when he stepped into the middle room he knew. There was a single bed positioned against a side wall. A cherry wood nightstand was next to it and a pine bookcase next to that. Another bookcase filled the entire span of the opposite wall with a desk positioned in the middle. Books and binders filled every surface in the room. A large map of the city of New Orleans and another of the state of Louisiana hung unframed on the wall over her bed. If it wasn't for a half-dozen strands of pink and white Mardi-

Gras necklaces hanging on the closet doorknob and a pair of fluffy purple slippers near the foot of the bed, he wouldn't have known this was a woman's room.

"It looks like you work in here instead of sleep. Hence, room for only the single bed." He sat on her bed and bounced a few times. The books that were stacked on the corner of the bed flew into the air, and one landed on the floor. "Comfy."

Jewell laughed. "Yeah, well. It does its job."

Beau tapped on the bed next to him for her to join him, and as she walked over, he picked up the book that had fallen. It was a Louisiana criminal law book. He felt the muscles in his jaw tense. "Changing professions?"

She took the book from him and placed it on the bedside table. "No. Research."

Beau nodded, feeling a little hurt that she didn't tell him more about why she had the criminal law book. Not that he needed to be told. He knew why she had it. "Jewell, if you need help with your case, I know good criminal lawyers who can help you."

She looked away. "It's all good."

"Don't think you can defend yourself." He turned her shoulders to face him. He wanted to shake her until she took her trial more seriously. It knotted his insides thinking she didn't have a good defense. "This is not a thesis on Civil War battlefields in Louisiana. This is out of your area of expertise. Don't take a chance with your life, you hear?"

"Yeah. I hear." She smiled, but Beau saw it wasn't genuine. Her eyes remained flat, worried. "I have a lawyer." She leaned into him. "Thank you." Then she kissed him. It was a kiss meant to distract, and that it did. When it came to kissing Jewell, it never took long for the rest of the world to fall away. He didn't know what power she had over him, but it was pretty damn potent.

The kiss ignited, leaving them in a hot tangle of desire until they were naked, panting and soaring to places that seemed to get impossibly better every time they were together. When they finally caught their breaths, Jewell settled along his side, her head resting on his chest, her arm reaching across it, her legs curved around his legs. He loved the way she wrapped her long legs around his, holding him tightly to her, like she was afraid he might leave. She held on to him with every part of her body, making him feel like it mattered. In fact, whether she was holding him with her legs, her hands or her arms, she held him with an intensity that made him feel so damn masculine. He could have beat his chest because of it, if he was inclined to roar like a jungle beast. She felt like everything good that brought him comfort and everything solid that brought him security.

That damn trial of hers had better go well, he thought. *She'd better be playing this straight with me. Pride be damned.*

"Jewell," he said, letting his fingernail scrape lightly along her spine.

"Yes," she murmured on a soft breath, sounding as content as a cat that had lapped a full bowl of warm milk.

He pressed a light kiss on her shoulder, feeling a warmth spread through him because he knew she was totally comfortable and relaxed with him. He understood that was a gift. Jewell didn't let her guard down and she certainly didn't release herself to enjoy being free knowing the trial could change that. She didn't trust herself or Mignon with anyone enough to let that happen. He hadn't realized how much he had wanted her to trust him until that moment. He slid his fingers through her long, silky hair, then contented himself, and her, by gently scratching her back with long easy strokes. She sighed.

He wanted her to always be this way with him. But, damn it, he thought about the trial again and knew that might not be possible.

"Humor me, *chère*. Tell me about your case."

She stopped breathing for a second, then, she sighed. "What do you want to know?"

He wanted to say 'everything,' but knew that would shut her down. *Everything* would be too overwhelming for her. "Do they have a good prosecutable case?" He heard her swallow hard and he held his breath waiting for her to answer.

"Yes."

Damn it. That wasn't what he wanted to hear.

"Jewell, sweetheart," he smoothed her hair with his hand. "Did you steal from them?"

She eased up to look him in the eyes. "Yes, Beau. I did."

***

Beau sat up on the side of the bed, while Jewell sat on the bed, leaning against the side wall, the quilt wrapped around her naked body like a cocoon.

Holy hell. She did do it. She was a thief. Shit.

He didn't believe it.

What the hell was wrong with him? He'd just heard her admit to doing it.

He needed to think. "Thank you for answering me." He rubbed his hands on his bare thighs just for something to do. "You want something to drink? Water?" She shook her head no.

Still naked from their lovemaking, he walked to the kitchen, not bothering to get dressed first. He came back with two cold bottles of beer. He handed her one. She took it. He sat on the bed, took a sip of his beer, and welcomed the cold to parch the dryness in his throat.

"Jewell, I know the family got the judge to issue a gag order despite that being unusual for this type of case. I know they wanted it to protect the Monroe family name and Genevieve Monroe's legacy."

"You know a lot." She frowned.

He took another sip. "I asked around about it. Spoke to the Monroe attorney..."

"You did what?" Her eyes widened, her spine straightened. "You had no right, Beau. You asked everyone about my case, but never asked me about it." She was breathing hard, erratic. Her eyes were bright with anger and hurt, and it felt like he'd been punched hard in the gut. "Did you talk to my opponent, my enemy, while you were pretending to be my friend? Right after you climbed out of my bed?"

"It wasn't like that, Jewell. Not like that at all." He reached for her. She slapped his hand away but didn't run from him.

She took a sip of her beer and looked at him with eyes so piercing that he sucked in a breath. "So, how was it, Counselor?"

He ran his hands through his hair. "I spoke to Frederick Henry, Ralph Bergeron and Claude Monroe..."

"Claude Monroe?" Her voice grew louder. "This is getting worse by the second." She blinked slowly like she was fighting back tears. It made his chest feel tight.

"Jewell, I spoke to them right after we had our talk on the porch steps at Sugar Mill." He kept his voice even, but he felt like he was pleading with her to understand. Damn, he really wanted her to believe him. That was a new feeling for him. "I wanted to go directly to the source to find out what they were claiming you had done because it was important."

"Shouldn't I have been the source?" Her eyes remained locked on his. The heat was still in them. She was angry, but at least she was listening.

"You wouldn't have spoken to me about this. You couldn't with the gag order. You didn't trust me."

"And you didn't trust me either. You wouldn't have believed anything I said." She looked away a moment, then turned back to him. "Go on. Tell me everything."

"I went to them because I had to know the details of what you were accused of because you were working and living with my family. I didn't know you then, Jewell, and you had access to their lives."

"And you wanted to protect them." She took a sip of her beer. Nodded. "You've made that clear from the beginning. They are your priority. As much as I hate to admit it, speaking to my accusers was logical." Her eyes met his again. The anger was still present but there was a little softening to them, too. "You've never pretended to want anything more than to protect them, have you?"

"I'm sorry, Jewell." And he meant it. "I don't want you to feel betrayed by my actions. When I met with them, it was before I got to know you...it was before we..." He ran his hand through his hair again. Before they what? What in the hell was he trying to say? "My family protected me when I needed to be protected. Hell, they did more than protect me. They saved me. They saved my brother. You know about my abusive parents." He placed his beer on the table next to the bed and rested his elbows on his knees. "What you don't know is that Ronald took Jackson and me home to live with him and Bernice the day he checked us out of the hospital." He extended his arms in front of him. "Both of my arms had been broken." He turned his palms up and dropped his arms. "My shoulder was dislocated. My nose was broken. Jackson had really skinned-up knees, a broken wrist. I jumped between him and my old man before he did worse to him." He sucked in a breath, as the memory of the horror of that day when his father beat him and his brother for ratting him out to old Mrs. LeBlanc whom he'd been scamming for a month. She was about to give him access to her bank account. "My mother was passed out on the old car seat that was used as furniture on the front porch. Or at least she pretended to be." He looked at Jewell. Tears were streaming down her cheeks. "I saw that she was awake. She just let our father, her bastard husband, beat her children."

"Oh, Beau. I'm so sorry." She entwined her fingers with his with one hand, while she still held the beer bottle with the other. "No child should be treated that way. Ever."

"No. No child or adult should be beat on for someone's sick, wicked, twisted pleasure." Jewell kissed his hand.

"I'm sorry. I understand why you feel so passionate about protecting your family. Why you care about them so much. Why you feel so indebted to them."

"It's more than that. I love them." He shrugged. "I care about them." He pulled her into his arms. "But I care about what happens to you, too."

"I'm glad the Bienvenus rescued you. You're a good man." She gave a short humorless laugh. "I don't like you butting into my business. It doesn't sit right, but I get it."

"I'm glad you do." He rubbed her arms. "Jewell, I'm concerned about your case and what you told me."

She eased back to sit on the bed, pulling the blanket over her naked breasts. "Yeah, well, I am, too."

"You know, Claude told me he'd drop the charges against you if you returned what you stole."

Jewell's eyes narrowed. "Really?" She turned the beer bottle in her hand. "Oh, he's talking about what he *thinks* I stole."

"I'm not following you." Beau picked up his beer and took a long drink. When she didn't expound on what she was talking about, he spoke again. "'What he *thinks* you stole?' Didn't you tell me you were guilty of the felony theft?"

"No." She said in a rush. "I said I stole from them. But I didn't take the items from the safe they're accusing me of stealing."

Beau sat up. "So you didn't take the family jewelry?"

"No."

"That's good. Right?" She nodded, then shrugged. "Did you see it in the safe?"

"Yes. When I left the house, it was all in the safe."

He didn't ask her if she was sure of that because he'd seen how thorough she was in her inventory methods. "Did you take photos of the jewelry while it was in the safe the way you did when you took photos of items at Sugar Mill?"

"Yes. The DA is using those photos as evidence that I had access and opportunity to take the jewelry."

Crap. Not good. "So, what else are they alleging you stole?" Before she answered, his head jerked up. "Was Mignon with you?"

Jewell frowned. "I know what you're really asking. No. She wasn't with me and no she didn't have access to the jewelry." She sighed. "It was one of those rare days that she was visiting with an old friend and didn't come with me. Thank God."

"Okay, so..."

"Beau, look, this is torturous," she said, interrupting him. "I know you're trying to strip apart this one thread before moving on, but what you really should be asking me is what I stole."

He nodded. "What did you steal?"

"I can't tell you."

"Damn it, Jewell." He threw up his hands. "This isn't a game."

"I know that."

"You either trust me or you don't."

"The gag order?"

"Hire me as your attorney," he said, meaning it.

"Like hell. I can't afford you. I saw where you live."

"Jewell," he had drawn out her name like it was an order.

"Okay. Okay. You're hired, but I'm not paying you anything because I intend on firing you in the next thirty seconds. I'm sure I can't even afford your thirty-second rate."

This was entirely too frustrating and unproductive. "As your attorney, you may speak about your case to me and not be in violation of the gag order. Tell me what you stole from the Monroe estate that you haven't been charged with taking."

She lowered her voice as if she didn't want anyone else besides him to hear her even though they were alone. "Personal family papers. Copies of family birth certificates. Legal papers of contracts Genevieve Monroe entered into with an individual for less than ethical, but not illegal, transactions. The kind of papers that would embarrass the Monroe family if they became public. And before you ask, this has nothing to do with Mimi and Martine."

Beau scooted back onto the bed next to her. He wanted more specifics than that. "You're sitting there so calm. What the hell? You don't look one bit remorseful or embarrassed that you did this. I don't get it. I thought I knew you better than this."

"I'm not remorseful." She stretched her legs in front of her. "I had no choice. The papers belonged to me, Beau. They belonged to me as much as they belonged to Claude Monroe's grandmother. And certainly more than they belonged to Claude."

"What the hell are you talking about?" His chest was starting to hurt. If she was this obtuse with her lawyer, she was in deep shit. He put his beer on the nightstand; half remained. It tasted sour in his mouth.

She handed him her beer, and he placed it next to his. She shifted on the bed so she was facing him. "Beau, you can't repeat any of this. Agreed? Even when I fire you as my attorney." He nodded. "Until the moment I read what was written in those papers, I didn't know. Right there, in Genevieve's office, I learned that Claude Monroe's father, the late Thomas Monroe, was my father, too. I only took the papers that proved that. Nothing more."

"Holy crap. That's a shocker."

"No kidding."

He took her hands into his. "So you were working for Claude Monroe, handling the assessment of the family estate, to which he was sole heir, and you discovered this information?" Was it purely accidental that she found the papers or had someone put it in front of her for her to discover? "Ralph told me he hired you. Did he do that of his own accord or had he done that because Genevieve asked for you to do the work in her will? Or had Claude requested him to hire you?

"I don't know who initiated it, but it was Ralph who contacted me," she said. "All I really know is that I took the papers, Beau, and I didn't take the jewelry and other items I'm charged with stealing. I also know, and now you do too, that I didn't tell the DA about the papers, either. I would've if he had asked me about them, but he didn't. I wouldn't lie about it." She looked at him a moment, and he knew she was trying to read in his eyes if he believed her. He wasn't sure she got her answer when she continued. "The way I figure it, if I go to the DA now and admit to taking Genevieve's personal papers from the same safe where the jewelry they say I stole was kept, it would incriminate me even more." She blew out a heavy breath. "I hate this. I'm an honest person. My ethics have always been stellar. My behavior with this has been incredibly difficult for me to justify. I want to go to Claude and his attorney and say, look, this is what happened. I'm innocent, but..." she shrugged.

"But they will say, sure, you just took the papers but you didn't take the valuable jewelry that's missing." Beau folded his arms over his chest. "And they'll probably go one step further and say that you may have even forged the papers to cause harm or to blackmail the Monroe family."

"Exactly." She said something in French and then shook her head. "Like I said before, this is incredibly difficult."

"Where are the papers now?"

"In my safe-deposit box." She gathered her hair and tossed it over her shoulder. "You know, I've gone over it in my head a thousand times, trying to figure out how I could've handled it differently. I couldn't. I don't have the emotional fortitude." She cleared her throat. "I was photographing the old coins in her office safe. There was a security guard in the room. I had hired him as I always do when I'm handling very expensive pieces. Anyway, at the bottom of the safe under a box holding her pearls was a large manila envelope hand-addressed to Genevieve. It was my mother's very distinctive, extra curvy handwriting."

"Go on."

"I opened it. I was still within my work guidelines to do so." She folded her hands in her lap. "In the envelope was a contract. My mother had signed papers stating she would never reveal the name of the father of her baby girl, Jewell Orleans Monroe. If she did, she would have to pay the sum of one million dollars for breach of contract. She was paid five hundred thousand dollars to enter into this agreement." Beau saw the pain in her eyes. "She was paid off to never reveal who my father was. She used that money to purchase the strip club she still owns today. The awful place that I've hated my entire life."

She tried to continue once, twice and even a third time, but her emotions were too wrenching and too close to the surface for her to speak. There were no physical tears flowing. These were the worst kind of tears that made a person weep from their soul. Beau could feel that kind of anguish charged in the air around Jewell. He wanted to gather her in his arms to soothe her and to soothe himself. He felt so damn helpless seeing her like this.

"I just kind of freaked when I found the papers," she finally said. "I felt the room start to tilt and blur. I tried to read the words on the contract again, but I couldn't see it. The sound of the fan overhead started to fade into a distant beat. It sounded hollow, like I was underwater. Yes. I felt like I was underwater. I suddenly couldn't breathe. I had to get out of there. Out of that room where my mother probably had signed this awful document that started the lies and embarrassment that shrouded my childhood." She pulled at a loose thread on the quilt. "It wasn't as horrific a childhood as yours, Beau, but it wasn't one that ever included a loving mother or father." She bit her bottom lip. "I took the papers. I wanted to take them home, lock the door to my bedroom, and read them when I was calmer. Also, in the chaos of my mind, I knew I wanted to take them to confront my mother to ask her why she'd done this. Like I didn't already know."

"Because you wanted to hear her side. You're a fair-minded woman. You wanted to know the truth."

She shrugged. "Maybe I was being a little pathetic too. Maybe I wanted to hear her say something redeeming, so I could discover my mother wasn't the narcissist I knew she was." She pulled a short beige thread from the quilt, wound it around her pinky. "She told me she signed the contract. She said she was seventeen and daring and naive enough to trap Thomas in the impossible situation. She was a minor. He was twenty-three. She called herself jailbait. She even admitted that when she trapped him with the pregnancy she hadn't considered that her being a minor would stop them from being able to marry. Genevieve told her that she wouldn't shame her family with her son marrying a pregnant minor...especially a pregnant mulatto teenager." She looked at Beau, swallowed. "My mom is half white and half black. Mimi got pregnant from a grand love affair she'd had when she turned forty. She had my mother when she was forty-one. Old enough to know better, she always told me. That was all I had known until the day we arrived at Sugar Mill. Mimi told y'all about her affair with a former pro football player. When I later questioned her, she told me he'd come to town while working for the NFL to get the New Orleans franchise started. It explains her obsession with the Saints."

"Jewell, your mother has always billed herself as being Creole," Beau said. "Her being interracial is no surprise and no big deal."

She smiled, and his heart felt like it was squeezed in a vice. "Thank you for saying that. But, it did matter to a lot of people when I was a child that she was interracial and that I was her illegitimate daughter. Especially to the mothers of the little girls I wanted to be friends with. I never got invited to sleepovers, after-school swimming parties or birthday parties. There was a fear that I'd expose those sweet innocent children to the decadent life of a Bourbon Street stripper because I must've had knowledge of that world since my mother was the queen of it."

She shrugged her shoulders as if it didn't really matter, but he saw in the tightness of her neck, the way her hands balled into fists, that it mattered to her. It mattered to her a lot.

"The truth is, I had been exposed way beyond what other kids had been, but not in the way they thought. I was an innocent. I saw no lewd and lascivious acts. Mimi wouldn't allow that. She protected me from that. God, Beau, I'm so grateful to her for that. Otherwise, I might've been that girl the PTA moms feared." She swallowed hard. Beau knew her emotions were barely contained. "I did have a promiscuous, narcissistic mother," she sighed. "She saw nothing wrong with introducing her daughter to the oversexed men she slept with, even going so far as being extremely affectionate with them in front of me. And she certainly had a lot of different men coming around. She'd claim to be in love with a guy one day, only to bring a new lover around the next day."

"I sort of understand why you developed your philosophy on sexual behavior being based on science."

"Oh, that didn't come from my mother," she said, defensively, but Beau wasn't buying it. "That was from years of study."

"Sounds like denial to me."

"No...I...it's not...it's physical anthropology...the study..."

"Whatever, Jewell," he interrupted her. "Off subject. Let's get back on subject." He began to pace. "The Monroes felt the same about your mother as your schoolmates' parents."

"Yes, but in a different way. It wasn't out of a sense of protecting her children that Genevieve was motivated. My mother simply wasn't good enough for her ilk, and her illegitimate grandchild wasn't either." She looked away. "You know, my mother said that she didn't regret getting pregnant for a second. She even said that...she got the most important thing in her life out of it."

Beau stopped pacing. "You."

"The Crescent City Lantern Club."

He moved to sit next to her. Gathered her in his arms. God, he needed her warmth against his chest. It was more than his understanding the chilling pain of the child just wanting their parent to love them. It was that he just couldn't stand seeing her suffer. He wanted to take that away from her. "That's a crap thing to say."

"Yeah, but it was the truth. She'd purposely gotten pregnant at sixteen to use Thomas Monroe's wealth and position. She didn't know his mother would be the one to give her what she wanted when she set out on her scheme. She thought she'd marry a good-looking, rich New Orleans man who'd shower her in diamonds, fancy cars, inappropriate clothes." She leaned her head back. "People use each other all the time. Thomas used her for a good time. She used him back."

She looked at him and Beau felt that she was telling him that was what was going on with them. It ticked him off. That wasn't what the hell was going on with them at all. But he wasn't taking the conversation there. Her legal problems were too serious for them to move to another topic that would no doubt end in an argument.

"Jewell, I don't like what I'm hearing about your case. How does your attorney plan to defend you? You have valid concerns about bringing in the fact that you took the papers, but does he agree with you?"

"It's not up for discussion. I don't want to bring my mother into this."

"You damn well should do whatever you need to do to win." He felt his ears begin to burn with his anger. "This is your damn life you're playing with here."

"I'm not playing, Beau. I need a not guilty verdict if I am ever going to do the work that I love and was trained to do." She got up from the bed with the quilt still wrapped around her. "How in the world will I be able to take care of Mimi if no one will hire me? I can't work for the Bienvenus forever."

"You can't support Mimi from jail, either," he snapped. "Damn it, Jewell. I sure as hell hope you have the best lawyer in New Orleans."

Jewell turned her back to him. "I thought you were my lawyer," she joked. "Oh, wait." She turned to face him. "Your thirty seconds are up. You're fired."

She walked out of the bedroom into the bathroom and closed the door. Beau heard the shower go on a few seconds later.

"Damn you, Boots," he said to the closed door. "I don't want to lose you now that I've just found you."

***

Jewell had been avoiding Beau for two days as she went back and forth to New Orleans with the moving crew to bring Elli and Ben's unwanted furniture to her warehouse. It broke her heart to see him with Nancy the few times he came by to check on her progress at Sugar Mill, but when she didn't make any extra effort to talk to him, he'd take the puppy and leave.

Jewell knew she wasn't being fair to him. He'd done nothing wrong. It was her. She was the one who was embarrassed about stealing the papers, about her mother entering into that awful contract with Genevieve Monroe and about any number of a dozen things. He was just being a friend. She didn't have time to fret over this, she kept telling herself. Their fling would've ended eventually anyway. Besides, relationships with men as good-looking and desirable as Beau never ended well. Hell, most relationships just didn't work out. Even good women like Mimi ended up alone.

"Mimi, you ready to go back to New Orleans?" she asked, deciding she could return to Cane to finish the work she promised to do for Tante Izzy if she wasn't convicted and locked away in jail.

Her grand-mère looked at her and smiled. She was doing a lot of that lately. It was as if she didn't understand the words Jewell was speaking. Jewell kissed her on the forehead and waved to Ruby and Tante Izzy, who had driven up.

"We heard you were heading back to New Orleans," Ruby said, walking up to her. "We wanted to say good-bye."

"Did you get dat truckload of stuff Pearl and some of da family sent over for you to sell for dem?" Tante Izzy asked.

"I got it." Jewell thought of the old beds, baby cribs, dressers and other used furniture that weren't antiques but would help poor families trying to furnish their homes. Those items would be perfect for the consignment store if Elli and her friend Abby were able to open it. "I'll do my best to sell the pieces for them."

Ruby looked at Mimi sitting on a lawn chair in the shade of a crepe myrtle near the barn. "I'm sorry she's gotten so distant" she said. "She looks happy, though. Wherever her mind has taken her, it seems to be a good place. You can thank God for that gift."

Jewell kissed Ruby on the cheek for those kind thoughts.

Tante Izzy looked at her, then lifted her cheek to Jewell for a kiss. She happily obliged. "I really love you, Tante Izzy."

She nodded. "What's not to love?" She shook her head. "My momma always said dat chil'ren are a blessing unless dey belong to a different woman." She laughed. "Not true for you. You're like my own."

Jewell hugged her. "Thank you." She looked at Ruby, who had tears in her eyes and was fanning her face. "Ruby? Are you okay?"

"Oh, it's just the menopause. I cry so easily and get hot flashes at the same time." She sniffed. "It has absolutely nothing to do with how much I'm going to miss you or how much my heart is breaking."

Jewell looked at Mimi, who was smiling up at a bird on a branch. She looked at Tante Izzy, who could recall stories of family from years gone by as easily as she recalled what happened yesterday. Why did some suffer with dementia while others kept clear minds to the end?

As she went to get Mimi, Jewell waved to the ladies who'd always have a place in her heart. She stopped. Turned. Tante Izzy's comment about her mother suddenly echoed in her head. "Tante Izzy," Jewell called to her as she rushed back to her. "You said your momma said that children are a blessing unless they are another woman's."

"Dat's right." She pursed her lips.

"Did she say anything else about other children or maybe the child from your father's first wife?"

"Hmmm, let me see, now." She scratched her head. "No, I don't think so." She narrowed her eyes, clearly thinking hard. "She didn't talk 'bout other chil'ren or Martine. She did feel sorry fer herself from time-to-time, though. She sure could do needlepoint, but she couldn't sew a real pretty dress. She'd complain dat she'd have to go to New Orleans if she'd want a good party dress because her favorite seamstress had done gone dere wit' her child to work fer da nuns."

Jewell smiled. "Her seamstress? Her French seamstress?"

"*Mais oui.* She sure was French. I remember her sayin' dat." She cocked her head.

"This seamstress had one child, you said?"

"I only remember momma talkin' about da one child and how her seamstress's talents were wasted on da nuns, not needing pretty dresses and all."

Jewell gave Tante Izzy a kiss.

She pulled out her phone and called Beau. She wanted to share the news with him. As she waited for him to answer, she watched Ruby and Tante Izzy walk over to Mimi to say good-bye. Tante Izzy leaned over and hugged Mimi so tightly she thought they might both tumble to the ground. Then Tante Izzy let her go and handed her the crystal salt and pepper shakers. Mimi laughed, recognition and joy shining from her face. "I need to put these back on the kitchen table when momma is finished sewing there." Mimi said, speaking for the first time that day. "Twinnie helps me. We get *madeleines* after." She smiled. "I like *madeleines.*"

"Who doesn't?" Tante Izzy said, winking. "It's your lucky day. I just bought some Girl Scout cookies from my niece, Molly. I'll get dem from my truck."

"Hello, Jewell," Beau said, answering the call.

Jewell had to clear her throat to speak; emotion made it difficult. "Hi, Beau."

"Are you okay? Mignon?" Hearing the concern in his voice made it impossible for her to speak. She nodded, then realized that he couldn't see her. "Good," she managed. "I'm calling with news." She told him about the conversation she'd had with Tante Izzy and what Mimi had said afterwards. "So, it looks like it was the seamstress who took Martine to New Orleans to live at the monastery with her and her daughter."

"I'm glad we got that question answered, Jewell." His voice deepened. His accent seemed heavier. "We still don't know which child died, do we?"

"No. It doesn't matter." She sighed. "We know that Mimi's Twinnie is no longer here for her to see or visit before..." Her voice caught. She cleared her throat again. "I know it would've been nice for your family to have closure, but for Mimi, we have that closure. I just wish I could've given her more of that memory before she lost all of her memories."

"Are you okay not knowing about your family history?"

"Yes. Mimi is my family no matter what her name really is."

Beau's voice softened. "Jewell, you're the best granddaughter she could ever have."

"Thank you. It means a lot to hear you say that." She shifted the phone to the other ear.

"I know you're going back to New Orleans, Jewell," he began, his voice stronger now, more confident. "How about I come by tomorrow after you and Mimi have had a chance to settle back into your home? I'll pick up dinner." He lowered his voice as if he didn't want someone in the room with him to hear what he was saying. "I'm already missing you."

She sucked in a breath, stiffened her spine. She'd miss him every minute of every day for the rest of her life, just as she already mourned losing Mimi's essence while she still lived on this earth. How would she get through this? God, would life in prison, where she would probably spend the next decade, teach her to accept what she couldn't have?

"No, Beau, this is good-bye," she said, not knowing where her strength came from, to keep her voice steady. Prolonging the good-bye meant she'd be tortured thinking of the day when it would come...and it *would* come. She inhaled deeply. "I'll always treasure what we had together. It's time for both of us to move on."

She hung up. "I love you," she whispered.

Chapter 19

Hello, God. You're the only one I can talk to now. People talk to me, though. When I try to talk back to them, the words mostly don't come out of my mouth. And, when they do, they're not in English. I don't remember English words most of the time. Momma is teaching Twinnie and me to speak English by singing songs to me when she braids my hair... I taught ma sucrée *to speak French by singing songs with her. I like songs...I need a bath.* Ma sucrée *sings to me while giving me a bath. In French. I like that. I don't like that she sounds sad.*

I don't like bubbles in my bath water.

I don't have much of a past or a future but I like this moment...it's my moment...it's all I have...I'm not a priest...one time ma sucrée *confessed to me that she understands her place in the world. I started to cry. She cried too. Her words hurt my heart. She says she'll be totally alone to walk, live and breathe and that's okay. I shook my head no, that it's not okay. And it's not true... the handsome Cajun man who looks at her with love in his eyes won't leave her to be alone. She started to sing again and I couldn't tell her about that man...what is his name? Oh, she's singing my momma's song. I miss my momma. Do you hear me God? I hope you speak French. Mr. Knucklehead...That's his name...the name of the Cajun man who loves* ma sucrée.

My boyfriend left me alone. Then I had Pauline. He had to go back to his wife. I didn't know he was married. I loved him. I don't want ma sucrée *to be alone... I'm*

going to say my prayers now, God. I sure hope momma
taught you how to speak French in heaven so you can
understand me.

***

"Well, I never thought I'd see the day." Ben walked
through the mudroom into the kitchen of Beau's house
without knocking. "You look like crap, cuz." With a laugh,
he went up to where Beau was sprawled on the sofa and
snatched up the bag of potato chips from his bare chest.

Beau glared at him. "Hey!"

Ben ate a handful of chips. "Is this your breakfast?"

"I think it was supper." Beau shrugged. "What
difference does it make?"

Ben glanced around the room. "I don't see any other
food or drinks out. There's just your dirty clothes and
shoes and socks tossed around." He smiled. "Yes, sir.
You're a mess, and your house is a mess. Hell, I better
check the weather forecast. We might have a blizzard
coming way down south here in Cane, since hell must've
frozen over."

Ben dropped across from Beau on the leather chair. A
few chips bounced out of the bag onto the wooden floor,
and he looked at Nancy lying on Beau's extended crossed
legs. "She must be as depressed as you not to come after
these chips," Ben said, calling for the sweet puppy. She
turned her head, but didn't lift it from where it was resting
on her crossed paws. Ben shrugged and ate a handful
more chips. He extended a chip to Beau.

Beau didn't bother responding. It took too much
effort, and he felt exhausted. Drained. He just continued
staring at the TV that wasn't on, thinking maybe he should
climb into bed and take a nap.

"Yep. You're a mess. This is a first," Ben said,
grinning. "I can't remember the last time I saw your hair
dirty, uncombed and sticking up like a porcupine's." He
nodded. "Wait, I want to take a picture." He reached into
his pocket to pull out his phone.

Since his cousin had clearly just come from working with a hunting dog, wearing camo jeans and shirt and smelling like the marsh, Ben damn well had no room to mock him. So what if he wanted to hang around in his gym shorts and no shirt.

"Say cheese." Ben snapped a picture and Beau threw a pillow at him. "Well, I'm glad to see you still have some fight in you." He nodded, then tilted his head to the side and stared at Beau's hand. Crap, Beau knew what he was looking at. He tucked his hand under his hip. "Is that a lady's pinky ring you have on? With pink stones?"

"Go to hell." Beau tossed another pillow at him.

Ben started laughing, and Beau had no doubt his laughter was rattling the dishes in the kitchen cabinet. "It is a pink pinky ring."

"It was a gift from Mignon, so shut up."

"Oh, man, it's worse than I thought. You miss the old lady, too." He shook his head. "So which bedroom you picked out as Mignon's?"

Beau answered without thinking. "Downstairs, so she wouldn't have to deal with stairs, of course. Crap..." He scratched his chest and looked at Ben. Yeah, he'd just told him how he'd been fantasizing about Jewell and Mignon moving in with him. He pointed a finger at his cousin. "Don't say a damn word. You hear me. Not a word."

Ben shrugged, smart enough to know that Beau was hurting too much to take any more teasing where Mignon and Jewell were concerned. He motioned to Beau's iPad, open near his side. "Have you been reading the news?" Beau nodded. "I guess you saw that Jewell's trial begins late this afternoon."

Beau sat up, lifting Nancy off his legs. He put her on the floor. She immediately trotted to the chips on the floor. Ben picked them up and went to throw them away in the kitchen garbage.

"I saw it. Nothing I can do about it. She doesn't want me in her life. Won't take my calls. Won't answer my texts." He stood and began to pace, but every muscle in his body ached. Including his heart. Hell. Maybe he was having a heart attack. What the hell did he care? He dropped on the sofa again. He was exhausted.

"Elli called Jewell last night to wish her luck and to let her know she was praying for her."

Beau nodded. "That's good."

"She told Elli she'd just come back from mass. Had lit four candles afterward." Ben sat on the sofa. "That's definitely a woman who's worried. I'd say even afraid." He picked up Nancy and started petting her. "Tante Izzy, Ruby, Pearl, Steve and a few other family members are going to the trial for moral support. Elli's going too."

"I'm really glad they're doing that. She needs friends. She has nobody." Damn it, he wanted to give her his support, too. When he'd told her that was what he was going to do a few days after she left, all she'd said in response was, "*No*". No reason for the *no,* just a plain, damn, hard-ass *no.* He was that unimportant to her. What they had didn't matter. It was freakin' biological anthropology to her. Nature and science.

He rubbed his chest. Leaned back on the sofa.

"You've never been dumped before, cuz." Ben grinned. "It sucks, huh? I bet there are women from here to Atlanta who'd love to buy tickets to see you like this. Lovesick." Beau nodded. The big ol' grin on his cousin's face pissed him off. "The thing is, you wouldn't be in this stinky state if she didn't matter to you." He shrugged. "Maybe you were right. She was a scam artist and you've been had."

Beau shot out of his seat. "That's bullshit." Nancy jumped from the sofa, barking at Beau, but when she saw his anger was directed at Ben, she started to bark at Ben. "You know that she's refused to pursue trying to find out if Mignon is Martine?" Beau was shouting now, he began to move. "All she really wanted to do was find Twinnie for Mignon. Just like she said. There was no scam. Once she found out where Twinnie was, she stopped looking into it."

"Oh, my mistake." Ben shrugged, walked into the kitchen and got a cold beer from the refrigerator. He returned to the sofa. "So, Elli was right. She wasn't scamming the family or going after the trust after all." He took a sip of his beer. "I find it interesting that you assumed she was trying to scam our family the instant you learned she was *accused* of theft for a New Orleans family. Talk about jumping to conclusions. Why is that?"

"Because I'm a jerk."

"Hell, you're just figuring that out now?" Ben shook his head. "Well, not that I'm one who wants to cut you any slack, but...did you ever think that her situation or what you thought was her situation pushed all the wrong buttons with you?"

He looked at Ben. What in the hell was he talking about? "What do you mean?"

"Your biological father button. The jackass." Ben leaned over and pushed Nancy's back end so she would sit. He rewarded her with an appreciated scratch beneath her ears. "I didn't think about it at first because what you said made a lot of sense, especially when Mignon opened the hidden nook. Then, Elli was so unwavering in her faith in Jewell's integrity that it got me thinking. It's when you least expect it that your past comes back to bite you on the ass. You couldn't possibly grow up with Cane's biggest scam artist and not have some baggage because of it." He stopped scratching Nancy to look at Beau and she tapped his hand with her paw. He patted her on the head and leaned back on the sofa. "You had warned me about him when we first met in kindergarten. Do you remember that?"

Beau thought back to the first day of kindergarten when they had tossed rocks in the schoolyard, talking to each other about swimming in the bayou, dogs and gators. It was crazy that he remembered those things but didn't remember talking to Ben about his father. He supposed it was because there were a lot of other good things to remember that day. "I remember thinking you were a pretty cool kid."

Ben laughed. "I liked you right away, too." Then his expression turned serious. "Beau, on that first day, you warned me to stay away from your father. You told me that if he saw my new belt with the shiny buckle, he'd pretend to be my friend and talk me into giving it to him. You even used the word scam, telling me about him."

"Crap. I don't remember that."

"I remember it clearly. I went home and asked my mom what the word scam meant. I hadn't heard it before." Beau folded his hands behind his head and looked out the clear glass window at the leaves waving on the trees just outside. "Hell of a thing for a kid to worry about enough to warn a new friend about it." Beau nodded, feeling his stomach knot.

"So you think those old fears, worries, troubles with my jackass father came to roost with Jewell?" He didn't need for Ben to answer to know the truth. "Damn." He sucked in a breath that seemed to weigh heavy in his chest. "I'm a nut job."

Ben smiled, saluted him with his beer. "Nah. That's just heavy shit for a kid to grow up with. I think you turned out okay for a knucklehead. Well, I did until you let Jewell walk away."

"I didn't let her..."

Ben spoke over him. "Have you figured out what a dimwit you are for letting the woman you've fallen in love with slip away?"

Beau looked at Ben, who was frowning at him. "Love her?" He blinked a few times. Everything looked blurry. "She's terrific. She's funny. Smart. Got an amazing heart. And, man, she does this thing with wrapping her legs around mine and draping her arm over my chest, right here." He pointed to his heart. "When she does that it feels so good, I just melt into her."

Ben was laughing so hard Nancy was dancing around his feet. "Oh, yeah. You've got it bad." He looked at a text that dinged on his cell phone and stood. "Wait 'til Jackson hears about this." He walked to the mudroom and shouted. "Hey Jackson, come check out your bro. He's a freakin' mess."

Jackson Bienvenu walked into the house, tucking his cell phone into the back pocket of his faded jeans. Beau jumped up off the sofa and ran to his younger brother who looked fit and healthy in his dark blue pullover shirt with US Navy written over the chest.

"Holy crap!" Beau hugged Jackson, so damn happy to see him. He knew it was a desperate hug, but man, he'd missed his baby brother. Jackson hugged him back. It had been almost a year since they'd last seen each other. "I didn't know you were coming."

Jackson shrugged. "Ben called last night. Told me you were in trouble. I hopped a red-eye for you, bro. I just got here." He held him away. "It's great to see you, Beau. But hell, man. You look like shit."

"So I've heard." He looked over his shoulder at Ben. "A number of times."

"Accurately so," Jackson confirmed. He patted Beau on the back and looked at Ben. "A woman did this to him?"

Ben nodded and started laughing again. Beau plopped on the sofa, smashing the bag of potato chips beneath him. He didn't bother removing it.

"I thought you were smarter than that. No attachments, no problems," Jackson smiled. "She must be something."

Ben grunted. "And to make matters worse, he's gone and fallen in love with a woman who's about to go to jail."

"Is she guilty?" Jackson asked, sitting on a chair near Beau.

"Yes and no," Beau answered. "Not for the felony theft she's charged with. Her lawyer will have a time proving it, though."

"She doesn't have a lawyer," Ben said. Both Beau and Jackson cursed at the same time. "She fired the jerk lawyer she hired. He's been neglecting her case because he had a more lucrative one to work on. She decided not to request an indigent defense because she told Elli that would've either delayed the trial, or she would've gotten a lawyer at the last minute that was no better than the one she fired." Ben shook his head. "Her reasoning was that she couldn't deal with a delay. She felt like she's been living in shackles, waiting. She needs a resolution, and getting an attorney at the eleventh hour didn't seem any better than defending herself."

Beau was on his feet. He ran his hands through his hair and looked at Jackson. "Give me fifteen minutes to scrape off the funk."

***

Mimi was sitting in the row right behind Jewell with Elli, Tante Izzy, Ruby, Big John, Pearl and four other Bienvenu family members she'd met, including the rubboard player from the Nonc Noon band. Mimi probably hadn't noticed, although Jewell had, that Tante Izzy, Ruby and Elli were each wearing one of the bright imitation stone rings Mimi had given each of them while in Cane. She'd given the rings as a sign of friendship and generosity. They now wore them as a sign of solidarity. Jewell wondered if the fourth ring, the one Mimi gave Beau, was still treasured as much or if he had tossed it aside. It really didn't matter, she realized, because Mimi was happy. That was what was important. She was now enjoying being with the chatty people around her, even though she normally would've been stressed and anxious over being in a place she didn't recognize with so much activity going on that she didn't understand. Instead, she was smiling and patting Ruby affectionately on the arm.

Jewell looked at the paper work in front of her, and her stomach pinched. She was nervous and frightened, but she was as well prepared as she could be. She'd gotten all of the files her former attorney's clerk had prepared for trial and used for the pretrial motions. There hadn't been as much as she had hoped, but it was a good start. And she even had the papers she'd taken from the safe in case she needed to use them, although she still didn't see why that would ever be a good idea.

Four law books, with relevant citations she was prepared to use, as well as trial procedural language she might need to refer to were tabbed with color-coded Post-its. A binder full of notes that she'd prepared for her opening remarks and for the cross-examination of the prosecution's witnesses was open on the desk and ready for her to use too. She'd decided she would approach the trial as if she was teaching a lecture, and hope the judge would be a good student. The DA had requested a trial judge decision instead of a jury trial decision, because Claude Monroe wanted to have as few people with knowledge of his case as possible. He didn't want a juror providing intimate details of the trial after it was over to a reporter, media outlet or personal social media postings. Jewell thought that not having a jury would work in her favor. She just had to convince one person of her innocence instead of twelve.

She looked at the prosecutor's table. Three lawyers were huddled together, whispering to each other while thumbing through black binders. They looked confident. Not nervous. They, unlike her, didn't look like they wanted to throw up. They had five times as much paper in front of them as she had.

Behind them sat Frederick Henry, Ralph Bergeron and Claude Monroe. All three men were wearing suits, leaning close to one another and speaking behind their hands. All three men stopped talking and looked at Jewell. Frederick stood and walked over to her. He extended his hand and she shook it.

"Dr. Duet," he said in greeting. "I know you're busy reviewing your notes, so I'll make this brief. My client, Claude Monroe, wants to once again offer you the opportunity to walk away from this trial before it begins. The charges will be dropped, if you return the jewelry to him. He simply wants what belongs to him." His eyes were steady on her. "He really would like to have those items because he needs them to help pay inheritance taxes. I'm only telling you this so you know that his offer is a serious one. He needs the money, and he doesn't care if you walk free."

"I wish to God that I had what he wants," she said, her voice steady. "It would be so much easier than going through this. Trust me. If I had stolen it, I would return it. But I didn't steal it. Tell Claude that. I have nothing. And he's not going to get any justice at this trial for the crime executed against him."

"As you wish." Frederick nodded and returned to his seat to speak to Claude.

"All rise," the clerk of the court announced and everyone stood. Jewell didn't have a second to think about Claude's last-minute plea. "Orleans Parish Court is now in session. The Honorable Judge Marcus Brunello presiding."

A short man with an average build and a full head of white hair walked up on the dais. He wore the traditional judge's black robe and a pair of reading glasses. When he sat in his seat, everyone returned to theirs. The courtroom fell silent. The only sound was of the courtroom stenographer adjusting her seat and Tante Izzy telling someone that the judge should put a Fanci-Full rinse in his hair.

The judge took his time positioning the papers in front of him. Jewell pressed the heel of her hand over the front of the skirt of her dark burgundy suit. She tried not to fidget with the hem of the matching form-fitting jacket or her straight hair that she had hanging loosely for the first time in years.

"Who is representing the defendant today?" Judge Brunello asked as he looked over the top of his black-framed reading glasses.

Jewell stood, her chair scraping against the white marble floor. She cleared her throat.

The doors to the courtroom burst open. "I am, your honor," a familiar voice shouted from the back of the courtroom. Heavy footsteps sounded as they rushed forward to the table where Jewell stood alone. "I'm Beauregard Bienvenu, your honor. I represent Jewell Orleans Duet."

Jewell looked at Beau. He gave her a sideways glance and a slight nod. She felt a wave of relief sweep over her. She hadn't asked him to come. Didn't want him to be there. But she knew she needed him.

She stared at him as he handed the prosecution and the clerk some legal papers having to do with who he was and his ability to be there in this court to represent her. In his dark gray suit, crisp white shirt, and polished shoes, he looked so virile, competent and confident. He moved easily in the courtroom before returning to stand next to her table. Another man, who had come in with Beau, remained standing near her desk as Beau delivered the papers. He looked so much like him, same height, same dark hair, and same smooth, good looks that she knew who he was immediately. This was his brother, Jackson, whom Ruby had told her had recently retired as a Navy attorney. Jackson also possessed an air of confidence that defied their childhood.

Beau looked at Jewell and smiled. "Have room for me and my brother at your table, Boots?"

She scooted to the middle seat. Jackson had taken the seat on her other side. For the first time in days, sandwiched between these two adept men, and especially being next to Beau, she felt that maybe things were looking up.

"You honor, may we approach the bench," Beau asked.

The judged granted them their request and he, Jackson and the prosecuting attorneys approached the bench. They stood there for about six minutes, with Beau doing most of the talking. Finally, the judge slammed down his gavel, his face red and angry. "Everyone in my chambers, now."

Beau came back to the table. "Let's go."

"What's going on?" she asked as she started to grab her binder and law books. Beau put his hand on top of the pile.

"No need for that," he said, taking a file Jackson handed him. "And no time to discuss what's going on, now." He leaned in closer to her. "*Do you trust me?*"

She looked deep into his clear green eyes. Of course she did. He'd been fair with her and her investigation to see if Twinnie existed. And she'd seen just how loyal he was when he committed to help someone. He was fierce in protecting them. She'd seen it with his family and even his awful client, Stanley Boudreaux. "Yes, Beau. I trust you."

"Let's go."

Tante Izzy started to follow them into the back, but the tall, heavyset bailiff stopped her. "*Mais* da judge said everybody."

"Not you, ma'am." A smile pulled at the corner of his mouth.

"Harrumph. Youz lucky I don't know you momma." She went back to her seat.

***

The judge had taken off his robe and sat behind his desk in a white dress shirt and solid red tie. The court reporter sat off to the side of him, hands on the keys ready to transcribe what they said. The prosecuting attorney and his two assistants were seated in brown leather chairs in front of the judge's desk to the right. Jewell, Beau and Jackson were in the same type of chairs on the left.

Judge Brunello steepled his hands on his desk. "So, your counsel has thrown a bit of a monkey wrench into the proceedings, Dr. Duet," he began, his voice even and commanding. "He said that you didn't steal the items listed in the indictment, but you did confess to taking some personal papers belonging to Genevieve Monroe. Is that true?"

"Yes, sir, it is."

"He also said that once produced, these papers will have me wanting to immediately dismiss this case." He grunted. "That's a big claim. Hence, why I decided to bring it to my chambers. I want to hear what you have to say outside the formality of the courtroom, Dr. Duet. Would you like to explain what papers you took?"

"I'd rather not say," she said, clasping her shaking hands on her lap. *God help me,* she prayed; she was a nervous wreck. She wasn't conditioned for this kind of interrogation or focus on her from someone in authority. She'd never been in trouble in her life before this. This had to be like a trip to the principal's office...on steroids. She saw the judge glance at her hands, which she held so tightly together that her fingers had turned white. He nodded. "Then I will hold your counsel in contempt of court for bringing us back here on a wild goose chase, and we will get on with the trial." He looked at Beau. "You also said that even if your client had taken the jewelry, she had every right to do so. Do you intend to prove that, or would you rather not talk about that, too?"

"No. We are prepared to prove that, your honor," Beau said.

The judged waved at him to be quiet and looked at Jewell. "Is he correct about you having a right to take the Monroe property?"

"Um." She hesitated, looked at Beau.

"Go ahead and answer him."

"I didn't steal the jewelry."

The judge's voice grew impatient. "Do you have the right to take possession of it if you choose, Dr. Duet?"

"Your honor," the prosecutor interrupted. "Can't we argue this during the trial?"

"We could, but humor me right now. I want to know what the hell is going on. We might be able save ourselves a hell of a lot of time, which this court and I are in very short supply of." He frowned. "Let's see if we actually have a case. Sometimes circumventing miles of paper work is the best course." He looked at Jewell. "Answer my question. Do you have the right to take possession of the jewelry if you choose, as your counsel said?"

"Um." She shrugged. She didn't want to contradict Beau. "Beau?"

"This is ridiculous, your honor," the assistant DA prosecuting the case said. "She obviously doesn't agree that she is the legal heir to the jewelry as her counsel contends."

Her eyebrows shot up. She looked at Beau. Legal heir. "Oh...my...God." Yes. She hadn't considered that. But could she prove it? Could Beau? She swallowed past the nerves. *Do you trust me* he'd asked her. *Yes, she totally trusted him.*

"Your honor," she began, her voice firm and full of confidence. "Yes. I am the legal heir."

Beau smiled. "Good girl. Smart girl."

"Explain," Judge Brunello huffed.

Beau started to tell him about the papers she'd taken and the judge stopped him.

"You tell me, Professor. One Tulane graduate to another." He sat back in his seat.

She told him the story of the papers she'd found, of the contract between her mother and Genevieve Monroe. And how Thomas Monroe was her legal father.

"Do you have proof of this contract?" he looked at Beau and the Assistant DA. "Does anyone here have those papers ready to be filed as evidence?"

"I do," Jewell and Beau said at the same time. They looked at each other. "I brought them with me, Beau."

"Good." His eyes crinkled in the corner. He asked her to tell Jackson where she had the documents and then sent him to get them. Beau faced the judge. "If the gag order is still in effect, your honor, yes, we are ready to file it as evidence," he told him.

The assistant DA shook his head. "This is ridiculous. These papers could've been manufactured. I need time to authenticate them."

"I've done that," Beau said, evenly. "I have an original notarized copy of them, your honor." Beau handed him the documents he had and the one Jackson had just returned to the chambers with. "I obtained the top document just an hour ago from Dr. Duet's mother, Miss Praline."

The judge raised an eyebrow and looked at her. "*The* Miss Praline?"

Jewell nodded.

"Let the record show that she said her mother is the famous...er...entertainer, Miss Praline of Bourbon Street." He looked up from the papers Beau had handed him. "Is that her legal name?"

Jewell nodded. "Yes, it is." She looked at Beau.

"At the time of the contract, she hadn't yet legally changed it to that, though. She was Pauline Martine Duet."

"Martine?" *What?* Jewell hadn't known that.

"The second copy you have is one Dr. Duet took from Genevieve Monroe's office. Her grandmother's office. It can be compared to this copy." He handed the contract to the judge.

The judge looked at Beau. "Do you have a birth certificate, counselor?"

Beau handed it to him. "There are two here. The last one that was created and the original. That one was issued by the state of Louisiana before Genevieve Monroe used her court contacts to have Jewell Orleans Monroe's birth certificate changed to Jewell Orleans Duet. Miss Praline thought it wise to obtain a second copy from the state before she signed the contract, just in case she needed it later."

"It all looks in order," the Judge said. "These are the original documents. Not copied ones."

"But your honor," the prosecutor protested. "I haven't had a chance to examine these documents. I should've had them in discovery..."

Beau handed the prosecutor and the judge each a notarized paper, and the prosecutor took the paper, read it, and didn't finish his argument. "This is a notarized statement signed by Miss Praline declaring that all of the documents I just presented were signed by her."

"I want Miss Praline sworn in by the court to state for a matter of record that this is her signature and all that has been presented is true," the prosecutor said. "And I want to ask for a delay to review..."

"She's just outside the courtroom and available right now," Beau said.

"She's here?" Jewell murmured to him.

The prosecutor and judge started to discuss procedure and how this, too, could be used as a contention in trial. As they argued over that point, Beau turned to Jewell.

"I had to bring her here," he said, his voice just a whisper. "I didn't have time to file motions for dismissal. If you had a good lawyer, like I thought you did, he would have already done that." When she started to respond, he put his finger to her lip. "Jackson and I did what we could in the little time we had this morning." Beau returned his attention to the discussion between the judge and the prosecutor. Jewell wanted to respond to him, but she knew now was not the time.

"Karl," the Judge said, speaking directly to the assistant DA. "If she swears that all that has been presented here in chambers is true, do you really want to continue with this trial and waste the taxpayers' money?"

"You want me to drop the charges?" The prosecutor shook his head. "Is that what you're suggesting?"

"I'm not suggesting anything," Judge Brunello huffed. "You can delay this trial and after a time bring it back to court, but the evidence won't be anything more than you have right here." He narrowed his eyes at the lead prosecutor. "Are you all really willing to risk moving forward and having the media get wind of what's going on here? Claude Monroe and his attorney have made it clear that they don't want the information of this case to become public knowledge. I think you all know the reasons." He looked at Jewell. "And now, since you appear to be an heir, you should ask your half-brother why, besides family legacy, he wanted to keep the family matters out of the press."

"Half-brother," Jewell whispered. She supposed she'd fleetingly thought about Claude being her half-brother, but had blocked it out because it didn't feel real to her. Her real family was Mimi. Now, in one stressful, complicated trial, she had a half-brother and was an heiress.

"I think when you discuss this with the Monroe counsel, they will want you to drop the charges. Just imagine what they'd make of the story of city philanthropist Genevieve Monroe paying off a Bourbon Street stripper that the now-deceased Thomas Monroe had gotten pregnant." He looked at Jewell. "Sorry, Dr. Duet, to speak so disrespectfully of your mother."

She nodded in acknowledgment, then turned to Beau. "I didn't want to involve her." He shrugged. She looked at Jackson. "Can we not have her involved in this, Jackson?"

"I'm not lead attorney, Jewell. Not my call."

Beau turned in his seat and looked directly in her eyes. "You agreed to trust me. Now trust me."

***

Jewell watched her mother take the witness stand, wearing a ridiculously low-cut, champagne-sequined halter top, wool champagne miniskirt and five-inch metallic silver stilettos. Her quarter-size diamond earrings caught the fluorescent lighting and shone like two suns on her earlobes. Her platinum blonde hair was pulled in a low-hanging side ponytail that fell into her cleavage. Her biceps self-portrait tattoo with long flowing hair in the colors of the rainbow caught the attention of Tante Izzy.

"Now dat's the kind of tat I want," she told Ruby. "Look at da colors." Ruby shushed her.

Miss Praline was on the stand for all of five minutes, but every man in the room thought she'd been there an hour. Claude, Ralph and Henry had been informed what had transpired in the chambers by the prosecutors and their red-faced, dour expressions said they didn't like it. When she stood to leave, she smiled flirtatiously at the judge, the assistant DA and Beau.

The judge called for a recess to allow counsel to attend to any necessary matters they needed to attend to related to the case.

Praline stopped at the defendant's desk and leaned across it to speak to Jewell. "Good luck, honey."

"Thanks." Jewell answered, but she knew the pause at the table and the low, sexy bend was meant for Jackson and Beau. Jewell leaned closer to her. "I was going to call you, Praline. I have a couple of questions about our family's history that Mimi can no longer answer. It might be a long shot..."

She looked at Beau and batted her long fake eyelashes. "Ask away."

"Martine. Do you know why Mimi gave you that middle name?"

Beau stopped looking through his papers and leaned against the desk to listen to Praline's answer. Jackson discreetly walked away.

"Well, how about that?" She laughed. "I thought you and Mignon were as close as two people could be. Didn't she tell you her little secret?"

Chapter

20

"What secret, Praline?" Jewell asked her mother, not pleased with her smug tone.

"You asked about my middle name." Praline looked at Beau and pointed a long crimson-tipped finger at him and cocked a brow.

"You can speak in front of Beau. He knows everything."

"Apparently not everything," she smiled. "Your great-grandmother was a kidnapper, my pretty daughter. Only, Mignon told me she was never sure if she was actually her biological mother. The woman was the only *mother* Mignon had known, though." She shrugged.

"Please go on. Tell us what you know," Jewell said, folding her arms across her chest.

"When she was dying, Mignon's mother told her that she'd been paid by the plantation owner's wife to take her stepdaughter from their Louisiana plantation. She moved to New Orleans and pretended the kidnapped girl was her three-year-old twin daughter. Mignon said she and Twinnie had looked so much alike that everyone believed the story. They even believed it."

Jewell's heart was pounding having the story confirmed. "One of the girls died when she was five years old. Do you know if it was the kidnapped child?"

Praline laughed. "That's the crazy part of the story. Mignon didn't know. She said that the two girls had called each other Twinnie as far back as she could remember. Since her mother was the plantation seamstress, she created the same dresses for the girls even on the plantation. It was tolerated because the girls were so close, Mignon figured." She patted her bright blonde hair. "In fact, your dear Mimi said, she really believed the other child was her twin. She'd been too young at the time to know any differently. When she discovered the truth, her mother convinced her that if she told anyone the story, they both would go to jail for kidnapping. Mignon said her mother believed if the sole surviving child didn't know her identity, she would never tell for fear she was the actual criminal and not the victim."

"So, Praline, no one knows if Mignon is Martine or if Martine died?" Beau asked, his voice even.

"You mean Rosary Martine, right?"

Beau and Jewell looked at each other.

"Oh, that's right." She waved her hand in dismissal. "Mignon said Rosary was the made-up name. One of them was Mignon. The other, Martine." Praline shook her head. "Honey, I am really shocked she never told you about this."

Jewell was too. She was hurt by it, too. Why hadn't Mimi confided in her? Her instincts told her that it was because of her chosen profession as a Louisiana historian and researcher. She wouldn't have wanted her to dig any further into the crime with the fears her mother had instilled into her. Not that those fears were logical. The fears of children, and even adults, when attached with strong emotions like dealing with the death of a loved one or fear of losing a mother had to create lasting scars. The dementia may have released her of those fears.

"And your middle name...?" Jewell asked.

"Oh, that. Mignon loved that child she thought was her sister so much she gave me her name as my middle name." Praline shrugged. "She said she was afraid to make that my first name because her mother had warned her that uttering the name could get them arrested."

Beau looked at Jewell, then Praline. "Thank you for the information." He smiled and extended his hand.

"Darlin', I don't shake hands with men," Praline threw her arms around his neck and hugged him. "You have my number. Give me a call sometime."

She stepped back, patted her hair again, then waved to Jewell as she walked around the desk.

"Oh, Miss Praline," Tante Izzy called to her. "I want to talk to you about some pole-dancin' lessons."

"Sure thing, honey," she replied. She waved to Izzy and left the courtroom without giving her a way to contact her. She hadn't greeted or acknowledged her own mother.

Jewell couldn't claim to be angry or disappointed that she didn't say hello to Mimi. She hadn't expected anything more from her than that. She was just grateful that Mimi didn't seem to notice or care.

"We'll talk about this later," Beau told her, calling Jackson back to the defense table as Claude Monroe's attorney approached them. Jewell sat down.

"Dr. Duet, I hope you're happy now," Ralph Bergeron said, his voice angry, but in hushed tones. He glanced at his boss Claude Monroe and Monroe's attorney who were huddled with the prosecutors.

Beau immediately moved to stand closer to Jewell, placing himself in a defensive position next to Ralph. She knew he'd protect her from this man who looked angry enough to spit nails.

"The only good thing to come of this disgusting episode in the honorable Monroe family history," Ralph continued, "is that the not-so-dear-Genevieve is rolling over in her grave, knowing her son's bastard child with the most famous stripper in New Orleans will inherit half of the Monroe fortune." He laughed, but it sounded more like a snicker. "It's just what the bitch deserves."

"I thought you were loyal to the family," Beau said. "What are you not telling us, Ralph?"

He looked genuinely shocked by his question. His eyes widened. "Nothing." He turned and rushed out of the courtroom.

"That was odd," Jackson said. "I think that there is much more to that man's story with the Monroes than we know."

"There is," Claude said, walking up to the table, scratching the peach fuzz on his chin. "My grandmother told him he'd be included in her will. He was not." He shrugged. "She didn't have a will. She didn't think she needed one since I was the only heir...or so she thought." He looked at Jewell. There was no resentment or ill intent in his expression. There was no warmth either. "She left him nothing after forty years of employment. No retirement, pension or bonus. He's bitter. He feels betrayed."

"I'm sorry for that," Jewell offered.

"Don't be." Claude absently thumbed through some papers on the table without looking at them. Jackson moved them and placed them inside a folder. Claude stuffed his hands in his pockets. "I think it's possible that Ralph stole the jewelry. He's said a few things over the last few weeks that make me think that might be true, especially now with this..." He pointed to the prosecution table. "I'm hiring a private investigator to see what he can find out."

"Good idea," Beau said, leaning against the table. "I've wondered why Jewell would've been hired, with her connection to the Monroes. Ralph had to know about it since he intimately worked for the family for so long."

"I think he wanted revenge against my grandmother," Claude said. "Again, that's from comments he's made. It's possible Ralph was hoping Jewell would blackmail me."

"He was with me in the office for most of the day the jewelry went missing," Jewell said, thinking about how oddly he'd acted just hanging around being creepy. "He had opportunity to take it, but I guess he always had opportunity as the trusted business manager. So why now and not another time?"

"Crime of opportunity, I suspect," Claude said. "He said he saw you rush out of the office like you'd seen a ghost. He let the security guard go home afterwards. Ralph could've easily gone back in and taken the jewelry."

"Innocent until proven guilty," Jewell warned them.

Beau looked at her and smiled. Then he turned to Claude. "The judge hinted there was more to why you all wanted to have a gag order for this case."

Claude nodded. "We told you about the security concerns and keeping our personal wealth private," he answered Beau. "Also, we may have to sell off some of our investments to pay the estate taxes. It will be better not to let potential buyers know how desperate we are. Simple economics." He looked at Jewell. "Um, if you have a free afternoon, maybe we can have coffee sometime. You know, might be kind of cool to have a sister."

She stood and walked up to him. She extended her hand to shake his and changed her mind. She hugged him. "I'd like that."

He smiled, looking timid and kind. "Oh, and Jewell. I've dropped the charges."

A few minutes later, the judge came back to the bench and announced that the case was dismissed. The Bienvenu clan stood and cheered.

After Jewell hugged and thanked all of the Bienvenus who'd come to support her, she walked up to her Mimi and squeezed her hands. "It's over, Mimi," she said speaking French, her voice unsteady with emotion. "No one can separate us now. It's you and me, together. You won't be alone." Jewell wiped away the tears on her cheek as she looked into her grand-mère's pale blue eyes.

"I have you, but who do you have, *ma sucrée*?" Mimi murmured also speaking French. Her voice just above a whisper. "You need more than me."

She shook her head. "I'm happy that we have each other." Jewell kissed her gently on top of the head. "I'm blessed. Now, let me gather my things and we can go home."

Jewell brought Mimi to the defendant's table and helped her sit in the chair behind it. Then she retrieved her books and binder. Beau was in front of the table talking to Jackson about the paper work they needed to complete.

"Congratulations, Jewell," Jackson said, shaking her hand once he and Beau finished speaking. "And I'm pleased to meet you."

"I'm happy to meet you, too. Thank you for your help, Jackson. I really appreciate it."

He nodded. "It was all Beau's doing. He had me run to your momma's club to find her and gather the documents. He did the rest."

Jewell introduced him to Mimi and he spoke to her a few moments. She smiled at him, and told him that he looked just like a man she once knew named Mr. Knucklehead. To Jackson's credit, he took her statement in stride, albeit with a huge grin on his face.

Jewell knew she had to thank Beau. It was crazy that her stomach was in knots and her heart was racing just thinking about doing it. She was so grateful to him. But she knew thanking him wasn't what was really upsetting her. That would be easy. Saying good-bye again would be hard.

She extended her hand to him. "Thank you, Beau. For everything." He looked at her hand and frowned. She swallowed past the nerves, the emotion. "I would be in jail right now if it wasn't for you." She forced a smile. "I owe you the damages for wrecking your car and now for my legal fees."

Beau grabbed her by the shoulder, then let her go. "Damn it, Jewell. You don't get it, do you?" He stuffed the folders into his briefcase and dropped it on the ground. "I don't want you to owe me. I just want you to...Oh, hell." He shook his head, reached into his inside coat pocket and pulled out an envelope. "You got most of the story from Praline. Here's the rest of it. This is for you. Tante Izzy took it upon herself to do it. I wasn't involved."

Jewell looked at the return address on the unopened envelope. GENE ID Foundation, Los Angeles, California. "What's this?"

"A DNA test. Fingernail analysis. Tante Izzy wanted to know if Mignon was genetically related to the Bienvenus." He hesitated, giving her a chance to understand what he was saying. "No one has seen the results. Read it if you want to know the answer to the final question in your search for Twinnie. Or tear it up. Our family has left that decision to you, to know if Mignon is Martine or not. We have all decided that whatever you tell us, we'll accept. We also have decided that we don't need DNA verification to have you and Mimi as part of our family." He touched her hand, started to take it into his, but stepped back. "That decision is yours."

She looked at the envelope and turned it in her hands.

"And, Jewell, you should know, that if Mignon is actually Martine, she's entitled to a very large inheritance."

"What?" She thought that maybe she should be angry that he'd never told her about the inheritance, but there had never been any reason she had a right to know of it. Besides, she knew how protective Beau was of his family. She respected and loved him for that. Those feelings came from deep pain and deep gratitude. He hadn't kept that information from her to hurt or deceive her.

He would've told her if she was entitled to know...which he was doing now—or giving her the chance to do for herself with the DNA test. Jewell shrugged her shoulders and laughed. "Beau, you might as well have told me I won the lottery. Not for the inheritance, but for the family I gained whether Mimi is a Bienvenu or not."

"Jewell." His voice deepened, softened. "Family isn't all about genetics and history. It's simply about...love. Love. Our family loves you and Mimi."

Jewell's eyes filled with tears. "Yes?" She lifted her chin. "But do you love me, Beau?"

He wrapped his hands around her wrists, held her at arm's distance away from him. "From the moment I saw you slip down the barn stairs with that silly headlight on your head and the clunky tool belt around your waist."

She stepped in closer to him. "Beau. I believed that man and woman only came together because of nature and science. I guess growing up with a mother like mine, I had to find a way to make sense of her claiming to fall in love dozens of times a year and jumping into bed with so many different men. I had to understand what it really was all about...to make sense of it...to make relationships between man and woman make sense, not my mother's irrational ones, but the way it was supposed to be." She shrugged. "I thought I had really figured it out. Until you made me realize an intimate relationship with a man and woman is much more than theories, hypothesis and linear thinking. It's poetry, not science..." Jewell's voice caught, she swallowed hard, fighting back tears. "It's song and dance...heart and spirit and maybe even a bit of science...chemistry."

"A lot of chemistry," Beau kissed the inside of her wrists. She shivered.

"Yes. A lot of chemistry." She smiled. Happy, warm tears that she couldn't hold back slid down her cheeks. "The bottom line is that you took me out of the science with your humor, your love of family, your values, your good looks. You captured my heart. You made me want to ...to create a history with you." She gently freed her wrists and wrapped her arms around neck; the envelope clutched in her hand was forgotten. "Oh, Beau. I love you."

"I love you, Boots. I'll love you forever." He leaned in and kissed her. It felt like a first kiss.

"You see dat, Mignon," Tante Izzy said, pointing to Jewell and Beau. "*Ta sucrée* and my Beau won't be alone anymore. And I didn't need to give dem da love potion."

"No, *you* didn't." Mimi squeezed Tante Izzy's hand and winked at her. "You see, Sugar Mill Plantation was all the love potion they needed. History and love and family come together there."

"You got dat right." Tante Izzy hooted. "You a sly one. Dat old-timer's didn't slow down you matchmakin' abilities one bit. You must be a Bienvenu."

"I'm sorry, but she isn't," Jewell said, walking up to the ladies with Beau. She turned the DNA report for her grand-mère to see. "Mimi, you are Mignon, just like you always thought you were."

"Well, I'll still t'ink of you as my big sister," Tante Izzy told her. "After all, you were sister to my big sister Twinnie. Dat makes us family."

Epilogue

"...and Elli thinks we can have the consignment store open within a couple of months, Beau," Jewell said, speaking in rapid-fire excitement with her eyes squeezed shut. "Thanks to you for giving us the huge, street level space in your downtown office building."

"Keep your eyes closed," Beau reminded her for the tenth time. "It wasn't being used. Besides, I like the idea of you working just downstairs from me."

"I like that, too. Mimi is excited to be part of it all. She's truly happy. We'll just have to keep an eye on her shoplifting the merchandise." Jewell laughed. "She's gotten quite good at it, to Ruby and Tante Izzy's dismay." The car slowed and Jewell heard the sound of the shell road crunching under the weight of the tires.

"Okay, now open your eyes," Beau said, stopping his new BMW Luxury SUV at the first of the sixteen two-hundred-year-old oak trees that created a dramatic canopy across the drive heading toward his house. This was the place they'd made love the first time.

Jewell smiled. "Why did you stop here?" Nancy jumped on her lap and licked her face. Ben had tried to take the sweet boxer pup back from Beau when he'd returned from Orange Beach, but Beau had told him that she was his little girl now, and Ben couldn't have her.

"Look," Beau pointed to one of the oak trees.

She adjusted her eyes to the soft late afternoon light to see where he was pointing. Her hands flew to her cheeks. "Oh, Beau." She rushed out of the car, leaving the door open behind her. The warm autumn breeze fluttered through her soft gold dress and her long loose hair. When Beau came around to join her, she took the hand of the man she loved more than she could ever have dreamed was possible. They walked to the first tree. She ran her finger along the deep lines where he'd carved their names into the thick rough bark of the old tree. A tree that would be there for hundreds of years more.

Beau loves Jewell

Then she spotted their names in the next tree and the next and the next...

He'd carved their names in every oak tree trunk lining both sides of the road except the last one. She threw her arms around his neck and leaped into his arms, wrapping her legs around his hips.

"I love you." She kissed him.

He eased her to her feet and walked away, casually and with his comfortable swagger, toward the last majestic oak. He leaned against it and looked at her, his eyes beckoning her to come to him.

"Wait," she said. "I have a present I want to give you." She thought of how this was the perfect time, right here, right now, to give him what she had planned to give him at his house. She ran back to his car and returned to where he was still leaning against the tree. She handed him the old Aguste François Bienvenu bible.

He opened it to where she had a ribbon marking the page for the family tree. She pointed to where she'd written his name in beautiful calligraphy. He smiled. "All the names are here." His eyes were so full of love. "Today is a day for gifts with a tree theme," he said, emotion making his voice thick. He started to close the bible and noticed the envelope he'd given to her in the courtroom. The one with Mignon's DNA results.

"This should remain with the family bible," she said. "It's part of the Bienvenu history even though Mimi isn't a Bienvenu. I've added a page in with the envelope that explains what happened to Martine when she was just three years old and how she was loved by Mignon Duet as if they were biological sisters...twins. I also shared what a brilliant and handsome man told me when he claimed my heart...that family isn't all about genetics and history. It's simply about...love."

He pulled her against him so tightly that she felt his heart pounding against hers. It felt right, good. She had never been happier. She glanced up at the bright blue sky peeking through the dark green oak leaves. But there was something on the tree behind Beau that caught her attention.

Another carving. A different one. She looked over his shoulder.

The outline of a rubber boot.

She smiled, and he sucked in a breath, dropped on his bended knee. Her hand went to her chest.

She looked at the thick, gray bark of the solid oak. Next to the carved boot, she read the words aloud...

"Marry me?" Her voice was barely a whisper and filled with so much emotion she could hardly breathe.

He handed her a small, sharp knife...she laughed, and started carving her answer into the tree.

Yes!

She turned to face him, her heart bursting with joy. "Yes, indeed, Beau. I'll marry you. Yes, indeed!"

Beau's eyes were bright as he reached into his pocket and pulled out the ugly pink ring Mimi had given him as a thank you for rescuing her from what she thought was a car fire the day she rear-ended Tante Izzy's truck. Jewell's throat tightened, her eyes filled with tears.

"This is Mimi's engagement ring," he began, his voice thick with emotion, "I intend to propose to her, too. I'll ask her if she wants to be part of my family. Our family. To be *my* grand-mère. To live with us."

"Oh, Beau, she already thinks of you as her grandson. She loves you." His beautiful green eyes held hers with all the depth of his love and vulnerability showing in them. "I love you." He swallowed hard, took her hand into his and slid a large round, heirloom diamond engagement ring onto her ring finger.

"I couldn't be happier," he said, pulling her toward him at the same time she threw herself forward. They stumbled off balance and tumbled onto the warm grass along the roadside. Nancy jumped on top of them with her muddy paws and excited licks.

"Life will always be a happy mess with you, Boots. I'm a lucky man."

Hope you enjoyed Jewell's story. Please take a minute and leave a review at Goodreads, Amazon, or wherever you purchased this book. Tell your friends, family and co-workers, and then stay tuned for the next tale from Tina DeSalvo...

Abby

Up next Abby and Jackson's story...

Jackson Bienvenu is home and ready to settle into life in Cane, working with his brother Beau in their successful law firm. Years travelling the world in his military JAG career are over and he's ready for a bit of peace and quiet. He agrees to hire Abby McCord, the best friend of his cousin's wife Elli, as a law clerk even though she is vastly over qualified and will probably bring her La-La Land craziness into his life because, well, because Elli asked him to and he never refuses family.

Abby has had a successful career as a top California-corporate lawyer, but beyond that she is privileged Hollywood Royalty. Her parents and grandparents are movie legends. Unfortunately, she has been forced out of work and out of town when she is thrust in the center of a media feeding frenzy after being named a suspect in the embezzling of the foundation that she and Elli co-founded.

Now the spoiled jet setter is complicating Jackson's life with her drama when all he wants to do is begin a laissez-faire existence in his laid-back Cajun hometown. On top of all of that, he knows that he and Abby are attracted to one another even though they are polar opposites. He likes dogs-she likes cats. He likes small towns-she likes big cities. He likes meat-she's a vegetarian.

Well, maybe there are some things that they both like.

About the Author

Tina DeSalvo enjoys using her imagination, humor, empathy and personal experiences to turn characters and situations into books that she hopes will entertain readers. Her first book, *Elli*, brought her in close contact with so many readers with whom she has loved sharing stories, laughs, tears and hugs. Tina has always been inspired by the people she meets and by hearing their personal journeys, not to mention the people she just observes along the way...so, watch out. You could be a character in her next book!

Tina is married to her handsome Cajun hero, and they live in Louisiana. They have two sons, a wonderful daughter (in-law) and three delightful grandchildren- Molly, Trip and Grey. By the time you're reading this, number four will be here!

If you'd like to know more about Tina DeSalvo, including info on her newest work, latest contests, where she's speaking or having a book signing, where she gets her ideas, or to see her photos from when she meets her cherished readers...please visit her website at www.tinadesalvo.com

Facebook: facebook.com/TinaDeSalvoAuthor

Twitter: twitter.com/Tina_DeSalvo

Instagram: instagram.com/tinadesalvo

Made in the USA
Charleston, SC
08 July 2015